D0250831

MORE RAVE REVIEWS FOR LYNSAY SANDS!

SINGLE WHITE VAMPIRE
"A cheeky, madcap tale…vampire lovers will find themselves laughing throughout."

—*Publishers Weekly*

THE LOVING DAYLIGHTS
"This madcap escapade [is] comic and campy."

—*Publishers Weekly*

WHAT SHE WANTS
"Ms. Sands gives romance readers what they want. [*What She Wants*] is charming, funny, and has very human characters."

—The Romance Reader

THE RELUCTANT REFORMER
"Lynsay Sands is a skilled writer. *The Reluctant Reformer* [is] a charming, entertaining read."

—All About Romance

LADY PIRATE
"Lynsay Sands has just the right touch of humor and the perfect amount of mystery to hold you in her grasp….*Lady Pirate* is a delicious treat."

—*Romantic Times BOOKreviews*

THE KEY
"*The Key* is a happy surprise…a whimsical tale that never sacrifices smarts for silliness."

—The Romance Reader

THE DEED
"Readers are swept up in a delicious, merry and often breath-catching roller-coaster ride that will keep them on the edge of their seats and laughing out loud. A true delight!"

—*Romantic Times BOOKreviews*

A WAIL OF A GOOD TIME

"I am the king and what I say is law, and I say you shall be wed!"

The Brat stared at King Edward for the longest time, appearing unsure how to respond; then suddenly she dropped her face into her hands and began to weep. It was no delicate female weeping, either, but loud and copious tears, sobs so noisy and dramatic that one could almost imagine she were acting. But Balan knew better.

He caught the astonished glance Osgoode sent his way, but continued watching the king. For his part, Edward did not appear so much surprised by this display as resigned to it, and perhaps somewhat pleased that she found the idea of leaving him unbearable. It seemed apparent he'd watched this scene played out on other occasions over other issues.

The woman carried on for several minutes while the entire hall looked on in horrified fascination.

"Oh, there, there," Edward said finally, patting her on the back. "I know 'twill be a trial to leave us....We shall miss you, too....Come child, do not cry so....You shall make yourself ill." The man tried many comforting words between her earsplitting yowls of sorrow, but the Lady Murie rocked in her seat, face covered and blubbering like nothing Balan had ever heard. When his words had no effect, Edward moved on to bribery.

"Pray, child, do not carry on so. We will find you the finest husband in all the land...and buy you a whole new trousseau...and have the biggest wedding ever...and you can even pick your own husband," he added desperately.

Her sobs finally slowed. She raised great, wet wounded eyes to the king, and stuttered "A-As...y-you...wish, s-sire."

The Brat

Lynsay Sands

LEISURE BOOKS NEW YORK CITY

A LEISURE BOOK®

MAY 2007

Published by

Dorchester Publishing Co., Inc.
200 Madison Avenue
New York, NY 10016

ISBN-10: 0-8439-5501-5
ISBN-13: 978-0-8439-5501-9

Visit us on the web at www.dorchesterpub.com.

AUTHOR'S NOTE

Dear Reader,

I have taken liberty with this story—well, I always do, but this is a date issue. St. Agnes day is January 21st, not in the fall as I portray it here. I hope you'll forgive this small liberty.

Chapter One

September 1351

Balan shifted in his seat and flexed his shoulders uncomfortably. His blue doublet was too small and restricting, but then, it hadn't been made for his large frame. It was his father's best, the one he'd always worn to court. That had been years ago, however; now its color was faded and it was threadbare in places. Still, it was the best Balan had. He had others that fit better, but none in good enough condition to wear here.

"Look at Malculinus over there, smirking like a fool," Osgoode said with disgust.

"He is smirking at us," Balan replied to his cousin, his mouth tightening. "Or, to be exact, at our garments."

"Then he *is* a fool." Osgoode snorted. "He looks a peacock in his own outfit. I ask you, would you be caught dead in a scarlet houpeland over a green doublet with purple cuffs? And who would then add a blue baldric edged with gold balls?" He shook his head. "The man has left his taste at home. He looks a complete idiot. Even in our slightly worn clothes we look better than he does in that garish spectacle."

Balan grunted, wishing it were true. Unfortunately, he feared he and Osgoode looked like exactly what they were: poverty-stricken warriors come to King Edward III's court in search of a wealthy bride to save Gaynor from a desperately hard winter.

"Well, 'tis true," Osgoode insisted. "The man is pathetic. I have heard he has his doublet padded. As for skill . . . he has none. Malculinus never practices at quintains or with the lance, nor has he been in battle. At least we have strength and skill at arms to offer. We have stories of our deeds. All he has is his father's gold."

Balan didn't comment; he heard the envy in his cousin's voice and knew Osgoode was feeling just as foolish and uncomfortable as he. Among so many finely dressed nobles, they were the poor cousins at the table.

"At least we have a better seat than he," Osgoode added, cheering.

Balan smiled faintly. His cousin's chest had puffed up. Their seats would indeed be the envy of everyone present, but they'd earned them with blood, sweat and loyalty. Balan and Osgoode had spent the better part of the last several years battling for their king against the French. In fact, they'd both still been away in France after the capture of Calais, when the plague had struck. It had probably saved them from joining all those Englishmen mowed down by the deadly disease. The plague had taken a terrible toll. At least a third—some said almost half—of England's population had fallen victim to the Black Death. They'd died and been buried en masse. Balan had returned to a country underpopulated and in chaos.

"Even Malculinus must envy our placement at the high table," Osgoode continued with a sort of glee. "We are close enough to hear every word the king says. 'Tis a fine reward for our fealty."

Balan merely grunted. While this had been meant as a reward, it felt more like a punishment: to be put so on display when their raiment was so poor. As for being close enough to hear the king speak, they were closer than that; they'd hear the man if he should pass wind! They were only two seats away from the monarch, or would be when he arrived.

Balan had barely finished that thought when the doors to the hall crashed open and King Edward III strode in. In his late thirties, the man was tall, strong and a sight to behold. His vestments were rich.

"Robert," Edward barked as he claimed his seat.

"Yes, sire?" A servant moved to his side with alacrity.

"Fetch me Murie."

Much to Balan's surprise, the servant didn't rush off at once to do the King's bidding, but hesitated, an alarmed expression on his face.

"Did you not hear me, Robert?" Edward growled. "Fetch me Murie."

Swallowing heavily, the servant nodded and acquiesced, backing reluctantly away.

Balan and Osgoode exchanged raised eyebrows. Both men had heard tales of the lovely Murie, the King's goddaughter and much feted favorite. It was said she was stunningly beautiful, with bright blue eyes and golden hair and a sweet smile. It was said the king had been charmed by her upon first sight and had doted on the girl since her arrival at court after the death of her parents, Lord and Lady Somerdale. It was also said he'd spoiled her rotten and that the girl was a horrible brat. In fact, her actions had earned her that very nickname at court. Judging by the servant's re-action to the idea of merely fetching the female, it seemed gossip must be true.

"Becker," Edward barked, and an aide stepped quickly to his side.

"Aye, sire?" the man murmured. "Is there something amiss, sire?"

"Aye." Edward announced heavily. "My wife has de-cided 'tis time for Murie to marry."

"Ah." The servant was well-trained and merely arched one eyebrow, pursed his lips, then breathed, "Oh dear."

"Aye, exactly," Edward muttered. "This news is not going to be well received by the child."

"Nay, well . . . Nay, I fear it will not," the servant ad-mitted carefully.

The king's expression was glum.

"However, she *is* well past the age of marriage, sire," Becker pointed out. "Perhaps 'tis indeed time she marry."

Edward sighed. "Aye. 'Tis time. There was no way for me to win the argument with my wife and convince her to put off the matter."

"Hmmm," Becker murmured. A moment later he said, "Well, perhaps Murie will take it better than we fear, sire. As I say, she *is* well past the age when young women usually wed. Surely she has realized it would eventually come to pass that she would be forced to do so. Mayhap she has already resigned herself to it."

"Do not be ridiculous," the king snapped. "We have given her everything she has ever wanted, and never once made her do a thing she did not wish. Why would she imagine that would change?"

"Aye, this is true, my lord," Becker agreed. "And I

fear, by all accounts, that Lady Murie does not wish to marry. She has said as much on several occasions."

Edward nodded unhappily. "I am not looking forward to the coming interview."

"No, I would imagine not, sire," Becker said.

"She is a charming child, but can be quite . . . difficult at times."

"Indeed, my lord."

King Edward shifted in his seat, then muttered, "Stay close. I may need you."

"As you wish, my lord."

The moment the two men fell silent, Osgoode clutched Balan's arm and whispered excitedly, "Did you hear that?"

Balan nodded slowly. "It would seem the king is finally going to force the Brat to marry."

"Aye," Osgoode murmured. "Aye." He was briefly lost in thought, then pointed out, "She is very rich."

Balan peered at him with dismay. "You were not thinking that I—?"

"She is *very* rich," Osgoode interrupted. "And we do need a rich bride to bring Castle Gaynor back to its former glory."

Unhappily, Gaynor Castle was in desperate need of coin to rescue it from ruin. The Black Plague had, in laying waste to a good portion of England, decimated the Gaynor and its nearby village. Half of the servants and villagers had died in horrifying waves of pustules and fever. Most of the other half had fled, either out of fear or in search of happier circumstances. There was only one solution: Finding their own villages and servants ravaged by the plague, many wealthier lords had given in to desperation and offered high wages to anyone who would work for them. These were the lords who'd replaced the people they'd lost to disease.

Gaynor had once been a wealthy estate. Unfortunately, Balan's father had spent a great deal of gold on installing a new fish pond two years earlier, and that had been followed by a wet season the summer before the plague, which had further eaten up their resources. By the time the Black Death hit, Gaynor was in no position to match the offers made by more fortunate holdings. They now found themselves without the manpower—or even the coin needed to bring in temporary manpower—to reap the harvest. The better part of the crop this year had rotted in the fields, further crippling the castle and its remaining inhabitants. They were in desperate straits.

On top of everything, Balan's father had been among the many who had perished when the plague rolled across the country, and Balan had inherited the man's title, castle, what loyal servants remained and all the attending troubles. Now they where all looking to *him* to return Gaynor to its former prosperity.

"*I*," Balan corrected sharply. "*I* am the one who needs a rich bride. *I* am the one who has to live with whomever *I* marry, and you are quite mad if you think I would even momentarily consider marrying the king's spoiled goddaughter."

"Well, I realize it would be a trial," Osgoode conceded. "But we must all make sacrifices in this time of need."

Balan scowled. "You keep saying we, but there is no we. *I* am the one who would have to marry *and live with* the wench, not we."

"I would if I could," Osgoode assured him, looking earnest.

Balan merely snorted.

"She cannot be as bad as all that," Osgoode said reasonably, trying another approach. "You could just marry her, bed her and then . . . then spend your days out in the bailey with us men, neatly avoiding her as much as possible."

"And only have to face her recriminations and whining every night?" Balan suggested dryly.

"Exactly." Osgoode nodded, then grinned and suggested, "She cannot whine and recriminate with her mouth full. Just keep her busy at night. That part shouldn't be too bad. By all accounts she is quite lovely."

"Of course she is lovely," Balan said, as if only an idiot would think otherwise. "That is why the king dotes on her. She arrived here, all big blue eyes and golden curls, and wrapped him neatly around her little finger. He denied her nothing. That's why she's an *enfant terrible*. And that is also why I shall not be marrying her," he announced firmly. A moment later he exclaimed, "Dear God, I cannot believe you would even suggest it! The Brat? Do you really want a woman like that at Gaynor?"

"Nay, but—"

"But nothing," Balan interrupted. "Besides, spoiled as the girl is, she would hardly look favorably on my suit. She would take one look at my clothing and laugh herself silly. And—seeing how he dotes on and spoils her—the king would hardly be willing to marry her off to someone with an estate in the sad shape Gaynor is in."

Osgoode frowned. Obviously, he hadn't considered that.

"Nay," Balan went on grimly. "He will want the best for his pet—the wealthiest, handsomest, most powerful lord he can find. Not a poor baron with a vast estate but nary a coin to his name."

"I suppose there is that," Osgoode admitted.

"Aye." Balan nodded, relieved at the concession. But that relief faded with his cousin's next words.

"Now that you mention it, I fear no lord will wish his daughter to be married into such circumstances. We have a tough job ahead of us in finding a bride for you, what with the resources Gaynor requires."

The two men fell into a glum silence as they contemplated the matter, and then both glanced around at the sound of the hall doors opening. The servant, Robert, led a petite blonde into the hall.

Balan sucked in a breath at his first sight of the notorious Brat. He'd never seen her before. He wasn't one for court, attending only those special ceremonies required as a member of the Order of the Garter; but Lady Murie Somerdale was something to behold. The famed golden locks were a halo around the sweetest of faces, framing large eyes the same periwinkle blue as the gown she wore. She had an endearingly tipped nose, soft rosy cheeks and large luscious lips that made a man think of kissing—and other, more carnal pursuits.

Balan let his breath out as he watched her move serenely across the hall, and wondered how serene she would be once she learned that she was to wed. To look at her, it was hard to believe she could be the horror everyone claimed.

"Good day, sire."

Balan almost sighed at the sound of her lovely voice as she greeted the king. It took some effort to force his eyes over to see the king's reaction. When he did, he saw that Edward's first response was to smile widely, but then the monarch scowled and looked away.

"Good day, Murie. I trust you slept well?" Edward asked, avoiding her eyes almost guiltily.

"Of course, sire," she assured him with a bright smile. "How could I not? I have the softest bed in the castle."

"The softest bed for the most delicate lady," he agreed, then cleared his throat and glanced around. He was starting to look a tad beleaguered, though all they had done was exchange greetings.

"Did you wish to speak to me about something, sire?" Murie asked as the king remained silent, his gaze searching the room as if for an escape.

Sighing, King Edward swung his gaze back to peer at her, raised his head and opened his mouth to speak, only to snap it closed again and turn to gesture irritably at the man seated beside him. "Get up, Abernathy. Give her your seat. I would have a word with my goddaughter."

"Yes, sire." The nobleman stood at once, but moving a few steps away paused and looked helplessly around, appearing lost and unsure about where to go. Seeing this, Becker gestured to Robert, who immediately rushed to the man's side. The servant led the noble Abernathy along the table to the only vacancy—one below the salt—murmuring assurances as he placed him that it was only temporary, that it was only until King Edward finished speaking to his goddaughter.

Balan and Osgoode exchanged another glance, anticipating what was to come.

The king took his time getting to the point. He hemmed and hawed and murmured trivial comments for the longest time, until Lady Murie finally asked, "Is there something troubling you, sire? You seem distressed this morn."

Edward scowled down at the table, then glanced at Becker for help. The aide immediately stepped to his side.

"Would you like me to do the honors, sire?" he asked humbly.

Relief immediately washed over the king's face. "Aye."

"Very good." Becker turned to Murie and announced, "I fear the king asked you to come here, my lady, to inform you that 'tis time you were wedded and starting your own family."

Much to Balan's interest, Murie did not at first seem angry. In fact, he would have said she appeared pleasantly surprised by the news, but then her mouth turned down and she scowled.

"Pray do not jest with me, Becker," she said. "The king knows I have no desire to marry and leave court. Why would he wish to force me to do so?" Her eyes narrowed on the hapless aide as she added, "Surely you are not suggesting that he has lost his affection for me, his dearest goddaughter, and wishes to send me far away where I can trouble him no more?"

Edward released something very close to a groan. It appeared that this beginning was not a good sign of what was to come.

"Nay, of course not, my lady," Becker replied quickly, utilizing the diplomacy for which he was famed. "You are very deeply seated in his majesty's affections, and while it will be a hardship on all of us to see you go, it is your own best interests he is looking to."

To Balan's eye, Lady Murie appeared to be winding up for a good screech when Edward muttered, "Oh, bother!"

Murie closed her mouth and turned to him.

"Murie, Phillippa has decided you must wed. She is firm on the matter and will not be moved. *And* she said I was being very selfish keeping you here at court and denying you the husband and children you were born to have. I am sorry, child. She will not back down once her mind is made up, and 'tis definitely made up now. She is most firm on the matter and will make my life miserable should I fight her on it." The king paused briefly and scowled as he realized everyone near enough to hear was listening to what he said, and he announced loudly, "I am the king and what I say is law, and I say you shall be wed."

Murie simply stared at him for the longest time, appearing unsure how to respond; then suddenly she dropped her face into her hands and began to weep. It was no delicate female weeping, either, but loud and copious tears, sobs so noisy and dramatic that one could almost imagine she were acting. But Balan knew better.

He caught the astonished glance Osgoode sent his way, but continued watching the king. For his part, Edward did not appear so much surprised by this display as resigned to it and perhaps somewhat pleased that she found the idea of leaving him unbearable. It seemed apparent he'd watched this scene played out on other occasions over other issues.

The woman carried on for several minutes while the entire hall looked on in horrified fascination.

"Oh, there, there," Edward said finally, patting her on the back. "I know 'twill be a trial to leave us. . . . We shall miss you, too. . . . Come child, do not cry so. . . . You shall make yourself ill." The man tried many comforting words between her earsplitting yowls of sorrow, but the Lady Murie rocked in her seat, face covered, and blubbering like nothing Balan had ever heard. When his words had no effect, Edward moved on to bribery.

"Pray, child, do not carry on so. We shall find you the finest husband in all the land . . . and buy you a whole new trousseau . . . and have the biggest wedding ever . . . and you can even pick your own husband," he added desperately.

Her sobs finally slowed. She raised great, wet wounded eyes to the king, and stuttered, "A-As . . . y-you . . . wish, s-sire."

Stumbling to her feet then, the Brat hurried from the hall, hands covering her face to muffle her loud sobs.

King Edward watched as the door slammed behind the girl, then shook his head with a heavy sigh and turned to face the table. He sat for a moment staring at the fare before him, a sumptuous feast all laid out and growing cold: No one dared touch it ere he began to eat. He suddenly stood.

"I have lost my appetite," he announced to no one in particular, and then he turned and walked to the door. "Come, Becker."

As the door closed behind the king and his servant, Osgoode asked uncertainly, "Do we get to eat now?"

Balan frowned and glanced around at the other nobles in the hall. They, too, looked uncertain. Were they now allowed to eat the fare provided, or expected to bypass it because the king had? When the others began to rise from the table, apparently deciding it was better to be safe than sorry, Balan shook his head. The girl's fit hadn't affected his appetite, but he would rather find a meal in one of the many alehouses of London than risk causing the king offense. They had best be off.

"I have been thinking," Osgoode murmured as the two of them made their way out of the keep and toward the stables. "Perhaps you are right. Murie is not the savior we need."

"No," Balan agreed, steering the man away from the stables and toward the gardens. If they were going to discuss this, it was better to do so in privacy. In the stables, there were many ears to listen in, and Balan knew Osgoode well enough that he knew they were going to discuss it. His cousin wasn't the most discreet of men. The man would voice his opinions on the matter whether Balan cared to hear them or not, so it was best to let him talk someplace he wouldn't be overheard.

"I cannot believe the wench!" Osgoode said as they reached the safety of the gardens.

Balan grunted and cast an eye around, to be sure that no one was near enough to overhear. They were in a secluded spot.

"Do not even think of marrying her," his cousin went on, as if he himself hadn't actually been extolling the virtues of such a union just a short time previous. "Not that she would be interested in you. Someone so spoiled would hardly look at you twice. Still, I would rather starve at Gaynor than have that weeping, wailing wench there. Dear God, she carried on so loudly they could probably hear it out here in the gardens. We could never escape the sound at Gaynor, not even in the bailey."

Balan would have criticized his cousin for the disrespectful address—Lady Murie might be a brat, but she should not be called a wench—but the man looked so dispirited at the realization that Lady Murie wouldn't do for a wife, he didn't have the heart. Besides, the behavior he'd witnessed in the hall was not that of a lady, so he supposed the term was not too inappropriate.

"Well," Osgoode said, forcing his shoulders straight and his head up. "There are plenty more ladies here at court to consider. Come, let us make a list."

Balan scowled as his stomach growled, reminding him of its emptiness, but he gave in and followed his cousin to a small stone bench. This was an important issue, after all; his stomach would have to wait.

"Let me see," Osgoode began as they both seated

themselves. "There is Lady Lucinda. She's quite pretty and well off."

Balan shook his head. "From what I heard, she is as good as wed to Brambury. Their fathers are negotiating the marriage contract."

"Oh." Osgoode frowned. "Well, then, there is Lady Julia. A bit temperamental, they say, but a beauty for all that—and soaking in coin."

"Plague," Balan muttered.

"I did say she was a bit temperamental, but really, Balan, there is no need to call her a plague. She is nowhere near as bad as Lady Murie, and beggars cannot be choosers."

"I was not suggesting she *is* a plague. She *died* of the plague," Balan said with exasperation.

"Oh. I had not heard that," Osgoode muttered. "Lady Alice?"

"She married Grantworthy last month."

"Really? I did not hear about that either." Osgoode thought for several minutes, then suggested, "Lady Helen?"

"She too was taken by the plague," Balan snapped. "Perhaps you'd best just stick to the ladies at court. Most of them are here searching for husbands because their betrotheds have died on them."

"Yes, yes," Osgoode agreed, and stopped to think again.

Balan waited patiently, his own mind picking through the eligible women.

"There are only three with the coin we need," Osgoode decided finally.

"I would have said two," Balan murmured. "Lady Jane and Lady Brigida. Whom did I miss?"

"Lauda."

"Malculinus's sister?" he asked with horror. He shook his head. "Not even for Gaynor."

"I was afraid you would say that," Osgoode admitted. "That being the case, there *are* only two—Lady Jane and Lady Brigida."

"Lady Jane is not a very good candidate," Balan said. "I have heard she has a secret lover."

"Hmm." Osgoode nodded. "I heard that, too. I also heard she may be with child."

They glanced at each other and said as one, "Definitely off the list."

"So, 'tis Lady Brigida," Osgoode murmured. His cousin sounded almost apologetic, and Balan knew there was good cause. The woman was frightening. Large and loud, she had the most god-awful chortle he'd ever heard. His future was looking most unpleasant.

"Emilie! I've been looking everywhere for you!"

Balan and Osgoode both glanced around. Even with both of them looking, it took a moment to realize the excited cry had come from the other side of the hedge behind their bench.

"Oh, good morn, Murie," a sleepy female voice answered. "I was just sitting, enjoying the day."

"You mean you were dozing off in the shade." A tinkling laugh sounded and Balan tilted his head curiously as he realized it was the Brat. He hadn't recognized her voice at first. It was neither the serene composed sound she'd had upon first entering the hall, nor the husky, sobbing whisper she'd had on the way out. This woman sounded bright and cheerful and carefree. Rather odd, considering her earlier upset at the king's announcement.

"It worked!" Lady Murie's voice came to them full of glee from the other side of the bushes.

"What worked?" the woman named Emilie asked, sounding confused.

"Your plan to get the king and queen to allow me to marry!" Murie said. "Oh, do wake up, Emilie, I am ever so excited."

"I am awake," the other woman assured her, sounding a little more alert. "Now, tell me all."

"Well, I have been strutting about the queen's solar all week, telling any of the ladies-in-waiting who would listen that I would never marry, that I was far too content at court to allow myself to be chained down by the shackles of matrimony in some far-off country estate." There was a *tsking* sound and then she added, "The queen did not seem to react at all, and I was beginning to think that it was not going to work. But then today, the king sent for me and announced that I am to marry! The queen insists on it!"

"How wonderful!" Emilie cried. "I told you it would succeed."

"Aye, you did." Murie laughed. "And you were right!"

"Of course I was." Emilie sounded very pleased with herself. Her tone was much drier when she added, "But it was an easy outcome to predict. Anything you do not want appears to be what Queen Phillippa wishes for you. It has always been so."

"Aye," Murie's voice dropped, becoming less excited as she added, "sadly, she has always seemed to dislike me, though I do not know why. I try so hard to please her, but nothing I do gains anything but criticism and derision. At least, I did try when I first came here," she corrected herself. "Of late I have simply been avoiding her and her ladies-in-waiting as much as possible."

"It is not you, Murie," Emilie said quietly. "It is jealousy that makes her so unbending when it comes to you. She dislikes that the king makes so much of you, even if he *is* just as doting on his own children. She resents every crumb of affection he shows you, as if it is stolen from the plates of herself and her royal offspring. And," she added solemnly, "Edward is not the most faithful of husbands. I think she fears his doting shall turn to something else should you remain here much longer. In fact, I am surprised that she did not command your marriage long ago."

Murie didn't comment.

"So, whom are you to wed?" Emilie asked after a pause.

"Oh!" Murie laughed. "I forgot to tell you. That's the best part. The king said I could choose my own husband."

"Really?" Emilie sounded amazed.

"Aye," Murie said. "I was a bit surprised by that myself."

"You must really have carried on to get that out of him," her friend said with a soft chuckle.

"Aye. Well, I could hardly hurt his feelings by letting him know I actually desire to leave court."

Emilie just laughed harder. When she could speak again, she said, "If anyone knew how sweet you really are —"

"I would be torn to shreds by the court harpies," came Murie's quiet comment.

"Aye." Emilie sighed.

"I really must thank you for all your help, Emilie," Murie went on solemnly. "Your advice has helped me survive my time here at court. I think I would have gone mad without it."

"Do not be silly," Emilie murmured. "You would have done just fine."

"Nay! They would have come after me like wolves. Only your advice has prevented it. Every time one of them seemed to be going on the attack, I just thought of what you said and either burst into great wracking sobs, or acted like an *enfant terrible*, a shrew. It has worked very well. Everyone just leaves me alone now. Even the queen does, for fear she shall have to listen to endless weeping and screeching."

"Well," Emilie said helplessly. "It was the only thing I could think to suggest. You simply are not cruel and grasping enough for court life, my dear. I saw it at once. Trying to meet the others on their own footing would have been impossible for you. You needed a good defense that could be used as an offense when necessary. Using the king's affection and behaving as if you had let it go to your head—that was the best way."

"Aye," Murie murmured, then gave a laugh. "Actually, it has proven quite fun at times. Although, sometimes even I am appalled by my behavior."

Balan suddenly felt Osgoode grab his arm, but he ignored his cousin and locked his eyes on Murie's happy face. By moving a branch down just the slightest bit, he'd found it possible to see the women on the other side. Both were blonde and lovely. Lady Emilie he recognized, and she was in the final stages of pregnancy. She had married his friend Lord Reynard the summer before. Reynard was clearly lucky in his marriage. Balan knew and liked Emilie.

As he watched, Murie suddenly frowned and glanced at Emilie with concern. "You do not think my reputation as a brat will affect my chances of finding a good and kind husband, do you?"

"Oh no, I am sure 'twill be fine," Emilie said, but Balan couldn't help noticing that she was looking a bit worried herself. She patted Murie's hand where it lay on the bench. Forcing the expression away and managing a smile, she went on, "As beautiful as you are, and being the king's most beloved goddaughter, the men shall be lining up to offer for your hand."

Murie blew out her breath. "I hope you are right."

"I know I am." Emilie patted her hand again and stood. "Come. Let us go to your room and consider the available men at court. We can make a list of them, and then find out which we think may suit you best."

Nodding, Murie stood to follow, only to pause as she spotted a pair of birds on a nearby branch. "Oh, look! Two male blackbirds, sitting together. That is supposed to be a good omen."

Emilie turned to glance at the birds, then shook her head with amusement. She murmured, "You and your superstitions."

"Well, it *is* supposed to be a good omen," Murie said, sounding embarrassed. She followed the other woman from their bower.

"Did you hear that?" Osgoode asked with excitement the moment the women were out of sight.

"Did you hear that?"

Balan and Osgoode peered at each other at the repeated question, which hadn't come from either of them.

"Is there an echo?" Osgoode asked, but Balan shushed him as he realized that the words had come from the other side of the bushes . . . and that the speaker was already continuing.

"Oh, this is too rich!" the man went on.

Pulling the branch aside again, Balan and Osgoode put their heads together so both could peer through. Beyond, Malculinus and Lauda Aldous stepped out of the bushes on the far side of the bower where Murie and Emilie had just been.

"Aye," Lauda said with a faint smile. "She is not the terror everyone thinks."

"And everyone is terrified of the girl due to her reputation," Malculinus crowed. "Halstaff has already claimed a sick mother as an excuse to flee court for fear she might consider him a candidate for her hand in marriage. And Harcourt swears he will do everything he can to escape her notice. The men are fleeing court like rats abandoning a sinking ship. There will be no competition at all for her hand."

"The way will be clear for you," Lauda agreed with a grin. "And just imagine the favor you will curry as the husband of the king's beloved brat."

"Aye." Malculinus almost sighed the word, his eyes faraway as he savored the idea.

"Still," Lauda said suddenly, "we should not count her won already. There are those desperate enough to court even someone they believe so unpleasant."

"Aye." Malculinus frowned. "Gaynor needs the coin. Did you see the clothes he and Osgoode are wearing? I would have been too ashamed to show my face at court dressed thusly."

Balan's mouth thinned at the insult.

"But I *want* her, Lauda," Malculinus went on with determination. "I want Lady Murie and the political connections she brings with her."

"Then we shall have to help her see that she should marry you," Lauda said calmly.

"How?" Malculinus asked abruptly. "Have you a plan? I know you do. I can see it on your face."

A slow smile drew his sister's lips apart, and she nodded. "Aye. We shall use her superstitious nature against her."

"Tell me," Malculinus insisted.

"Not here. Someone could come upon us at any time and overhear," she cautioned. "The maze is a safer place to have this conversation. Come."

Nodding eagerly, brother followed sister out of the bower.

"Come on," Osgoode hissed, standing to follow.

"Where?" Balan asked suspiciously.

"You heard them—they are going to the maze to plot. We have to find a way to listen." When Balan just stared at him, he frowned and added, "Surely you are not going to leave them to trick Lady Murie into marrying that snake? She hardly deserves such a fate. Besides, now that we know she is not the brat everyone believes, you should court her yourself. She could save Gaynor!"

Balan still hesitated, and his cousin repeated, "She does not deserve being tied to that man. I hear he beats his horse, and you know what they say about a man who beats his horse."

" 'He beats his wife twice as hard,' " Balan recited with a frown, not at all liking the idea of Murie marrying someone who would beat her.

"Aye. Surely you know you would be the better husband. You are always gentle with beasts and women. Besides," Osgoode added, "if you do not marry her, it will be Lady Brigida."

Balan winced, then stood with a nod. "Very well, we shall make sure Malculinus does not do anything to trick the girl," he agreed. But he added firmly, "That is all."

Chapter Two

"Move over a little; I am standing half in the bush here," Osgoode muttered.

"Hush, they will hear you," Balan growled back under his breath. He added, " 'Sides, I have nowhere to move. I am half in the bushes as well. Now just hush and listen."

Ignoring the way his cousin continued to shift and mutter, Balan turned his attention to Malculinus and Lauda Aldous on the other side of the hedge. They'd had no difficulty keeping up with the pair making their way into and through the maze to a spot they deemed suitable; the problem had come when Balan and Osgoode needed a place close enough to listen but not be seen. They'd finally settled on a dead-end aisle between the hedges that backed onto the spot the couple had chosen. Unfortunately, it was really far too narrow for the two of them to hunker together comfortably, but neither of them wished to miss what would be said.

"It is St. Agnes Eve tonight," Lauda announced, as if this were a matter of some importance.

Balan didn't see what the significance could be, but then, apparently, neither did Malculinus, who asked with irritation, "So? There will be a feast tomorrow. How does that help me?"

"It does not," Lauda said patiently. "It is St. Agnes *Eve* and Lady Murie's superstitious nature that are of import here."

"Tell me," Malculinus demanded.

"Surely you have heard what they say about St. Agnes Eve?" Lauda asked, and Balan could hear the frown in her voice. "If a girl fasts all day or eats something rotten before bed . . . when she goes to sleep she will dream of the man who will be her husband."

"Ah!" Malculinus gave a small chuckle. "So you will remind her of this superstition."

"At dinner," Lauda agreed.

"And . . . ," Malculinus began. "And . . . what? Hope that she dreams about me?"

"Nay. Hope is a fool's tool," Lauda said with derision. "The Lord helps those who help themselves. So, we shall *ensure* she sees you."

"How?" Malculinus asked.

"She obviously will not have fasted all day, so I will suggest she eat something rotten," Lauda said simply. "And then I shall offer to find this rotten item for her."

"But that will not ensure she dreams of me," Malculinus protested.

"It will," Lauda assured him. "Because this rotten item I *find* shall be something I have prepared beforehand with special herbs to make her woozy and sleepy and not likely to fully wake until morning. You will slip into her room in the middle of the night, make a noise or even shake her shoulder if you must. Better yet," she said with sudden inspiration, "kiss her awake, and when she opens her eyes, she shall see you and—"

"And immediately start screaming for the guard," Malculinus said with disgust. "Have you lost your mind? Are you *trying* to get me drawn and quartered?"

"Nay," Lauda said with exasperation. "Did I not just say that I would give her a drug to keep her woozy and sleepy through the night? She will not scream for the guard. She will wake up, see you and then fall right back to sleep. But when she wakes in the morning, she will recall seeing your face and think that she has dreamt of the man she must marry."

"Oh . . . I see," Malculinus said with sudden understanding. He murmured thoughtfully, "That might work."

"Of course it will work," Lauda snapped. "Now, come; I needs must send my maid to fetch the necessary herbs to achieve the right effect."

There was the rustle of leaves as the pair moved off.

"We have to do something!" Osgoode said. "They are plotting against the poor girl. She will find herself married to that idiot."

Balan merely grunted, considering.

"We cannot have that!" Osgoode pointed out. "What are we going to do?"

Balan was silent for a moment more, then shook his head. "Nothing."

"Nothing?"

"There is nothing we need do," Balan decided, having thought it out. "The girl has the entire court believing she's a spoiled brat. Surely she is not foolish enough to believe this nonsense about eating something rotten on St. Agnes Eve and dreaming of the man who will be her husband. Let them carry out their plan; it will not work. And as an added benefit, they might destroy themselves."

"I wish I had your confidence," Osgoode said, his mouth tight. "But what if Murie truly is superstitious, and if Lauda convinces her to eat something rotten? What if Murie wakes in the night to see Malculinus . . ." He raised his eyebrows. "She may very well believe. She may think he is the one, marry him, and 'twill be all your fault for doing nothing to prevent it."

Balan scowled at the suggestion and paused to reevaluate the possible danger. He was sure Murie was intelligent; the fact that she'd fooled all of court suggested as much. But she had made that comment about the two blackbirds being a good omen, and, he feared, could indeed be superstitious despite her intelligence. Added to that, Lauda was very clever; she was renowned for a sneaky, conniving wit that could be dangerous. She might indeed be able to convince Murie to try this superstitious ritual; either as a lark or to simply prove it wasn't true at all. And, if she did, the plan might actually work.

"Very well," he said at last. "We will endeavor to sit by her at dinner tonight, in order that we know whether Lauda convinces her to try or not. If Murie agrees, we will intervene."

"Aye." Osgoode let out a slow breath, some of the tension leaving him; then he nodded and said with a grin, "I shall distract Malculinus, and you can sneak in and wake Murie so that it is *your* face she sees."

Balan peered at him with exasperation. "Nay. I will not."

"Why not?" Osgoode asked. "It would ensure she married you, and you would be a better husband than Malculinus. In fact, I would venture to say you would be a better husband to Lady Murie than most of the men at court. I have known you long enough to say with assurance that you would be faithful and kind."

"I am not going to stop Malculinus from committing such a scurrilous deed only to do the same myself," Balan said firmly.

Osgoode sighed, beleaguered, and shook his head. "If you will not take advantage of opportunities dropped in your lap, Balan, it will be a miracle if we get you married to anyone."

"So be it," Balan replied. "Now, come. We missed out on the nooning meal, and all this plotting and sneaking about has only sharpened my appetite. I wish to go and find something to eat."

"The duck is lovely," Emilie commented.

"Aye," Murie agreed.

"Then why are you not eating any of it?" Emilie asked.

"What?" Murie glanced at her friend in confusion, then peered down at her trencher and the untouched food upon it. Heaving out a breath of air, she confessed, "I am thinking."

"You are *fretting*," Emilie corrected. "And I have no doubt it is over whom you should choose to marry."

"Well, 'tis an important matter," Murie pointed out. "I will spend the rest of my life with whomever I choose. And will have to let him bed me. And will bear his children. And . . ." She shrugged helplessly. "What if I choose the wrong one?"

"You shall not choose the wrong one. I shall ensure that," Emilie said with a grin. She added more seriously, "Let us think on this. Is there anyone on the list of available lords we made whom you are interested in or think a likely possibility?"

Murie considered the matter, then blinked and admitted with dismay, "I know not. I have avoided everyone and stayed to myself for so long, I know none of the men at court."

"Well," Emilie said reasonably, "then you shall have to get to know them. There are many men here at court who are fair of face, wealthy and charming."

Murie waved her words away. "What does it matter if they are 'fair of face'? A fair face can easily hide a cruel heart—as I have learned well these years at court. As for wealth, I have no need of it. My parents left me well endowed. And charm is lovely, but it cannot keep you safe in troubled times."

"Then, what would you look for in a husband?" Emilie asked.

"Oh . . ." Murie pursed her lips. "I should like him to be kind and gentle to those weaker than he. And intelligent—that is most important. I should not like a stupid husband, else we could never find common ground. And he must be strong enough to keep us safe when war threatens. And he should be a good lord, one who knows how to manage his property so that his people can prosper."

She fell silent and Emilie patted her hand. "Those are all fine attributes, and I am sure that if we think on it, we can find someone to fit the bill."

"Why not let St. Agnes help?"

Surprised, Murie turned to the woman on her other side. Lady Lauda Aldous generally didn't have a kind word to say to her. In fact, Lauda usually ignored her completely. At least, that had been the case for the last five or six years, as Lauda had left court to return to her family home. Before that, she had been one of Murie's most vicious tormenters. Murie had been surprised to find the woman settling into the seat beside her at dinner. Despite them both being adults now, she had actually found herself tensing in expectation of the old verbal assault that would have been forthcoming when they were children. Much to her relief, the attack had never come. Instead, Lady Lauda had merely smiled, wished her a good evening and turned her attention to her meal, not speaking another word. Until now.

"Excuse me? Did you say let St. Agnes help?" Emilie asked with a disbelieving smile. She leaned forward to see past Murie to Lauda.

"Aye." Lauda gave an embarrassed laugh. " 'Tis silly, really—never mind. Just ignore me."

"Oh, no," Murie said, quickly offering a smile. "You have me curious now. Tell us what you meant."

Lauda shifted with apparent discomfort, then admitted, " 'Tis just that your concern over choosing a husband made me think of what they say about St. Agnes Eve."

"What do they say about St. Agnes Eve?" Murie asked with interest.

"Well . . ." Lauda leaned toward her conspiratorially. "According to the old beliefs, if you fast all day, when you go to sleep on St. Agnes Eve, you will dream of the man fated to be your husband."

Murie and Emilie just stared at her blankly, and Lauda gave another embarrassed laugh and shrugged. " 'Tis a silly superstition, I know, and it probably does not work, but would it not be wonderful if it did?" She gave a little sigh. "I am in much the same position as you, Murie. My betrothed was taken by the plague, and Father wishes me to select a husband while we are at court. But . . ." She peered around the crowded hall. "There are so many, and I hardly know any. I have no idea whom to choose."

" 'Tis a difficult decision," Murie acknowledged, somewhat surprised to find she had anything in common with this girl who had tormented her throughout her youth.

"Aye, and it affects the whole of our lives," Lauda murmured. She added wryly, "But I suppose I have missed out on allowing St. Agnes to assist me with the matter. I did not remember, and so did not fast."

Murie smiled faintly, thinking with amusement that it would have been nice to at least try. Not that she would have based any decision solely on the result. However, a little help from the saints would always be nice.

"Actually, Lauda," Malculinus suddenly commented from beside his sister. "You have not missed out at all. The saying is that if you fast all day *or* eat something rotten before bed, you will dream of the man you are meant to marry. You could still eat something rotten and test this belief."

"Really?" Lauda peered at him with apparent uncertainty. "Are you sure, Malculinus?"

"I believe he may be right," Emilie spoke up, drawing Murie's wide eyes. "Now that you remind me, I have heard the saying before, and I do recall some mention of rotten meat."

"Well, there!" Lauda said brightly, flashing a smile at Murie. "You can still test the theory and see if it is true."

Murie bit her lip uncertainly. Fasting all day was one thing, but the idea of eating rotten meat wasn't very appealing. Unfortunately, it was too late to choose the first option. Wrinkling her nose, she suggested, "Why do you not do it tonight, and if it works, I shall try it tomorrow."

"It only works on St. Agnes Eve," the woman reminded her, shaking her head. "Nay, I fear you would have to do it tonight."

"What of you?" Emilie asked, and when Lauda looked at her in alarm, she reminded her, "You keep saying Murie should, but you have to choose a husband, too."

"Oh, I do not think—" Lauda began quickly, but Malculinus interrupted.

"Of course she will try. Murie and Lauda can do it together." When his sister turned on him sharply, he shrugged and said, "Well, you *do* have to choose a husband, and Murie does not wish to try this on her own. Mayhap dreams will supply the answer to your waking mind's concerns."

Lauda scowled, but then turned back to Murie, who commented, "As lovely as it would be to have some aid from the saints, I am not sure I want to eat rotten meat to—"

"No, of course not," Lauda said. "Forgive me for suggesting it. Your stomach is surely too delicate. I suppose I shall have to test it out on my own."

Murie stiffened at the suggestion that she was somehow weaker. "My stomach is no more delicate than anyone else's."

"Well, then, perhaps you are afraid," Lauda suggested mildly.

"I am not afraid." Murie scowled.

"Good. Then we shall do it together."

"You shall both do it!" Malculinus laughed. "How charming. I can hardly wait until morning to hear the results."

"Oh, but—," Murie began in protest. She hadn't meant her words to be taken as agreement. She really had no desire to eat something rotten, even if it did mean she would get the answer to whom she should marry.

"Very well," Lauda interrupted, getting to her feet. "I shall go to the king's cook right now and see what he has for us. He must have some bad meat somewhere. Perhaps he will be kind enough to cook it and to add in some spices and herbs to make it more palatable."

"Nay, Lauda, I—," Murie began, but the woman was already away. Murie watched her disappear out of the hall and then sank back into her seat with a small sigh.

"Surely you are not going to go through with this?" Emilie said. "I thought this was a joke. You cannot mean to really do it."

"Nay, of course not," Murie assured her friend. "I will tell Lauda so as soon as she comes back."

"Oh, good." Emilie shook her head. "While I mean no offense to St. Agnes, it does seem a silly superstition—and eating rotten meat could be dangerous."

Murie nodded and turned her attention back to the food on her trencher, then merely pushed it around with disinterest as she found herself repeatedly glancing toward the doors as she waited for Lauda's return. And waited. And waited.

The meal was over and everyone was beginning to rise from the tables when the woman finally reappeared. Murie prepared to explain politely but firmly that she'd no intention of participating in the exercise, but Lauda didn't give her the chance.

"Oh, I am so sorry I took so long. The king's cook took forever to even trouble himself to talk to me. He then took his time about finding something suitable, and insisted I stand there and wait while he prepared it. But I have it, *finally*," she added with a small laugh, and held up two bits of meat on a small pewter plate.

Murie eyed the bits of meat with distaste and started to shake her head. The moment she did, alarm claimed Lauda's expression. "You are not going to refuse after all the time and trouble I took to get this, are you?"

Guilt making her grimace, Murie said, "I am sorry, Lauda, but I never meant—"

"You do not have the courage," Lauda said on a disappointed sigh. "I should have realized. You never did have any backbone. And being famous as a spoiled, wailing brat can't be for nothing."

Murie stood up abruptly, her mouth open to reciprocate, but then she spotted the avid faces of those around her, and she closed it again. She'd tried to stand up for herself on first arriving at court. She'd been a sad, lonely child, newly orphaned and lost, in need of friends and sympathy and affection. Instead, she'd found herself the target of the other girls who'd spotted her pain, seen it as weakness and circled like wolves for the kill. Murie had tried to fight back, but it had left her in constant conflict. One girl would attack her and, whenever she tried to defend herself, the rest would jump in. Six months later, beleaguered and miserable, she'd simply wished she'd died along with her parents. If Emilie had not arrived at court then and befriended her, Murie wasn't at all sure how things would have ended. Fortunately, Emilie had; had seen what was happening and given her advice. It hadn't perhaps been the best advice in the world, considering her reputation, but Murie felt sure it had saved her sanity. All she'd had to do was break into noisy sobs, and the girls usually backed off and left her alone, eventually not even bothering to attack her anymore.

An added benefit was that the queen had found her weeping and wailing so tiresome that she'd stopped insisting Murie remain close by, allowing her to slip away on her own and read or practice some of the various hobbies she'd acquired over the years.

The Brat. Murie's pride wouldn't stand for the label anymore. She wished to marry and wanted a husband who would respect her. Despite Emilie's assurances, she knew the label would damage her chances. She wanted it forgotten.

Expression grim, she held out her hand. "Give it to me."

Lauda handed over one of the pieces of meat, and Murie immediately popped it into her mouth. She grimaced at the vile taste. One of the herbs or spices the cook had used to hide the rot was bitter and nasty. It was so bad she nearly spat the meat back out, but determination made her chew and swallow. Pausing, she glanced at the other piece and arched an eyebrow. "Well?"

Lauda smiled and ate it.

"There we are then," Malculinus said. Lauda's brother was grinning widely, but then, he wasn't the one who'd had to eat the horrendous meat. "I can hardly wait until morning to learn what happened. May I say I hope you both have sweet dreams?"

Murie made no reply; she simply turned and left the hall.

"Are you all right?" Emilie asked as they made their way toward their rooms. "You keep rubbing your stomach. That meat hasn't made you feel sick, has it?"

"A bit," Murie admitted with a grimace.

Emilie shook her head, clearly exasperated. "I do not know why you allowed her to cow you into eating it. You do know this is all nonsense, do you not?"

"Of course," Murie muttered.

"Oh, aye," Emilie continued dryly. "I know you too well, Murie. You are the most superstitious person I know and probably believe you *will* now dream of the man meant to be your husband. The only reason you hesitated was the unpleasant task of eating the rotten meat."

Murie neither admitted nor denied this claim. She

really wasn't feeling at all well. Her stomach was roiling, and she was actually feeling a bit woozy.

"The meat is not resting happily, is it?" Emilie asked with concern as Murie rubbed her stomach again. "Is it revolting?"

"Aye," Murie admitted, then gave a short laugh as she added, "in more ways than one. That meat tasted absolutely vile."

"Hmm. I am not at all surprised to hear it." Emilie's gaze was concerned.

"Here we are," Murie said, gesturing to the door they'd reached.

Emilie glanced at it—the door to her chamber—frowned and said, "Mayhap I should sit with you for a bit. Just to be sure you are all right."

"Do not be silly," Murie said, touched by her concern. Emilie had always been a good friend. "Nay. Reginald would worry if he returned to your chamber to find you missing. Besides, I shall be fine. I am going to go right to bed . . . hopefully to have sweet dreams. It would be a shame to have eaten that vile meat and not be rewarded for it."

Emilie sighed. "Well, all right, but have Cecily sleep in your room, and tell her to come fetch me if you start feeling any worse," she ordered.

Murie just smiled, refusing to make a promise she didn't intend to keep. She had no plan to make her maid sleep in her room. To distract her friend from noticing she'd not promised, she asked, "Are you not going to wish me sweet dreams?"

Emilie chuckled softly and shook her head. "Very well, sweet dreams."

"Thank you," Murie murmured.

Shrugging, Emilie gave her a hug. "I suppose stranger things have happened. Mayhap Malculinus is right and your mind will supply the answer to your heart's question."

"Aye," Murie said as her friend opened the door. "Sleep well, Emilie."

"And you," Lady Emilie answered, slipping inside.

Murie grimaced as she turned away and continued up the hall to her own room. It seemed questionable whether she would sleep at all tonight. Her stomach really was not happy to have the rotten meat in it. On the other hand, she was also quite exhausted and even a bit woozy. She didn't know why that should be; she'd hardly had any of the wine or ale that had poured so freely tonight, but there it was.

"My lady." Her maid, Cecily, smiled widely and popped up from the window ledge where she'd been seated while mending an undertunic. She set the garment aside and hurried forward as Murie closed the door. "Did you have a good evening?"

"Not really," Murie admitted wearily.

"Oh?" Cecily set to work helping her to disrobe.

Murie was silent for a moment, then asked, "Cecily, have you ever heard of a superstition connected to St. Agnes Eve? Something about—"

"Dreaming about the man who will be your husband?" Cecily finished with a nod. "Aye. In fact, my sister once tried it."

"Oh?" Murie said. "What happened?"

"She dreamt of a stranger. Met him a week later, and they were married six months after that," she announced.

"Really?" Murie smiled, hoping that her upset stomach might not be for nothing after all.

"Aye." Finished with the fastenings of the gown, Cecily helped her mistress slip out of it, then helped Murie out of her undertunic as well.

"Have you ever tried it?" Murie asked. She moved to the basin of water on the stand by her bed and dipped in a bit of linen.

"Aye," the girl said slowly.

"And did you dream of a man?"

"Nay. Not that I recall." She smiled wryly and put the gown away. "Though, that was years ago, and I am not yet married. Mayhap I never shall be, so there was no one to dream of."

"Oh, I am sure that is not the case," Murie said quickly. But while Cecily had been a young woman when she'd first come with Murie to court after the death of Murie's parents, that had been ten years ago. She was growing long in the tooth and very well might never marry. Frowning at the thought, Murie ran the damp cloth over her face and arms, then donned the fresh tunic Cecily held out.

"Will there be anything else, my lady?" Cecily asked as Murie crawled into bed.

"Nay. Thank you, Cecily," she murmured wearily.

"Good night then, my lady. Have sweet dreams."

Murie glanced toward the door with a start, but it was already closing behind the woman. "Sweet dreams," she murmured with a little sigh, then turned on her side in the hopes of easing her tummy upset.

Wouldn't it be wonderful if she did dream of and marry a wonderful man? Murie really did wish to marry, for various reasons: Marriage would get her away to her own home where she need not deal with the cruelty and avarice of the courtiers. It would also give her children, and Murie had lately found herself yearning to have a child of her own. She would love it as she'd been loved before her parents' deaths.

Unfortunately, with her eye on the end result of getting the king and queen to agree to her marriage, she'd really not considered whom it would be to. She'd assumed that the king would choose her mate, and now found herself quite lost on the matter. Not to mention she was terrified of making a mistake in her choice and landing with an abusive or cruel husband.

Sighing, she turned onto her back again, thinking it would definitely be helpful should St. Agnes decide to give her a dream of whom she should marry. However, she very much feared she wasn't even going to be able to sleep with her stomach as upset as it was. And she could not dream did she not sleep.

Murie had barely finished having that thought when her eyes began to droop and she drifted into slumber.

"Where is the man?" Osgoode muttered impatiently.

Balan shrugged in answer. They had managed to situate themselves near enough to the quartet at dinner to hear Lauda convince Murie to try the St. Agnes Eve ritual, and had decided to intervene. They'd kept Murie in their sights all evening, then followed her and Emilie back to their rooms. Now they waited behind the cloth draping one of the hall windows outside her chamber, watching for Malculinus to make his appearance.

"Dear God, will he wait until just before dawn?" Osgoode asked in vexation.

"That is doubtful," Balan assured him. "Surely he risks the herbs Lauda put on the meat wearing off if he waits too long."

"Aye." Osgoode nodded, then suggested, "Speaking of those herbs, after we stop Malculinus, mayhap you should just slip into Murie's room to see that whatever it is she was given has caused her no harm."

"No," Balan growled. "I am *not* going to go in and let her see me."

"But it would assure she marries you, and marrying her would save our people, Balan. Many will starve to death over the winter do we not soon have an influx of coins. And surely she would choose you to husband anyway if she knew you. In fact, if you were not so shy—"

"Shy?" Balan interrupted, glancing at his cousin in disbelief. "I am not shy."

Osgoode snorted. "Balan, I have known you my whole life. You are so shy you do not even *speak* to women. And do not claim you speak to camp followers; they need little enough said to them. Besides, it is ladies I am speaking of."

Balan shrugged. "I do not speak to women because I have nothing to say to them."

"Bollocks," Osgoode said. "You are shy. But I could help you with that. I am quite successful with the ladies. I could teach you how to romance them and impress them and—"

"Osgoode," Balan interrupted. "Somehow I do not think that the skills you use to woo tavern wenches would stand me in good stead with Lady Murie."

"Women are women, cousin," the other man responded. "Whether lady or tavern wench, they all like to be complimented and feted and told they are special. If you were to just go in there and—"

"Nay."

"Balan, please. If you would just—"

"Nay," he grouled. "You will not convince me to take advantage of Malculinus's trickery and show myself to her, Osgoode, no matter what approach you use. Now let it go."

"Oh, very well," his cousin muttered. "I just

think— Is that not him?" Osgoode interrupted himself to ask.

Balan glanced up the hall in the direction from which he'd expected Malculinus to come, but saw nothing. Frowning, he glanced the other way, toward Murie's door, and stilled when he saw Malculinus standing two doorways beyond. The man's clothes were rumpled, his hair was a mess, and he was busily kissing a woman in the door, quite thoroughly.

"Is that not Lady Jane?" Osgoode asked, but then, before Balan could answer that, yes it was, he added, "I guess the rumors are true, and she really does have a secret lover. I wonder if she is really with child, too."

Balan grunted.

"Mayhap he does not intend to go through with the plan," Osgoode suggested. "Lady Jane is nearly as wealthy as Lady Murie."

"Wealth is not a concern for Malculinus," Balan reminded him.

"Aye, but she is a lady in good standing . . . well, other than the fact that she has taken him on as a lover," he muttered. "Besides, surely even *he* is not despicable enough to go straight to Murie's room from the arms of his lover?"

Balan didn't respond. Malculinus was turning Lady Jane and pushing her back into her chamber. After giving her a playful swat on the behind, he pulled the door closed. The man then paused for a moment, as if waiting to be sure she didn't open the door again. Finally he started up the hall, straightening his clothes and running a hand through his hair.

For one moment, Balan thought Osgoode might be right and Malculinus would bypass Murie's room, but Malculinus stopped. He cast a quick glance about to be sure no one was around to see, then eased open Murie's door and slid inside.

"Do something," Osgoode hissed.

Balan was already slipping out from behind the curtain.

Chapter Three

Balan managed to open the door just enough to slip into the room without drawing Malculinus's attention. Easing it silently closed, he paused to allow his eyes time to adjust to the darkness. A dying fire in the grate cast some weak light, but not much. It was enough for him to see that Malculinus was already at the bed, gently shaking Murie's shoulder in an effort to wake her.

"Murie? Wake up," the man whispered, scowling when she showed no sign of stirring. "Lauda must have been too generous with her herbs. Ah, well—perhaps a kiss will wake you."

Grimacing at the very idea of the despicable cur pressing his lips to Murie's, Balan snatched a statuette off the table by the door and crept swiftly behind him. As silently as he moved, he must have somehow given himself away, for Malculinus started to glance over his shoulder just as Balan reached him. Balan brought the statue sharply down on his head.

The thud was loud in the silent room, and Malculinus moaned as his feet went out from beneath him, but a quick look showed Balan that neither sound had woken Murie.

The hearth was on the other side of the bed, leaving this side in shadow. Balan stared down at the dark heap that was Malculinus, started to bend over to grab the unconscious man to drag him out of the room, but paused as his eyes slid back to the sleeping woman in the bed. He'd thought her beautiful when he'd seen her in the hall at midday, but she was even more stunning by firelight. Her features looked serene and mysterious in the shadowed room, and the weak light from the flames painted her hair with both light and dark brush strokes.

She must have been suffering a restless sleep; she'd kicked off her linens and furs and lay with her tunic tangled around her thighs, leaving her alabaster legs to glow softly in the dim light.

Balan's eyes traveled over rounded hips to the soft swell of her belly, and finally to the neckline of her tunic. The cloth there had been disrupted by her tossing and turning as well. The tie at the neck had pulled loose and lay wide open, leaving her upper chest and part of one breast exposed.

Balan found himself staring at the curve of that breast. Were he to lean down and shift the cloth the tiniest bit, her nipple would be in full view. The thought made him lick his lips as he tried to commit this image to memory so that he could pull it out and enjoy it again later. He had no idea how long he stood there, but knew it was too long when a moan sounded from the heap on the floor.

Glancing down, he scowled at Malculinus for interrupting his pleasure. He then dropped to his knees to find the man's head, and to plow a fist into the side of it to ensure he didn't make any more noise. At least, that was the plan. Unfortunately, the moment he caught him by the head to lift it, Malculinus squealed like a pig at the slaughter.

Cursing under his breath, Balan gave him a knock-out blow, then glanced worriedly toward the bed, freezing when he saw that the man's scream must have woken Murie. She was leaning over the side, blinking sleepily as she peered at him where he knelt in the darkness.

"Who are you?" she asked with confusion, and it was obvious by the way she could barely keep her eyes open that she wasn't fully awake. "Are you my husband?"

Balan hesitated, surprisingly tempted to take advantage of the situation and say yes. Should he do so, however, he'd be no better than the man lying in the shadows at his knees. Cursing his conscience, he reluctantly growled, "Nay."

"Who are you then?" Murie asked with bewilderment.

"No one," he assured her. "I am not here."

"Are you not?" Murie asked.

"Nay. You are asleep. Lie down," Balan ordered.

She pondered that briefly, and a thought seemed to occur to her. "Oh, aye, of course. You are not my husband yet. You are the man I am fated to marry."

Balan's eyes widened with alarm as she lay back down. Oh, this was so wrong. She now thought he . . . She . . . Hell!

He bit his lip, uncertain how to rectify matters but knowing he had to. After a hesitation, he shifted closer to the bed on his knees and then half stood to peer down at her. Murie had followed his instructions, lying back and apparently promptly going to sleep. His gaze slid to her gown to see that her brief spate of activity had disrupted the cloth further, and her nipple was now in plain view. Balan sucked in a breath and squeezed his fists tight to keep from reaching out to touch her.

God, he wondered; what had he ever done to deserve this kind of torture? First, the plague had decimated his people—though that had wiped out half of England, so Balan supposed he shouldn't count that as a personal assault by the Fates. But, thanks to circumstances he *could* blame on the Fates, Gaynor had not rebounded as well as some others estates. Then his father had died, leaving the burden of Gaynor and its people in his hands. And now this temptation.

A small sigh slid from Murie's lips and she shifted, disrupting her gown further until a whole breast popped out, round and firm and very inviting.

"Damn," Balan breathed. It was impossible to think of how to rectify the situation with that staring him in the eye.

After another moment wasted debating the wisdom of the action, Balan reached out to try to slip the breast back into her gown. It was a two-handed job, one hand needed to shift her breast and the other to tug at the cloth, but both hands froze as Murie moaned and arched into his touch.

His gaze shot to her face, and Balan saw that her eyes were starting to blink open. He did the only thing he could think to do—he kissed her. His reasoning was, it would both keep her from screaming at the realization that someone was pawing her, as well as give him time to think of some way to fix the mess.

It was flawed reasoning, he now realized. If just having her naked breast inches away had been distracting to his thinking processes, actually kissing her completely stole his ability to think. The woman was a warm and sleepy bundle, her mouth soft and accepting, and she tasted of honeyed mead. He was lost.

Balan had started out with a rather chaste kiss, just covering her mouth with his own, but when she sighed against his lips and stretched before him, he was helpless to stop from deepening the kiss, slipping his tongue out to urge her lips apart and then thrusting it forward to claim her.

This had a most gratifying effect. Murie groaned deep in her throat, and he felt her small hands clutch weakly at his arms as she rose up in bed, pressing her breasts against him. His hands immediately accepted the invitation, quickly returning to her chest, though this time he was trying to get her breast back out of her gown rather than put it away.

Finally freeing the coveted orb, Balan squeezed it gently in his hand. He swallowed her next groan with glee, suddenly finding himself eager to draw more happy noises from her. He was just shifting to lay himself on the bed when a deeper sound reached his ears.

Balan had so forgotten where he was and how he'd come to be there, that for a moment he was flummoxed as to where the noise had come from. But when something brushed weakly against his ankle, he was recalled to his circumstances. Without lifting his mouth from Murie's, he swung out with his fist, making a satisfying connection with what felt to be Malculinus's forehead. The soft thud as the man fell back to the floor made him sigh into Murie's mouth.

What he was doing was terribly wrong. He was taking advantage of Malculinus's scurrilous plot. He was mauling a drugged girl in her bed.

The last thought was like a bucket of icy water to the raging desire this slip of a girl had so innocently reared in him. Easing from the kiss, he slowly withdrew. Brushing her hair back as their lips parted, he whispered, "Sleep."

Murie sighed a sound of sleepy disappointment, but appeared to have fallen back asleep before the sound died on her lips. It made Balan realize how effective the herbs Lauda had given Murie were. He doubted if the girl had really been awake at all to begin with.

Sighing in disappointment, he turned to survey the heap that was Malculinus, then stooped to lift and swing him over his shoulder. Straightening, he turned for one last glance at Murie's sleep-rumpled state. Her hair was splayed across the pillows, her arms up by her head, her knees half bent to the side and her body more revealed than hidden by the gown now tangled around her hips and hanging off her shoulder.

It was a vision he'd give almost anything to wake to in the morning.

Turning resolutely, Balan carried Malculinus out of the room and pulled the door gently closed behind him.

"What happened?" Osgoode hissed, hurrying to his side. "Did she see him? Did she see you? Did—"

"Shut up, cousin," Balan ordered wearily. "Let us get this . . ." He scowled at the unconscious man over his shoulder. "Let us just get him to his room and find our own beds."

For once in his life Osgoode did not push his luck, but fell silent in accompanying him to Malculinus's room. Fortunately, the man must have dismissed his servant before slipping away, for they found the room empty and the bed turned down. Balan and Osgoode undressed the lord and put him into bed in the hopes that he wouldn't remember anything in the morning, and would think that he'd stumbled back to his own room and gone to sleep.

Of course, Balan realized, the man would have a splitting headache in the morning, which might work against them. But he little cared. It was nothing less than Malculinus deserved.

Murie woke with a smile on her face and stretched sleepily in bed. She felt marvelous, and she'd had the most wonderful dream. She'd dreamt a man had come to her in the night and— Her eyes blinked open.

She'd dreamt of a man!

Sitting abruptly up, Murie stared around her room. He wasn't here of course; she'd dreamt him. But he'd seemed so real. She could still taste him on her lips and smell him on her linens. . . .

"Oh my," Murie breathed. She'd eaten rotten meat on St. Agnes Eve and dreamt of a man with long dark hair, dark eyes and the body of a warrior.

"Oh . . ." Her eyes widened as she recalled his lips and hands on her. If the man was half as good in reality as he was in her dreams, she could hardly wait to meet and marry him. There would be nothing to fear in the marital bed.

Laughing, she tossed her linens and furs aside and leapt from bed, eager to go below and break her fast. She was famished this morning . . . and her husband-to-be might be in attendance at court. She hoped so. She couldn't wait to meet him and find out his name and have him kiss her again. Her toes tingled at the very idea. That kiss had been—

"Ouch," Murie muttered, raising her foot to look at it. She'd stepped on something hard-edged on the floor, but while sore, her foot was unmarked. Rubbing the spot, she peered across the rushes, eyebrows rising as she spotted a bit of shiny gold.

Murie released her foot and bent to pick up the object, eyes widening at the cross on a gold chain upon which she'd stepped. She examined the item curiously. It wasn't hers, and she'd never seen Cecily wear it. She turned it over in her hand and began to bite her lip, worrying at its origin.

The click of the door opening distracted her, and Murie glanced over to see Cecily stick her head into the room. Spotting her mistress up and about, the servant smiled and entered bearing a basin of fresh water.

"Did you sleep well, my lady?"

"Aye." Murie set the cross on the table by her bed and followed the maid to where she set the water by the window.

"Did you dream of anyone?"

Murie glanced at her with surprise. She recalled talking about the St. Agnes Eve superstition with the maid the night before, but didn't remember mentioning that she'd eaten rotten meat.

"Well?" Cecily asked curiously. The maid then tilted her head, eyes narrowing. "You did, did you not?"

"Aye," Murie admitted. By now, she realized, news of what she and Lauda had done was probably all over court. After all, the woman had gotten the rotten meat from the cook, and anyone sitting near them last night had been able to hear their discussion.

"You did!" the maid squealed excitedly. "Tell me all. What does he look like? Is he handsome? Do you know him?"

"He was very handsome," Murie acknowledged, an image of the stranger's face rising up in her mind. It was a strong, handsome face, with deep brown eyes, a straight nose and the sweetest lips—Murie unconsciously raised her hand to her own mouth at the memory. Their kiss was a little fuzzy in her mind, not as clear as reality would have been, but still, she could recall the feelings that kiss had stirred and could even still taste him on her tongue. She could not smell him anymore, though, not now that she was up and about, and she suddenly wondered if the rest of it would fade as quickly. Murie hoped not; she'd never been kissed before, and it had been quite the most exciting thing she'd ever experienced. She really didn't want to forget.

Realizing that she was rubbing her upper lip with her fingers, Murie forced her hand away and began to wash, saying, "I put a cross on the table by the bed. Go look and make sure it is not yours."

The maid moved dutifully across the room and picked up the cross. "Nay, my lady. 'Tis not mine."

"I did not think so," Murie said, troubled. She briefly considered that it might belong to her dream man and that he wasn't a dream at all, but she didn't recall him wearing anything of the sort.

"Most likely one of the servants dropped it while replacing the rushes yesterday," Cecily suggested. "Or it may have been caught up in the rushes themselves."

"Oh." Murie released a breath of relief. "Aye. That must be it. Set it back on the table, and I shall ask Becker to check with the staff and find out if someone has lost it."

Cecily set the cross on the table as instructed, then walked back to her side, asking, "Did your dream man say or do anything?"

Murie's hand slowed, the damp linen washcloth pausing over her left breast. She was reluctant to answer, really wishing now that she hadn't admitted to the dream. She suddenly didn't wish to share her dream man with anyone. She wanted to remember and savor what she'd experienced, and telling others seemed to lessen the experience somehow.

Raising her head, she forced a smile and lied: "Nay. And that is all I am telling you for now. Come; help me dress. I am famished this morn and would go down to break my fast."

Cecily looked disappointed but refrained from questioning her further. After helping her mistress get ready to face the day, she followed Murie out of the room and accompanied her below. Emilie and her husband, Lord Reginald Reynard, were just leaving their room as they approached, and both smiled upon spotting Murie and her maid.

"Good morn, Murie! Are you feeling better?" Emilie asked, waiting so that they could all walk together.

"Aye, thank you for asking," Murie answered. She smiled in greeting to Lord Reynard. Handsome and strong, the man adored his wife and treated her as such. Murie couldn't have chosen a better husband and was happy for her friend's happiness.

They all made their way below, chatting about this and that and sundry, and once they reached the hall where the tables were set up and food was being circulated, Lord Reynard ushered them to an open spot above the salt. He then kissed his wife's cheek and excused himself to have a word with one of the other knights, promising to return quickly.

Emilie watched her husband go with a fond smile. "He will get caught up in a political discussion, and it will be the end of meal before he thinks to come back and eat."

"Don't you mind?" Murie asked.

"Not at all," Emilie said with a laugh. "It is rare we come to court, and I like to see him enjoy himself. He has been working so hard since the plague rolled through." Her brows drew together with concern as she watched her husband disappear into the crowd.

Murie nodded solemnly. Castle Reynard had been more fortunate than most, losing few of their people, but the plague was terrifying all the same. Murie had been worried sick about her friend all through that horrible time, and knew Reginald had been as well—especially after he'd learned his wife was with child. If he'd lost her and the babe, Murie suspected it would have been a blow from which he might not have recovered.

"Besides"—Emilie turned back to Murie with a laugh—"I think he just rushes off to allow me time alone visiting with you. He knows how close we are and how I look forward to seeing you."

Murie smiled widely at this claim and gave her pregnant friend a hug. "And I always look forward to seeing you as well. You are the closest thing I have to family, Emilie."

"Oh, hush. Do not speak so loud. You shall hurt the king's feelings should it get back to him," Emilie cautioned.

"Aye," Murie agreed, glancing around to see if anyone was close enough to have heard. She really didn't wish to hurt the king's feelings. He'd been kind in his way, and she was grateful for it, but the man was rarely here. He was more like an uncle to her, while Emilie was like a sister.

"So, how did you sleep? Did you dream of your future husband?" Emilie teased, clearly to lighten the subject.

When Murie hesitated, Cecily burst out with the news, saying, "Aye, she did—and he was very handsome!"

Emilie's eyes widened incredulously at the maid, then she shifted to a blushing Murie. "What?"

"I . . . well . . . I am sure it was just a dream," Murie said finally. Trying to drop the subject, she added, "You do not think that Reginald minds that we are so close, do you? He—"

"Oh, no, no, no," Emilie said firmly. "You are not changing the subject. Tell me all. Did you really dream about someone?" When Murie nodded and shifted uncomfortably, Emilie asked, "Was it someone you know?"

Murie let out her breath in defeat. "Nay, I do not know him."

"You do not?" both Emilie and Cecily exclaimed at once.

"Is he handsome?" Emilie asked after taking some time to get over her apparent surprise.

"Aye, he is very handsome," Murie murmured.

"What does he look like?" Cecily asked.

"Yes," Emilie echoed eagerly. "What does he look like?"

"Well, his hair was very dark—black, I think—and he looked . . . like him!" she finished with amazement as her glance landed on a man seated across the hall. Murie stared at the man in the faded blue doublet with wide, fascinated eyes. Her chamber had been dark in her dream, and she hadn't seen him as clearly as she was seeing him now, but she was sure it was the same man. He had the same long black hair that had felt so soft as it brushed against her cheek, the same proud face, the same wide shoulders she recalled clutching in her dream. The man was gorgeous.

"Who?" Emilie glanced around, trying to follow Murie's suddenly stunned gaze. "Which one is he?"

"The man in the blue doublet and green cote-hardie. Just across the room. With the dark hair and strong wide shoulders and soft lips."

"Soft lips?" Emilie's head shot back around.

"Well, he had soft lips when he kissed me in the dream," she said. Then she frowned. "But firm. Soft but firm."

Emilie stared at her, wide-eyed for a moment, then allowed curiosity to draw her gaze to the man in question.

"Lord Gaynor," she murmured.

"Gaynor," Murie echoed, testing the name on her lips. It was a fine-sounding name. Strong and solid. The man looked strong and solid as well.

"You must tell me everything," her friend demanded. "From the beginning of the dream to the very end. I want to hear it all."

"She saw you."

"What are you talking about?" Balan asked, trying not to look guilty as his cousin claimed the seat beside him.

"Lady Murie. On my way around the hall, I passed by where she and Lady Reynard are seated, and I overheard her telling Lady Emilie that you were the man she dreamed of last night." Pausing, he arched one eyebrow and said, "Why did you not tell me she saw you?"

Balan shifted uncomfortably. "Because I was hoping she would not remember it when she woke."

That wasn't really a bold-faced lie. Part of him, the more honorable part, truly wished she'd forgotten. That part would rather win her hand more honorably. The other part, however, couldn't care less how he won her and really hadn't wanted her to forget him at all. It wanted her to remember, demand a fast marriage and have her greet him stripped naked in every private corner of this castle. Not that there were many private corners at court.

"Only you," Osgoode said with a shake of the head.

"I—," Balan began irritably, but Osgoode interrupted.

"There is more. I was not the only one to hear. Lauda was loitering nearby. She appeared about to hail them, but paused when she heard what Lady

Murie was saying. She got most agitated as she listened and then rushed around the room. I followed, of course."

"Of course," Balan said. His cousin loved this sort of thing.

"Aye, and she went straight to her brother."

"And?" Balan asked, knowing there would be more.

"And she is still there. See?" Osgoode gestured along the tables, and Balan followed his pointing finger to where Malculinus Aldous sat listening as his sister spoke most animatedly. She was obviously not at all happy, and when she gestured in his direction and both Aldouses glanced his way, Balan found his mouth splitting into a wide, sharklike smile, teeth bared. It wasn't that he was happy about all of this, but he thought it could only be a good thing if they realized he knew what they had been up to. Perhaps it would prevent their trying any further nonsense.

"I wonder if they will be able to sort out what happened," Osgoode said, watching the pair.

"Probably, or very close to," Balan murmured. The Aldouses turned away from him and huddled together, whispering furiously.

"They are plotting again."

"Aye," he agreed with irritation. So much for his having any sort of influence on them. "I wish I knew what they were saying."

"You will," Osgoode assured him. When Balan glanced over sharply, he shrugged and explained, "I sent my page to spy on them."

Turning back to the pair across the room, this time Balan noted the lad loitering nearby. He was sitting cross-legged in the rushes, playing with a dog. No one was paying any notice at all.

Balan smiled slowly. "William is a good lad."

"Aye, he is. And he is excellent at such tasks. The boy will recall and recite every word to me when he gives his accounting."

Balan nodded and turned his attention back to the bread and cheese before him.

"So . . ." Osgoode prompted.

Balan glanced at him warily. "What?"

"After all those protestations of not stooping to his level, you not only let her see you, you kissed the girl."

Balan shifted uncomfortably. "I did not intend either outcome."

"But once she'd seen you, you thought you may as well go the whole journey and kiss her," Osgoode said, nodding with condescension.

"I kissed her because she woke up while I was trying to right her nightgown!"

"Ah." The word sounded understanding, but Osgoode's expression was less so. Biting his lip, the man asked, "And how did her gown come to need righting?"

"She is apparently a restless sleeper," Balan muttered, then glanced to the side to see his cousin making a face. "What the hell are you grinning about?"

"Well, it is not often I get to see you so uncomfortable," Osgoode pointed out with amusement. "And besides, we are saved. You have won the fair maid's hand. She sounded quite taken with you as she described her 'dream' to Lady Emilie."

"She was telling her about it?" he asked with alarm, wondering how much Lady Murie remembered. Did she recall waking to find him seemingly groping her breasts in the dark?

"Aye, and it was all 'heated embraces, flames of passion, and burning kisses.'"

Balan stared, aghast, wondering if those herbs Lauda had given Murie had somehow distorted the actual event, combining the fire and his kisses in her mind. Not that it hadn't been hot and passionate for him, too, but there seemed to be a lot of references to fire in the descriptions Osgoode was giving. Perhaps the herbs or the gamy meat had made her feverish.

"Well . . ." Emilie sat back in her seat and fanned her face with one hand. "It sounds as though it was . . . well . . ."

"Aye." Murie sighed. "It *was.*"

Emilie eyed her for a moment, then said, "The St. Agnes Eve nonsense aside, Lord Gaynor is a fine man. I know Reginald thinks highly of him. And the king."

"That is a good sign. I respect your husband's opinion, and if the king thinks highly of him, too, surely he would not protest our marriage."

"Aye," Emilie nodded and added, "he served the king in battle at both Crecy and Calais, and is said to be a fierce warrior."

Murie smiled, pleased at this news. A strong sword arm to defend the home was important.

"I have never heard whispers about ill treatment from him toward man, woman, child or animal. It seems he is fair and honorable in all his dealings."

"That is promising as well," Murie said happily.

Emilie smiled, but then cautioned, "There are some murmurs that Castle Gaynor suffered heavily from the plague. I know his father was among those who died, and Balan returned to find he'd inherited many troubles."

"Balan?" Murie said with confusion.

"That is his name," Emilie explained.

"Oh . . . Ba-lan," she murmured, trying the name out. It was lovely to her ear. Balan and Murie.

Emilie bit her lip on a smile and then said, "Anyway,

I understand he is in some financial difficulty at the moment because of it. I am sure it is only temporary, however—"

"My parents left me well off. Financial difficulties are of little consequence." Murie waved the concern away easily, her mind immediately going back to his name. Balan, Lord Gaynor. Balan and Murie. Lady Gaynor, she thought, and wondered what Gaynor Castle was like. She hoped it was by water and not too far inland. Murie loved the water. "Where is Gaynor?"

"In the north. I believe it is on the seashore, but am not sure. I know there is a river nearby," Emilie answered. "The best part of all this is that 'tis far enough away that you would not be expected to return to court very often."

"That is definitely good news," Murie admitted. She'd come to loathe court life. The debauchery, the intrigue, the cruelty . . .

"Hmmm," Emilie said thoughtfully, her gaze moving over Balan, Lord Gaynor. "I suppose the only question that remains is whether the two of you would suit."

Murie nodded, trying to act halfway intelligent and sensible, rather than flighty and eager. Her gaze slid back to the man who might be fated to be her husband. Balan seemed deep in conversation with the man seated beside him, who was also attractive, but in her opinion could not hold a candle to Balan. He was paler in coloring and not quite as broad-shouldered or strong-looking. "Who is the man beside him?"

"His cousin, Osgoode. He went off to battle with Balan in France. It was the reason they were not here when the plague struck. Reginald thinks much of Osgoode, too."

"That is nice," Murie said. "Does he live at Gaynor?"

Emilie nodded. "His mother died giving birth to him, and so he was raised at Gaynor after his own father died. He and Balan are as close as brothers."

Murie nodded. "Is there any other family?"

"I believe Balan has a younger sister. The mother died in labor with her, and now that their father is dead, she is orphaned."

"Like me," Murie murmured, her heart aching for the unknown girl. Though, the child was fortunate to have her brother to look after her; Murie had had no one once her parents died. Well, the king and queen had taken her in, of course, and she'd been fortunate in at least earning her godfather's affections. But it had been the queen's affections she'd truly desired. She'd wanted a mother's love and approval, something no amount of doting by the king could make up for. Perhaps she could give Balan's sister what she herself had not gained. "What is her name?"

"Hmm? I believe it is Juliana, but I am not at all sure."

"Juliana," Murie echoed, thinking the name quite lovely.

"So?" Emilie queried lightly. "Are you ready?"

"For what?" Murie asked with confusion.

"To meet him."

"Meet him?" Murie gulped. "Why?"

Emilie laughed, them said patiently, "To speak with him and see if he is suitable."

"But . . . *now?*"

"There is no time like the present," Emilie assured her. "This way you can decide if he is worth troubling with or not. If so, you may spend more time with him. If he does not seem suitable, you can move on to other candidates."

"But . . ." Murie glanced down at the gown she wore,

a white surcoat over a plain gray cotehardie. Had she known for sure she would meet the man from her dream today, she would have dressed more attractively.

"You look fine," Emilie assured her. "Come. Balan has spent time at Reynard. He stopped there on his way home from France. I know him, and he will not think anything of my stopping to greet him."

"Oh," Murie murmured; but her mind was in a panic as she stood to follow Emilie around the room.

Chapter Four

"They are coming this way!"

Balan nearly choked on the bread he was swallowing when Osgoode hissed at him in a panicked voice. Grabbing up his mead, he gulped some to help wash down the bread, and then glanced around to see Lady Emilie and Murie coming across the hall. They could have been headed anywhere and to speak to anyone, but the way Reginald's wife was eyeing them with determination suggested that they were indeed coming to see them.

"Sit up," Osgoode ordered. "And run your hands through your hair. Oh, dear God, what are we going to do?"

Balan rolled his eyes. "I thought you were an expert on women. Why ask me? Besides, stop panicking. If they are coming here, it is to speak to me, not you."

"That is why I am panicking," Osgoode assured him. "You do not speak much—not to women. Not even to men, really."

"I am the strong and silent sort," Balan growled.

"Well, strong and silent will not win you a wife. I prithee, Balan, please talk to the woman. Give her a compliment or two or—" Osgoode cut himself off as the pair drew near enough to overhear. Turning abruptly in his seat, he concentrated on his meal, as if he hoped the women might think they hadn't been noticed.

Balan shook his head at this behavior, then hesitated, unsure what he should do. Should he follow his cousin's lead and act as if he were unaware of their approach, or smile in greeting now that they were drawing nearer? He knew and liked Reginald's wife, and was glad she would be the one to introduce he and Murie properly; it should help ease things. Actually, as he watched the women approach, he suddenly recalled a conversation at Reynard Castle when last he was there. Reginald had been forced to make an appearance at court, and Emilie was excited at the opportunity to visit her friend. Balan had been startled to hear Lady Emilie and Murie were friends at the time, having heard the famous stories about the Brat and her antics for years, but Emilie had assured him the girl wasn't what the stories claimed at all and that he should wait to judge for himself.

Balan had just shaken off the suggestion at the time.

Yes, he now believed her words. Murie *wasn't* what everyone perceived her to be. Her behavior was just an act to protect her in the cold, cruel world of court. Balan honestly found it amazing that she'd survived as well as she had and suspected the friendship with Emilie had been her saving grace. He'd yet to meet a kinder, more understanding woman than Reginald's bride. He'd even felt a pang or two of jealousy over the man's good fortune in marrying Emilie.

"Good morn, my lord," Lady Emilie said.

Balan jerked his gaze back into focus at the greeting, his eyes widening in surprise that they had already reached him. Aware that Osgoode was glancing around in feigned surprise himself, Balan stood and nodded to the two women.

"Murie, this is Balan, Lord Gaynor, and his cousin, Osgoode," Emilie said politely. "And this, gentlemen, is Lady Murie of Somerdale."

Balan nodded again, grunting when Osgoode jumped to his feet, jarring him in the side with an elbow. *Not* accidentally, Balan was sure.

"Ladies! How lovely to meet you both," his cousin cried happily. "Of course, Lady Emilie, we have met before, but it is always a pleasure. And doubly so because you have brought such a flower of beauty with you."

Balan turned wide eyes on Osgoode, sure he'd lost his mind. He'd never heard his cousin sound like such an ass.

"Good morn, Osgoode." Emilie laughed, then glanced from one man to the other. "Murie was hoping for a walk in the gardens, and I was happy to join her, but we cannot find Reginald to accompany us."

"Actually, I believe he is approaching now," Balan said, glancing past her.

"Ah." Much to his surprise, the woman didn't look pleased. She turned to see her tall, fair-haired husband indeed hurrying toward them.

"I am sorry, love," he said, reaching her side and bending to press a kiss to her cheek. "Lord Abernathy wished to discuss something of import, and I lost track of time."

"'Tis all right, husband," Emilie said, but she appeared vexed.

"Your wife was just informing us that she was hoping

for a walk in the gardens with Lady Murie, but she could not find you," Balan announced, hoping to ease any tension.

"Oh." Reginald frowned at his wife. "Er . . . well, actually, I was just coming to explain that I have to meet with the king. He sent Robert to fetch me, and I said I would be along at once, but I wished to explain that to you."

"Oh." Rather than appear put out by this news, Emilie brightened, beaming at the man as if he'd just said something terribly clever. All signs of annoyance gone, she assured him, "Oh, that is all right, husband. I am sure Lord Gaynor and Osgoode would be willing to accompany us on our walk."

"Oh my, yes. We would be honored," Osgoode said quickly. His voice was bluff and deeper than usual. It made Balan glance at him in bewilderment, not having a clue what was wrong with him.

"You see? They will accompany us. All is well," Emilie said, patting her husband's arm.

"Good, good," Reginald replied—but his eyes were narrowed on his wife with something like suspicion. His gaze then moved to Murie, and finally to Balan. When Lord Reynard cocked one eyebrow in question, Balan shrugged. It was becoming obvious that Lady Emilie was trying to help lady Murie spend some time with him. However, he wasn't going to explain that to Reginald. Not now, and not later. He had no desire to explain the debacle of last night.

"Well," Reginald said. "I should be off. Enjoy your walk."

He bent to press a kiss by his wife's ear, taking the opportunity to whisper something that made her scowl. He then straightened, nodded to the rest of them and departed.

"Well, shall we, gentlemen?" Lady Emilie asked brightly. Before anyone could respond, she stepped forward to take Osgoode's arm in a firm grip and began to walk.

Murie smiled at him shyly, so Balan offered her his arm. She placed her hand lightly on his forearm, and they began to follow the other couple. They left the castle and made their way into the royal gardens.

Emilie and Osgoode were walking a couple of steps in front of them, but it was a miracle the two didn't trip over anything in their path: Both spent more time glancing anxiously back at Murie and Balan than paying attention to where they were going. Emilie was casting them worried looks, and Osgoode kept raising his eyebrows and giving Balan meaningful glances. Fortunately, Murie didn't appear to notice. Balan had no idea what his cousin's problem was, but he suspected it had to do with him speaking to the woman. Unfortunately, Balan found he couldn't think of a thing to say. Every time he looked Murie's way, his attention got caught on her lips and he remembered the kiss they'd shared last night, and his thoughts went south, not offering the sort of elevated conversation he supposed Osgoode wanted.

Apparently deciding as one that he and Murie were in need of intervention, the pair suddenly broke apart and dropped back to walk on either side of them: Emilie on Murie's side, Osgoode on Balan's. It was no surprise when his cousin jammed his elbow into his side, obviously hoping to jar him into speech, but Osgoode was saved from a good cuff to the head by Emilie's sudden speech.

" 'Tis a lovely sunny day for a change and yet not too hot," she said cheerfully.

"Aye, 'tis," Osgoode agreed at once. "Very nice for

summer. And yet not too cool either. I do hate when the cold winter winds arrive. So does Balan," he added informatively.

"Aye, winter is Murie's least favorite time. She likes this time of year, though she does think fall is lovely with all its colors," Emilie went on, then briefly fell silent and began to worry her lip. Suddenly she stopped, brightening as she said, "Balan, I was telling Murie about your sister, Juliana. She is ten, is she not?"

"Aye," Balan answered.

Emilie frowned when he said no more, then asked, "She is faring well, I hope?"

"Aye," Balan said, then grunted and turned to glare at Osgoode, who had elbowed him once more.

For his part, Osgoode glared right back. He leaned forward past Balan to the ladies and said, "Juliana is faring very well. She is missing her father, of course, but Balan is doing his best to fill the hole his passing left."

Balan arched an eyebrow at the bald-faced lie. Much to his distress, his father had blamed Juliana for her mother's death and had never forgiven her. He hadn't been cruel to the child, but had basically ignored her all her days, leaving her to the care of servants. The girl could hardly miss someone she'd never really known. There was no hole for Balan to fill.

The words had apparently touched Murie, however, for she smiled sweetly upon him and murmured, " 'Tis very kind of you, my lord. I am sure she appreciates your efforts. I know I should have been grateful to have had an older sibling to take over my care after my parents died."

"Aye," Emilie agreed. Leaning forward to look past the girl, she explained, "Murie was only ten when she was orphaned and brought to court."

Balan nodded, catching Osgoode's elbow when it jutted toward him again. Aware that the women had noticed it, he merely gave his cousin a warning glare before releasing him, and said, "Careful, cousin. 'Tis slippery, and you might lose your footing."

Osgoode's mouth twisted with displeasure. He said to the women, "That must have been difficult for you, Murie. Court is not the most clement of environments."

Murie looked uncomfortable, and it was Emilie who answered. "It was very difficult for her. The other girls were jealous that the king made so much of her looks, and they were very cruel."

Osgoode murmured a sound of sympathy and said, "Balan suffered something similar in his youth. We were sent to Lord Strathcliffe's to train, and Strathcliffe took a liking to Balan, showing him favor. Though it was no fault of his own, the other boys hated him for it. They were constantly picking fights."

Balan scowled. While this was true, it had happened a long time ago, had made him a stronger fighter and better warrior, and was hardly worth mentioning now. Or so he thought until Murie squeezed his arm and gave him a shy, sympathetic smile. Hmmm.

"No doubt you have heard that the king decided it is time for Murie to marry and has given her leave to choose her own husband," Emilie said suddenly, drawing a horrified gasp from her friend. Ignoring Murie, Lady Reynard went on, "It is such a serious and difficult decision to make."

"Aye," Osgoode agreed. "Balan must marry as well, and he is finding it so."

Balan almost groaned aloud. The pair was embarrassingly obvious. He very much feared that, given more time, the two would be proposing for them soon. Fortunately, that didn't come to pass. Or perhaps unfortunately, he acknowledged as Malculinus and his sister, Lauda, stepped out onto the path.

Judging by Lauda's flushed face and Malculinus's out-of-breath state, Balan would have guessed that the pair had run to get ahead of them to appear.

"Why, Lady Murie, Lady Emilie," Lauda greeted, smiling widely. "How fortuitous to meet up with the two of you here." Balan didn't miss the fact that he and Osgoode were completely ignored.

"Aye," Malculinus agreed, still gasping for breath. He really needed to start working out with his men, Balan thought with disgust. Some time working with the quintain or exercising his sword arm would put him in shape. But that wasn't likely to happen. He happened to know Malculinus's sire had been paying scutage for years to prevent his having to serve his military time.

Which was probably a good thing, Balan decided, as the man caught his breath. In the shape he was in, Malculinus would be dropped in the first battle he dared enter, though it was doubtful he would ever have the courage to bother.

"We were just wondering if you had dreamt of anyone?" Malculinus finally got out. He'd taken a moment to collect himself.

Balan's mouth tightened at the question and at the way the man was looking at him with slight triumph. He had a feeling the Aldouses had come up with a way to reveal that last night had been no dream, and without revealing their involvement in the matter.

He tensed, prepared to plow his fist into the man's head again, when Murie said, "Nay, my lord. I fear I did not dream at all."

If Malculinus and Lauda appeared shocked by these

words, it was no more than he himself felt. Osgoode's expression also seemed to suggest surprise.

Only Lady Emilie didn't react to the claim, merely smiled and said, "I fear it was just a silly superstition after all."

"I . . . You . . ." Malculinus paused and stared at Murie, seemingly at a loss. It appeared his plan was foiled.

"Are you sure you did not dream of anyone?" Lauda asked with a frown, and Balan felt sure that, if it were acceptable, she would have grabbed Murie by the throat and shaken her until the truth came out. However, they weren't alone, and she could do nothing when Murie shook her head.

"I am quite positive," she replied, and then asked, "Why, Lauda? Did you dream of someone?"

The woman stiffened, then suddenly looked pleased. "Ayc. I did."

"Really?" Emilie asked with interest. "And who did you dream of?"

"I . . . he was a stranger. Tall, fair and handsome," Lauda remarked, then eyed Murie. "I felt sure you would have dreamed, too."

It was obvious the woman was hoping that by claiming she'd dreamed, she would encourage Murie to admit as much herself, but Murie merely shook her head apologetically. "I am sorry, Lauda. Mayhap I did not have enough of the rotten meat."

Lauda let her breath out on a sigh, scowled and then said, "Mayhap."

"Well," Emilie said brightly. "We were enjoying a nice walk on this rare sunny day. I suppose we should continue."

"We will join you," Lauda suggested, an obviously forced smile on her face.

Emilie's smile became decidedly annoyed, but there was little she could do without appearing rude. Unable to dissuade the Aldouses from joining them, she did the next best thing and latched on to Malculinus's arm. "How lovely! I can ask Malculinus about something I have been wondering for quite a while. How do you feel about . . . the French?" she ended at last, drawing the man determinedly forward and away from Murie and Balan.

Lauda scowled and opened her mouth to speak, only to snap it closed again in surprise as Osgoode took her arm and began to urge her forward. "I shall escort you then, Lady Lauda. How fortunate I am— getting to walk with three such lovely women in one day." Balan bit his lip to keep from laughing as she found herself led firmly away.

"Well," he said, turning back to Murie. "Shall we?"

Murie nodded silently, and allowed Balan to draw her hand through his arm to continue their walk. Her mind was in an uproar. It had been Emilie who suggested that she not admit she'd dreamt of anyone last night. She'd made the comment right after hearing the details of the dream. Murie had been grateful for the suggestion. While she hadn't minded telling Emilie about it, she hadn't felt at all comfortable sharing the dream with Cecily and wasn't happy with the idea of having to share it with anyone else, either. She felt sure this was the best way to deal with the matter, and had found it surprisingly easy to lie to Lauda and Malculinus when the question came up. Not that she would have admitted to it in front of Balan, anyway. It was one thing for Emilie to know about it; quite another for the man who had kissed and caressed her so sweetly in her dreams.

Besides, this seemed to her to be a good test of the superstition. She knew about the dream, but Balan did not; and so, if they ended up together anyway, then surely it was fated.

Forcing a smile, she glanced toward Balan, wishing he would say something to break the silence that had swallowed them now that Emilie and Osgoode were no longer doing the talking. She tried thinking of something to say herself, but had spent the past several years trying to avoid conversation with everyone but Emilie, leaving the queen's solar and roaming the garden and castle on her own. She'd been too successful. It seemed she now had no idea how to carry on a normal conversation. At least, she hadn't yet come up with anything to say. And he was equally silent. It was difficult for her to get to know him and figure out if he would suit her as a mate should they not speak.

Finally Murie said, "Emilie says you and Reginald are friends?"

"Aye."

She waited for him to expound on that, but he didn't. Frowning, she asked, "Have you known him long?"

"Aye."

Again she waited for him to expound, and again he didn't. Murie bit her lip. He wasn't being very helpful. "Emilie says you have gone to battle for the king?"

"Aye."

"In France?" she prodded.

"Aye."

"Crecy? Calais?" she asked through gritted teeth.

"Aye."

Murie finally turned on him with irritation. "Do you actually speak, my lord? If so, I would consider it rather kind of you to help out with this conversation, rather than leaving me to carry it on my own."

"Aye. I speak," he answered. Then he fell silent.

Murie thought she might swoon. The man had issued three whole words! Dear Lord, be still my beating heart, she thought, frustration clawing at her stomach. The man was—

"However, I am more comfortable speaking to men than women. I have spent more time around men," he explained.

Murie was just softening at this explanation, thinking it was admirable of him to say it when so many men seemed to dislike admitting a failure—at least the king did—when he added, "I often find it more trouble than it is worth. Women are such emotional creatures and often seem to lack in the basic sense that God gave men. It is difficult not to offend them."

"What?" She gasped in dismay.

"See? I have offended you."

"Aye, of course I am offended, my lord," she said with exasperation. "You have just claimed that women are too stupid to bother talking to."

"Nay, you misunderstood me," he said quickly.

"It must be because I am so lacking in the sense God gave men," she snapped. Turning on him she added, "I shall have you know, women have just as much sense as men. More, even."

"Oh, now—," he began, but she interrupted again.

"Aye, they do. I assure you, I am every bit as intelligent as a man."

"I am sure you are," he murmured soothingly, but it was too late.

"Do not patronize me, my lord," she snapped. "I am as intelligent as a man, and I shall prove it. In fact, we shall have a duel of intelligence to prove women are just as smart as men."

"A duel of intelligence?" he echoed with surprise. "What exactly is that?"

Murie bit her lip, then admitted, "I am not sure. However, despite my lack of intelligence, I will endeavor to think of something and let you know."

With nothing else to say to the man, she turned on her heel and hurried to Emilie's side.

"I am finding it a bit inclement out here, Emilie," she said when her friend saw her. "I think I shall return inside."

"I shall join you," Emilie agreed.

"As will we," Lauda announced, pulling free of Osgoode. She gestured for her brother to join them, and followed the two women starting back toward the castle.

"Is Lord Gaynor not coming as well?" Malculinus asked with interest, moving up on Murie's side.

"I have no idea," she answered honestly.

"I see," Lauda said slowly, then commented, "Are you sure you did not have a dream?"

"I have answered that question several times now, Lauda," Murie pointed out with irritation. "I am *quite* sure."

"Aye, I am sorry I keep asking. It is just that I feel so bad. We both ate that rotten meat, and yet I am the only one who had a dream. I feel guilty that I talked you into it at all," she continued. "Especially now that there is some question as to whether the rotten meat part actually works."

Murie stopped and turned sharply. "What do you mean? What question?"

Lauda bit her lip and admitted, "Well, one of the ladies heard what we were doing last night, and she told me it only works if you fast all day. Only then shall you dream of the man meant to be your husband. If you eat rotten meat, you shall dream of the man you should *not* marry."

"What?" Murie stared at Lauda with horror.

"Aye." Lauda nodded. "So, I suppose it does not really matter that you dreamed of no one. But eating that rotten meat was a waste, I guess."

"I do not recall that being part of the legend," Emilie spoke up, scowling. "I do not recall there being anything at all about someone you not marry."

"Aye, well, neither do I," Lauda agreed earnestly. "But then, I did not recall the mention of rotten meat at all yesterday, and you said you had some vague recollection of it. This lady seemed to know the belief well and seemed firm on that point. Anyway," she decided, waving the matter away, "it matters little, as Murie was not made ill, nor did she dream of anyone."

"Aye," Emilie said heavily, casting an anxious glance at Murie as they entered the castle. Then, with feigned cheer she said, "Oh, look, here we are back inside. You must come up to my room with me, Murie. I have a gift I meant to give you."

"Of course," Murie agreed, despite the fact that her friend had already given her a gift; it was obvious she wished them to speak alone. Either way, Murie was glad for the excuse to get away from Lauda and Malculinus Aldous. She needed to think about things. She was very confused. She'd dreamt of Balan and his passionate kiss and assumed the man was to be her husband, but then he'd made that comment about women being emotional and lacking sense.

Murmuring good-day to the brother and sister, Emilie drew Murie's arm through her own and led her toward the stairs. They ascended in silence, but Murie was aware of the concerned and curious glances Emilie kept casting her way. Finally, the woman said, "I gather the walk did not go well. Was the conversation stilted?"

"Would that it were," Murie muttered. "At first he would not speak at all. The man was silent as a stone. And when I confronted him on the matter, he explained that he did not often take the trouble to talk to women, as he found more often than not it was not worth his trouble. Women, it seems, are emotional creatures who are not gifted with the same strength and intelligence as men."

"What?" Emilie asked in amazement. "But we talked when he visited Reginald."

"Aye, well, mayhap you are the exception to the rule, then," Murie muttered.

They were both silent for a bit, and then Emilie said, "Nay. I do not believe it. You must have misunderstood him, Murie."

"I did not misunderstand," she assured her friend.

Emilie shook her head. "Then he must have been teasing you." When Murie did not allow that to be possible, in fact, insisted it wasn't, Emilie went on, "I think you need to ignore all this superstition business, Murie. You have to ignore what Lauda said regarding dreaming about a man after eating rotten meat meaning you should not marry him. 'Tis all nonsense."

"If you thought it was nonsense, why did you introduce me to him after you learned I dreamt of him?" Murie asked.

"Because I know him, and the moment you mentioned him I realized that he would be a good husband to you. He is honorable and kind, and he too needs to marry. Gaynor needs a bride with enough wealth to help set it back to rights. The superstition had nothing to do with it." Emilie sighed. "Murie, you cannot base such an important decision on anything as whimsical as a superstition. You mentioned that you know none of the court's available men, but I do, and truly, Balan is one of the best. Perhaps *the* best. I think the two of you would suit each other beautifully, and you know I love you like a sister and would not lie about such a thing."

Murie let her breath out slowly and bit her lip, then confessed, "I have challenged him to a duel."

"What?" Emilie turned on her in horror.

"Not with swords or anything," she explained quickly. "A duel of intelligence."

"Oh." Emilie relaxed and continued to walk, then asked uncertainly, "And what exactly does that consist of?"

"I am not sure," Murie admitted. "I have to come up with something."

"Hmmm . . . Well, I suppose a duel of intelligence is all right. It gives you an excuse to meet again, and will give you both a chance to get to know each other better," Emilie said, nodding. "Aye. It may even be a good thing. I shall help you come up with something, but please believe me, Murie, when I say I really think he was teasing you. He has always treated me with the utmost respect. I have never got the smallest inkling that he thinks little of women."

"I shall keep that in mind," Murie promised—and she would. But she was distressed by the possibility that they'd got the St. Agnes belief wrong, and that dreaming about Balan might mean she shouldn't marry him. In fact, she was so distressed that she thought it would be a good idea to check with the wisest person she knew.

Unfortunately, that would be Becker. But she could not go ask Becker, because that might make the king think she believed his aide was smarter than he, and would be insulted. No, she'd have to go to the king while Becker was there and see what they both had to say.

"Are you coming?" Emilie asked when she realized Murie had paused.

Her thoughts scattered, and Murie glanced up and managed a smile. She would have to see the king and Becker later. She didn't want Emilie knowing she wished to inquire. Superstitions were the one place the two women did not agree. Emilie was always lecturing her on the subject, but Murie could not help herself. The world was a big, scary place. She'd learned while very young that Fate could be a cruel master, any little bit of wisdom helped, and anything that gave optimism was a good thing. There were some days that only the sight of two blackbirds together or spotting a white butterfly in the summer were the only things that gave her hope for the future.

"Aye, I am coming." Murie picked up her skirts and hurried along.

"What did you say?" Osgoode asked harshly as soon as the others were out of hearing.

"I do not know what you mean," Balan replied, wishing he knew himself what he'd said to muck things up so badly. He knew what he'd meant to say—that he found he didn't understand females, that they seemed more emotional than the men he was used to and seemed more complicated than the plain-spoken and sensible men he knew—but apparently he hadn't expressed himself well. Murie seemed to think he was suggesting women were simple and stupid rather than complicated and emotional. He wasn't admitting that to Osgoode, however.

"Oh, bollocks!" his cousin cursed. "You must have

said *something* to upset her. She could not wait to get away from us."

"Perhaps she just found it inclement, as she claimed," Balan suggested, wondering if—once she calmed down a little—he might be able to get her to stand still long enough for him to explain. He'd meant no insult or slur on women. He loved women.

"I knew you would be hopeless when it came to talking," Osgoode said. "I can only hope the fact that she thinks she dreamed of you will get her past this upset."

Balan didn't respond. He was rather hoping the same thing himself.

"There will be dancing after the feast tonight," Osgoode said.

Balan nodded absently. He had quite forgotten that this eve would be the feast and celebration for St. Agnes. He shouldn't have forgotten, not after all that nonsense last night, but those shenanigans were exactly what had driven the feast from his mind.

"Mayhap we should practice dancing this afternoon," Osgoode said thoughtfully.

"Dancing?" Balan said with alarm.

"Aye. Despite Lady Strathcliffe's best efforts to teach you, you were never more than adequate while we were squiring—and I do not think I have seen you dance since."

That was because Balan hadn't danced since. Never more than adequate was a kind description of his abilities. He hadn't cared for the pastime, and it had shown in his lack of skill.

"Aye, come, we will practice the steps."

"Nay. I have things to do," Balan said with irritation. "Important things."

"There is nothing more important than winning

Lady Murie for your bride," Osgoode said firmly. "Unless you wish to marry Lady Brigida instead? Perhaps you've found yourself forming a *tendre* for her?"

Balan let his breath out on a sigh. "Oh, all right."

Chapter Five

"Balan, pray stop stepping on my toes," Osgoode said through gritted teeth.

"You are the one who insisted on this ridiculous venture," Balan ground out, releasing his cousin's hand with disgust. He'd always found dancing a useless waste of time. Why women insisted on the foolish exercise was beyond him. He was sure men would never bother if women did not insist. His opinion being so, he found it difficult to concentrate on the complicated steps. His mind tended to wander to more interesting matters, and he soon lost track of what he was supposed to be doing, which led to losing his place in the dance, or worse, trampling on Osgoode's toes.

"You need to at least be able to dance with the woman tonight after the feast without crushing her feet if you wish to impress her at all," Osgoode insisted. "It would not be so important had you not managed to insult her on the walk."

Balan scowled. He still was not sure how he'd managed to mess things up so badly. But it had led to this last hour of misery, going through the steps of the dance with Osgoode. He felt ridiculous dancing with his cousin and would have called a halt to the practice if not for the news Osgoode's page had gained while listening in on the conversation between Malculinus and Lauda Aldous.

Of course the pair had been quite distressed by the news that, rather than Malculinus, Murie claimed to have dreamt of Balan. The two had spent several moments trying to sort out how that had happened, until Lauda had forced Malculinus to confess that while he did recall going to Murie's room, he had no recollection of actually either waking or kissing the girl. He'd also admitted that he was not sure how he made it back to his room. The last thing he remembered was approaching her bed and then waking up in his own. He'd woken with a splitting headache and three bumps on his head.

Lauda had pretty much put together what had happened. Her opinion was that Balan had taken advantage of their plot, knocked Malculinus out and woken the girl himself on purpose. The Aldouses had no idea that Murie's seeing him had not been part of Balan's plan. As he'd suspected out in the garden, the pair had come up with a way to try to expose his presence in her boudoir: to claim that Lauda had seen him enter Murie's chamber, but hadn't realized it was Murie's until she'd seen her coming out of it this morning—else she would have surely called the guard. Of course, that plot had been ruined when Murie denied dreaming of anyone.

Positive that the pair would not now let the matter lie but would come up with another plan—either to expose Balan's presence in Murie's room last night or to find another way to trick the girl into marrying Malculinus—Osgoode and Balan had sent their spy to trail the brother and sister and see if he could learn what they might come up with.

"Come." Osgoode moved back across the room and turned to face Balan. "We shall start again. This time, try to recall you approach me on my right."

Heaving a heartfelt sigh, Balan took up his position, then nodded to his squire. The fifteen-year-old promptly began to play a tune on his lute, and Balan and Osgoode began again to dance.

"Perhaps a test of knowledge?" Emilie said.

Murie stopped pacing to contemplate the suggestion, then asked, "What kind of knowledge?"

"History?" Emilie suggested after a moment to consider.

Murie wrinkled her nose and shook her head. "I have never fared well at history. I always get dates and names mixed up."

"Ah." Emilie's eyebrows drew together in concentration. The two women were briefly silent. "What are you good at?"

Murie stopped pacing and pursed her lips in thought. "I am quite good at chess."

"Chess!" Emilie stood. "That is perfect! I know Balan plays chess. He has done so with Reginald at Reynard."

"Good," Murie said, relieved to have the matter settled. After the last hour of pondering the possibilities, and not coming up with anything suitable, she'd begun to think it was an incredibly stupid idea to challenge him to a duel of intellect. But Murie was very good at chess. She often played the king—or at least had in the past. Much to his chagrin, she'd begun to win quite frequently, and he'd stopped playing with her.

"Let us go find Lord Balan and tell him what we have come up with," Emilie said. "Mayhap you can even play now."

Nodding, Murie led the way to the door. The moment they were in the hall, however, she began to grow nervous.

"I have not played the game in a while," she confessed with worry. "King Edward has refused to play with me because I keep beating him. I hope I have not lost the skill."

"Nay, I am sure you will be fine." Emilie patted her shoulder reassuringly.

The two women looked for their quarry first in the hall. They did not see either Osgoode or Balan, but Emilie did spot and recognize Osgoode's page loitering near the fire. The boy was not far from Malculinus and Lauda, who were seated in chairs by the fire, their heads close together in conversation.

Not wishing to draw the attention of the pair, Emilie caught the boy's eye and waved him over. The lad hesitated, then ran to them and eventually related that Balan and Osgoode had retired to their chambers to prepare for that evening.

Thanking the page, the women made their way through the castle halls to find the rooms Balan and Osgoode shared, wondering as they went what exactly the two were preparing. They still hadn't come up with an answer by the time they reached their destination.

"Here we are," Emilie said as they paused outside the door. They glanced at each other with raised eyebrows as they heard the sound of a lute from inside, and then she knocked. When a moment passed and there was no response, she knocked again.

"They are not answering," Murie pointed out. The door remained firmly closed.

"I do not think they can hear us knocking over their music," Emilie said with a frown.

"Mayhap we should come back later." Murie shrugged, not at all distressed by the delay. She was suddenly feeling a need to practice chess. It *had* been a while since she'd played, and she didn't wish to make a fool of herself after insisting she was as intelligent as any man.

Unfortunately, Emilie shook her head. "Nay. 'Tis better to get this over with."

"Well, I do not see how we are going to do that if they do not answer the—" The words died on her lips as Emilie opened the door. Both women stared wide-eyed at the occupants of the room. A young lad with a lute was the source of the music, but it was Balan and Osgoode who had the women gaping. The two were dancing—or trying. While Osgoode seemed to manage the steps just fine, Balan appeared to be having difficulty.

"Watch the toes!" Osgoode squawked as Balan—concentrating on the hand he was taking—took one step too close and stomped on his cousin's foot.

Emilie pulled the door quietly closed again and turned to grab Murie's arm. She hurried her away from the door as they both burst into giggles.

"Oh my," Murie breathed once they had turned the corner and her laughter had eased. "Whatever were they doing?"

"I think Osgoode was giving Balan lessons in dancing," Emilie said. "Most likely to impress you tonight after the feast."

"Oh, I had forgotten about tonight," Murie admitted. She generally tried to avoid court feasts and balls when Emilie was not in attendance, and generally she got away with it. However, Emilie was here, and Murie would no doubt be expected to attend this event, especially now that she'd been ordered to marry.

"I suppose you have not decided on what to wear," Emilie commented.

Murie shook her head.

"Well, as the men are busy, mayhap we should delay the game of chess and go look into that. I am sure you have something suitable."

"I do not understand it," Emilie said, frowning around the ballroom. "The entire court knows you must marry. Where are all the men?"

Murie shrugged unhappily. "Probably hiding, for fear I shall look in their direction and they shall be stuck with a *brat* for a wife."

"Oh, nay," Emilie said, but she looked worried. And well she should, too, Murie thought. She'd caught more than one whisper suggesting that this was exactly the reason for the sudden shortage of men at court. Some of the women found it amusing and were tittering over the fact, while others were annoyed with Murie for scaring off the men when they too needed to find husbands. Lord Malculinus Aldous was one of the few men who had not fled, but that had left him to plague Murie all evening, and she'd found she could not turn around without tripping over the man.

"Well, at least Malculinus does not seem afraid of me," she said with forced cheer. While she found the man's constant attentions irritating, at least she had someone to dance with. It would have been wholly humiliating had even he turned away from her. In fact, she thought she should have looked kindly on him for that alone. However, there was something about the man that put her on her guard.

"Aye. But there is something about Malculinus that I do not trust. Every time he comes around, I find myself fighting the urge to snatch you away and hide you," Emilie confessed, She grimaced. "I suppose I am being silly. Lord Aldous has not set a foot wrong."

Murie didn't comment, but she found it interesting that they'd both had the same reaction to his presence.

"I wonder where Balan and Osgoode are," Emilie said—not for the first time. "It seems obvious they planned to attend, else why practice dancing?"

"Hmmm," Murie murmured, wondering the very thing herself. In fact, she'd found herself searching for him among those in attendance and watching for his arrival when she realized he was not yet there. However, it was growing late, and he still had not yet appeared. She supposed she shouldn't be so concerned with where he was. After all, if Lauda were right, her dream had meant that she shouldn't marry him. Considering his opinion of women, she could understand that. On the other hand, she had to wonder why they would share such a passionate kiss in her dream if she wasn't supposed to marry him.

Shrugging the matter aside, she glanced up to see Reginald approach. Reaching them, he pressed a kiss to his wife's forehead, then offered Murie a greeting before turning back to Emilie to say, "You look pale and tired, wife."

"I am fine," she assured him. "You worry too much, Reginald. Do not fuss so."

"You are carrying our child, Emilie," he reminded her. "Our first child. I will fuss if I choose."

"He is right, Emilie," Murie agreed. "You do look pale. Mayhap we should call it a night."

Emilie snorted. "You are just hoping for an excuse to leave the ball."

Murie shrugged. "There seems little reason to be here if Malculinus is going to be the only one to ask me to dance."

Reginald frowned at her comment, then turned to his wife to ask, "Where is Balan?"

Murie sent an accusatory glance Emilie's way. It seemed obvious her friend had shared her dream and the events that followed with her husband. Of course, she'd suspected she would. Emilie's marriage was a true love match. Still, it deserved a glare.

"We were just wondering that ourselves," Emilie admitted, sending Murie an apologetic grimace.

"I know he intended to attend; I spoke to him earlier," Lord Reynard said. "He borrowed a doublet from me."

Murie's eyes widened in surprise, but Emilie leaned close and whispered, "See? He did plan to attend— and even hoped to impress you, else he would not have borrowed a doublet from my husband."

"It would have impressed me more if he had attended," she said dryly. Then she narrowed her eyes on Reginald and suggested, "Mayhap he heard from someone that I plan to challenge him to a game of chess and was too afraid to come."

"Do not glare at *me*," Reginald said with amusement. "*I* did not tell him about the chess game. Although, I hardly think that would scare him off. The man is quite good at chess. He has even beaten me several times."

Murie wrinkled her nose at his arrogance. She'd known for ages that the man considered himself a genius at chess. Unfortunately, Murie could not deny it. While she hadn't played him, she'd seen him play here at court, and she had to admit that he was quite good. It made her positive that she would be better off practicing before playing Balan. It would hardly prove her intellect if he beat her.

"Come." Reginald put his hand under Emilie's elbow. "You are going to bed."

"But Murie—" Emilie began to protest, only to have him interrupt.

"Murie does not want to be here and would most likely appreciate the excuse to retire herself," he said firmly.

"Aye," Murie admitted with amusement. "I am ready to quit the ball. There is little of interest for me here, and I would rather be gone before the wine and ale takes effect and loosens everyone's tongues." Those who attended court were unpleasant at the best of times, but she knew from experience that drink could make them worse. Murie really would rather not be around for it.

"Oh, very well," her friend muttered, and the very fact that she gave in so easily proved how weary she really was. It made Murie peer at her with concern. In truth, Emilie was far along in her pregnancy and probably should not have traveled to court. In fact, Murie had been surprised that Reginald had allowed it. However, Emilie confessed to Murie that she'd threatened to follow him on her own if he tried to leave her behind. Knowing she was just stubborn enough to do it, Reginald had given in. Not happily, however.

"Are you coming?" Emilie asked as Reginald started to lead her away.

Murie hesitated, then said, "I will say good night to the king first. You two go ahead without me."

Emilie opened her mouth, no doubt to offer to wait, but Reginald began to pull her firmly away.

"The girl lives here, Emilie. She will make it to her own chamber safely enough."

Murie smiled faintly at Emilie's expression as she gave in and allowed her husband to lead her from the ballroom.

Once the Reynards were out of sight, rather than make her way to the king, Murie turned and made her way out of the castle. She had no intention of wishing the king good evening. She had no desire to be asked if she'd chosen a husband yet. However, she really wasn't tired either. She found herself oddly restless instead and hoped a walk around the gardens would wear her out.

However, Murie hadn't thought ahead. The garden was one of those places where amorous couples sought out privacy. After running into the second couple occupied in carnal endeavors Murie turned back with a sigh, thinking she could find something to occupy herself in her room, where she was safe from seeing things she really had no desire to see.

She'd made it perhaps halfway back through the gardens when Malculinus suddenly stepped into her path. Murie froze like a squirrel spotting a predator, but she forced a smile to her lips. "Lord Aldous. I thought you were at the ball with everyone else."

"I saw you leave and thought you might desire some company," he replied with a smile.

There was nothing in the least threatening about him. He was neither standing too close, nor leering in any way that could be considered improper, and yet she was suddenly on the alert. So much so, when she spotted Balan approaching along the path, she hailed him with relief.

"My Lord Gaynor! Lord Reynard asked me to give you a message," she called out to ensure he did not turn off the path before reaching them. She then glanced at

Malculinus and smiled apologetically. "Excuse me, my lord, I promised to tell Lord Gaynor something."

Slipping quickly past Lauda's brother, she hurried to Gaynor's side and took his arm to lead him toward the castle. When she glanced back several moments later, Malculinus stood where she'd left him, watching with narrowed eyes.

"What was this message you spoke of?" Gaynor asked once they were out of Aldous's earshot.

Murie bit her lip and admitted, "I fear that was a lie, my lord. There is no message. I simply did not wish to be alone with Malculinus in the garden and made that up as a way to escape him without being rude."

"If you did not wish to be alone with him, why did you accompany him here?"

Hearing the shortness of his tone, Murie glanced at him with irritation. "I did not 'accompany him' anywhere. I came out here for a walk, and when I turned back he was there."

The harshness left Balan's face and he said, "And you were not comfortable alone with him?"

Murie shrugged. "Let us just say that I was uncomfortable with the situation."

"You have good instincts," Balan assured her. "I would not trust him alone with you, either."

Murie glanced at him with surprise, but didn't comment.

"Are you enjoying the ball?" he asked after a moment of silence.

Startled, Murie answered, "I would hardly be out here if I were enjoying it, would I?" She smiled faintly and asked, "Why were you not at the ball?"

Balan was silent so long, she felt sure he would not answer. Finally he admitted, "The doublet I planned to wear met with an untimely accident." He paused, then turned toward her. In the moonlight, she could see that he wore a pale doublet, but there was a large stain in the center.

She eyed it for a moment and asked, "Did you not have something else to wear?"

"Nothing fine enough for a court ball. In fact, I have nothing suitable for court at all. Gaynor was hit hard by the plague, and we are in temporary financial difficulties. I borrowed this doublet from Lord Reynard and shall now have to replace it."

Murie was silent, unsure how to respond. Honesty did not appear to be a problem with this man. She suspected most men would not be so open about their difficulties, temporary or not, but he'd stated them as a simple fact.

Rather than address his poverty, she asked, "How did the doublet get stained?"

"That is a question I myself would like to hear the answer to," he replied, his expression grim. "I laid it in my chamber after borrowing it from Reginald, went below with Osgoode, and when we returned ink had been spilled on it."

Murie's eyebrows rose at this explanation. It sounded as if someone had deliberately stained his tunic while he was out of the room; though, why anyone would do that was beyond her. Unless they hadn't wished him to be able to attend the ball. But why would anyone want that? And who?

The garden was lit by torches, but the path was still shadowy. Distracted as she was by their conversation, Murie was not watching where she was going as closely as she should have. When she put her foot down on something in the path, her ankle suddenly twisted out from under her. Murie cried out and instinctively grabbed for Balan's arm. He immediately paused and turned to steady her; then, seeing the pain on her face, scooped her into his arms. He carried her to a bench set off from the path and gently set her down, kneeling before her to examine her ankle.

Flushing with embarrassment—he dared to look under her skirt?—Murie tried to brush his hands away, but he was not one to be put off. Balan examined the ankle carefully, removing her shoe and pressing the skin around her heel and shin until she gasped.

"It is not broken," he said, "but 'tis swelling."

"It will be fine," Murie assured him, wishing he'd stop.

He did stop, but still held on to the foot as he raised his head to peer at her. After a hesitation, he said, "You misunderstood me in the garden today. Or perhaps I misspoke," he added quickly as her eyes narrowed. "I was trying to explain that I find women much more complicated and confounding than men. We are simple creatures, with simple needs and simple conversations. Women tend to wish to discuss more . . . er . . . emotional matters. They—I have been told—enjoy protestations of undying love and compliments to their beauty, and these are not areas in which I excel. And so, rather than unintentionally offend a lady or drive her to distraction with my silences," he added, smiling wryly at her, "I tend to avoid them altogether. Thus, I am poor at the art of conversation."

Murie relaxed. "Lady Emilie did tell me that she was sure you meant no insult."

"Nay. I did not."

She smiled and added, "We spent a good deal of time thinking up ways to have a duel of the intellect."

"Did you?" he asked with amusement. "And what did you come up with?"

"A game of chess," she admitted. "I am quite good—

or I used to be. I have not played for a while. The king would no longer play with me because I kept beating him."

Balan's eyes widened, and he threw back his head with a deep laugh.

Murie smiled, even though she wasn't sure what he found funny. His laughter was just so lovely that she could not help smiling.

When he finally sobered, he said, "I should very much like to play chess with you someday, my lady. I quite enjoy the game, especially when 'tis challenging."

"Then I shall do my best to challenge you," Murie replied.

Balan smiled and stood. "Now," he said, offering her his arm, "if your ankle is quite recovered, I shall see you to your room."

Murie stood and slid her hand onto his forearm, marveling at how natural the action felt. They walked in silence back to the castle, but this time it was companionable. Murie felt no desperate need for conversation; she was content to just walk. At her door, they both murmured good night, and she slipped inside with a little sigh.

"My lady." Cecily smiled and rushed to her side as Murie moved farther into the room. "Did you enjoy the ball?"

"Not really," she admitted.

The maid's eyebrows rose. "But you are smiling."

"Aye." Murie laughed softly, then shrugged. "I went for a walk afterward in the gardens and ran into Balan."

"Lord Gaynor?" the maid asked with concern.

"Aye."

"My lady," Cecily murmured, then frowned and bit her lip as she helped remove Murie's surcoat.

"What is it, Cecily?" Murie asked.

"It is just . . . I should have mentioned this earlier, but there was really no opportunity."

"What?"

"Well, when I left last evening, I noticed Lord Gaynor lurking out in the hall with Lord Osgoode, and I did wonder . . ."

"What?" Murie repeated with a frown.

"Nothing." The maid shook her head and folded the surcoat, then came to help with her gown. "I was talking to Mydrede today."

"Were you?" Murie said, her mind still on what Cecily had just told her.

"Aye. I asked her about ways to divine who your mate should be."

Murie nodded and forced herself to pay attention to the conversation. Mydrede was the oldest servant at court; a woman always happy to pass on any bits of wisdom, such as how to counteract the evil eye. "Why would you do that?"

Cecily shrugged. "I heard today that they are debating the trustworthiness of the St. Agnes Eve ritual. Some seem to think that by eating rotten meat you will dream of the man you should *not* marry."

"Aye, I heard that myself," Murie admitted with a frown. She'd quite forgotten that on her walk with Balan. She also hadn't had a chance to ask Becker about it yet.

"Well, I asked Mydrede for other ways to sort it out," the servant explained. "I know 'tis a difficult decision, and you are finding it upsetting."

"Aye," Murie agreed. The maid had finished with the lacings and had lifted her gown up over her head. The truth was, Murie rather liked the idea of marrying Balan, and had ever since her dream. Now people seemed to be suggesting she shouldn't.

Sighing as she was freed from the gown, Murie let her hands drop. "What did she tell you?"

"She gave me many methods," Cecily announced with enthusiasm. Setting the gown aside, she reached into a small bag at her waist and pulled out various leaves and little seeds.

"What is that?" Murie asked, leaning closer to eye the items. "Ivy. Clover . . . An ash leaf?"

"Aye. If you put the ivy leaf in your pocket, the first man you meet shall be the man you marry and similarly with the clover . . . though, that you put in your right shoe. The ash leaf works the same, though you have to recite a poem. Let me see . . ." She paused and scrunched her face up with concentration for a moment, then nodded. "It goes 'Even ash, even ash, I pluck thee off the tree. The first young man that I do meet, my lover he shall be.' And then you put it in your left shoe, and the first man you meet shall be your husband."

"But the poem says *'I pluck thee off the tree,'* and I did not pluck it. You did," Murie pointed out with a frown.

"Oh, aye." Cecily appeared disappointed.

"What are those seeds?"

"Oh." She brightened again. "These are apple pips. You put them on your cheeks, naming each for a possible husband, and the one that stays on the longest is the name of the man who will be your husband." Cecily was licking and sticking the pips to Murie's cheeks even as she spoke.

Not wishing to dislodge them, Murie tried to speak without moving her mouth and cheeks. "But I have no names to give them."

"Of course you do, my lady. There are several single men at court right now. Why, Lord Aldous is one. He is wealthy and handsome. And then there is . . ." She frowned.

"You see?" Murie said, and raised her hands to wipe the pips from her cheeks. Turning, she moved toward her bed. "I am tired, Cecily. We can talk more about what you learned from Mydrede in the morning. I do appreciate it, though."

"Aye, my lady," Cecily said, sounding disappointed.

Trying to cheer her, Murie suggested, "Mayhap you could show me where to find the ivy, clover and ash leaves, and we can try them all tomorrow."

"Aye." The servant managed a smile, then moved toward the door. "Good sleep, my lady."

"Good night," Murie replied as the woman left. Climbing under the linens and furs, she settled herself on her side and stared into the flames of the fire Cecily had built up. It was late summer, and while the days were still warm, the evenings were beginning to cool; a fire helped keep the chill out. Murie gazed into the flickering flames, and she ruminated that Balan had a lovely laugh. And kind eyes. And she wished he'd kissed her in the gardens so she would know if his kisses were as exciting in real life as they had been in her dreams.

Frowning, she rolled onto her back and pondered the matter of the rotten meat. Did it mean she shouldn't marry him? She wished she knew. Murie would have thought that Mydrede would have known, but had she, Cecily would have mentioned the answer one way or another, so she supposed she didn't. Becker would know, however, She reminded herself of that, and determined once again to speak to Becker and the king first thing in the morning.

Chapter Six

"Now . . ." King Edward turned to Murie with a raised
eyebrow as his receiving room emptied out. "What was
so urgent that you needed to speak to me alone?"

Murie flushed. She'd found it almost impossible to
sleep last night, her mind flittering between thoughts
of Balan and worries as to what her dream truly meant.
Was he to be her husband? Or was he not? She'd de-
bated and fretted over the issue back and forth until
finally the dawn had begun to break. Murie had immediately tossed the linens and furs aside and leapt
from bed. She'd been dressed and gone from her
room ere Cecily even arrived . . . only to find she was
up and about far too early, and the king had not yet
even left his bed.

Irritated that everyone else appeared to have no
problem sleeping, Murie had taken herself off to the
gardens to sit in the bower and think on Balan some
more. She'd replayed the kiss from her dream over
and over in her mind, and spent more time there than

she'd intended. By the time she made her way back into the king's receiving room, it was already full of others awaiting their turn to see him. Murie had been vexed when she'd spoken to Robert, who was in charge of who entered next.

Apparently, fearing the tears and fits that the disgruntled man read on her face, he had promised to get her in as quickly as was possible, to arrange for her to have a private audience.

"Murie?" Edward prompted when she did not speak.

She grimaced at his impatience, understanding it when he had so many to see, but at a loss as to where to start this conversation. Her gaze slid to Becker. She'd been relieved to find the aide with the king. He usually was, but there were times he was off doing something for his sire and was not nearby. Fortunately, such was not the case today.

"Murie?" King Edward repeated, his voice gone hard, indicating that his patience was at an end.

She opened her mouth and blurted, "Sire, have you heard about the ritual to find a husband on St. Agnes Eve?"

"Ahhhh." He nodded with sudden understanding, then said, "I had heard that Lady Aldous talked you into testing the superstition."

"Aye." She shifted uncomfortably under his amusement.

He arched an eyebrow. "Did you dream of anyone?"

"Aye," she admitted, blushing at the memory of the dream.

"Really?" He straightened up with surprise. "I was told you had not."

Murie grimaced. Word spread through court faster

than a squirrel could dart through. That was something else she would not miss once she married and left.

"Only Lady Reynard and my maid know I did dream of someone," she confessed. "I did not wish the whole court to know I had, and who it was."

"Ah." He nodded. "That was perhaps wise."

Murie nodded and glanced at her hands.

"Who was it? Someone you have known and thought handsome for a long time?" he asked indulgently.

Murie glanced at him, startled by the suggestion. "Nay. In truth, I had never seen the man before I dreamed him. I had no idea who he was."

His eyes widened. "Really?"

"Aye," she answered, then got to the point. "Do you know the proper tale, sire?"

He sat back, expression confused. "What tale?"

"About St. Agnes," she explained patiently. "On St. Agnes Eve, Malculinus said that if you either fasted all day or ate rotten meat, you would dream of the man meant to be your husband. But yesterday morn, Lauda said someone told her that if you *fasted* the man you dreamt of would be your husband, but if you ate rotten meat the man you dreamt of was someone you definitely should not marry, and I was hoping you could give me the truth of the matter."

"Ah, I see." He nodded, then said, "So, you are confused as to whether this dream man is the one you should marry, or one you should definitely not marry."

"Aye."

"Well . . ." Edward frowned, then glanced at Becker. "Which is it, Becker? You are more knowledgeable on such superstitions than I."

Murie blinked in surprise at the king owning up to his ignorance and asking his aide, but then she realized that was what an aide was for. And, perhaps true wisdom wasn't in knowing everything, but in being willing to turn to those who do know what you don't. After all, no one could know everything.

Becker did not hesitate. "I believe Lord Malculinus had it right last night, sire. Fasting or eating the rotten meat would make you dream of the man meant to be your husband. As far as I know, there is no mention of anything making you dream of one you should not marry. In fact, such a bit would be rather silly. 'Tis obvious if you *should* marry one, all the rest are ones you should not."

Edward nodded and smiled at Murie. "There you are, then. Whoever this man you dreamt of is, he is the one meant to be your husband." He smiled faintly. "You really dreamed of someone?"

"Aye." She blushed again.

"And it is someone you have never seen or met before?" he asked with interest.

"Aye," Murie murmured.

"Hmmm." Edward's expression became concerned. "Murie, I appreciate that you do not wish to marry and leave us, but you cannot use a dream man as an excuse to delay in choosing a husband. Phillippa will not give ground on this."

"Oh, nay, sire," she assured him quickly. "I would never do that. Besides, when I went down yesterday morn to breakfast, I saw the man from my dream."

"You did?" The king looked stunned. "Well, who is it?"

Murie hesitated. "Lord Gaynor."

"Lord Gaynor?" Edward repeated sharply. "No, he has not been to court in years. Not until the day before yesterday, and always left as quickly as he arrived, usually avoiding the feasts and balls."

"He has been here before then?" Murie asked with

surprise, for truly, she'd never seen him before that morning.

"Aye, but you could not have met him and gained a *tendre* for him," he pointed out. She realized that he'd originally thought her dream a result of her own subconscious desires.

"Oh, nay, I had no *tendre* when I dreamt of him," she assured the king. "I had never seen his face before. And truly, I almost feared he was a figment of my imagination until I saw him."

"But . . ." Edward looked confused, then asked with bewilderment, "You really ate some rotten meat and dreamed of a man you had never before seen?"

"Aye," she answered.

"I see," Edward said. "And it was Gaynor. You are sure?"

"Oh, aye. I pointed him out to Lady Reynard when I spotted him, and she knew him. She is the one who told me his name, and I am sure she is right."

"Aye. I am sure she is," he agreed. He glanced to Becker. "Gaynor."

"Aye, sire."

"He is a good man."

"Aye, sire," Becker agreed. "Balan. A fine and faithful warrior. His father passed during the plague, and he has inherited the holding."

"Aye." The king nodded. "I was thinking to reward him for his loyalty in France, and this would be a fine reward."

"Aye, sire," Becker agreed.

Murie's eyes widened in alarm. "Sire, I have not told him I dreamt of him, and I will not do so until I am sure we suit. And then, of course, he may not wish to marry me," she pointed out, hoping Edward would not interfere. "You said I could choose my own husband. What if it ends that we cannot love each other?"

"Love?" Edward looked at her with surprise. "You do not base marriages on love, child. I did not even know Phillippa when it was decided we should marry."

"Aye, but you did say I could choose my own husband," she reminded him.

"Aye, and you have," he pointed out. "You are the one who came to me with his name."

"But . . ." Murie bit her lip, trying to think of a way to tell him to mind his own bloody business without causing insult. It didn't seem possible, however. Besides, he probably wouldn't listen. The man was lost in his thoughts.

After a moment, Edward glanced about, seemingly startled when he spotted her still there.

"Oh. You are excused, Murie," he said at once, then turned to Becker and commanded, "Have someone fetch Gaynor."

Murie groaned inwardly, but didn't see how to sway him from whatever course he'd decided on. She stood with resignation to leave.

"Murie, I want you at the head table for sup tonight," the king announced as she reached the door. She turned back, eyes wide.

"But I was to sit with Lady and Lord Reynard."

"Reynard?" Edward glanced to Becker. "He is—"

"Aye, sire," Becker murmured, apparently not needing to hear the entire question.

Nodding, Edward said, "They may join you at the head table. Now go, child. I have business to attend."

Blowing her breath out on a sigh, Murie escaped while she could, but as she hurried toward her room, she wondered what she'd set in motion. Unfortunately, she suspected she knew. She quite liked Balan and found him attractive, and his kisses in her dream had been divine; however, she had no desire to have him forced into marrying her. What if he did not like her or find *her* kisses divine? Nay, she needed to—

Her thoughts came to a shuddering halt, as did her feet, at the sight of the man moving up the hall.

Balan.

She stared at him; then, without thinking about it, her feet carried her past the others in the hall and directly into his path, forcing him to halt.

"Lady Murie," he said with surprise.

"Aye." She nodded, bit her lip and blurted, "My lord, I must speak with you."

"Very well," he said.

Murie hesitated, her gaze shifting anxiously over the people passing by.

Balan arched an eyebrow in question. "What is it?"

"I . . ." Murie bit her lip, her gaze following those passing closest to them and knew a blush was coloring her cheeks. She really didn't wish to speak to him on this subject at all, but even more so, did not wish to speak about it where others might hear. This was embarrassing enough without that added humiliation.

Seeming to recognize the problem, Balan glanced around, then took her arm and led her down the hall, then below stairs and out of the castle. He walked her across the upper ward to where Edward's tower was being built. Fortunately, it was a rainy day and the men were not working, but the walls were begun and offered them some shelter from the weather. Murie had to walk carefully to avoid sinking in the mud.

Seeming to note she was having difficulty in her dainty shoes, Balan suddenly swept her up in his arms and carried her to a stone where she could safely stand.

Murie managed a slightly embarrassed smile as he straightened from setting her down.

"Thank you, my lord," she murmured, peering at him curiously. She was now as tall as he, their faces on a level, and she'd not seen him this close before. His eyes were really quite lovely, a deep dark brown that was almost black. And he had the longest eyelashes she'd ever seen; startling on a man.

"My lady?" he said when she remained silent. "You had something you wished to tell me?"

"Oh, aye," she said, and began to worry her lip. How to tell him? This was all so terribly embarrassing. Why the king felt he had to intervene, she did not know. If he would just leave her to deal with the matter on her own as he'd promised . . .

"My lady?" Balan prompted. There was a slight smile on his lips, and his eyes locked on her mouth as she nibbled at her lip.

Forcing herself to stop, she opened her mouth, closed it again, tilted her head thoughtfully and then opened her mouth again, only to exclaim in horror, "Oh, gawd!"

Balan blinked in surprise, then caught her hands in his. "Just take a deep, calming breath and tell me what is on your mind."

Murie did as instructed and sucked in a lungful of air, let it slowly back out and blurted, "The king!"

"What about the king?" he asked.

"Oh, 'tis awful, my lord. I never meant for it to happen; I just wanted to ask if he knew the rules, but he decided it was a fait accompli and now he will surely start spouting orders and telling everyone, and 'twill be so embarrassing and I do not know what to do to make him—"

Her words ended on a startled gasp as he covered her mouth with his. The panic immediately slid out of her, and a little sigh escaped as his mouth brushed over hers, soft and caressing.

"There," he said softly as he drew back. "Are you feeling calmer?"

Murie blushed but nodded.

"Good. Now—calmly—what is this about the king?"

"Oh!" Murie's eyes widened with renewed alarm. "I never meant for him to take it as he did, certainly not until I had spoken to you, but I—"

Her words died another abrupt death as his mouth covered hers again, this time moving more firmly, and then his tongue slid out to urge her lips apart and he was suddenly invading her as he had in her dreams. Moaning, Murie found her arms wrapped around his neck and their bodies pressed together. It was heaven.

When he broke the kiss, she was panting softly and much slower to open her eyes. As she did, he smiled and said, "Are you feeling calmer?"

Murie nodded vaguely.

"Good, do you think you can explain things without becoming hysterical?"

"Was I hysterical?" she murmured.

"You seemed to me to be, and I thought a kiss much more pleasant than a slap."

"Oh, aye," she agreed on a sigh. "In fact, mayhap if you were to keep kissing me, I could explain better. It does seem to distract me from the worry of it all."

He chuckled and bent to press a kiss to her cheek, following an invisible trail to her ear, where he nibbled lightly before trailing down her throat. "Is this helping?"

"Oh, aye," Murie breathed, leaning into him.

"Speak," he ordered, his hands moving restlessly up and down her back and pressing her close against him.

"I told the king I dreamt about you and—ohm, that's . . . mmmm," she groaned as his head dipped and he nibbled at her collar bone. "Would you mind if we were wedded?"

He stilled—his mouth, his hands, his very heart she suspected, stopping—then slowly lifted his head. Murie bit her lip and avoided his eyes, then grimaced and admitted, "I do not know if you heard about the St. Agnes Eve—"

"Aye," he growled.

"Well, Lauda, Lady Aldous," she explained, "she talked me into eating rotten meat."

"I know."

"You do?" Murie said in surprise.

"My lady, I doubt if there is anyone at court who has not heard."

"Oh." She wrinkled her nose and said, "Well, I told everyone that I had not dreamed that eve, but I did. Of you."

When he didn't squawk in horror at the news, she continued. "But the next day Lauda said that she was told that rotten meat made you dream of the man you should *not* marry; only fasting allows you to dream of the man you *should* marry."

"You do not suppose she was lying, do you?" he asked in a dry tone.

Murie blinked in surprise. "Why would she lie about such a thing? Especially when I claimed I had not dreamed of anyone." She shook her head and said, "Nay, I do not think she lied, but did wonder if this lady she spoke of might be mistaken. So, this morning I went to the king to ask which version of it was true, and Becker said—Becker is very smart, you understand; he knows everything. I always go to him when I am uncertain about knowledge. Unfortunately, I have to go through the king to get to him, because if the king thought I was going to Becker rather than him, I think his feelings would be hurt and—"

This time, rather than kiss her to silence her nervous rambling, Balan simply covered her mouth.

"You went to the king to ask about the true version of the superstition. Nod or shake your head."

Murie nodded.

"And you told him you dreamt of me?"

She nodded.

"And now he has decided we should marry?"

Murie nodded again, and when his hand dropped away, she blurted, "I did remind him that he promised I might choose my own husband, but he seemed to think the dream was my choosing and told Becker to fetch you. But I did not wish you to walk in there unprepared, and if you do not wish to marry me, I surely understand and will not be offended and will do my best to talk him out of it. Though the king can be rather obstinate on some points, and I—"

Balan kissed her to silence her again, this time covering her mouth in an aggressive, demanding manner. It left her breathless. When he pulled away, Murie was swaying on her feet, her eyes unfocused.

"We shall marry," he announced, and turned to walk away.

Murie blinked after him, the shock quickly clearing her mind. She then hopped off the tower stone and hurried after him, slipping and sliding in the mud but uncaring that it was ruining her gown. "Really?"

Pausing, Balan turned to glance at her, then frowned and scooped her into his arms. "Is it what you wish?"

"I . . . You . . ." Murie paused, blew a stray hair out of her face and peered up at him, her body relaxed in his arms. "Well, St. Agnes seems to think it would be a good idea."

His eyes narrowed, mouth twisting with displeasure. "For any reason other than that?"

She considered the matter, then admitted, "I think you are very handsome."

"You do?" he asked. When she nodded shyly, he stared at her. "And I find you lovely."

Murie smiled and added, "And Emilie and Reginald and even the king seem to think a lot of you, so I already know you are a good man."

"And you are not the horrible brat everyone believes you are."

Murie blinked at the back-handed compliment.

"Anything else?" he asked.

She blushed but admitted, "I like your kisses, my lord."

A grin took his mouth, and he bent to lightly press another to her lips.

"We shall deal well together," he decided, and turned to continue on to the castle, carrying her in his arms.

Murie stared at his strong face and gave a little sigh, then slid her arms around his neck. It seemed that the decision was made; she would marry Balan. Her mind immediately began to make plans: She would have a new doublet sewn for him for their wedding, a fine new doublet made from the best materials and of colors that would suit him. And she would commission a dress for the child Juliana to be given when they reached Gaynor. And she would order all the things she thought Gaynor might need. The list was endless.

With nothing to delay it, and wishing Emilie and Reginald to be able to attend, Murie did not protest when the king decided the wedding should be a week hence. It meant she would spend the week running in circles trying to get everything done, but with the help of Emilie, Becker and several other servants, she handled everything she wished and even managed to present herself at the wedding both on time and dressed in a lovely new gown of pale blue, with a surcoat of burgundy to match the doublet and houpelande she'd had made for Balan.

Murie was most gratified when her husband arrived in the new garb. He looked very handsome and even regal.

The wedding passed in a blur for Murie; all she could later recall was a buzzing in her ears and being surrounded by people. She was most grateful when it was over and Balan was pressing the wedding kiss to her lips. It was a quick, perfunctory kiss, nothing like the kisses in her dream or the ones in the shelter of the tower wall, but she hardly expected such in front of so many people.

Taking her hand, Balan led her back through the well-wishers and in front of the procession back to the hall for the feast to follow. That too passed in a blur for Murie. She had a vague recollection of Balan feeding her sweetmeats and pressing a chalice of wine to her lips with concern on his face, and saying something about her being quite pale; and then the queen was beside her with her ladies-in-waiting and Emilie at her back, announcing it was time for the bedding.

Murie would have liked to have swooned then and slept through what followed, but she had too hearty a constitution for that. She stayed awake all through the chatter and—not always kind—teasing of the women as they stripped her of her clothing and then put her in the bed. Only Emilie's reassuring murmurs, glances and pats on the hand kept her from striking out at one of the court cows or bursting into sobs. And this time her sorrow would have been for real. Fortunately, Emilie was there, her presence a calming influence that kept Murie teetering on the edge of panic but not falling.

Once in the bed with the linens drawn up, the worst of it should have been done, but Murie found what followed just as distressing. The queen gave her an encouraging smile and moved to open the door. The men immediately burst in, the king leading the procession and Balan in the middle being half dragged, half carried as if he were a prisoner of war. Osgoode and Reginald were among the men who immediately began stripping him, and Murie watched wide-eyed as her new husband was denuded before her.

He really was an impressive sight, with his wide strong shoulders and muscular chest tapering to a flat stomach. Mary swallowed as her eyes dropped lower, then quickly turned her gaze away and tried to pretend she was anywhere but there. The men finished stripping her husband and then pulled the linens away, briefly revealing her own nudity as they slipped him into the bed at her side.

Murie was in such a state, she hardly heard the ribald jests and approving comments before the linens were replaced and the room began to empty out.

Balan watched the last of the people vacate the room before turning to peer at his wife. Murie looked like a deer spotting danger: eyes wide, body seemingly frozen stiff.

He sighed to himself. This was going to be a long night. He would have to handle her most delicately, ease her into this business of the marital bed. She would be a virgin after all, with a virgin's sensibilities and no doubt all sorts of ridiculous beliefs put into her head by the church, beliefs about the relations between a husband and wife and all that they should and shouldn't do.

Shaking his head, he turned carefully in the bed so as not to startle or frighten her, intending only to assure her all would be well; but before he could speak, she threw herself at him, plastering her mouth to his. After the briefest startlement, Balan shrugged and slid his arms around his wife, using one hand to hold her head at an angle he liked, and began to teach her how to kiss properly.

Chapter Seven

Murie moaned in relief as her husband kissed her back. She'd sat there worried and anxious and . . . well . . . really, terrified of what was to come, but then she'd recalled her dream and knew that if he would just kiss her, all would be well. However, he'd not hurried to accomplish the task, and finally, panicked to the point that she was ready to hop out of bed and flee the room, when he'd turned to her, she'd simply taken the matter into her own hands and kissed him herself.

Fortunately, he'd not been offended and after a brief pause, slid his arms around her.

She felt his tongue slide insistently along her lips, and she opened for him as she recalled that dream kiss. As in the dream, his tongue immediately slid inside, and Murie moaned as it rasped over hers. Balan tasted of ale and the beef they'd had at the feast, and she quite liked the combination, but then she forgot all about it as his hand found her breast under the linens.

Gasping, Murie found herself arching into his touch as excitement tingled through her.

"Oh, husband," she breathed as he broke the kiss to run his mouth to her ear. Her eyes popped open with surprise at the heat this caress unfolded within her. She'd never thought of her ears as good for anything but hearing. Apparently, that wasn't so. She tilted her head slightly to give him better access, and her gaze landed on the chest across the room. She blinked with surprise as she recalled the horseshoe and rabbit's foot she'd collected for the wedding night.

Murie immediately tugged free of her husband's embrace, probably only managing to do so because she took him by surprise.

"What—?" Balan's question ended on an *oomph* as she unintentionally kneed him in her scramble to get out of the bed. Realizing what she'd done, she removed her knee, ending up straddling his hips over the furs as she eyed him with concern.

"I am sorry, my lord. Did I hurt you?"

Balan released a small whimper but shook his head. Relieved, she smiled and continued her rush over to the chest. Dropping to her knees in the rushes, she threw it open and began to dig under the clothing for the items she sought. She'd hidden them under her gowns so Cecily wouldn't see them.

"What are you doing?"

Murie glanced to the side with surprise when she realized he'd followed and now stood beside her, a frown on his face as he watched her digging frantically through the chest.

"I put . . . Oh dear," she murmured as her gaze got caught on the appendage jutting out from between his legs. It hadn't seemed nearly so large when they'd put him in the bed . . . nor had it been red and angry-looking. She must have really done damage when she'd unintentionally kneed him.

"My lord, you are all swollen and red. I *did* hurt you," she said with alarm, catching the bobbing member in her hand so she could take a better look. It was difficult to see if she'd done any damage with it waving in front of her face like a priest's finger during a lecture.

Murie heard him groan as her hand closed around it, and she took this as a sign that he was sore.

"Is it tender?" she asked with concern, glancing up at his face. Balan's eyes were squeezed shut, but popped open at her question, and he stared down at her with disbelief.

"What?"

"Well, 'tis swollen from the blow you took," she pointed out.

"Blow?" he asked faintly, and she leaned closer and gently blew on him to help ease any stinging she may have caused. His flesh was very warm. Hot, even, as wounds often were.

"Aye. Would you like me to rub it? Would that help, do you think?" she asked, glancing up at him again.

Balan stared down at her incredulously. "Rub it?"

"Aye, as I would a sprained ankle or—" Her explanation became a startled gasp as he suddenly tugged her to her feet. The gasp stopped when he covered her mouth with his, and Murie's thoughts halted as their bodies came together and he thrust his tongue into her mouth.

Moaning, she let her hands slip up his arms and held on as he kissed her most thoroughly. Truly, these kisses were even better than the ones of the dream. In her dream, her breasts hadn't been rubbing across his chest, her nipples tickled and excited by the small, springy hairs there. And in her dreams, his injured appendage had not been pressing insistently against the apex of her thighs, causing little jolts of excitement to course through her and a heavy, pooling sensation in her lower belly.

Balan's hands slid down to clasp her behind, and he lifted her suddenly, rubbing her center most aggressively against his injured limb. Murie groaned at the sensations that suddenly rioted through her, but she reluctantly broke the kiss to gasp, "I should look at your wound."

"Later," he muttered, nipping at her chin then kissing her again.

Giving up for the moment, Murie followed the urge to wrap her legs around his hips, her feet hooking one over the other for purchase as her arms tightened around his shoulder. She began to kiss him back, her tongue meeting his and slipping into his mouth. The shift allowed his appendage to poke at her most private area, and Murie wiggled tentatively against him, using her hips and thighs to do so.

Her movements seemed to affect Balan strongly. Growling deep in his throat, he started to walk to the bed, but then Murie recalled the items in her chest and let her feet unhook, and she dropped away. Caught by surprise, Balan could not stop her from thumping to her feet on the floor.

"I have to get the rabbit's foot and horseshoe," she explained, trying to race around him.

"What do you want with a horseshoe and a rabbit's foot?" he asked, sounding a little grumpy. He caught her arm.

Murie turned back to explain, but she paused at the sight of him. He looked quite adorable, with his hair all mussed from her fingers and his lips swollen from her kisses.

"Murie?" he repeated, giving her arm a gentle shake. "What do you need with those items?"

"Oh!" She blinked and smiled. "They are good luck charms said to increase fertility." She tried to tug free of him again, but he wasn't releasing her.

"Leave them," he ordered, drawing her back against his chest.

"But—"

He silenced her protest with another kiss, this one more determined. When he released her waist to slide his hands up to cup her breasts, she sighed in defeat and forgot about the charms. She could use them the next time, she assured herself. He'd begun to knead.

When he broke their kiss, she was at first disappointed. But then his mouth dipped down to cover one of her nipples, which she saw had become swollen and erect as they only did when she was cold. She started to protest, then jerked up onto her tiptoes and cried out with surprise at her body's response. This was . . . this was . . .

"Oh, *husband*," she breathed, leaning back to make it easier for him and feeling the edge of the bedside table against her bottom.

Balan's response was to draw on that nipple and then nip it teasingly. His hands slid to her waist and ran lightly over her bottom and hips. Murie found herself twisting first one way and then the other, then thrusting her hips forward, her thighs opening slightly as he clasped her bottom.

Balan dropped to his haunches before her, his mouth trailing over the suddenly quivering muscles of her belly and then along the outside of her leg, then drifting to the inside of her knees and urging her legs apart. His mouth moved slowly up along the inside of her thigh.

Murie gasped for breath, little mewling sounds emitting from her lips, her bottom resting more heavily against the bedside table and making it rock as she shuddered and bounced against it. She came to rest fully upon it, however, when he suddenly caught her legs and drew them over his shoulders, burying his face into her center.

Murie cried out and clutched at the edges of the table, her fingers digging into the wood as his tongue ran over the very core of her. This was . . . this was . . . Oh! This had to be bad. Nothing that felt this good would ever be approved by the church, she was sure.

But as Balan continued to lave and pleasure her, Murie didn't care what the church thought; she only cared that he didn't stop, didn't end this wicked torment. And then it was suddenly too much; she was going to explode, and she wanted him to end it.

Panting out a protest, she released the table and grabbed at his head with one hand, her fingers tangling in the soft strands of his hair and tugging insistently. Balan ignored her wishes, and instead of stopping, stepped up his actions until Murie gave up trying and grabbed the table again, her hips lifting and thrusting of their own accord. She rode the waves he was creating in her. Suddenly she stilled, her whole body pausing, every fiber straining toward something . . . and then she bucked against him with a scream as the explosion she'd feared arrived, sending her body into convulsions she'd never before experienced.

Murie was not really aware of Balan allowing her legs to slide off his shoulders or his rising before her, though she did instinctively clutch at his arms when he stepped between her legs, but she was completely unprepared when he suddenly drove his swollen appendage into her still-quivering body, filling her as she'd never been filled. She gasped against his ear, her body stiffening around him, and Balan paused, merely holding her for a moment.

"Are you all right?" he asked after several heartbeats.

Murie let her breath out and turned stunned eyes to him. "Aye."

Balan hesitated, then asked, "Does it still hurt?"

"Does what hurt?" she asked with bewilderment, for truly she had no idea what he was talking about. When she recalled that it was supposed to hurt the first time, she blushed. "Oh—nay, my lord husband."

Balan smiled faintly and then withdrew from her body, and Murie found herself clutching at him with her hands and legs around his hips, trying to stop him. Before she could protest, however, he was sliding back into her, and she dropped her head to his shoulder and moaned.

"Pray, do that again," she whispered as he paused once more.

Chuckling softly, Balan caught her under the bottom. He lifted her from the table to turn and lay her across the bed, coming down on top of her without their needing to separate.

"Do you like this, wife?" he asked as he withdrew and thrust again.

"Aye," Murie moaned, flattening her feet on the bed and thrusting her hips into the action. "I am sure 'tis a sin in the church's eyes, but aye, my lord, I like it very much."

"So do I," he whispered against her lips, then covered her mouth with his and thrust his tongue into her even as he thrust his hips forward once more. The two of them fell silent then but for moans, sighs, groans and growls, working together toward what Murie now knew was a sort of heaven. She cried out again as he took her there once more, but this time he cried out too and went as well.

Murie woke to find herself curled in her new husband's arms, her body semi-excited once more. It shouldn't be, she thought sleepily. Her husband had woken her twice in the night, reaching out for her in the dark and covering her mouth with his, even as his body shifted to blanket her. He was a most vigorous lover, and she couldn't help thinking that the horseshoe and rabbit's foot may have been efficacious despite not being under the bed. Mayhap just being in the room was enough to have an influence.

A tingling in her breast distracted her from such thoughts, and Murie stretched on her side with a little sigh as she became aware of her husband's hand moving over it. She'd awoken several times to find him cupping her breast in his sleep, but now he was not asleep—or if he was, he was having interesting dreams. His hand was not simply cupping her; it was holding her, lifting, kneading, and his thumb was rubbing back and forth over an already erect nipple.

Murmuring his name, she shifted, pressing her bottom backward into her husband's groin and smiling as she felt his semi-erect state. The horseshoe and rabbit's foot were definitely working, she thought with a sigh, reaching back to find and clasp him in her fingers. She'd soon realized that the red, swollen state she'd thought she'd inflicted with her knee had nothing to do with injury, and had quite enjoyed it each time it had occurred. Now she ran her hand down the length of him, encouraging him to return to that state again.

Balan caught her by the chin and turned her head to the side for a deep kiss, then suddenly rolled away from her out of bed. Startled by his sudden abandonment, Murie sat up in bed and watched with amazement as he moved to the basin of cold water from the night before and began to quickly wash himself.

"My lord? Are we not going to . . . ?" she began uncertainly, then paused and blushed, incapable of giving voice to her expectations.

Balan tossed the damp linen he'd been using to wash himself into the basin, then walked back to bed and leaned on it with his hands to bend down and kiss her on the lips. It was a very quick peck, ending before she could respond. Then he straightened and turned away, saying, "I promised Reginald I would meet him in the bailey this morn to practice at swords. We have neither of us been getting any practice since coming to court."

"Oh." Murie gave a little sigh of disappointment and slid out of bed to move to the now abandoned basin of water and perform some quick ablutions of her own. "Well, Emilie is expecting me this morning as well. So mayhap it is for the best."

Balan chuckled and moved up behind her. His leather leggings pressed against the back of her thighs as he wrapped his arms around her, and he kissed the side of her neck.

"I am very pleased with you, wife," he whispered into her ear. "You are very enthusiastic in your duties, and I like that."

Flushing, Murie pushed his arms away and moved over to snatch up the fresh gown Cecily had laid out. She pulled it on over her head and moved to the door, saying a tad stiffly, "Well, I am pleased to hear it. 'Tis a wife's place to please her husband."

Ignoring his chuckle, she pulled the door open, relieved to find Cecily there, hand raised as if to knock.

"Just in time, Cecily," she said, smiling at the woman. "I will need help with my laces."

"Of course, my lady." The maid followed her into the room as Balan tugged on his cotehardie.

Murie was silent as Cecily worked at the lacings on the back of her gown, her eyes eating up her husband as he finished strapping on his sword and boots. Cecily finished with her lacings and caught up Murie's surcoat to drop it over her head. When the cloth was pulled down from in front of her face, Murie blinked in surprise to find her husband standing in front of her. He smiled at her expression and bent to kiss her most thoroughly, despite Cecily's presence, then started for the door, only to pause and swing back. Returning to their bedside, Balan picked up a small dagger there and slid it into his belt, then glanced down and paused, eyes widening with surprise.

"Odd, I thought I had lost this," he said, bending to pick up something from the floor.

Murie glanced curiously at the item. Her eyes widened as she saw it was the cross she'd found in her room the morning after she'd dreamed of Balan. She'd had Cecily set it on the table, but apparently it had gotten knocked off onto the rushes at some point last night. She didn't have to think hard to guess how.

"Hmm, it must have been caught up in my clothes," he commented, and fastened it around his neck; then he stopped to press another kiss to her now cold lips on his way out of the room.

Murie stared after him, pale and shaken.

"Is that not the cross you found the morning after you dreamt he came to you?" Cecily asked quietly.

"Aye," she breathed.

Cecily was silent for a moment then said, "I did tell you I saw him lurking outside in the hall that night."

"Aye," Murie repeated.

"You do not think he—?"

"Aye!" Murie cried, and hurried for the door, her only thought that she needed to speak to Emilie. Her friend would know what she should do. She *always* knew what to do. She would help fix this.

"Slow down," Emilie said with concern moments later when Murie burst into her room and babbled a stream of nonsense. "Tell me slowly. I do not understand. Balan found a cross in your room?"

"Aye. Nay. Aye, but . . ." She paused with frustration, took a deep breath to calm herself, then started again. "I found a cross in my room the morning after the dream. I thought nothing of it at the time. I did not know whom it belonged to, but thought perhaps it had fallen from someone's throat in the hall and gotten caught in my skirt and fallen off by the bed as I disrobed . . . or perhaps a servant had lost it while cleaning the room."

"Aye," Emilie said patiently. "I understand."

"Well, this morning while he was dressing, Balan spotted the cross on the floor and—"

"You left it on the floor?" Emilie said in surprise.

"Nay, I put it on the table. It must have got knocked off somehow," she said, blushing as she recalled what Balan had done to her on the table and just how it had probably gotten knocked off. Giving her head a shake, she went on: "Anyway, he picked it up, saying he thought he'd lost it and that it must have simply been caught in his clothes. And then he put it on."

Emilie nodded. "He has worn the cross ever since his father gave it to him some years ago."

Murie scowled impatiently. "Do you not see? It was

his cross . . . in my room . . . the morning after I dreamed he came to me and kissed me."

"Ah." Emilie sat back. "I see. You think it was not a dream at all, but that he came to you in person and kissed you in your bed." She paused, looking startled, and then exclaimed, "Before you were married! Why, that is scandalous. That is—"

"Not a dream at all," Murie said grimly, trying to return to the point. "I did not dream he was there; he *was* there. Why?"

Emilie blinked. "Why?"

"Aye. Why? We had never met before. I had never even seen him before I woke up to find him kissing me. But it was the night I was supposed to dream of the man I was fated to marry, and I woke up thinking that was him!"

"Oh, I am sure that had nothing to do with it," Emilie began, but she was looking concerned.

"Nay? Then why did he come in and kiss me—a veritable stranger?"

"Mayhap he was drunk and stumbled into the wrong room, and when he saw you sleeping there he was so overcome he could not resist kissing you," she suggested.

"Cecily told me the day after the dream that she'd seen Balan lurking in the hall when she left that night. I did not think anything of it at the time, but now . . . Lurking in the hall does not suggest he stumbled into my room by accident."

Emilie was frowning. "Murie, I prithee do not overreact to this. I am sure there is a perfectly good explanation for everything."

"Like what, pray tell?" she asked dubiously.

"I do not know," Emilie admitted. "And you will not either until you ask Balan. Just ask him."

Murie was silent for a moment, then stood with a small nod and moved to the door. "Aye, I shall ask him if he was in my room that night and why."

"Good. I am sure it will all work out."

"Aye." Murie slipped out of her friend's room and pulled the door softly closed behind her. She then paused and peered around. She needed to talk to Balan, but this was a serious matter and must be approached carefully. She was married to the man now, with no way out until one of them died. This had to be handled delicately.

Most delicately, Murie thought as she moved up the hall. She would go for a walk and consider how best to approach the matter before confronting her husband. And then she would stop at the chapel and pray her husband's answers were acceptable and did not prove he was a tricky, cheating lord who had taken advantage of the St. Agnes Eve superstition to get her to marry him because he needed coin for his castle.

"Balan, there is trouble. Murie *knows!*"

"Knows what?" Balan asked. He and Reginald had been headed back to their rooms, but came to a halt as Osgoode rushed up.

"That you were in her room that night. That it was not a dream," his cousin explained, his voice worried.

"Oh-ho. What is this?" Reginald asked with interest.

Balan ignored him and said, "And she married me anyway?"

"Nay." Osgoode waved that possibility away with exasperation. "She did not ken ere the wedding; she realized it this morning when you picked up your cross from the table. It had not been caught in your clothing; you apparently lost it the night you were in her room.

She found it the next morn and put it on the table. You must have lost it in your struggle with Malculinus."

Balan frowned, one hand rising to touch the cross at his neck. "Nay. There was no struggle. But mayhap it fell off when I picked him up."

"Hmm, that is possible," Osgood agreed.

"Oh, now, you have to explain this," Reginald said firmly. "A struggle with Malculinus? In Murie's room?"

Balan grimaced, but quickly explained the events of that evening to his friend.

Reginald nodded solemnly when Balan had finished and then glanced at Osgoode. "And you say Murie knows Balan was in her room that night, really kissing her?"

Osgoode nodded.

Reginald sighed. "This could be a problem, Balan. Murie will not be pleased if she thinks you tricked her into marriage. Neither will the king if he hears of it." His gaze suddenly returned to Osgoode. "How did you find out that she knows? Is word of it already spreading around court?"

"Nay. At least, I do not think so," Osgoode said. "I had my page follow Murie this morning, just to make sure Malculinus and his sister did not try to pull another stunt or cause trouble. He says she rushed out of the room shortly after Balan left, and he followed her to your room and listened at the door to what was said, then came to report to me directly after they spoke."

Reginald did not look pleased to hear that Osgoode's page had eavesdropped through his door, but then neither was Balan pleased with the information obtained.

"You are not to set that boy on my wife again," Balan said with irritation. "She is *my* wife. If I deem she needs following, I shall arrange it. And she does not need following."

"Well, obviously she does," Osgoode argued. "Had I not commanded Robbie to follow her, we would not now know about this problem and could not do anything about it."

"That is true enough," Reginald pointed out, some of his annoyance fading.

"Aye." Osgoode nodded, then turned a raised eyebrow to Balan. "Now, the question is . . . what are we going to do about it?"

Balan scowled for a moment, then said, "*We* are doing nothing."

"Nothing?" Osgoode squawked, and then rushed after him as Balan continued up the hall. "Balan, you have to tell her what Lauda and Malculinus planned. 'Tis the only way to make her understand that we never intended her to see you, that we only meant to stop Malculinus."

"I fear he is right," Reginald said with concern. "You really should tell her, Balan. She may be thinking all sorts of things right now."

Balan paused and turned to face both men with a weary expression. "Do you really think she would believe me?"

Osgoode and Reginald exchanged glances, both seeming to realize it wasn't likely.

"Then what are you going to say when she asks you?" Osgoode asked.

"When she confronts me, I will admit I was there," he said simply.

Reginald winced, and it was Osgoode who spoke. "Can you not deny it? Can you not simply suggest you were there at another time? Claim you entered the

room by accident earlier in the day when she was neither there nor sleeping. That you hadn't even realized
it was her room, and—"

"I am not going to lie to my wife," Balan said firmly.
"A marriage begun on lies is no marriage at all."

"But you have to give some sort of explanation—"

"Nay," he said firmly. "I will not give explanations
she will not believe. Nor will I lie. She has to learn to
trust me. A wife should trust her husband, and Murie
cannot do that until she knows me better." Turning, he
started to walk again. "She will soon learn what I am
like by living with me and seeing how I deal with her
and others. Mayhap then, when I know she will believe
me, I shall tell her about that night."

Sighing, Osgoode shook his head and fell into step
beside him. "You are in for a troubled marriage,
cousin."

"I fear he is right," Reginald said with concern.
"That being the case, might I suggest it is in your best
interests to leave court as soon as possible." When
Balan paused to peer at him, he shrugged and said, "If
Murie is noticeably unhappy so soon after wedding, it
shall surely draw the king's notice."

"Or she may run to him herself with the problem,"
Osgoode put in.

"Either way, you could incur the king's wrath," Reginald pointed out.

Balan frowned. "How would I explain leaving so
soon? We are expected to stay another week."

Reginald shifted, then said, "I could go to Murie
and tell her that I am worried about Emilie. That she is
tired and drawn of late, and I fear for her and the babe
and wish to get her home where it is less wearying and
she may relax."

"All of which is true," Balan said. He cocked his

head. "But how will that convince Murie to leave? Especially if she is upset thinking I tricked her into marrying me?"

"The two women are as close as sisters. While it has the unfortunate effect of making Emilie determined to remain until you and Murie leave, it will also ensure Murie puts Emilie's health and well-being above her own marital troubles. I would ask her to leave early and that our parties travel together to Reynard so that she will be there to help should a problem arise along the way."

"Which would solve both our problems," Balan said solemnly. "I have seen you watching your wife with worried eyes."

"Aye. She is tiring much more quickly than she used to. She claims 'tis normal and she is fine, but . . ."

Balan placed a hand on his friend's shoulder and nodded.

"This is perfect," Osgoode said, drawing them all out of their somber mood. "Emilie will be home where she may rest, and Murie away from court and the king until this matter is resolved between you."

"Aye." Balan nodded.

"And, of course," Reginald added, "once at Reynard, your party is more than welcome to rest a day or two, or even a week before continuing on."

"I may take you up on that. I think Murie would enjoy it," Balan said. Then he frowned. "I am not so sure the king will take our leaving early well, though."

"That is a consideration," Reginald admitted.

The three men were silent for a moment, each considering the matter. Then Balan sighed and said, "I shall have to broach the matter carefully."

"Aye," Reginald and Osgoode agreed.

"Come," Balan said, turning away. "We will have to

think on this, and I think better with an ale in my hand."

Murie watched the men leave from the opposite end of the hall. She'd been looking for her husband and had just started around the corner to the hall near their chamber when she'd heard Osgoode hailing the two men. Pausing abruptly, she'd ducked back out of sight and listened to the entire conversation.

Leaning her back against the wall now, she closed her eyes and allowed a small smile to curve her lips. Emilie had been right. It hadn't at all been what she'd thought.

So, the trickery had been Malculinus and Lauda's. . . . She shuddered at the thought of waking to find that man's lips on hers. She might very well have been fooled into marrying the deceitful lord.

But Balan had saved her from Malculinus's machinations. What a wonderful husband she had!

Her smile widening, Murie pushed away from the wall and started up the hall the men had taken, sure they were far enough away that she would not run into them. She wished she could say with honesty that she would have believed Balan if she'd had the chance to confront him and he'd told her the true state of affairs, but she feared he was right. In truth, she hardly knew her husband and might very well have taken him for a liar. Overhearing this conversation, however, had gone a long way toward increasing her trust in him. Not only had he had honorable intentions the night he was in her room, he'd flat out refused Osgoode's suggestion to lie to appease her. She had a good man for her husband. She owed St. Agnes a good deal for sending Balan to her.

Murie paused and pursed her lips thoughtfully as she reached the stairs. She was not at all upset about leaving court early. She too was worried about Emilie; besides, she had no great love for court. She only feared that the king could be difficult about such things and might not take Balan's request well if he used the wrong approach. She, on the other hand, had a great deal of experience in how to handle the king. She would deal with the matter for him.

Chapter Eight

" 'Tis busy," Reginald murmured as he peered at the lords milling around them. They had already given their names to Robert, making their request to see the king, and had found a spot to wait in the corner. "We shall be lucky to get in to see him at all today."

"Aye." Balan scowled at the crowded waiting room outside the king's chamber. He'd been hoping to get Murie away from court today to prevent their marital problems becoming fodder for the court, but at this rate, it wasn't looking likely.

"Is that not Murie?"

Balan turned at Osgoode's surprised words and saw his wife bustling out into the hall. She moved quickly, a smile on her face, looking neither left nor right, so she did not see the three of them.

Frowning, Balan took a step to follow her, intending to ask what she'd been about, only to pause as he heard his name called.

"Lord Gaynor?" the speaker said again, closer this time.

Balan tore his gaze from his departing wife's back and peered at Robert as the man reached his side. "Aye?"

"You may see the king now."

"What of Lord Reynard? We asked to see him together," he said, glancing toward his now frowning friend.

"I was told to send for only you," the servant said simply. "This way, please."

After the briefest hesitation, Balan nodded and followed.

His eyes sought Edward the moment he stepped through the door. There was no fury or upset apparent on the king's face, but that wasn't necessarily a good thing. He was well aware that His Majesty could hide his emotions when it suited his purposes. If Murie had been here to complain about her husband tricking her, Edward might very well hide his emotions until he was ready to tear layers off Balan's back.

"Ah, Balan." Edward smiled in greeting. "Good. I asked you here to speak about Murie."

"Actually, I asked to speak to you for the very same reason," Balan replied. Worry drew his brows together.

"Really?" Edward glanced toward Robert in question, and the man nodded.

"He arrived and asked to see you just before you ordered me to send for him," the servant explained.

"Ah." Edward nodded. "That explains how you got here so quickly. Good, well, as I am the king, I will speak first, and then you may speak of your issue."

Balan gave a half bow. "As you wish, sire."

Edward nodded and got right to the point. "Murie is concerned about Lady Reynard's health. The two have been friends for years, and she holds a great deal of affection for Lady Emilie—an affection that is returned. Unfortunately, it would seem this affection may be endangering the woman's health. She is with child and should really be at home resting before the babe comes, but she wishes to stay here and visit with Murie as long as she can. Murie feels that, were she to leave court, Emilie would agree to leave as well and return to her home."

"Ah," Balan said, realizing slowly that she'd not come to tattle to the king, but had done his work for him. What was the minx up to? He merely said, "Aye, Lord Reginald was saying something similar to me just this morning. In fact, that is why I wished to speak to you."

The king smiled. "Good, then we are in accord. I have agreed to forgo the celebrations we had planned and allow your party to leave early. Today, even." He paused and arched an eyebrow. "Is that a problem?"

"Nay, sire," Balan replied.

"Nay. I did not think it would be. I know how you dislike court, Balan." He added, "And you most likely have a lot to put to rights at Gaynor to prepare for the winter."

"Aye, sire," Balan admitted.

Edward nodded. "I have not yet had the chance to say it, but I was sorry to hear of your father's death. He was a good man."

"Aye. Thank you, sire," Balan said softly.

Edward nodded again. "Well, you may leave as soon as you are ready, without need to see me again before you go. Murie is, no doubt, already in her . . . er, your chamber, directing the servants in packing."

"Thank you, sire."

Edward acknowledged his words with a slight incline of his head. "You may go."

Murmuring a farewell, Balan bowed and backed away, then turned toward the door, only to pause as Edward called out. "Take heed, Balan." He glanced to his aide and then back. "Becker does not think it necessary that I tell you this, but Murie is not as weak as everyone thinks she is. That weeping and carrying on . . ." He smiled faintly. "She is very bad at it."

Balan's mouth dropped open. He stared at his liege for several heartbeats, then asked, "You knew she was feigning all those tears?"

"Certainly," Edward said.

Balan nodded slowly. "And yet you never called her on it?"

Edward shrugged. "It amused me. Besides, it kept the other girls from harassing her further, while preventing the need for myself to intervene and adding to their ire."

While Balan processed that, the king added, "The females tormented her horribly when Murie first got here. So badly, I think it would have twisted the mind of a lesser person, but she has handled it beautifully. Had she continued trying to stand up to them as she first did, they would simply have moved in for the kill. Instead, little Emilie advised her to weep loudly and annoyingly, and it worked."

"You knew Emilie was the one who advised her to do this?" Balan asked, amazed.

"My wife is not as oblivious as she likes to let people think," Edward replied solemnly. "And she has more affection for the girl than she lets on. She could not show it for fear of making things worse. While she could have forced the girls to behave while in her presence, she could not be with Murie all the time, and Murie is proud enough she would not tell, no matter what horrible things the others did out of the queen's presence." He allowed that to sink in, then grinned and added, "Besides, Osgoode is not the only one who can set servants to spying. There is nothing that goes on in court that I do not know about." He began to chuckle at Balan's alarmed expression, then added, "Treat her well. You will soon realize that she is a blessing to you."

"I believe I already do, sire," Balan said quietly.

"Then we are satisfied. You may go."

Balan turned away, and this time managed to leave the room without being stopped. He was shaking his head with wonder as he rejoined Osgoode and Reginald.

"Well?" the two men asked as he paused before them in the waiting area.

"We leave at once," Balan said, leading them away from the others. He added wryly, "Well, as soon as we can get the women packed and ready."

"Was it very difficult to convince him?" Osgoode asked curiously as they headed back through the castle.

"Nay. Murie had already been to ask the same thing."

"What?" Osgoode glanced at him with surprise.

"Apparently, that was why she was there to see him. She was concerned about Emilie and thought that if we left, Emilie might. She had already asked and been granted permission to leave early."

Balan did not share all the other things he'd learned in that room. He felt it was not his place to do so. Someday he might tell Murie that her weeping and carrying on had never fooled the king and queen, but it was no one else's business.

"Well," Reginald said slowly. "Murie is quite fond of Emilie and not fond at all of court. I suppose I should not be surprised, but . . ." He peered at Balan. "Should she not have approached you rather than the king?"

"Aye," Osgoode agreed. "And what of her upset over learning you had really been in her room and it was not a dream?"

Balan shook his head with amusement. "You are always looking for trouble, Osgoode. Stop looking this gift horse in the mouth. I am just grateful it is all going as we planned. I will be glad to get home to Gaynor sooner than expected; and I know you, Reginald, are glad to be able to get Emilie home as well."

"Aye." Reginald smiled. "I should go break the news to her."

"And I should go have the boys pack our things," Osgoode said.

"Aye," Balan agreed. "I shall go and see how long it will take Murie to be ready to go."

Nodding, Osgoode set off. Balan followed Reginald to the stairs, but he was frowning as he considered they might not be able to leave today. He, Osgoode, and the Lord and Lady Reynard had only come to visit, so had just what they had brought to take away. This, however, had been Murie's home for ten years. She would have a lot to pack, he realized.

They reached Reynard's room, and the men parted, Balan continuing on toward the room he'd shared the night before with Murie. However, he paused when Reginald opened the door to his room and several women's voices could be heard. One of them was Murie's.

Returning to Reginald's side, Balan peered in to see his wife fussing around Emilie, helping her and her maid pack away her things.

"Oh, good. You are already packing," Reginald said to catch their attention. The three women turned as one.

"Aye." Emilie smiled widely at her husband. "Murie

is eager to get to Gaynor to see her new home, and she managed to convince the king to let her leave early. And, as you have been fretting so about our leaving, I thought . . ." She paused and bit her lip, then said, "Well, I did not mean to presume, I just got excited. And if you do not wish to leave yet—"

"Nay, that is fine," Reginald assured her, moving into the room to slide an arm around her. "I am glad to leave."

Balan watched him press a kiss to his wife's forehead and then glanced for his own wife. Murie was watching the other couple with a smile, apparently not at all concerned that Balan might not wish to leave. He did wish it, but she could hardly know that, and while he'd told Osgoode not to look a gift horse in the mouth, Balan could not think it a good thing that the woman cared so little for his opinion and intended to do as she liked regardless of how he felt.

This, however, was not the time to broach such a subject. He really did want to leave. If she showed such presumption again, he would tackle it. For now, he was annoyed but would let it ride.

"How long will it take you to pack, wife?" he asked, drawing Murie's attention.

"Not long. The servants are packing as we speak," she assured him. She added wryly, "The queen got wind that we were leaving and sent several of her servants to help. I was told to take myself out of the way, so I came to help Emilie."

Murie was smiling as she said the words, but he could see the hurt in her eyes, and it was obvious to him that she thought the queen had sent the servants along to speed up the process, to be free of her as quickly as possible. Balan decided he would have to tell her the truth of matters sooner rather than later. He understood why Queen

Phillippa had refrained from showing her attention, and it was true doing so had probably saved Murie even more torment, but it had left the girl feeling uncared for and unvalued. Balan would not have his wife feeling that way.

"With all that help, they shall probably be done within the hour," Murie finished.

"An hour?" Balan's eyes found Reginald's and saw the man's surprise equaled his own.

"I had best get the men together," Lord Reynard declared.

Balan nodded and backed out of the room into the hall. "I will go let Osgoode and the boys know."

"I am surprised they didn't take exception to our presumption," Emilie said as the door closed behind the men.

Murie shrugged. "They wished to leave. We made it so that they may."

"Aye, but as far as they know, we do not know they want to leave. To them it must appear as if we are just forging ahead with our own plans, uncaring of what they want."

"Oh." Murie frowned as she realized this was true. While she knew they had planned this and had simply facilitated what she could, they had no idea she knew. Sighing with exasperation, she snatched up an undertunic to fold. "Being married is far more complicated than I expected. Suddenly, everything is an issue, and he must be considered in all things."

"Aye," Emilie murmured. Then she grinned. "But it does have its rewards as well."

Laughing at the twinkle in her friend's eye, Murie hugged her and returned to packing.

With the three of them working, it was less than the hour she'd suggested before they were done. Leaving

Emilie to wait for the servants to carry her chest below, Murie went to check on her own belongings, surprised to find the queen herself in her room, directing the servants.

"There you are, dear." The woman smiled. "I think we are nearly done. At least, with the clothes you shall need for the next few weeks until the remainder are sent on to you. They shall be sent along with the items you ordered as soon as those are got together, and Edward has agreed to send soldiers to guard your things on their journey."

"I . . . Thank you, Your Majesty," Murie whispered, wondering if the woman was being so kind just because she was so happy to be rid of her.

"Murie."

"Aye?" she said warily as the servants trooped out with the two chests they'd packed, leaving her alone with the queen.

Phillipa closed the door behind them and turned to face her. "I wanted to tell you before you go how very proud I am of you."

Murie blinked in surprise. "You—Proud?" she asked weakly.

Queen Phillippa nodded. "Aye. I know the girls and young women were awful to you here at court, but you never once asked my aid in handling them. You dealt with it in your own way. Other girls were constantly running to me, weeping at this cruelty or that, but not you. You faced your own problems and found your own way through them." Crossing the room, she clasped Murie's shoulders and said, "Out of all the girls who have been here over the years, I know I can let you go and not fear there is a situation you cannot handle. I know you will be fine and will be able to cope with any matter that comes your way in life. I am proud of you."

"Oh," Murie breathed, and she blinked her eyes rapidly to try to dry the tears pooling there. She did not wish to weep and make a fool of herself.

The queen smiled at her expression, then bent to press a kiss to her cheek. "Be happy, child."

Murie raised a hand to her cheek to touch the spot the woman had kissed and watched silently as the queen left the room. Her heart was aching from just those few kind words, and they put an entirely different light on the past ten years of her life. She just wasn't sure how.

"Wife?"

Murie turned to see Balan in the doorway, eyeing her in question.

"Are you well?" he asked with concern. "Have you been crying?"

"Nay," she said quickly and flashed him a smile. She moved toward him. "I am fine, husband."

He stared at her silently for a moment, then grunted and caught her hand to lead her into the hall. "The horses are ready, and the wagon's packed. Osgoode is waiting with them. We are to meet Reginald and Emilie down by the stables."

"Aye, my lord," Murie said.

They walked quickly down the hall. Her eyes were skating over the trappings and décor of this castle, which had been her home for ten years. She was happy to be leaving, and yet some part of her felt sad as well. She had no idea why. Murie had suffered little but misery in this place. Still . . .

Mayhap it was because leaving meant the end of her childhood and the beginning of a new phase of life. She pondered the matter as they made their way to the stables.

"All is ready." Osgoode greeted them as they reached

the wagon and the small group of armed men on horseback waiting nearby.

Murie glanced around, noting her chests on the wagon, as well as Emilie's. They had been arranged to leave a small pocket of room where several furs lay. She glanced at those curiously, then peered around the gathering. "We have beat Emilie and Reginald here."

"Aye. They shall be along soon, though I am—" Balan paused abruptly and turned his head, a hand rising to his nose as he began the repeated gasping inhalations of an oncoming sneeze. Eyes widening in alarm, Murie reached out quickly and slapped his left cheek, forcing his face to the right just as he sneezed.

Balan turned to her with confusion the moment he'd recovered himself. "What—?"

" 'Tis bad luck to sneeze to the left ere a journey, my lord. You must always try to sneeze to the right if you are planning a trip."

"I see," he said solemnly, his shoulders relaxing. His tone was rather dry, however, when he asked, "Is there anything else I should know about sneezing?"

"Never sneeze near a grave, and—"

"Here we are!" Emilie cried gaily, and Murie gave up her explanations in order to smile at the woman whose husband led her over. "I hope we did not hold you up too long. Reginald felt he should make his farewells to the king, else we would have been here much sooner. Fortunately, he did not have to wait too long to see him."

"That was fortunate," Murie agreed, and thought that Edward must have realized Lord Reynard was stopping to beg leave and so had seen him quickly to allow them to get on their way.

"Come, wife." Balan took her arm to lead her to her mount.

"Emilie is not riding in the wagon, is she?" Murie asked with surprise. Reginald had lifted his wife up into the back.

"Aye," Balan said as he caught her at the waist to set her on her horse.

"But—" Murie broke off with surprise as he stopped lifting her and kissed her quite thoroughly.

"Wife," he said when he'd finished.

"Aye?" She sighed, her eyes slowly opening.

"I was sneezing to my right. You turned my head to *your* right, which was my left." He grinned at her blank expression, then set her in the saddle and turned to walk to his own mount.

Murie stared after him with dismay, realizing what he'd said was true. They had been facing each other, and she had turned his face from her left to her right, which meant she'd turned his face from his right to his left. Oh, this didn't bode well for the journey at all!

They rode through the afternoon and well into evening before Balan and Reginald deemed it time to stop and make camp. Murie knew they had traveled so late to make up for leaving court so late, so she had not complained, but she was grateful to be off her mount.

She was doubly grateful when her husband proved himself very considerate by suggesting he take her down to the riverside to clean up while the rest of the men prepared camp.

Yes, she'd chosen her husband well, Murie decided with a contented smile as he grabbed her hand and led her into the woods around the clearing the men had chosen. So distracted was she with her own satisfaction, they had gone quite a way before she began to pay attention to the trees and vegetation around them.

It was pure chance that she glanced down and spotted the St. John's wort.

"Oh, nay, my lord! Be careful!" Murie cried, catching at Balan's arm and trying to bring him to a halt. She sighed with exasperation. "Too late."

"Too late for what?" Balan asked with bewilderment. She bent and urged his foot out of the way, then tried to fluff up the plant he'd crushed with his step.

"You must never step on St. John's wort," she lectured. "A fairy horse will rise up under you and carry you away."

Balan watched his wife's useless efforts to fix the plant, baffled, and then realization struck. This was one of her silly superstitions. Smiling faintly, he caught her upper arm and drew her back to her feet. "I think we can do away with that worry."

She peered at him in confusion. "Why?"

"Because I am still here. No fairy horse rose up and took me away," he pointed out.

"Oh." She sighed, leaning into him as his thumbs caressed her cheeks. "Husband?"

"Aye," he murmured, fascinated by the way she was turning in to his touch like a putted cat.

"I like it when you kiss me."

His mouth curved in a smile. "Do you?"

"Mmmhmm." She nodded.

"Would you like me to kiss you now?" he asked, aware of several changes taking place in his body at the prospect. Just the thought had his shaft stirring to lazy life.

"Yes, please," she whispered, tilting her head a little more so that her lips were on offer.

Smiling, Balan shifted his hand, giving up caressing her cheek to catch his fingers in her hair. He held her in place as he lowered his mouth to hers.

Murie let her mouth open on a satisfied sigh. Taking advantage, Balan slid his tongue out, growling deep in his throat when she slid her arms around his neck and tried to move closer against him. She was shorter than he, however; Balan had had to bend to kiss her, and she could not get close. Releasing his hold on her hair, he reached down to catch her by the behind, squeezed her buttocks firmly through her gown and lifted her up to press her firmly against him.

Murie gasped into his mouth, her nails digging into his shoulders. Immediately an erection sprang to life under his cotehardie. Impatient, Balan let her slide back down to the ground and then set to work at the laces on the back of her gown until the collar slipped away, sliding down her shoulders. Giving up on the laces, he tugged the cloth down her arms until her breasts popped free, then immediately he caught one in his hand.

Murie groaned and arched her back, her hands clutching at his arms and tugging in a silent demand for either one of two things: an end to the torment or a plea for more. Smiling against her mouth, he broke their kiss and immediately ducked his head to close his mouth over the nipple of the breast he was cupping.

His wife's response was most gratifying. Crying out in excitement, she switched her hands to his hair and alternately tugged at the strands and pushed at his head, as if unsure whether she was trying to stop him or urge him on. As she couldn't make up her mind, Balan ignored her and did as he wished, his attention wholly focused on suckling the sweet nub in his mouth, drawing on it and nibbling lightly by turn as he kneaded with one hand the soft plump flesh. But soon that was not enough, and he straightened, catching her mouth once more with his.

Murie kissed him back desperately, a constant keening coming from her throat as her breasts rubbed across the rough cloth of his cotehardie. When she slid one tentative hand between them and pressed it against the erection so evident beneath his clothes, Balan growled into her mouth, his hips thrusting forward of their own accord.

Opening eyes he hadn't realized he'd closed; Balan spotted a tree a couple of feet behind Murie, and he urged her backward without breaking their kiss. Pressing her against it, he reached for her skirt, rucking it up her leg until he could slip his hand beneath. Murie gasped and sighed and moaned by turn as his fingers ran up her outer thigh and then dipped around and inside.

Her legs briefly squeezed his hand as it slid between her thighs, but then eased apart to allow him access. Balan murmured approvingly when he found her warm and wet. The approval wasn't needed; his wife wasn't in any state to listen. She was sucking almost violently on his tongue, and her hand squeezed him almost painfully through his clothes.

Apparently unhappy with the interference, she released him, then found her way under the clothes to his erection. Grasping him firmly in hand, she pulled him toward her, making her desire known. She wanted him inside her.

Balan ignored the silent demand. Instead, he slid a finger lightly over her quivering flesh and then drove it into her. Murie broke their kiss and threw her head back with a cry, her body jerking and her hand along with it. He cried out as well.

Giving up tormenting her, Balan removed his hand from between her legs and slid it around to her behind. The moment he lifted her, Murie wrapped her legs around his hips, pulling him tight against her even as she released his erection to hold his cotehardie out of the way.

Balan groaned as he pressed against her slick core. Pinning her against the tree, he shifted slightly and slid into her. A relieved sigh slid from his lips as her body closed around him, welcoming him to her heated depths. He then covered her mouth with his again, withdrew himself and slowly thrust forward.

Murie kissed him back, her tongue dancing with his even as her body arched and shifted and urged him on. Aware that he was close to spilling his seed, but unwilling to do so until she'd found her release, Balan caught her by the hips and swung away from the tree, then carried her quickly to a slanted boulder at the riverside, each step threatening his control.

Pausing at the boulder, he laid her on the higher end so that her body was at a downward angle. Without the need to hold her, he was free to touch, and he took full advantage, cupping her pale breasts in both hands and kneading briefly before sliding his hands down over her stomach, then across the crumpled material of her gown and further. One hand stopped at the core of her and began to caress, but the other continued on down to one ankle to catch and lift it before him.

Murie's eyes popped open, and she stared wide-eyed as he leaned it against his chest, then held it to help brace himself as he drove into her with more urgency. But her eyes soon closed and squeezed tight shut, her face tightening until she suddenly twisted her head to the side with a scream of pleasure.

Only then did Balan allow his seed to spill. Giving up his caresses, he clutched her leg with both hands and thrust one final time, his head falling back as he released his own shout of victory.

Chapter Nine

"Is everything all right?" Emilie asked as Murie rejoined her. The men had built a fire, and she was seated by it, enjoying its heat.

A bit chilled from the dip in the river she'd just taken, washing after the episode with her husband, Murie was grateful for the fire. She began to brush her hair, hoping to dry it more quickly.

"Aye, of course I am fine," she said with surprise. "Why would you think otherwise?"

"Oh, no reason," Emilie assured her. Then, eyes twinkling, she added, "The men were a bit concerned by the shouts and screams coming from the woods, but Reginald assured them that all was likely well and kept them from running to your rescue."

Murie stared, her face flushing with embarrassment; then she scowled and wrinkled her nose. She said by way of explanation, "I saw a snake."

"I am sure you did," Emilie said meaningfully, and Murie blushed harder.

"I did not mean—" she began, but when her friend burst into a fit of giggles, she gave up and joined her.

"I am glad that part of your marriage appears to be going well," Emilie said as their giggles died. "I imagine it could be most difficult did you not . . . er . . . find some common ground in the marital bed."

"Aye," Murie agreed, her eyes finding her husband and watching him talk to Reginald. The two men were laughing, and she had no doubt Lord Reynard had just told him that the men had thought to rescue them. His gaze found hers, and he smiled. Murie admitted, "He makes my legs weak and my body quiver."

"Aye." Emilie sighed, her eyes seeking out her own husband. "So did Reginald."

"Did?" Murie asked with alarm.

"He has not touched me since we found I was pregnant," she admitted unhappily.

"Oh." Murie bit her lip, her gaze slipping back to the man in question. "He is most likely afraid of hurting you."

"That, or he finds me hideously unattractive now that I grow heavy with child," Emilie said with forced cheer.

"Oh, Emilie, I am sure that is not it," Murie assured her. "Anyone can see that Reginald adores you."

"Then why does he no longer touch me?"

"He is always hugging and kissing you," Murie pointed out.

"That is not the same thing, Murie, and you know it. That is affection. I want . . ." Her eyes returned to her husband, a battle of wants and needs warring there.

"You want to feel desired, not just cared for," Murie remarked with quiet understanding. She'd only been married two days and a night, but even so, she did not think she'd be very happy were Balan suddenly to stop wanting to make love to her.

Emilie heaved a sigh and waved her hand vaguely. "It will be all right. I am just huge and miserable right now. Everything will be fine once the bairn is born . . . which I hope will be soon."

"Not too soon," Murie said with a half laugh. "Pray, let us get to Reynard Castle before it arrives. I should not like to help you deliver the babe out here in a rough camp without aid or herbs or medicinals to help."

"Well, not *that* soon," Emilie agreed. "I still have a couple months to go."

Murie nodded.

"Ladies." Reginald smiled as he led Balan over. "As Balan and Osgoode did not bother bringing a tent for the journey, and we did, I have offered my place in the tent to you, Murie. I shall join the rest of the men by the fire while you and Emilie rest inside this night."

"Oh." Murie's eyes slid to her husband. She'd rather hoped to sleep curled in his arms by the fire. It had been nice waking in his arms last night. She'd felt cared for each time she'd awakened. Her husband didn't appear to feel the same, however.

"That is a good idea," Emilie murmured.

Forcing a smile, Murie nodded. "That is very kind of you, Reginald. Thank you."

Despite her up-front agreement, as the men walked away Emilie said unhappily, "Now he does not even care to sleep with me."

"Aye, and apparently Balan does not wish to sleep with me, either," Murie muttered.

Both women sighed as they watched their husbands cross the clearing.

* * *

Despite the absence of her husband, or perhaps because of it, Murie slept late the next morning. When she woke, the tent was empty, Emilie having risen and left. Cecily had, apparently, already been; there was fresh clothing lying on the furs at the foot of the pallet she'd slept on. Reaching for the undertunic, Murie donned it, then stood to don the gown as well, then ran her fingers through her hair before making her way out of the tent.

She stepped out into the clearing to find it a hive of activity. She was the last to rise, and men were rushing this way and that, packing things and preparing to break camp.

"Wife."

Murie turned and offered a shy smile at her husband. "You slept well?" he asked.

She nodded, eyebrows rising. He looked a bit pale and haggard. It seemed obvious from that, and from the scowl gracing his face that he had not. Still, she asked politely: "And you?"

"It rained last night," was his answer.

"Ah." Murie bit her lip and gave a start when he took her elbow to lead her into the woods.

"You did not sleep much on our wedding night, so I let you sleep in this morn. However, because of that you will not have time for proper ablutions ere we go," he announced. They walked the trail to the river's edge. "I was just coming to wake you when you stepped out of the tent. We are leaving as soon as the tent and furs are packed on the wagon."

"Oh," Murie murmured, and soon found he was not exaggerating about time for proper ablutions. He allowed her a moment to relieve herself of her full blad-

der, then led her to the riverside to splash water on
her face and hands before hurrying back to camp.

Murie saw with some amazement that, despite how
quick she had been, the tent and all its trappings were
already broken down and stowed away, and everyone
was mounted—except Reginald, who was lifting Emilie into the wagon as they entered the clearing. Murie
had barely noted all this when Balan suddenly caught
her by the waist and lifted her. Glancing around with
surprise, she saw that they had reached her mount,
and then he was sitting her on the mare's back, and
she was scrambling to hold on to the pommel.

"I—," she began with bewilderment, then paused as
her husband suddenly held up a bag.

"Cheese, bread and an apple—to break your fast as
we ride," he announced.

"Thank you," Murie said, accepting the bag and
watching as he turned to mount his own horse. She
was still not quite awake and was feeling a bit over-
whelmed by the speed of things this morning, but
movement drew her gaze to the wagon to find Emilie
smiling and waving at her, and she felt herself relax a
little as she smiled and waved in return.

A high-pitched whinny and snorting drew her eyes
sharply to her husband and his mount. Balan had apparently just mounted, but the stallion, Lightning, was
not pleased for some reason; he was reacting badly. He
was rearing and snorting and pawing the air as he
squealed in what sounded to be pain. Murie's eyes had
barely begun to widen with alarm for her husband,
when the horse suddenly stopped rearing and charged
off into the woods.

Murie did not even think about it; she simply
slipped her leg over the pommel so she was astride her

mare, and dug in her heels to send her horse charging
after him. A shout made her glance over her shoulder
as she charged into the woods, and she spotted Reginald right behind her with several of the men. Then
she turned forward and concentrated on catching up
to her husband.

Murie had a fine mare, a gift from the king and
queen on her sixteenth birthday, but Lightning was a
warrior's steed, used to moving quickly while carrying
a man heavy with armor and weapons. Balan was not
in armor today, nor did he have a heavy shield or
weapons, and the lack of weight and whatever had distressed the animal combined to make the beast move
like the wind. She had no hope of keeping up, let
alone overtaking her husband and helping.

Fortunately, Reginald's war horse could, and Murie
released a little breath of relief as he overtook her and
drew closer to Balan. Murie watched with wide worried
eyes as he finally reached Balan's side, a dangerous maneuver in the woods, and then her husband was leaping
from Lightning's back and almost on top of Reginald.
The two men teetered briefly, and she feared they
would both lose their seat, but they settled, and Lord
Raynard allowed his mount to slow and stop. Balan's
steed had slowed the moment he was out of the saddle.

Murie drew her mount to a halt as she reached
them, her eyes moving anxiously over her husband to
be sure he was not injured. Once assured that he was
well, her worry turned to anger.

"I told you not to step on that St. John's wort," she
said with vexation as she reined in.

"What?" Balan asked with confusion. He slid to the
ground.

"The St. John's wort that you stepped on yesterday,"
she reminded him from her saddle as Reginald also

dismounted and moved to catch Balan's now calm horse. "Do you not recall? I told you it is said that should you step on St. John's wort, a fairy horse will rise up beneath you and carry you away. You must be more careful where you set your feet in future, husband. I could have lost you."

"Murie," he said patiently. "I stepped on the St. John's wort yesterday, not today. And a fairy horse did not rise up and ride off with me. *My* horse did."

"Aye, but the saying does not say *when* the fairy horse will rise, or how," she pointed out. "Mayhap it possessed your mount and tried to ride off with you. Had Reginald not caught up . . ." She shook her head with distress and pleaded, "Pray, just be more careful where you are stepping."

"Lightning was *not* possessed by a fairy horse," Balan said with exasperation. Turning, he stomped over to join Reginald, who was unsaddling his sweating mount.

"Nay. Your horse was not possessed," Reginald agreed grimly, and Murie could see that he was holding up something as her husband reached his side; but she could not tell what it was until he added, "Someone put a thistle under your saddle. The moment you put weight on it, it dug into the animal's back and sent it wild."

Eyes widening, Murie slid off her mount and hurried over to see. It was indeed a thistle he held, a particularly large and thorny one. Frowning, she asked, "You do not suppose the fairy horse left that behind to fool us into thinking it was not a fairy horse?"

"Murie!" Balan snapped.

"What?" she asked warily.

"I . . . You . . . Just get on your horse," he finished with a sigh.

"You had best not risk trying to ride your mount right now," Murie heard Reginald advise. She turned with a little flounce and stomped back to her own horse. She'd only been trying to help. And really, it couldn't be coincidence that he'd stepped on St. John's wort just last eve and been carried away by a horse this morn. Why did he not see that?

Muttering under her breath, she led her mare to a small boulder—much smaller than the boulder Balan had laid her on when they'd stopped to make love last night, she thought as the memory rose up in her mind. Shaking her head to free herself of the thought, she stepped up onto the boulder, jammed her foot in the stirrup and pulled herself into her saddle.

"Nay, you are right," Balan was saying as she sat and gathered up the reins. "I suppose I shall have to leave him riderless for the day."

Murie had just turned her horse back the way they had come when her husband called out. "Wife! Wait a moment."

"What?" she snapped, glancing over her shoulder with irritation.

"I shall be riding with you."

"Hmmph," Murie muttered, but she kept her mare where she was as Balan began to lead his mount toward her.

"I can lead him back," Reginald offered. "You shall have your hands full holding on to the reins and Murie."

"Thank you," Balan agreed. Murie simply scowled down her nose at him where he paused beside her mount.

" 'Tis *my* mount. All you need hold on to is me,"

she said firmly. She would not have her mare usurped by him.

Balan didn't reply; he merely mounted behind her so that his chest pressed insistently against her back, an unmovable wall. He then took the reins and turned the horse around.

"You were going the wrong way," he murmured in her ear, then took her hands and wrapped them around the reins again. "Now you may go."

Murie grimaced, then paused, her head jerking up as a plaintive, trilling sound filled the air.

"A curlew," she whispered with dread.

"What is it?" Balan asked, leaning around to see her face.

"That was the call of a curlew," she said in hushed tones. " 'Tis a very bad omen. It foretells a death—or is that only if you hear it at night?" she fretted.

"Wife, just get us back to camp. I do not have the patience for your silly superstitions at the moment." Balan's tone was short. Unnecessarily so, Murie decided as she urged her mount into a walk. She was really quite annoyed with him. First he'd yelled at her, and now he snapped at her; and he thought her a fool and—

She blinked and glanced down in surprise as his hands slid up to cup her breasts through her gown.

"What are you doing?" she asked in a squeak, her head swiveling around to be sure Reginald couldn't see what he was about.

"Holding on, so I do not fall out of the saddle," he said, beginning to nuzzle her neck.

Murie sucked in a breath to tell him to stop, then let it out in a quick whoosh as he found her half-erect nipples and began to toy with them.

"Husband," she reprimanded breathlessly, her head tilting to the side to offer him better access—wholly of its own accord; she was not instructing it to do so.

"Aye," he growled, his teeth grazing her throat. "I am your husband."

Murie was trying to sort out what that announcement meant, when one hand left a breast to slip between her legs, pressing the cloth of her gown against her. Murie groaned and started to sink against him, then sat up abruptly as Reginald rode near. Fortunately, Balan was quick to shift his hands to more acceptable spots, and Lord Reynard seemed oblivious to what he'd interrupted.

"It probably would be better not to ride your mount at all today," Reginald repeated reluctantly. "I suppose we could delay leaving and camp here until the morrow."

"Nay," Balan said. "Murie will ride in the wagon with Emilie, and I shall ride her mare."

Murie found her earlier annoyance returning. She'd been about to offer to do just that—give him her mount and ride with Emilie—but she hadn't got the chance; instead, he'd announced the plan like it was law. It would have been nice had he bothered to ask. He seemed to like to boss everyone about.

"Never fear, this will not slow us down," Balan assured his friend. "By my reckoning, we shall be there by the morrow."

Seeing the relief on Reginald's face, Murie forced herself to relax. Of course Lord Reynard was worried about Emilie and would not wish the journey slowed, and of course her husband had realized that and made a decision meant to get them to their destination quickly. She really shouldn't be upset that he was such a high-handed, bossy, annoying—

Murie's thoughts flew from her head as she was suddenly lifted bodily out of the saddle. While she'd been distracted, thinking up descriptions for her overbearing husband, they had arrived at camp, he'd dismounted and was now setting her on the ground.

"Go hop in the wagon and reassure Emilie that all is well. She is looking worried," Balan ordered, turning her toward the wagon and giving her a pat on the bottom. Grimacing, she went.

Balan watched his wife go, smiling at the way she was muttering under her breath; then he tore his gaze away and nodded to Osgoode.

"What happened?" his cousin asked with concern, moving past him to look at his mount. "Why did he bolt like that? Lightning has never acted so before."

"Someone put a thistle under the saddle," Reginald explained, dismounting to join them.

"A thistle?" Osgoode asked. "On purpose?"

"Well, it could have got there accidentally," Reginald said doubtfully. "But it was placed so that it would do no harm until weight was put on the saddle."

"On purpose then," Osgoode agreed with a frown. He glanced at his cousin. "You could have been killed."

"Aye." Balan took the saddle Reginald had carried back before him on his horse and handed it to one of the men to pack on the wagon.

"I shall go check on Emilie and be sure this upset did her no harm," Reginald said.

"Thank you for your help, Reginald," Balan called with belated but real gratitude. He could have been killed in the incident and might have been had his friend not thought quickly.

"You do not suppose Murie is the one who . . ." Osgoode let his words trail off as Balan turned to glance at him. His cousin's expression was troubled.

"What?" he asked, not understanding.

"Well, I was just thinking . . . she never confronted you about being in her room. And she seemed eager to leave court, even though she has to be upset with you for what she thinks is tricking her into this marriage."

"Aye, and . . . ?" Balan asked, not sure where Osgoode was going.

"Well, mayhap she does not intend to confront you about that night. Mayhap she is so angry she has decided to . . . er . . . end the marriage."

Balan peered at him as if he were mad. "There is no way to end the marriage, Osgoode. It was consummated. 'Tis done. She is stuck with me."

"Until death do you part," Osgoode agreed meaningfully.

"You think she is trying to kill me?" Balan asked with shock. He immediately shook his head. "Do not be ridiculous." Turning on his heel, he stomped to his wife's mare and mounted, but the thought was in his head now and not easily shaken. It troubled him for the next hour as they rode, his mind inundated with questions such as: Why had she not confronted him about being in her room? And, why had she arranged to get them away from the castle so quickly?

She had not approached him with the matter as a wife should, but had gone to the king and arranged it so that Balan could not have refused had he wished—ensuring they would be off in the woods where accidents were less likely to be witnessed or questioned. Not that anyone would question them, since no one at court knew she had any reason—or thought she did—to be furious with him.

* * *

"Balan has been sending you odd glances all day. Did the two of you have a spat?" Emilie asked as they relaxed around the night's campfire.

Murie cast a glower over her shoulder toward her husband. He was on the other side of camp, talking to one of the men, but he was also watching her with narrowed, thoughtful eyes. She wasn't really annoyed anymore, but if he was annoyed with her, she would be annoyed right back. After all, she was the one who had been riding in the wagon all day, not he. And it had been damnably uncomfortable. She had no idea why men seemed to think that women were better off in wagons when they were jostled and bounced around at least as much as on a horse. Her whole body felt battered and bruised. And now her stomach was out of sorts too. It had not been a good day.

Sighing, she rubbed her stomach absently and turned back to stare blindly at the dancing flames, then recalled that Emilie had asked her a question. "Nay, not really. He is annoyed with me because I was sure it was a fairy horse carrying him away this morning."

"What?" Emilie asked, startled.

Murie quickly explained about her husband stepping on St. John's wort and her fear that he would be carried away by a fairy horse—or a horse possessed by a fairy horse, she added meaningfully.

Emilie burst out laughing. "Oh, Lord, Murie. Your belief in these silly superstitions is the only thing that keeps you from being a perfect woman."

Murie frowned. "I am sorry, I—"

"Nay, do not apologize," Emilie said quickly. "If you were perfect, I would have to hate you on principal alone."

"Oh," Murie said, unsure how to reply. When they

fell silent again, she found her eyes drifting back to her husband. She'd hoped he would take her to clean up after their journey again tonight and perhaps kiss her again, and . . . Well, but he hadn't. Reginald had seen both women down to the river and turned his back while they tended to matters. Balan, it seemed, was too busy to be bothered.

Realizing she was scowling at him again, Murie started to turn away, then froze as she noted his coloring. It might have been just the effect of the firelight, but he looked slightly gray.

"Murie, are you feeling all right?" Emilie asked. "You keep rubbing your stomach and your color seems off, though 'tis hard to tell in this light."

"Nay," she admitted unhappily. "My stomach is bothering me. I think it did not like the journey in the wagon. I do not know how you stand it."

"I did not have a choice. The only way Reginald would allow me to travel to court was if I rode in the wagon," she said. "And I did so want to see you."

"Oh," Murie breathed, tears coming to her eyes. "You must truly love me. Thank you, Emilie."

"Murie?" There was sudden real alarm in her friend's voice. "Are you all right? You look—"

"Are you supposed to have two faces?" Murie interrupted with a frown. Then she felt herself slumping forward.

Chapter Ten

"How are you feeling?"

Osgoode's voice drew Balan's eyes open where he lay prostrate on the ground in a small copse. His answer was to groan and roll to his side and begin to retch yet again. It seemed all he'd done through most of the night: tossing up everything he'd eaten until now it was just dry heaves.

"Well, the good news is that it probably is not Murie trying to kill you," Osgoode announced cheerfully. "She is sick as well."

"What?" Balan asked in alarm, then broke off in another fit of dry heaves.

"Aye. It seems that while she personally cooked your meal, it smelled so good, she ate half of it herself before bringing it to you. She would not have done so had she deliberately poisoned it. So, either this poisoning was an accident, or someone else poisoned the meat she left roasting over the fire while she went to the river with Emilie and Reginald."

Balan flopped onto his back with a groan. "That bit of meat she brought me *was* small."

"Aye," Osgoode said solemnly. "Had you eaten the whole piece yourself, and had Murie not eaten half, Emilie is sure you would now be dead."

"How is my wife?"

"A little worse than you," Osgoode answered. When Balan's eyes popped open, he pointed out, "She ate half the meat, therefore half the poison, and she is not as big as you. It has hit her a little harder. She is hallucinating as well as vomiting."

Balan forced himself to sit up and tried to crawl to his feet.

"Emilie is watching her," Osgoode said. "There is no need for you to—" He gave up and started to help his cousin, knowing how stubborn Balan could be.

The few feet back to camp made for a very long trip. The world seemed to have taken on an appalling tendency to wobble under Balan's legs, and his vision seemed slightly impaired so that the world seemed to move in and out of focus. He was grateful when they reached the tent and Reginald rushed from the fireside to hold the flap open. Osgood helped him stumble inside. His cousin then helped him to the pallet where Murie lay and released him to step aside. Balan immediately collapsed beside his wife.

"Oh, Balan—you look better," Emilie said from the other side of the pallet, where she knelt pressing a damp cloth to Murie's face. But even in the state he was in, Balan could hear the lie in her voice and see her concern.

"I am better," he assured her, and then added in dry tones, "I made it all the way from the tent flap to here without having to vomit."

"Oooh," she murmured, then scowled at both him

and his cousin. "Reginald told me what you and Osgoode thought. Murie is *not* trying to kill you."

Balan would have scowled at his big-mouthed cousin and friend if he could have, but it seemed too much
effort.

"She intended to confront you about being in her
room that night, and about it not being a dream, but
then she came upon you talking to my husband and
Osgoode about it in the hall. She heard the explanation you gave Reginald. She also heard his concern for
me and that you intended to ask early leave from the
king. Murie was afraid Edward would not permit it
should you ask, so she went to him herself." Emilie
paused to glare at Balan. "She would not put a thistle
under your saddle, and she certainly would not poison
your meat and then eat half of it herself."

Balan heard Osgoode say something, but forced
himself to concentrate on Emilie's face. He could hear
the indignation and anger in her voice, so wasn't surprised to see it reflected in her expression as she
glared at him.

"Aye," was all he managed to say. Then he passed
out beside his wife.

Murie opened her eyes and started to stretch, then
paused as she realized there was an arm thrown over
her waist. Moving carefully, she turned her head to
glance past her shoulder and saw her husband. She
peered at him with surprise. The question as to what
he was doing in the tent with her had barely risen to
mind when she realized they weren't in the tent at all.
Her gaze slid around the room in confusion; then she
eased out from beneath her husband's arm and got
shakily to her feet.

Her legs were not happy with her weight and seemed

to be threatening to give out beneath her, but Murie needed a privy and could not wait for them to make up their mind as to whether they would hold her up or not. One of her gowns lay crumpled in the rushes by the bed, obviously left there after being removed from her. She picked it up, gently shook it out and donned it, then made her way carefully to the door, holding on to the wall to keep her balance as she went.

"Murie! What are you doing up?"

Emilie's alarmed voice drew her head around as she slipped into the hall. She smiled at her friend, relieved to see her. She had no idea where they were.

"Where are we?" she asked as her friend reached her side.

"Reynard Castle," Emilie answered, taking her arm to steady her. "You should be back in bed. You have been very ill."

"I need the privy," Murie replied, resisting all efforts to turn her back to the room.

"Oh." Emilie hesitated and then sighed, slipping an arm around her waist. "Come, then. I will help you."

"Thank you," Murie said.

Her gaze slipped around what she could see of the castle. She'd never been allowed to visit Emilie away from Windsor Castle; Emilie had always had to come to see her. "Your home looks nice, Emilie," she said as they moved up the hall.

Her friend chuckled. "It is. But you have only seen your chamber and the hall. You shall see more before you leave," she promised.

"I do not remember arriving here," Murie admitted. "The last thing I recall is stopping for the night after riding in the wagon all day."

"Do you remember feeling sick?"

"Aye." Murie wrinkled her nose. "My stomach did not like riding in that wagon."

"It was not the wagon ride," Emilie said quietly. "You were poisoned."

"What?" Murie paused to glance at her with horror.

"It was not meant for you," Emilie explained quickly. "We think Balan was the target, but you ate half the meat you cooked for him."

"The meat was poisoned?" Murie asked with confusion. "But I spiced and cooked it myself."

"Aye, but you left it roasting and came down to the river to bathe, remember?"

"Oh, aye," Murie recalled, and remembered something else: "I told Balan that hearing the call of the curlew foretold death. If I had not eaten half that meat, it would have been so."

"Er . . ." Emilie bit her lip to hide a tolerant grin. "Well, anyway, they think it was poisoned while we were at the river. And they *do* think that your eating half probably saved Balan's life."

"I ate more than half," Murie admitted with a grimace. "I did not mean to, but it was so good, and I just kept picking at it."

"Aye, well, you saved his life by that action, but nearly lost your own. You were terribly sick."

"Oh," Murie sighed. "Well, I do not mind so much. 'Tis better to be ill than lose my husband."

Emilie smiled faintly. "Balan was most concerned. Sick as he was that night, he dragged himself to your side. Mind you, he fell unconscious directly afterward, but not until he had reached you."

"Oh!" Murie breathed.

"And then, the next morn, he took you up on his horse before him for the last part of the ride. Reginald and I said that we could wait until you had recovered to continue home, but he wanted to get you indoors and to Reynard where my maid, Marian, could tend you."

"Marian." Murie smiled at the name. The woman had cared for Emilie since she was a child and was very knowledgeable about medicinals and such, but she'd also been terribly kind to Murie whenever the two had met at court. Murie had been sorry when the woman announced that she was far too old to be making the journey anymore, and had ceased accompanying her mistress. That had been the year before Emilie married Reginald. The maid had eventually moved to Reynard, but that was the last move she'd made. She now stayed at Reynard all the time. "How is she?"

"Getting old," Emilie said on a sigh. "It scares me to see how paper thin her skin is getting and how fragile she grows. I fear I shall lose her soon."

"Nay," Murie said with certainty. "She is a strong woman. She will live to see all your children born— and perhaps even their children as well."

"I hope you are right," Emilie replied.

They reached the privy and fell silent, Emilie waiting outside while Murie attended her needs. She then helped Murie back up the hall, but as they neared the stairs, Murie said, "I am hungry."

"That is a good sign. After I help you back to bed, I shall find you something to eat."

"I do not want to go back to bed," Murie announced stubbornly. "I want to be up and visiting with you."

"Perhaps later," Emilie suggested.

"But I want to visit with you now."

"Then I shall sit with you," Emilie said patiently.

"Balan is sleeping in our room. We cannot visit there. Can we not go below? I could see more of your castle that way."

Emilie's lips began to twitch, making Murie narrow her eyes.

"What is it?" she asked.

"I had forgotten that when you were sick was the only time you truly lived up to your reputation," Emilie said with amusement. "You were always a poor patient."

Murie made a face but didn't deny it. She'd always found herself impatient with illness, not wanting to be held back by it. Perhaps because she knew others would see it as yet another weakness and a good opportunity to launch further verbal assaults.

"Very well." Emilie led her to the top of the stairs and paused there to call out, "Reginald! Pray, come help me bring Murie below."

Lord Reynard had been seated at the trestle table in the hall, but he was on his feet and up the stairs in a trice. "Should she be up?" he asked his wife with concern as he paused before them.

"Aye, she should," Murie snapped. He was ignoring her as if she were too ill to make up her mind for herself!

One eyebrow arching, amusement tugging at his lips, Reginald shrugged and scooped her into his arms to carry her downstairs. "Very well, but you shall be the one to explain to Balan when he gets up. He will not be pleased, I am sure. I know I would not be, were Emilie up and about so soon after being so ill."

Murie scoffed. "Then I suspect you will find yourself annoyed with her every time she is ailing, because Emilie is no better a patient than I, if I recall correctly."

Reginald chuckled, his chest vibrating against her side, and Murie smiled. She added, "Have I ever told you how grateful I am that you love my friend and are a good husband to her?"

"Have I ever told you how grateful I am that you did

not ask the king to have me drawn and quartered for marrying her and stealing her away?" he returned.

Murie scowled over his shoulder at his wife. "You told him about that?" she asked with embarrassment. She'd been most distressed to learn her friend was to be married to some lord from the north. Emilie's parents' castle had been close to Windsor, and her visits prior to that had been most frequent. Neither of them had been pleased that she would be married and moved so far away. Murie had toyed with the idea of asking the king to prevent it, but then Reginald had arrived at court, and the couple had fallen so obviously in love that Murie had not.

Shaking her head at Emilie's unrepentant grin, Murie turned to Reginald and said, "I would have, had you not been so perfect for each other."

"Then I should tell you that I am grateful you have always been a good friend to my wife, Murie Somerdale," he replied solemnly.

"That would be Lady Gaynor, Reynard! And just where the hell is it you are taking my wife?"

The three paused at the foot of the stairs, and Reginald turned back with Murie still in his arms to stare up at Balan.

Murie bit her lip. Her husband was wearing only a cotehardie and no leggings, and his hair was standing up every which way, and he really looked angry. It was enough to make her burst into speech.

"Good morning, husband. I got up on my own. I had to go to the privy. Fortunately, I happened upon Emilie in the hall, and she showed me where it was, but when she tried to get me to go back to bed, I explained that I am very hungry, so she asked Reginald to carry me down here, and now I am going to sit at table and eat because really I have been very ill, and I do need to build my strength back up, and I did not wish to disturb you while you were sleeping." She paused in her almost panicked explanation to take a breath, then asked, "Did you sleep well?"

A sudden burble of laughter from Emilie made them all glance her way. She held an open hand before her face and shook her head. "I am sorry. Ignore me. It is probably being with child making me hysterical."

"That, or the fact that my husband is standing up there in no leggings, flashing himself to all and sundry in the hall," Murie said. She glanced at Balan, trying not to stare up his cotehardie. "Really, husband . . . perhaps you should finish dressing."

Balan did not cover himself or look embarrassed. He merely scowled harder, then turned to stalk back to their room.

Reginald continued on to the table, carrying Murie, a giggling Emilie following. Murie said wryly, "Well . . . now *everyone* knows how well endowed my husband truly is. Is that not nice?"

"Already?" Murie stared at her husband in dismay. He'd been glowering and glaring since returning to the great hall fully clothed, but she'd not thought that he was annoyed enough to cut short their visit to Reynard and make her leave the day after they got there.

"We have to get to Gaynor and prepare for winter," he said.

"Aye, but you said we might stay a week—or a few days at least. I heard you tell Reginald that," she accused.

"Aye, and we have been here a week."

"What?" She gaped at him in disbelief, but recalled from what he'd said to Osgoode back at court that he wouldn't lie to her. Still . . . Her gaze shot to Emilie for confirmation.

The woman nodded solemnly. "You have been very ill, Murie. It hit you much harder than it did Balan. You were delirious for this whole week."

Murie slumped in her seat with dismay, not having realized how long she'd been under the weather. She did not even recall waking since arriving at Reynard, yet they said she'd awakened several times this last week. Incredible.

"I am sorry that you will not get to spend more time with Emilie while you are conscious," Balan added, "But we cannot spare the time. We will give you this day to recover and visit, but we will have to continue on in the morning. Reginald has offered us the wagon for the remainder of the journey so that you may rest."

"Rest? In that hellish contraption?" she asked. She shook her head. "Oh, nay. I shall ride a horse. I am *not* riding in the wagon."

"We are almost there."

Murie glowered at her husband from where she was bouncing about in the back of the wagon. He looked so bloody cheerful, while she was horribly miserable. She wanted to snatch his smile right off his face. It had been a long and horrible journey. The only good thing about it was that it had been just one horribly long day in length. They had set out at sunrise—just Osgoode and Balan; and Murie and Cecily in the wagon; and of course the wagon driver, who would be making the return journey with an escort of two soldiers on the morrow after resting at Gaynor for the night.

Balan and Osgoode had not bothered with men-at-arms for their journey to court. Her husband had explained that all the men he'd brought back from battle had been needed to help keep Gaynor running now that so many servants had fled or died; he hadn't wished to take them away when they were so badly needed at home. Besides, while he'd gone to court hoping to gain a bride, he'd not expected success to be so quick.

Without men to help guard their party, Balan had insisted on a grueling pace, not stopping to eat but eating in the saddle—or in the back of the wagon as was the case for Murie. However, food was not the only reason to stop. Murie had been suffering with a full bladder for much of the last two hours—not an easy thing when one was being jostled. Now she feared she might not make it to the castle without embarrassing herself.

As she was annoyed with her husband, Murie was reluctant to ask for anything, but she had no choice. Heaving a put-upon sigh, she called out and gestured him over to the side of the wagon. Peeling his mount away from Osgoode's, Balan immediately moved to her side, keeping pace with the wagon as he raised an eyebrow in question.

"I need to visit the woods," she announced.

"What?" he asked with disbelief.

"I need to visit the woods," Murie repeated through slightly gritted teeth.

"Why?" He frowned.

"To . . . I . . . To visit the woods," she said lamely, blushing bright red. She could not believe he could not grasp the concept. For heaven's sake, surely he must need to relieve himself by now, too!

"I believe she needs to tend to privy business," Osgoode said helpfully, having moved to ride beside Balan.

"Oh!" Balan's eyes widened with understanding, he asked in mild irritation, "Well, why did you not just say so?"

"I did," she muttered.

Her husband urged his horse up beside the driver to tell him to stop, and Murie was out of the wagon almost before it did. She immediately forced her stiff legs to carry her into the woods along side the path, not bothering to wait for accompaniment. She did not care if it annoyed her husband that she was traipsing off by herself; she had to go and had to do so now, and she was annoyed with him anyway for making her ride in the cart. He could be annoyed back if he liked.

She carried out her business quickly and with much relief, then returned to the horses and wagon much more slowly than she'd left, uneager to climb into the uncomfortable contraption again. Oddly enough, it seemed a much longer walk back than it had been out.

"Murie!" Balan yelled.

Frowning, she paused and glanced back the way she'd come, wondering how her husband had got behind her.

"Murie!" Osgoode's voice called from the same direction, and she turned and started that way, frowning with concern at the anxiety in their voices.

"Aye!" she shouted, moving a little more quickly. She hadn't retraced far when Balan and Osgoode stepped out of the woods, relief on their faces.

"Were you lost?" Balan asked, looking her over as he approached.

"Nay, of course not. I was just coming back."

"You walked out a terribly long way and took so long we were worried," Osgoode explained. Balan was urging her back the way they'd come.

Murie bit her lip and realized she'd been heading *away* from the lane where the wagon waited. How had she got herself turned around like that? she wondered. The question flew from her mind, however, when the call of a cuckoo sang out nearby. Murie immediately threw herself to the ground and began to roll.

"Wife!" Balan was at once kneeling at her side, forcing her roll to an end. "Are you all right?"

"Of course," she said, sitting up. "But you really should not have stopped me."

"What were you doing?" he asked with bewilderment.

Murie frowned. "Did you not hear the cuckoo? Nay, of course not, else you would have rolled on the ground, too."

There was a moment of silence, and then Osgoode cleared his throat and asked, "Why would Balan have rolled on the ground, too?"

"Because 'tis good luck to do so at the first sound of the cuckoo's call," she explained. "I would not normally do so, for fear I might ruin my gown, but with someone trying to kill my husband, it seems a good idea not to take any chances or miss any good luck we may gain. After all, I may be annoyed with him right now, but I am sure 'tis a temporary situation. I shall forgive him eventually. I would not wish him dead ere that happened."

"Ah," Osgoode murmured. His worried gaze found Balan, who stayed silent.

Murie frowned at her husband's unreadable expression, then shrugged, stood and continued the way they had been heading. Behind her she heard Balan mutter, "I have married a mad woman."

"Aye, but at least you know she is not trying to kill you," Osgoode replied with amusement.

Murie whirled on them. "You may laugh if you wish, but did you not sneeze to your left ere we began this journey, husband? And have we not had bad luck? And then, did you not step on St. John's wort and get carried away by a horse? And did we not hear a curlew before you were poisoned? Aye." She nodded grimly. "Laugh if you wish, but each event has been foretold by unlucky omens. You mark my words, you shall be grateful for my silly superstitions someday."

Turning on her heel, Murie flounced back to the wagon and crawled miserably into the back. The men remounted. She'd barely settled herself when her husband rode up and leaned over the side, hooked an arm around her waist and lifted her out onto his lap and the saddle.

"Thank you for troubling yourself to roll on the ground—even though it might ruin your gown—to gain some good luck for me," he whispered in her ear as she remained stiff in his arms.

Murie released a little sigh at his words and sank into the comfort of his arms. This really was much better than the wagon.

"You are welcome, husband," she murmured. "And thank you for removing me from that horrible wagon."

"I could hardly have you riding up to the castle scowling like thunder. You would scare off the few servants we have left," he said, then smiled at her as her glower returned. "Aye, just like that."

Murie went stiff in his arms and tried to turn to ignore him, but Balan leaned down and began to nuzzle her ear. He whispered, "Besides, it allows me to do this."

Murie gasped as his tongue slid out and whorled around her ear, the action having a surprising and immediate effect on other points of her body. Her stiffness was suddenly gone, and she pressed into him, her head turning to make his suckling easier.

Chuckling at her response, Balan caught her by the chin and turned her face until he could kiss her, his tongue thrusting into her mouth and claiming ownership.

A shout drew them apart, and Murie turned to look forward as they broke from the trees through which they'd been passing for the past hour. She got her first view of her new home. The fields still had much of their produce on the vine, rotting. The village ahead and some distance to the right looked oddly still. The castle on the hill was large—and surprisingly lovely.

"We lost many people to the plague," Balan explained quietly, his eyes sliding over the fields. "My warriors have been reduced to trying to reap the harvest, but of course there are not enough of them, and they are not as skilled or quick as the peasants would have been. Much of the crop has been left where it grew."

"The land will be very fertile next year then," Murie noted. "The soil will benefit from our loss."

She sensed the way his eyes shot to her, but she herself was busy looking at the man hurrying toward them up the lane. He was not a warrior, his body thin and undernourished. His hair was of a salt-and-pepper shade that suggested he was older than his spry behavior suggested, and his face was weathered with both age and exposure to the elements. He was one of the survivors of the village, she supposed.

He paused before them, and Balan reined in. It must have been he who had shouted a moment ago; there was no one else to be seen on this lonely lane.

"My lord, you are returned," the man said, smiling widely. "We heard news you were on the way and that you had yourself a beautiful bride." He turned an unabashed grin to Murie. "We are so very happy to have you at Gaynor, my lady."

"Thank you," she said, smiling in return.

"Murie," her husband said. "This is our stable master, Habbie."

Once she'd murmured a greeting, Balan asked the man, "What are you doing out here?"

"Oh, I was thinking to find a little something for the horses," Habbie said with a shrug. "But 'tis all pretty much beyond being useful."

Murie followed the old man's sad gaze over the fields, concern drawing her eyebrows together. "Is the situation so desperate, husband?" she asked.

"Aye," he replied with a sigh. "Hop on the wagon, Habbie. You may ride with us back to the keep."

Nodding, the man moved to the wagon. He spoke a greeting to Cecily in the back, then mounted the bench to sit beside the driver, and they were off again.

Murie examined everything much more closely now. The crop had obviously grown well; the only problem had been bringing it in, as her husband had said. That was important. This was healthy land, then, and likely to grow just as lush and strong a crop next year. Gaynor would recover.

The village was distressing to see. Even from the lane, Murie saw that it was inhabited by only ghosts. Neither person nor animal stirred as they rode past. Doors and window shutters on the small, thatched cottages stood free, slamming open and closed in the breeze. The small gardens around the buildings that had once boasted herbs and spices were now growing wild and filled with weeds.

Murie was relieved when they had passed by. Then she noted the huge mounds that lined the path on each side of them, and she didn't need Balan to tell her that this was where they had buried their dead. So many dying so quickly had forced them to dig mass

graves. Fear had been a part of that as well. The
plague had made its way through all of England, including Berkshire, where Windsor Castle stood. Fear
of the plague had been horrifying and had induced
people to do the most appalling things.

Balan's arms closed more securely around her waist,
drawing her from her thoughts. She forced a smile for
his benefit. Then they were passing over the drawbridge and riding into the castle's outer bailey.

Here there were obvious signs of the plague's effects
as well, but they were only due to neglect and lack of
manpower. The bailey at least had people in it, mostly
men. Obviously they were warriors: most wore tabards
and armor as they walked the walls or manned their
posts. Others as big and brawny as those in uniform
were wearing more serviceable clothes for labor,
rough tunics and faded leggings.

Murie eyed all the men curiously, but couldn't help
noting that every single man turned toward their small
procession with wide relieved grins and obvious welcome. Emilie had mentioned that Gaynor suffered under the plague, but the expressions on the faces of the
men told her more than anything how bad things were
and how much hope they were pinning on her. She decided then and there that she would not let them down.
She would do all in her power to make things better for
those here . . . and to keep their lord, her husband, safe.

Despite her annoyance with him, Murie had been
pondering the matter of how to keep her husband safe
as she rode in that horrible wagon. Someone had put a
thistle under his saddle in the hope that he would fall
from his mount and break his neck. When that had
not worked, they had resorted to poisoning him, and
only her inability to cook without picking at the food
had saved him. Well, all right, she'd more than picked.

Anyway, someone wanted her husband dead, and she intended to find out who and why, and to stop them. She'd already started making a list of the things she would need to do to keep him alive; now she just needed to sort out a plan for catching the culprit.

Chapter Eleven

"Here we are."

Murie glanced around as her husband slid from the saddle and reached up to lift her down. Smiling at him as he set her on her feet in front of the stairs to the keep, she glanced around as people began to draw near. Most of them were men, as she'd noted, but now the keep doors were open, female faces peered out with excitement. Women began to hurry down the stairs, followed by two small boys and two men, one tall and slim, and one short and round.

"Who are these?" she asked Balan as she waited for the group to reach the foot of the stairs.

"The cook and steward," her husband answered.

Murie nodded. Both men were wearing brown tunics made of very rough and heavy cloth, as were most of the people at Gaynor, but it didn't take a genius to guess which was cook and which steward. Obviously, the round little man with the welcoming smile worked in the kitchens, and the tall, skinny, scowling man was the steward.

She blinked in surprise when Balan began introductions, and it turned out she was wrong:

"Wife, this is Clement, our cook," he announced, gesturing to the tall, skinny man.

Murie's eyes widened in alarm. In her experience all cooks were short and round or tall and round or round and round. They were always round. They got that way from sampling their food, or so she'd always assumed; but this gentleman was tall and thin. So, either his food was terrible, or . . . She blinked as his name sank in. Clement? Didn't that mean kind, or something? There was nothing the least bit kind-looking about him.

Well, this wasn't very promising, she thought as she nodded politely, almost afraid to speak and give the man an excuse to be rude. He truly didn't appear a very friendly sort.

"And this is Thibault. He is the steward here."

Murie was almost as happy to turn her attention to the little man as he apparently was to receive it.

"Oh, my lady! You cannot know how happy we are to receive and welcome you into our small family. You bring hope to all of us. I pray you will be very happy here, indeed," he cried effusively, clasping her hand and pressing a kiss to the back of it.

"And this is Gatty," Balan continued, gesturing to the oldest of the women present. "She has been my sister's nursemaid since she was born."

"My lady," the woman murmured.

"And these are her daughters Estrelda and Livith. They are maids in the keep."

"My lady," the two dark-haired girls chorused, giving pretty little curtsies.

"And this is Gatty's son, Frederick." A boy nodded and smiled shyly, eyes large in an elfin face.

"And this . . ." Balan stepped forward to catch the last little boy by the collar who'd tried to shrink behind Gatty. He pulled him out front, finishing, "Is my little sister Juliana."

Murie stared wide-eyed at the child. Her hair had been hacked off quite viciously, and it hung in short, uneven clumps around her head. Her face was filthy, as was the rest of her, including her clothes, which were the same rough cloth everyone else here seemed to be wearing. There was nothing that could have told Murie she was a girl, though Murie still felt horrible for making the assumption.

Taking a breath, she managed a smile and held out her hand. "How do you do, Juliana?"

The girl reacted like a trapped animal. With her brother and the others behind her, hemming her in, and Murie in front of her, her eyes darted left then right before settling on Murie with a sort of panic. She blurted, "Yer stupid and ugly, and I do not care if you like me. I hate you!" The girl then stomped on Murie's foot and turned to run across the bailey as fast as her little legs would carry her.

"Juliana!" Balan roared furiously, even as he stepped forward to sweep Murie into his arms. Casting a scowl after the retreating child, he hurried up the stairs with Murie, his gaze concerned as he glanced at her. "Are you all right? Did she break anything?"

"Nay, of course not," Murie assured him, holding on for dear life as she was jostled in his arms by his jog up the stairs. "You need not carry me, husband. She merely stomped my toe."

"Aye," he muttered. "And I shall tan her bottom for it when she finds the courage to return."

"Nay," Murie said sharply, and kicked her feet now that he was carrying her into the keep. "Put me down, please."

"Not until we reach the table. I wish to examine your foot."

Murie drew a breath for patience. Her foot was fine; a bit sore, but fine. The girl hadn't stomped as hard as she might have, and Murie hated being fussed over.

At the speed Balan was moving, they reached the trestle table in moments, and he set her down in the head chair, then knelt to lift her skirt and remove her shoe.

"Husband, please. I am fine," she insisted, then sat back abruptly as she realized they were not alone. Osgoode, Cecily, Habbie, the servants and soldiers and even the wagon driver from Reynard were now crowded around them, most hunched forward, eyeing her toe with concern. The only one missing from within the walls was the young girl who had caused all this fuss. She was off alone somewhere in the bailey, no doubt weeping from fear of her brother's retribution.

Putting aside the child for the moment, Murie felt a blush rise up her cheeks at so many eyes on her ankle and foot, and leaned down to hiss in a whisper, "You are showing my naked ankle and foot to everyone."

"What?" Balan asked absently.

"She says yer showing her naked ankle and foot to all," Habbie announced helpfully.

Balan glanced about with surprise, then promptly dropped her skirt and stood, forcing everyone to straighten away from them. He scowled at the gathering, then reached out to pat Murie's shoulder. "I do not think 'tis broken."

"I did tell you that, my lord husband," Murie replied with a scowl.

"Aye, she did," Thibault agreed, eager to be of assistance. "Outside, in front of the steps."

"Aye, well . . ." Balan frowned slightly and glanced around. "I shall leave you in Gatty's capable hands. She shall give you a tour of Gaynor and explain how things work. I must get a reporting of what has occurred in my absence and see that all is well."

"Of course, husband," Murie said, managing a smile.

"If Juliana returns while I am gone, you just send her out to me, and I shall tend to her," he said as he started to turn away.

Murie's mouth tightened. "Husband?"

"Aye?" he turned back.

Terribly aware of the people surrounding them and of her desire to make a good impression, Murie forced a smile and said, "Do you not think I should be the one to deal with Juliana?"

"Nay."

Her smile twisted into a scowl, but she forced it back into a smile. "I am sure you would agree that it would be better if I deal with her."

"Nay," he repeated.

"Husband," she tried again. "I am the injured party here, and I am now her sister and guardian. I should be the one to deal with the child."

"Nay."

"It is like talking to a boulder," she muttered to herself. "Honestly, Emilie could have warned me he was as stubborn as a stone wall."

"Wife, I can hear you," he said dryly.

"So can we," Gatty spoke up, amusement sparking to life in her eyes.

Murie scowled at them all and suddenly announced, "I am quite overwrought. I think I shall cry."

Osgoode's eyes widened in horror, remembering. He beseeched his cousin, "Balan, please, let Murie handle the girl."

"Aye," Thibault agreed. "We do not want the lass unhappy here."

"I am sure she will not hurt Juliana," Habbie added.

Balan ignored them all, his gaze locked on Murie as he returned to stand before her. He froze, staring silently at her for the longest time, then asked, "How will you handle it?"

"I will not hurt her," Murie assured him with annoyance. "I shall simply talk to the child. Obviously she is very unhappy. She has been orphaned, like I myself was, and was terrified I would not like her or some similar thing. She responded out of fear. I will just reassure her and . . . talk to her," she ended helplessly.

Balan was silent for another moment, then bent to kiss her lightly on the lips. At least, it started lightly, but when Murie instinctively let her mouth open he couldn't seem to resist deepening it, if only briefly. As he ended the kiss, he whispered, "You are too soft."

Murie scowled at the claim as he straightened.

"I shall allow you to handle her this time," he announced, ignoring her expression. "But you may tell her from me that if she does something like that again, I shall deal with her immediately—and much more firmly than you."

Murie smiled widely. "Thank you, husband."

Nodding, he started to turn away, then turned back to add, "And Murie?"

"Aye?"

"You are very bad at pretending to sob. Even the king said so."

Apparently satisfied by the stunned look on her face, he turned and marched to the keep doors.

"I think I shall join Balan." Osgoode excused himself with a smile, then turned to follow his cousin.

Balan reached the keep's main doors, paused and turned back with a scowl. "Anselm, I am wanting an accounting," he said.

"Oh, aye, my lord." A soldier broke away from several others and hurried after Balan, who had turned and marched out of the keep. At the door, he also paused and scowled. "Are the walls to be left unmanned?" he said.

Murmuring amongst themselves, most of the soldiers who'd swarmed inside with them stepped reluctantly away and began to make their way after Anselm.

Murie glanced around almost expectantly, but no one else made a move to leave. It seemed that none of the others felt any great need to get back to whatever they had been doing. Instead, they stood there smiling as if she were a performing jester about to tell a joke or juggle something.

"Yer the king's goddaughter," Frederick said suddenly into the silence, only to be cuffed by his mother.

"Yer not to speak 'til yer spoken to," Gatty reminded

"Nay, 'tis all right," Murie said quickly, and she offered a smile to the boy before saying, "Aye, I am. How did you know that?"

"Lord Aldous and his party stopped here on their way home and told us," the boy said, his chest puffing up with importance. "He said Lord Balan had married the spoiled, sobbing goddaughter of the king known as *the Brat* and should have been home with her by now. He was wondering if something had happened to slow down your party."

Murie managed not to react to Malculinus's unpleasant description and once again thought she was most fortunate she had not married the man.

" 'Tis sorry I am, my lady," Gatty murmured, catching her son by the ear and dragging him backward. "He should not have repeated what Lord Aldous said."

"Nay, 'tis all right," Murie said, and sank thoughtfully back into her chair. So, Aldous wondered if something had happened to slow down their party? As far as she'd known, Lauda and Malculinus were still at court. Glancing at the people surrounding her, she asked, "When were they here?"

"Nearly a week ago," Clement answered.

"They must have left on our heels. They would have had to, to reach here a week ago. We were at Reynard a week."

"So, you simply stopped to visit Reynard? There was nothing that happened to slow you down?" Gatty sounded relieved and explained, "We were all growing quite worried as the days drew on."

"As it happens," Cecily said, drawing everyone's attention from her mistress. "Lord Gaynor was nearly killed twice on the journey from court, and my lady once. In fact, if not for my lady, Lord Gaynor would most like be dead. Someone poisoned his meat, you see, but she ate half of it and thereby saved his life. She nearly died herself. She was unconscious and delirious the entire week we were at Reynard."

Murie flushed as everyone peered at her wide-eyed. Really, Cecily could have kept the exact method of how she'd saved Balan's life to herself and allowed the staff to draw their own conclusions. There wasn't much less flattering than the truth.

Realizing that a curious silence had fallen over those around her, Murie glanced about to see everyone staring at Cecily.

"Oh dear!" She stood and moved to her maid's side, her expression apologetic. "I am sorry, Cecily. You should have been introduced as well. Everyone, this is my maid, Cecily. She accompanied me to court as a child and has been with me these past ten years."

There were murmurs of greeting all around, and Thibault stepped forward, wringing his hands nervously. "Is it true, my lady? Did someone try to kill you and his lordship?"

Murie hesitated. Balan had not seen fit to inform his people of what had happened on the journey out, and she did pause to wonder if she herself should, or leave it in his hands. It did seem that the cat was rather out of the bag already, thanks to Cecily's comments. And besides, it was probably prudent to keep the people informed as to what was going on so that they might keep an eye out for trouble and help keep Balan safe until Murie could find the culprit.

Decision made, she settled back in her chair and considered the faces around her. These were the servants loyal to her husband, those who had remained behind while others left in search of greener pastures. Or more money, as the case may be. They deserved to be aware of what was going on.

"Aye, someone tried to kill my husband twice between court and Castle Reynard," she announced, then waited for the sudden murmuring of those around her to quiet. "Someone put a thistle on his horse's back, under his saddle, so that when he mounted and put weight on it the stallion reared and ran off with him. Fortunately, Lord Reynard gave chase and managed to catch up to the panicked animal, and my husband was able to leap from his mount to Reynard's."

"Oh, my lady, his lordship could have been killed!" Thibault said with distress.

"I do believe that was the whole point," Clement pointed out.

"And the second time was by poisoning?" Gatty asked.

"Aye." Murie grimaced. "I chose to make my husband's sup when we camped the second night. I skinned and dressed one of the rabbits the men brought back and roasted it over the fire."

"How did someone poison it if you are the one who prepared it?" Clement asked with arched eyebrows.

Murie glanced at him sharply, her eyes narrow. "I left it briefly while Reynard took Emilie and myself down to the river to clean up. When I returned, it was nearly finished, and it smelled so good I began to pick at the meat. We both fell ill not long after eating."

"Did no one see the culprit near the meat while you were gone?" one of the remaining soldiers asked.

"Emilie—Lady Reynard," she explained for those who did not know her friend, "told me that her husband did ask that night, but no one seemed to see anything."

The man nodded thoughtfully and asked, "And no one saw anyone near Lord Gaynor's horse on the morning it bolted?"

"Nay," Murie said; but she wondered if Balan had thought to ask. She hadn't thought of it herself until the soldier mentioned it just now, and she didn't recall her husband speaking to anyone. They had returned to camp, he'd tied his stallion to the back of the wagon and then mounted her mare and they had left. Of course, that did not mean that he hadn't asked later, but she did wonder if—in his rush to get them to Reynard—he'd not overlooked the necessary inquisition.

"You do not look sure," the man-at-arms pointed out.

Murie shrugged and said apologetically, "I never

thought to ask my husband. And I am not sure that he thought to ask around."

"He would have asked," the soldier assured her. "If he has not said anything, or confronted anyone, then no one was seen."

Murie nodded and glanced around at the people surrounding her. "Obviously, we must keep an eye out for him."

Everyone nodded.

"I was thinking about how to keep him safe on the ride from Reynard," she confessed. "And I do have some ideas."

"We will help," Gatty said solemnly. The others nodded.

"What ideas did you have?" Thibault asked eagerly. "Is there anything we can do tonight?"

"Naught but keep an eye on him," Murie said with a sigh, her gaze moving toward the keep doors. It had been late in the day when they arrived, the sun finally setting. It had still been light out as they rode up, but the gray light of coming dusk. Though, she acknowledged that could last a long time at this time of year, when the days were still longer than the nights. "But I shall need to find some things on the morrow and may need direction as to where to find them."

"Certainly, anything you need," Thibault said.

Murie nodded. "We shall discuss it in the morn. In the meantime, it has been a long journey, and I daresay my husband and Osgoode would enjoy a meal of some sort when they return from speaking to . . . Anselm, was it?"

"Aye," Gatty said.

"A meal is it?" Clement muttered bitterly. He nodded. "Certainly. I can make fish stew, fishcakes, or fish roasted over the fire."

Murie bit her lip at this news. "I gather there is little but fish available?"

"There is *nothing* but fish available," Clement announced.

"Nothing?" Murie said with dismay.

"Nothing," the cook repeated. "It is fish to break our fast, at the nooning and at sup."

She shook her head with disbelief. "There must be something else, surely? A chicken that lays eggs? A bit of beef? Pork, even?"

"Nothing," he repeated.

"But . . . I mean I knew that Gaynor was short on people to bring in the harvest and so the ground went fallow, but surely the plague did not strike the animals as well?"

"Saying the fields went fallow suggests that the harvest was plowed under and left to fertilize them," Clement pointed out shortly. "With so few of us here, we could not even manage that. The crops have been left to rot where they grow."

"My lady," Gatty said quietly, casting a sharp gaze at the cook. "Allow me to explain."

Murie nodded, and Gatty continued: "Half our people were taken by the plague. A good portion of the remaining half fled for fear of contagion. This left very few to try to keep body and soul together. With no one to watch over them, many of the animals wandered off or simply died of starvation. And then we began to hear tales of lords willing to pay large sums of money or rewards such as fine cottages and extra food for workers to tend their fields. Most of those remaining promptly picked up and left.

"Unfortunately, many of those also chose to take what livestock was left behind . . . in lieu of payment, they claimed," she added bitterly. "Those of us stand-

ing before you now are all who stayed behind and remained loyal to our lord, and we were left with little
more than what we could harvest from the fields or
the orchard . . . and the new large pond. Fish."

Murie sank back against her seat, her eyes slipping
over the people around her. They all wore rough
woolen clothes made from a cheap brown fabric. Each
had a hollow look about the eyes—including the round-
ish Thibault—that suggested they had lost weight of
late. And they had the slump-shouldered bearing of
the defeated. Their morale was obviously low; but
then, Murie supposed, if all they'd had to eat for the
last year was fish—morning, noon and night—she
could not blame them.

Truly, while Murie had known things went badly at
Gaynor, it was heartbreaking to realize just how bad.
But then, it had been bad everywhere. The plague had
struck London violently, taking almost half of the population. Everywhere had been chaos. Many of the no-
bility had fled to the country, hoping to find safety
there, but the majority of Londoners had not had the
option A good number had become nothing better
than animals and, seeming to think it was the end of
days, they had consumed all the drink and food they
could, moving from empty dwelling to empty dwelling, whether homes of the already deceased or of own-
ers who'd fled to the country. They'd taken what they
wanted with no one to stop them. Meanwhile, others
had simply shut themselves in their homes and tried to
avoid and ignore anything that went on outdoors in
an effort to stay safe. The terror had been so bad that
brother abandoned brother, son abandoned parent,
and even mothers abandoned their children at the
first sign of a cough or a redness, all for fear it was the
plague.

Of course, Murie had only heard of this second-hand. She, like everyone else connected to the king, had been locked up in Windsor Castle where the revelry was nonstop and seemed almost manic. One would almost have thought that no one at court had any idea of what was going on outside . . . if it were not for the fact that it was on everyone's lips. And the king's favorite daughter, Joan, had been taken by the plague. She'd died in Bayonne at the age of fourteen. She'd been on her way to marry Peter I of Castile.

"Very well," Murie said finally. "Fish roasted over the fire sounds delightful, and I thank you for troubling to make it. I shall speak to my husband about purchasing some livestock when he returns from getting his accounts from Anselm."

Nodding stiffly, Clement turned and made his way to a door that she presumed led to the kitchens.

They were all silent, and then Gatty stepped forward, her shoulders squared. "Well, his lordship said I should give you a tour. Where would you like to start, my lady?"

Murie waved a hand vaguely. "Wherever you deem it best to start, Gatty. You know this castle better than I."

Nodding, the servant turned and gestured the others out of the way. As they moved to the sides, she announced, "The great hall."

Murie stood, smiling faintly, and moved toward the small grouping of chairs around the fire across the room. The chairs were well-made, no doubt having been commissioned during better times. A chessboard populated with finely carved game pieces was obviously also from earlier days. Murie took it all in, then turned to survey the rest of the hall. It was large, with tapestries hanging from the walls. From a distance they appeared dull and colorless, but on approaching them, Murie saw that this wasn't the case at all; they were simply coated with dust and soot. Obviously, with so few people left to manage the castle, a chore such as beating and cleaning the tapestries would go long neglected.

"We have done the best that we cou—" Gatty began with a hint of defensiveness, but Murie cut her off.

"It shall be beautiful again once we have the man-power necessary to set things to rights," she said quietly.

Gatty peered at her for a moment and then allowed her shoulders to relax. "Would you care to see the kitchens?"

Murie nodded and followed.

The kitchens were large, made to feed hundreds, as one would expect in a castle this size, but only a small corner showed any recent use. Murie supposed it didn't take much room to make fish stew for so few people, and it appeared Clement was the only person generally here of late. However, she had no trouble imagining it as the hot, bustling beehive of activity it must once have been. She was determined to see it returned to that state.

"My daughters often help Clement in the kitchen as well as with serving the food," Gatty announced quietly. "However, before the plague they were housemaids."

"And they shall be again," Murie assured her. She turned to leave the kitchens.

"Did you not wish to see the pantry?" Gatty asked, following her.

"There is time enough for that tomorrow," Murie said, not wishing to see the empty shelves. She was depressed enough by all these people had endured, and simply wished to get the tour over and done.

They moved above stairs, and Murie was silent as Gatty showed her room after room. Juliana's bedchamber was small and mean, with little in the way of comfort. There was a bed, a chest and filthy rushes on the floor. There was not a single tapestry covering the windows to help keep the breeze from creeping through the rickety shutters. Murie could only imagine how cold that must be in the winter.

"How . . . Why?" Murie asked, turning to Gatty.

The woman's mouth tightened, but this was the only sign of her anger. She said, "Lady Gaynor died giving birth to Juliana. Lord Gaynor had loved his wife dearly and blamed the child for her death. He never forgave her. He brought Juliana to me moments after her mother died, handed her into my care and—as far as I can tell—never gave her another thought. I did the best I could, but with her father treating her so coldly and uncaring of her comfort or happiness . . ." She shrugged wearily.

"And what of Balan?" Murie asked.

Gatty's expression softened. "He loves the child dearly, but he has been away battling for most of her life. He tried to reason with his father when she was first born, but there was no arguing with the old man's grief. His lordship has tried to make things better since his return, but Juliana has been so long without—"

"She no longer thinks she deserves it and cannot accept it," Murie finished on a sigh. It seemed she had more than a newly orphaned child to deal with. In truth, Juliana had been orphaned at birth, losing both parents with her mother's death. Unfortunately, her father had stayed around to torment her with his lack of love.

"Aye." Gatty hesitated and then said, "I hope you will not be too hard on the child for what she did to you in the bailey. She is—"

"You need not fear," Murie interrupted. "I was orphaned at ten and raised at court. It is not the best place for a child to feel loved and nurtured. I think Juliana and I have a lot in common."

Gatty relaxed and even smiled faintly. "Thank you."

"There is no need to thank me," Murie assured her, hesitated and then announced, "I would appreciate it if you would disregard whatever gossip you have heard about me, whether from Lord and Lady Aldous or elsewhere, and judge me on my own merit."

"I never judge on gossip, my lady. Besides," she added with a grin, "we had all already decided you could not be the brat you are reputed to be, else his lordship would never have married you."

Murie raised her eyebrows slightly. "Not even to save you from the winter ahead?"

"Not even then," Gatty assured her. "He would have continued to hunt game and done what he had to, to keep us all alive, and waited until he found someone he felt he could deal well with. Balan is smart enough to know that a lord's marriage affects the castle and its inhabitants as much as the couple themselves. A battling couple can bring about divisions in the people beneath them as each takes sides."

Murie's was taken aback by this bit of wisdom, but she asked, "Then there is sometimes food other than fish?"

"Aye, but not often. There's too much to do around here to take the time for hunting more than once every couple of weeks. And there hasn't been anything but fish since his lordship and his cousin left for court. That left us with even fewer men to work, and no one could take the time to hunt."

"I see." Murie glanced around Juliana's room one more time, then headed for the door. She would begin to make this room more hospitable first thing on the morrow, right after she tended the great hall.

"The master's bedchamber is the only room left above stairs," Gatty commented as she pulled the door closed behind them.

Nodding, Murie followed along the hall to the last room and managed not to gasp in horror when the woman pushed the door open for her to enter.

"This . . . This is . . ." Murie shook her head, unable to give words to how horrible the room was. The rushes here—as in the rest of the castle—had not been changed for quite a while, perhaps not since before the plague. They were a stinking, soggy mess. And whereas the rest of the castle had shown the neglect of the last year or better, this room had obviously been neglected much longer. Cobwebs strung the ceiling overhead; a huge, heavy, framed bed was the only furnishing; and its curtains hung in tatters around it, no protection at all from the draft allowed in by the open and broken window shutters. A fireplace sat cold and empty.

"The old lord insisted on keeping the room exactly as it was when Lady Gaynor died ten years ago," Gatty explained quietly. "He would not allow us in to clean."

"But . . ." Murie shook her head.

"We only managed to change the rushes when he was away from the keep, and then we all pretended, including he, that it had not been done."

"Aye, but why has Balan not—"

"Lord Balan has been sleeping in the garrison with the soldiers since returning from France."

"Oh," Murie said weakly. It seemed obvious she could not join her husband in the garrison, but they could not possibly sleep here. Yet, it was late in the day to make other arrangements.

Obviously moved to pity by her hopeless expression, Gatty suggested, "Mayhap with some fresh linens and furs it shall not be so bad for one night, and then on the morrow we can perhaps do something with the room to make it more comfortable."

"Aye," Murie said weakly.

"I am sorry," Gatty said with a sigh. " 'Tis a poor homecoming to be sure, but with so few of us left, we are kept running from morning till night and simply did not have the time to—"

"Nay, of course not," Murie interrupted, straightening her shoulders. " 'Tis fine. If you would send Cecily up and have someone bring along my chests, she and I can set to work preparing it for the night."

"I could help," Gatty offered.

Murie shook her head. "I have taken enough of your time. You go about whatever you would normally be doing. We shall tend this."

Nodding, the woman turned and left the room, and Murie spun in a slow circle, her eyes roving over everything as she tried to decide where to start.

The bedcurtains were the biggest eyesore; not just dirty, but ragged. In the end it was those she decided to tackle first. Hitching up her skirt, she marched across the room to the side of the bed, grabbed two handfuls and gave a firm tug. The next moment she was bent over, coughing up the dust and debris that had billowed around her in a gray brown cloud from the musty old cloth.

Finally able to catch her breath, she waved her hand in front of her face to displace the remaining dust cloud and peered up at what she'd achieved. Her shoulders slumped as she saw that the cloth was so fragile that it had torn away where she'd grasped it and no higher.

Murie glared at the results, then squared her shoulders and clambered onto the top corner of the bed.

Clinging to the post there, she reached up to grab the cloth as near to the frame as possible, having to stretch up on to her tiptoes to manage the task.

"Oh! My lady! What are you doing? Get down! You shall hurt yourself!"

Murie glanced down with surprise to find Cecily had arrived. Her maid was looking absolutely frantic as she rushed across the room to her side.

"I am just going to pull down these curtains. I thought if we remove them and remake the bed with fresh linens, it would do for the night." She reached up again, tugging at the cloth, adding, "I wish we could change the rushes as well, but that is not possible at this hour. Those shall have to wait until the morrow."

"My lady, this is . . ."

Murie glanced down again to see the maid staring around the room in horror. Sighing, she turned back to give the cloth another tug.

"It is rather awful, but—Aiyeee!" Murie squealed as the cloth suddenly tugged free and she lost her balance, falling back on the bed. A cloud of dust immediately rose up to envelope her, and then Murie gasped in alarm as the bed itself suddenly collapsed beneath her, crashing to the floor.

Chapter Twelve

"My lady!" Cecily hurried forward and began to crawl across the remains of the collapsed bed toward her. "Are you all right? Were you hurt?"

"Nay, I am fine." Murie sat up to peer around and forced a smile for the woman, but was unable to maintain it and finally let her breath unhappily out. The room looked no better from this angle than it had standing.

"There most-like were no fresh linens to replace these anyway," Cecily said as she peered at the ruined bed, wrinkling her nose. "It seems little enough is done around here, I doubt laundry is at the top of their list of concerns."

Murie frowned, not having thought of it herself, and then her gaze swiveled to the door Cecily had left open. Men began to cart in her chests.

"Oh." The first man paused sharply as he spotted the pair on the ruined bed, forcing the others to an abrupt

halt as well. The four men simply stood there staring
for a moment, and then one said, "We can fix it."

"Do not bother," Cecily began. "We have no—"

"Aye, do," Murie countered, scrambling quickly up.
Cecily followed.

"But, my lady—"

"There may be linens in one of my chests," Murie interrupted hopefully.

"What?" Cecily said. "I hardly think—"

"Everyone at court knew Gaynor was in a bad way,"
Murie pointed out. She rushed over to the first chest
the men were now setting down and threw the lid open
to begin rifling through the contents. "The queen may
have had the forethought to send some of my own
linens with me in case they were needed. Queen Phillippa is very good with such details."

"But . . ." Cecily's words died on her lips as Murie
gave a sudden squeal of glee and pulled out a set of
pure white linens.

"Oh, what a wonderful woman!" Murie exclaimed
happily. "I shall have to write and thank her for such
forethought."

Shoulders slumping, Cecily simply shook her head
and got out of the way. The men had moved over to
take a look at the bed. "You cannot sleep in this chamber. Is there nowhere else—"

"Certainly," Murie said dryly. "My husband and I
could sleep together in the men's garrison this night."

The comment made all four men pause and turn to
gape at her.

"Well," the one who had suggested he'd fix the bed
said finally. "You would be most welcome there, my
lady."

Murie turned to Cecily, arching one eyebrow.

"I shall fetch a broom to sweep out these rushes. We

may not be able to replace them until the morrow, but at least the chamber will smell less," Cecily said with defeat. She hurried from the room.

Murie set the linens back in the chest, where they were safe from getting dirty, and stood to inspect the room. Her gaze landed on the bed as the men began to raise the frame, and she hurried forward. "Wait! I should like to remove the curtains before you put the frame back up."

"We'll do it for you, my lady," one of the men said, and proceeded to rip off the curtains nearest him. The other men immediately began removing the rest of the tattered cloth, dropping it in piles on the floor. They managed the task much more quickly than she would have, Murie noted and was grateful for it. There were enough other things for her to do.

Leaving them to their work, she bustled out of the chamber and to the stairs, encountering Cecily on her way back up, broom in hand.

"Do you know what they did with the furs and pillows from the wagon?" Murie asked. Emilie had kindly left the items in the wagon for her journey from Reynard to Gaynor, claiming she'd no need of the items at the moment and was happy to loan them to her for the trip home. While they would have to be sent back with the wagon driver the next day, she and Balan could at least use them this night.

"I believe they are still in the wagon," Cecily said.

Nodding, Murie moved past the girl. "I shall go find them. You start sweeping up the rushes."

The great hall was empty as Murie moved through it; no doubt the servants and soldiers had all returned to those vital tasks their lord's arrival had interrupted. Murie didn't encounter anyone until she was halfway across the bailey, when two of the men came rushing up.

"Are you looking for your husband, my lady?" one of the men asked. He added, "I am Erol, my lady."

"Good eve, Erol." Murie flashed him a smile, then said, "Nay. I am not looking for my husband."

"What are you looking for then, my lady?" the other man asked. "Mayhap we can help you. Oh, and I am Godart."

"Good eve, Godart. I am looking for the wagon my chests were on. I presume I will find it by the stables?"

"Aye," both men said.

"Was there something you needed from the wagon? Mayhap we could fetch it for you," Erol suggested.

"Oh, nay," Murie replied. "I would not trouble you or take you away from your work. I can manage."

" 'Tis no trouble," Godart assured her.

"Nay, no trouble at all," Erol agreed.

Murie simply smiled and shook her head. It was obvious the men were eager to please, but she suspected this had more to do with the fact that they had few women around than anything else. As far as she knew, Gatty's two daughters were the only single females. She supposed they must be very popular with the men.

They had reached the stables, and Murie bustled inside, eager to find the items she sought. Instead, she found Balan's sister seated on a stall post next to Gatty's son, Frederick, watching Habbie brush down Balan's stallion. The girl was busy chattering away to the stable master, so she did not notice Murie and the men enter. By the time Juliana realized Murie's presence and slipped off the post to make a run for it, Murie was close enough to catch her by the arm and draw her to a halt.

"My lady!" Habbie said with surprise. His gaze slid from her to the squirming child she held and back before he said uncertainly, "Can I help you?"

"Aye." Murie smiled pleasantly and ignored Juliana's struggles. Her hold on the girl was firm. "There were some furs and pillows in the wagon that rode in with us. I intended to fetch them myself, but mayhap you can show these gentlemen where they are to bring them to the lord's bedchamber for me, as I think my new sister and I have some things to discuss."

"Oh . . . er . . . aye. Of course, my lady," Habbie murmured, his concerned gaze returning to the child.

"Very good," Murie said with a smile. She turned to leave the stables, pulling Juliana with her.

"I ain't going with you," the girl snarled, trying to kick her. Unfortunately, it was difficult to kick when she was racing to stay on her feet with Murie dragging her out of the stables.

"Of course you are," Murie said. "Surely you wish to get to know your new sister?"

"Yer not my sister," the girl snapped.

"I am married to your brother, Juliana. That makes me your sister."

"My lady, we have the things you asked for," Godart said, gasping as he hurried to her side.

Murie glanced around to see all three men now trailing her and all three out of breath. It seemed obvious that they had rushed to gather the things she'd asked for and hurried after her, concerned for the child. She supposed she could not blame them; they did not know her and so could not be sure she would not beat the child or perform some other equally fearsome punishment as retribution for the earlier kick. They would learn in time.

"Thank you," she said, not slowing her step. She had no desire to be kicked again.

"Would you like one of us to take Juliana to your husband for you?" Erol panted.

"Certainly not. You were there, surely you heard my husband say that I may handle the matter myself?"

"Aye," Habbie agreed. "But—"

"But nothing, sir," Murie said firmly and gave him a reassuring smile. She could handle this. She wasn't sure how, but she would handle it.

They had reached the keep by then, and Murie mounted the stairs as quickly as she'd crossed the bailey: not so fast that the girl could not keep up, but quickly enough that her attention was distracted by the effort. The men followed across the great hall and above stairs and finally into the bedchamber. They arrived just as the four men who had been fixing Murie's bed trooped out with the ragged remains of the curtains.

Murmuring her thanks for their help, Murie slipped past and into the room, drawing Juliana with her.

Murie did not pause inside, but now walked around dragging Juliana with her. She was afraid that, should she stop, the child would strike out at her again; and if her husband heard about it, he would surely take over the matter himself. It was not that Murie feared Balan would beat his sister, though she suspected he might take her over his knee. But she didn't wish to see the child punished at all. Murie found herself feeling great empathy for the girl, and all she really wanted to do was hug her and assure her she was loved and cared for and everything would be all right. But she first needed to get past the hard, defensive outer layer the child wore like armor.

She pondered the matter as she glanced over the repaired bed. It looked much better without the tattered cloth hanging around it and with the nasty old linens removed. It looked as if the men had beaten the dust out, too. Relieved, Murie turned her attention to how much progress Cecily had made with the rushes. The woman had cleared away one corner of the smelly floor covering and was still working industriously.

Noting the weariness Juliana was beginning to display, Murie slowed her steps and turned to the men. "Very well, gentlemen, thank you so much for helping me gather these things. If you would be kind enough to set them on the chests over there, Juliana and I can start making the bed."

The girl's steps had begun to falter, but this comment seemed to perk her up. She snarled, "I'll not."

"You will," Murie assured her calmly, circling the room once more.

"You cannot make me." The girl tried to tug free once more, but Murie had a firm hold on her arm.

"Godart?" Murie said as she started around the room for the third time. "Am I right in assuming that you are one of Balan's soldiers?"

"Aye," the man answered. Then he added, "We take turns manning the walls and guarding the castle, or doing the labor that needs doing around here. This week is my week for labor."

"I fear today is your day to be a guard," Murie countered. "Please stand by the door and ensure Juliana does not leave. She will not exit this room until I say so, and I will not say so until she has done what I have asked of her."

The man nodded, and Murie released Juliana. The child hesitated the briefest moment, probably torn between kicking her again and fleeing. In the end, she chose fleeing and made a rush for the door, but Godart was immediately in front of it, between her and freedom. Juliana didn't slow; she charged him in a bull-like fashion, crashing into his legs and proceeding to kick and strike out at him with her small fists.

Murie winced and sent him an apologetic glance, but the man just smiled and shook his head. He wore boots and leather leggings, and apparently this was enough to protect him, for he truly did not seem to be suffering any pain. He simply stood there, immovable, allowing the girl to wear herself out. Having just jogged across the bailey up the stairs and around the room several times, it did not take the child long to give up. Apparently, seeing how ineffective her attack was, she then tried to squeeze her way around him to reach the door handle. Godart let her, but was leaning against the door so it did her little good. After tugging uselessly for several minutes, she turned to glare around the room.

"Your brother said that I may handle the matter of your kicking me in greeting," Murie said, drawing the girl's gaze. "I would prefer to be friends with you and even proper sisters. However, if he does not feel I handled it effectively, he shall surely punish you himself and no doubt much more harshly than I would, and then you would no doubt blame me and never be willing to be friends with me.

"I am sure he will think helping Cecily and I clean this room is punishment enough," she added quietly. "And that way, perhaps we could talk, and you could get to know me better and decide if you might wish to be friends."

The girl hesitated, scowling. "I do not want to be friends. And once you get to know me, you will not wish to be friends either."

"Oh, that is where you are wrong," Murie assured her, moving to collect the linens from where she'd set them earlier. "I already quite like you." A glance to the side showed the girl looking uncertain.

"Why?" Juliana asked suspiciously.

"Because you remind me of myself at your age."

This comment made the girl's eyes widen in complete and utter disbelief.

Before any doubt could be voiced, Murie announced, "I too was orphaned at the age of ten."

That made the girl pause, so Murie continued: "My mother fell ill with the red plague."

"The smallpox?" Juliana asked uncertainly.

"Aye." Murie carried the linens to the bed. "The servants were afraid of contracting it and neglected her terribly. When my father found out, he took over her care; trying to get her to eat, cleaning her sores and bathing her to try to bring down her fevers. He stayed with her night and day, neither eating nor sleeping himself so that, by the time she died, he was sick as well and too weak and exhausted to fight the illness himself. He went very quickly."

"My father nursed my mother as well," Juliana said quietly, automatically taking the end of the linen Murie handed her. "She had childbed fever, though, and I do not think men get that."

"Nay," Murie agreed.

"But you went to court," Juliana pointed out, her eyes narrowing. "And the king is said to have spoiled you."

"Aye, I was sent to court to live with my godfather the king. And aye, 'tis said that he spoiled me. However, the truth is, the king was always terribly busy and had very little time for me," Murie assured her. It was true. While the king had spoiled her and his own children when at court, until the plague hit, Edward had very rarely been there. Usually he'd been mounting some campaign or other in Scotland or France. Murie could count on the fingers of one hand how many times she'd seen him during her first five years at court.

"What of the queen?" Habbie asked, reminding Murie that the men were still present. She didn't mind, however; the stable master had asked the question, but his gaze was on Juliana, trying to gauge how she was reacting to the news.

"The queen was very busy too," Murie said quietly. "And then, she already had children of her own to tend, and between that and state business she had little enough time for another child. I was pretty much on my own at court except for my friend Emilie."

Murie commented when Juliana remained silent, "Gatty seems very nice."

"Aye . . . but she has her own children, too, and everyone here is always busy. Frederick is my friend," Juliana added quietly, as Murie folded the edge of bed linen under the straw-stuffed mattress and then imitating the action herself.

"And what do you and Frederick do to have fun?" Murie asked, moving to the foot of the bed to tuck in a corner. The girl began to talk, and Murie glanced toward the men and nodded silently. After a hesitation, they nodded back and reluctantly left the room. A glance toward Cecily showed she'd paused and leaned against her broom to watch and listen as well, but now she shook her head and returned to sweeping up the rushes.

Murie turned her attention back to her new sister, smiling faintly as the child revealed some of the pranks she and Frederick had got up to. It seemed obvious the girl was intelligent and really very tenderhearted under all the anger bubbling on the surface, and she could have wept for Juliana; but she didn't. Instead, she vowed to ensure Juliana felt loved and valued as she'd never felt herself since the death of her parents.

* * *

"I hope Murie had Cook make something for us to eat. I am famished," Osgoode said as he and Balan mounted the steps to the keep.

"I am sure she did. She must be hungry as well," Balan answered, running a hand through his hair. He too was hungry. He was also a tad weary. The week of worry at Reynard had taken its toll. Balan had spent many sleepless nights watching over his new wife as she struggled, her feverish body fighting to rid itself of poison. He'd tried to comfort her when she wept for her parents, to soothe her when she cried out and fled from demons in her dreams, and had even had entire conversations with her about things she liked or disliked, though she didn't appear to remember any of it when she woke up.

During that time, Balan had learned that his wife was as tenderhearted as he'd suspected, was more intelligent than he'd realized and that she'd somehow managed to make a huge space for herself in his heart. He'd believed they might deal well together, else he would never have married her, but now he found himself wishing for more than "dealing well." He wanted her to love him. Balan did not necessarily want to love her in return, for that was a messy female emotion and a sticky web in which he would rather not find himself caught. But he did wish for her to love him. He simply didn't know how to achieve that.

"If she has," Osgood said dryly, distracting him from his thoughts, "I bet it is something with fish in it."

Balan gave a harsh laugh, knowing there was little question. Anselm had already told them the men had not managed any hunting at all while he was gone. Not that he'd expected it.

The great hall was quiet and empty when they entered. Balan remembered a day when just the opposite would have been the case, when the walls seemed to ring with chatter and laughter as people bustled in and out about their business. However, the plague had changed all that. He sincerely hoped to see the day when it was happy again, and with Murie's help hoped that day was not too far off.

The two cousins headed for the door leading to the kitchens in the hopes of finding food, but paused when the door opened and Clement stuck his head out.

"Oh. You're back," he said as he spotted them. "Good. I've roasted some fish over the fire as your wife said you'd both be hungry."

"Where is my wife?" Balan asked, then frowned when the man disappeared back into the kitchen. He took another step toward the door, but paused when it opened again and Clement stepped out with three trenchers stacked on top of each other, each full of fish.

"Her ladyship is up preparing your bedchamber for the night," Clement answered, shoving the trenchers at them. "You might want to let her know the food's ready before it gets cold. I've to clean the kitchen."

The moment Balan took the trenchers, Clement turned and marched away.

"He grows surlier with each passing day," Osgood said, taking one of the trenchers.

Balan shrugged. "He is doing the best he can with little in the way of supplies, and everyone is groaning at the results."

"Aye." Osgoode wrinkled his nose at the fish on his trencher and turned to move toward the trestle tables. He paused to ask, "Are you taking that up to Murie?"

"Aye. Did you wish to join us?"

Osgoode grinned. "I would not be so cruel. Enjoy

your wife—I mean enjoy *your meal with your wife*," he corrected, eyes twinkling.

Chuckling, Balan turned and made his way to the stairs with the two trenchers. His parents' private chambers had been above stairs ever since they added the second floor to the keep some twenty-five years ago. Balan had been too young to really remember what it had been like before, and had not taken over the master bedchamber upon returning to find his father dead and Gaynor in chaos. He'd taken one look at the ruined room and decided to make his way to the garrison to bunk with the men who had gone off to battle with him.

He couldn't imagine that his wife would be able to make the room inhabitable in such a short time, but he was pleasantly surprised upon reaching the open door. The filthy rushes that had coated the bedroom floor had been removed and the floor swept clean, furs thrown down beside the bed and in front of the fire to make it more comfortable, presumably until fresh rushes could be gathered and strewn. Furs had also been hung over the rickety shutters at the windows. The smelly, molding, rotted curtains had been removed from the bed and fresh linens and furs now covered that as well.

A fire had been set in the fireplace. It wasn't really needed at this time of year, but something sweet had been added to the wood to fill the room with a much more attractive scent than the overpowering and unpleasant stench Balan recalled from the last time he'd entered.

His gaze slid over the hard work done and to the two females in the room. Murie and Juliana. The little girl stood in front of the fireplace wearing a pale yellow gown that was a little big on her.

"Osgoode thought you were about the size of Lady Greyville's daughter, and so we used her for sizing," Murie was explaining as she finished the fastenings of the gown. " 'Tis obvious the girl is a bit bigger than you, but you shall grow into it quickly, and we can put temporary stitches in until you do."

Juliana was silent, her eyes wide as she touched the frock.

"And mayhap we can do something about your hair tomorrow," Murie suggested gently.

"I cut it myself," Julianna admitted, putting a self-conscious hand to her head.

"And you did a fine job," Murie assured her quickly. "But 'tis difficult to cut your own hair, and there are a couple of places where it could use evening out."

Juliana nodded and confessed, "I thought if I looked more like a boy, my father might like me better."

Balan felt his heart squeeze at these pain-filled words and silently cursed his father for neglecting his sister. In his pain, the man had cared little about the suffering he was causing his child. Balan had tried to reason with him, but—obstinate as ever—he'd just waved the words away and refused to discuss Juliana.

"Oh," Murie breathed, and Balan could feel her empathy for the child. She bowed her head and was silent a moment, then straightened and took the girl by the shoulders. Solemnly she said, "I am sure he liked you fine in his deepest heart, Juliana, but men have trouble expressing themselves sometimes."

"Nuh-uh." The child shook her head. "He showed anger well enough."

"Aye, well, that seems easy enough for all of them to show," Murie agreed dryly. She added, " 'Tis the finer emotions they have trouble with."

"He hated me because I killed Momma," Juliana

said, her eyes suddenly afraid. It seemed obvious to Balan she feared Murie would no longer like her once she knew this fact, or what the girl thought was fact, and he found himself squeezing his fingers around the trencher hard enough to crush the crusty, hollowed-out bread.

"You did not kill your mother, Juliana," Murie said in a firm voice. "She fell ill with a fever after giving birth to you. That was not your fault. It happens sometimes, and no one can say why—else we could stop it. It could happen to me, and it would not be my child's fault," she added, and Balan felt his eyes widen at the horrible suggestion. But she continued: "And I hope you would love and comfort my child for me in my stead, did that happen, not blame it for something it was not responsible for."

"Aye," Juliana promised solemnly.

"Good." Murie smiled at the girl and stepped back. "I think you look lovely in the dress. Howbeit, mayhap you should remove it until we can take it in and take up the hem. I would not see you trip and come to harm on the stairs."

Nodding, Juliana allowed her to undo and lift the gown clear.

"Will I still be able to play with Frederick in the dress?" the child asked worriedly as she put on her leggings and cotehardie.

"Well . . ." Murie paused and frowned, then suggested, "You could if you were to keep wearing your cotehardie during the day and then changed into the dress for sup."

"Oh!" Juliana grinned. "It would be like being a boy like Frederick during the day and a girl like you at night!"

Murie laughed as she carefully folded the gown. "Aye, that it would."

Once dressed, Juliana said, "Thank you, Murie. 'Tis a beautiful dress. I have never owned anything so lovely."

Murie smiled and shrugged. "I thought it would be nice to bring my new sister a gift, to show I am glad to be a member of your family."

"We *are* sisters, are we not?" the girl said happily. "I think I shall like having you for a sister. I am glad Balan married you." Juliana hugged her quickly and then turned to flee, pausing with a start when she spotted her brother.

"Good eve, Balan. Murie is nice," she announced as she skirted him for the door. "I have to go tell Gatty about my dress."

Balan watched his sister go running down the hall with a light step he'd not seen since his return from France. Once she'd disappeared down the stairs, he shifted the trenchers to one hand, closed the door with the other and turned to face his wife. Much to his amazement, she was watching him almost warily. He understood why when she spoke.

"I did punish her. She helped me make the bed and hang the furs and find herbs for the fire," she said quickly. "The dress was a reward for her hard work."

Balan smiled faintly and, moving forward, pointed out: "You commissioned the gown ere you ever met her or knew there would be something to reward."

"Aye, well, I thought she might like it."

Balan paused before his wife and started to reach for her, only to come to a halt when he recalled the trenchers in his hands. He peered at the roast fish with a frown and then glanced at Murie. "I brought you food."

"I am not hungry right this moment, I—" Her words ended on a gasp of surprise as he suddenly dropped the trenchers on the fur next to them and caught her in his arms, his mouth covering hers, hard and demanding.

Her kindness to his sister had touched him, and as he'd watched he could imagine her with their own children: teaching them, comforting them, mothering them. It had made his heart ache with a sort of yearning that he did not understand but that he wanted to express. He wanted to devour her; he wanted to hold her so tight that she became a part of him he was never without.

Saying so would probably alarm the woman, however, so he expressed himself the only way he knew how. Mouth covering and filling hers, he ran his hands up and down her body, pressing as close as he could get while they were dressed. Of course it wasn't enough, and he soon swept her into his arms and carried her to the bed. Unwilling to be parted from her for even a moment, he let her feet drop so that she hung in his arms and then tumbled them both onto the bed, his mouth breaking away on a shout of surprise. The bed had collapsed beneath them!

Eyes wide, he peered around at the buckled frame and then down at his wife in surprise. She shook beneath him with silent laughter.

Sobering as his eyes met hers, she murmured, "I think we may need a new bed, my lord husband."

"Aye," he agreed on a husky growl. Then he kissed her again, his hands beginning to remove her gown. They could worry about a new bed on the morrow. He had other matters to attend tonight.

Chapter Thirteen

Murie opened her eyes and found herself staring at an empty expanse of bed. Sitting up, she peered around the room. Her husband had already risen and started his day . . . and without waking her.

Scowling, she pushed the linens and furs aside and climbed to her feet from the collapsed bed. She'd hoped to talk to Balan about perhaps getting some livestock and more servants for the castle, but he'd quite distracted her last night and now had slipped away while she slept. It wasn't a good start to the day.

Muttering under her breath, she crossed to her chest of clothes and began pulling out gowns and surcoats until she settled on something she felt like wearing. Murie had a rather large selection, thanks to living at court, where fashion was nearly a religion and becoming more so all the time since the plague. It was almost as if everyone were insisting on vast variety and color to make up for the misery they'd gone through.

Settling on a deep red gown with a black surcoat

that should manage for a busy day of cleaning, Murie began to tug the clothes on, pausing when the door opened and Cecily looked in.

"Oh, you are up." The woman smiled but raised her eyebrows at the fact that she was already dressed. "Are you not going to wash up first? You always wash in the morning."

Murie opened her mouth to say she couldn't be bothered this morning, that she was just going to get filthy cleaning and thought it better to just take a bath that night, but the woman stepped into the room with the customary basin of water.

"Oh, bother!" She promptly tugged off the gown she'd just put on and stomped over. "Where is my husband?"

"He rode out with Osgoode hours ago," Cecily informed her. "I have no idea where they were headed. He simply told me to let you sleep as long as you liked, as you are still recovering from the poisoning, then left."

"Hmm." Murie scowled at the linen cloth as she ran it quickly over her body. She supposed it would be fish to break her fast, as well as at lunch and sup. Not an appetizing prospect, she thought, then chided herself. She had naught to complain about. The people here had been eating fish at every meal for months, and she'd not yet eaten it once: They had never got around to eating the fish Balan had brought up with him last night.

"I suppose everyone else is up and about their duties as well?" she asked.

"Aye, though little Juliana has been hanging about in the hopes that you would rise and hem her dress," Cecily said with amusement. "You have won a heart there."

"She is a sweet child," Murie murmured, her face softening into a smile.

"Aye, I sensed that the moment she kicked you," her maid commented.

Murie merely chuckled and finished her ablutions, then crossed the room to re-don the red dress. As she pulled on the black surcoat, she asked, "Lord Reynard's wagoneer has not yet left, has he?"

"Aye, he was gone almost on Lord Gaynor's heels."

Murie *tsk*ed at this. "He left without Emilie's furs and pillows."

"He said she would not need them returned for a while, as they have plenty at Reynard, and they could stay here." Cecily picked up Murie's gown from the night before and clucked over the state of it. Murie flushed, but otherwise ignored the reprimand; Balan had been a bit impatient removing it and had left it a tangled heap.

"So? What completely unsuitable task are we going to perform today?" Cecily asked as she straightened and folded the dress. "Shall we clear and scrub the great hall floor, or chop wood for the fire?"

"You have been spoiled by too much time at court," Murie said with gentle amusement. "Do you not remember life at Somerdale? Surely it was not all gentle ladylike pastimes there?"

"Aye, I remember," Cecily said quietly. She put the dress away.

"I wonder how Somerdale fared through the plague," Murie said, suddenly worried. She had been so distracted with the happenings at court and in London that she hadn't given her childhood home a thought since the plague struck. But then, it had been so long ago, and the people there were all just fuzzy images and echoes in her mind.

"They fared no better than anywhere else," Cecily

informed her. "One third to one half of the villagers and servants were taken by the plague, including William the steward."

"William the steward," Murie murmured, a faded image of the man coming to mind along with a memory of Cecily giggling at something he said. She seemed to remember that all the maids had found him handsome and giggled in his presence. "I wonder if the king has replaced him, or if it is something Balan need tend to."

"I would not know, my lady. I only heard how Somerdale fared secondhand from one of the maids of the neighboring castle. Her lady was visiting court and passed the news to me."

"I had best mention it to Balan then," Murie decided, and headed for the door.

"What do you wish me to do today, my lady?" Cecily asked, trailing along.

Murie paused at the door to consider. There was so much to do; it was difficult to decide where to start. She really needed to tour the castle again—more slowly this time so that she could sort out what needed doing most. But there was no need for Cecily to waste time trailing her around.

When Murie realized she was absently scuffing her toe against a hard bit of something long-ago spilled on the wooden floor, her gaze swept the bedchamber and she nodded. "Why do you not gather rushes for the floor to start with?" she suggested, opening the chamber door. "If you do not think you can manage the task on your own, take one of Gatty's daughters with you."

"Aye, my lady," Cecily said, and the two left the room.

Leaving Cecily to go about her own task, Murie started a tour of the upper floor before going below to break her fast. Truly, the idea of fish was not tempting.

And a more thorough going-over of each room on the upper floor simply reaffirmed what she'd noted the night before: They all basically needed as much effort as her bedchamber. The last two chambers of the four could wait, but she would definitely like to see Juliana's room made more hospitable.

As if thoughts of the child brought her running, Balan's sister was the first person Murie saw as she descended the stairs to the great hall. The girl rushed to greet her, Frederick on her heels and questions on her lips.

"Are you going to cut my hair today, Murie? Are you going to hem my dress?" she asked excitedly. The girl's eagerness was enough to decide Murie on her first tasks.

"I shall certainly cut your hair right now if you like," she assured the child, and then added, "and I shall certainly pin your dress directly afterward. Howbeit, I will not hem it until this evening when we are relaxing around the fire after sup."

"Oh," Juliana's shoulders drooped with disappointment. "But then I shall not be able to wear it tonight."

Murie bit her lip and sighed. Some things were simply too important to be left, and an injured young girl's feelings were far more important than cleaning this or that. "You are right, and so I shall hem it when we break for the nooning meal instead. How is that?"

Juliana brightened at once. "That would be wonderful!"

"Go sit at the trestle table while I fetch the items I need to cut your hair," Murie instructed.

"Aye, Murie. Thank you, Murie. You are the best sister a girl ever had, Murie."

The child raced off toward the tables with Frederick on her heels, and Murie watched them go with a smile.

"Bribery will get you far with her, I think. No one has ever troubled themselves to use it."

"Clement." Murie sighed as she turned to the speaker. "Is there something I can help you with this morning, or have you just come to devil me with your surliness?"

He blinked in surprise at her tone. Presumably, no one normally dared confront the man on his moods for fear he might spit—or worse—in their food. Come to think of it, Murie thought suddenly, mayhap hers wasn't the smartest move.

"Actually, my lady," he said finally, in a much more amenable voice, "Cecily mentioned that you are touring the castle once more to see what needed doing, and I hoped you might see your way clear to touring the kitchens first so that you would be done and out of the way when it came time to make the nooning meal."

Judging the request to be perfectly reasonable, Murie gave a nod of assent and promised, "Directly after I deal with Juliana. Would that be sufficient?"

"Aye. Thank you." Clement gave a very formal bow and turned to walk away, then paused after several steps. "I shall bring you the implements needed to repair the child's hair," he said, looking back.

"Thank you," Murie said slowly, perplexed as she watched him leave. It seemed snapping at him had a beneficial effect.

"You have taken Clement in hand as well, I see," Gatty said, making her presence known.

"Aye, it would seem so, though I am not at all sure how I managed it," Murie admitted.

"You did not toady," Gatty said simply. "Even the old Lord Gaynor tended to tiptoe around the man and let him get away with more than he should have. Clement grew too big for his britches because of that."

"Are you saying he was as surly before the plague as he is now?" Murie asked with disbelief.

"You thought his having nothing but fish to work with had caused his moodiness?" Gatty guessed. When Murie nodded, she said, "I suspect Lord Balan thinks the same, but it is not the case. He was cantankerous from the day Lord Gaynor lured him away from our neighbor Lord Aldous."

"Aldous is a neighbor?" Murie asked sharply.

"Aye, our closest, and Gaynor and Aldous have always been at odds. Balan's father and the old Aldous both loved Lady Gaynor, but Lord Gaynor got her. Aldous never forgave him, and the two have been feuding ever since, though not openly. It seemed to transfer naturally to the sons. Malculinus and Balan both trained at Strathcliffe and were constantly at odds from what has been said. Though, as with the fathers, not openly. I gather Malculinus used to get a bunch of bullies together to harrass Balan, never actually doing the dirty work himself. But then, he was always a small, frail lad and would not have been able to stand in a fair fight."

"And Lord Gaynor hired Clement away from Aldous Castle?"

"Aye. More than fifteen years ago. Those were better days, of course. Lady Gaynor was still alive, and Gaynor was healthy and prosperous. 'Tis only when Lady Gaynor died that things began to slip. Lord Gaynor seemed to lose interest in everything around him at that point. And then, the summer before the plague hit, he suddenly found a renewed interest in Gaynor and decided we needed a bigger, finer fish pond. He spent a great deal of money on the task, and it was fraught with difficulty. The moment the men started the project, the heavens seemed to open up and pound us with rain that simply did not stop."

"I remember that summer," Murie admitted. "Many lost their crops to the mud and damp."

"Aye, we did as well. So the pond ate a good portion of our income. Then the crops failed, and the plague hit. Had Lord Gaynor not built the pond, we would have been in a much better position to keep servants."

"Mayhap," Murie said thoughtfully. "But then you would have had more mouths to feed and no fish to feed them."

The maid looked startled, and Murie shrugged. "Who is to say there would have been enough people here to tend the animals and keep them from wandering or being stolen? We are close to the border of Scotland up here, and they are famed for reaving. Mayhap it was more fortunate than you think that Lord Gaynor put in the new pond. Fish may get tiresome in a hurry, but they are good for keeping up one's strength." Her gaze slid across the great hall as the door to the kitchens opened and Clement reappeared. "Now, if you'll excuse me, I must tend Juliana's hair and then tour the kitchens and gardens."

Murie was no expert on cutting hair. In fact, she'd never cut hair before in her life, but there was simply no way she could make more of a mess of the child's—no doubt once beautiful—chestnut locks than Juliana had made herself, so Murie approached the task with more enthusiasm than was probably warranted. The project turned out surprisingly well. She managed to turn the hacked mass of hair into an even bob of sorts.

She was most pleased with the results, and Juliana seemed so as well. After showing absolutely everyone she could find—which turned out to be only Clement, Thibault, Gatty and Frederick—the child rushed upstairs to change into her new dress. Aware of the day slipping away, Murie worked quickly at pinning up the gown, then sent the girl off to change again while she herself headed for the kitchens. Once she'd inspected, she moved on to the gardens outside. And while she'd only intended to look, the sight of parsley made her gasp in alarm and immediately drop to her knees. She was tearing the plants from the ground when an alarmed cry rose up behind her.

Glancing over her shoulder, she stared in amazement at the horrified expression on the cook's face.

"My lady!" Clement bellowed, finally finding his voice as he charged toward her. "What in God's name are you doing?"

"I am removing the parsley," Murie said soothingly. " 'Tis all right. I shall replant it outside the gates."

"But I do not want it outside the gates. I needs must have it close by to cook with," he protested.

" 'Twill be little enough effort to walk a ways to get it rather than risk a death in the castle."

"What?" he asked with bewilderment.

"Do you not know that growing parsley in the garden means there will be a death in the house before the end of the year?" she asked with exasperation. "Honestly, you are practically ensuring my husband's death with such nonsense. Well, I will not have it! I am moving the parsley outside the gate, and you can just walk that little distance to get it when you need it."

Clement simply stared with a sort of befuddled expression, seemingly at a loss for what to say. His gaze was mournful as he peered at the parsley she was gathering.

"Did you come out here for a reason, Clement?" she asked.

"Aye," he breathed after a moment, then seemed to

give himself a shake. "His lordship and Osgoode returned with a boar from their hunt, and I came to find the herbs I should like to stuff it with."

"Oh." She smiled brightly. "Stuffed boar for sup! That shall be lovely."

"Aye," he agreed.

"Is my husband in the great hall, then?" she asked, gathering the plants she'd uprooted. She could finally speak to the man—or so she thought. Clement soon disabused her of that possibility.

"He was," the cook said. "But I gather the boar put up a battle and both men were bloodied. They rode down to the river to bathe rather than trouble me to boil water and haul it above stairs for them."

"Oh." Murie shifted from one foot to the other and asked, "Is the river far?"

"Nay. Not far," Clement said, his gaze locked on the parsley. His look made her nervous. She very much suspected he would like to wrest the plants from her and put them back exactly where she'd taken them from, despite being warned of their horrible effects.

Easing a wary step away, she turned and headed out of the garden. "Well, I shall simply walk down to the river after replanting the parsley. I should like to have a word with my husband."

Murie could hear the cook's sigh as she walked away, but she ignored it. Honestly, how he could fret over having to walk a little distance when it might save a life, she didn't know.

Still . . . she didn't end up planting the parsley outside the gate. The saying was only that growing it in the garden was bad, so she planted it nearby, on the edge of a short row of apple trees. Satisfied that it wasn't in the garden, but Clement might be a little less distressed that it was not so very far away, she straightened and brushed off her hands and headed out of the bailey to find Balan.

She was most grateful that he'd spent the morning hunting. Truly, stuffed boar sounded a nice treat. Murie had never cared much for fish, and the idea of being forced to eat it three times a day was a terrible trial. Actually, it was making her feel rather ill, which it had never done before, but there it was. That was the reason it had been no hardship for her to miss the meal last eve, and why she'd found herself "forgetting" to break her fast this morning in all the fuss of cutting Juliana's hair and touring the kitchens.

She'd been quite pleased with the kitchens, actually. Clement had done a wonderful job of keeping them up. While everywhere else seemed to need whitewashing and new rushes and even new furniture, the kitchens were in tip-top shape, simply needing supplies and some servants to bring it back to life. Murie had expressed her pleasure to Clement. The man had said stiffly that it was his job, but he'd also blushed, and she'd seen the spark of pleasure in his eyes. She suspected that everyone had been so busy tiptoeing around him all these years, they had neglected to compliment his efforts as well. A little credit where credit was due might make the man a bit more bearable. He would never be as dear and cheerful as Thibault, but she thought his personality might improve with some work.

"Murie."

Pausing, she glanced up with surprise as Osgoode appeared on the path ahead. He was walking toward her, wet hair slicked back from his face and damp clothes clinging to his body. Smiling, she said, "I see you saved the ladies some work and washed your clothes along with your bodies. Is my husband still bathing?"

"Aye." Osgood grinned. "Balan likes water. The man will sit in a bath until the water is cold while bathing indoors, and he's even worse outdoors. Not me," he added. "I like to get in and out."

Murie smiled faintly, but refrained from pointing out his in-and-out method left much to be desired—he still had blood on his neck below his ear. Then she realized it was a graze, and she frowned. "Clement said the boar gave you a battle. You were hurt."

"What? This?" He wiped at his neck and shrugged. " 'Tis naught. The boar was stubborn and did not wish to land on our table."

"Was Balan hurt as well?" Murie asked.

"Nay. He is swifter of foot than I. Besides, he was on top of the boar. I was foolish enough to dismount in front of the beast before he was quite down. Balan had to leap off his mount onto the animal's back and slit its throat. This is from me running away—right into a branch while looking behind me to see how close the beast was," he admitted, laughing and rubbing the spot.

Murie shook her head. Boar hunting was one of the most dangerous sports. Boars often did not go down right away, and the arrow or spear that pierced them usually just made them angry and stronger.

"Well, I am off. I want to be sure Clement has all he needs for dinner. A fine beast like that boar deserves to be cooked properly."

Murmuring farewell, Murie watched Balan's cousin off and then turned to continue on to the river. She had no idea how far it was, but suspected she must be close. At least, that was what she thought at first, but after five minutes, she realized it was farther than she'd expected. Not far, exactly, just not as close as she'd thought. Still, she enjoyed the walk, noting a birch

tree here and an ash tree there, and even a clump of
wild onions and a small carpet of clover. These were
all very good luck when carried on a person. Deter-
mining that her husband needed all the luck he could
get, she stopped to pluck a twig from the birch and
then an ash-key from the ash tree before spending several moments hunting until she found an even ash
leaf. She searched the clover for a four-leafed one, but
after several minutes gave up for another time and
continued along the path, eventually coming to the
river.

Much to her dismay, the clearing was empty. Murie
paused and frowned, wondering if she'd missed her
husband and he'd walked right by her while she was
on her knees in the clover. The sound of splashing
from farther downriver answered that question; obviously the men had moved from the main clearing to
ensure they didn't startle any of the castle women who
might unsuspectingly approach.

Clucking her tongue, Murie moved to the edge of
the river and peered in the direction from which the
sound had come. Her heart stopped when she saw a
bit of blue cloth floating on the surface of the water . . . the same color as the new doublet she'd had
made for Balan's wedding and which he'd worn since.

Staggering quickly along the water's edge, Murie
hurried to the shore directly beside it . . . and found
herself staring at her husband's back. He was half sub-
merged under the water.

Screaming his name in fear and horror, she charged
into the river, cursing as her gown immediately grew
wet and heavy, clinging to her legs and slowing her
down. It seemed like hours passed before she managed to gain his side. Grabbing him by the back of his
doublet, she turned him quickly in the water and

slipped a hand under his head to lift it up, then peered at her husband's pale face with dismay. He wasn't breathing; she was too late, she thought with alarm, but then ground her teeth and started to rise, intending to drag him toward shore.

She paused when she spotted blood on the hand she'd had beneath his head. Lifting his head further, she shifted the wet strands and gasped at the sight of the deep, wide gash. Someone had hit him on the back of his head with . . . something. Her eyes examined the shoreline, and her mouth tightened. There were several likely rocks on shore that could have managed the job. Someone had tried to kill her husband again!

Standing abruptly in the water, she caught Balan by the shoulders and dragged him toward land.

Moving him was easy in the river, where the water helped buoy him up and all she had to do was pull and direct him, but once she reached shore, the task became almost impossible. Murie would never know where she found the strength to draw him out of the water, but she did, alternating between pulling and pushing at various parts of his body. She pulled his arms out first, then ran around to grab his ankles to drag those so that he ended bowed backward on his side, his stomach and chest still mostly in the water. Murie then moved to his torso and placed one hand on his belly and one on his upper chest and began shoving with all her strength, trying to push him completely out of the water.

She wasn't sure how many times she'd pushed at him when he suddenly gagged and coughed up what appeared to be half the river. He followed that with several more coughs, then rolled onto his back with a groan and fell silent.

"Husband?" Murie whispered, hardly believing he lived. Dropping to her knees, she brushed the damp hair back from his face and looked him over. His coloring seemed a little better; less gray, and with a tinge of pink to it now. But he was still unconscious.

Biting her lip, she tapped his cheek a couple of times and then sucked in a deep breath and gave him a sound whack across the face. She'd hoped that would wake him, but it didn't have the desired effect.

Sighing, she sank back on her heels and peered around, trying to think of what to do. Instinct was yelling at her to run and get help, that she couldn't possibly get him back by herself, but her instincts were also telling her that whoever had done this might yet be lurking, awaiting an opportunity to finish the job. She would not leave Balan alone . . . but she needed to get him back to the keep.

How? Her mind screamed the question, and then her gaze landed on the doublet she was unconsciously clutching. She stared at the cloth hard for a moment, then shifted her gaze to her own gown and finally to the uneven ground. There were two branches almost large enough. . . .

Murie shook her head. Nay. She could not; not even for her husband would she . . .

But the idea had taken hold, and she didn't have a better one.

Finally, admitting with much regret that there was nothing else for it, Murie stood and began to strip.

Chapter Fourteen

"She *what?*" Balan roared, but his head was immediately pierced by a thousand sharp needles of pain. He'd woken in his collapsed bed just moments ago, not to find his caring wife there tending him with adoration, but Osgoode sitting on one side and his wife's maid, Cecily, on the other. Cecily had told him that Murie had saved his life after finding him unconscious in the river. Osgoode had told him how.

Holding his throbbing head and squeezing, in an effort to press back the pain as well as ensure his head didn't explode, Balan repeated a little more quietly, "She what?"

"She stripped naked and then stripped you naked and used the clothing and two branches she found nearby to make a sort of litter, then dragged you all the way back to the castle," Osgood repeated, eyes shining.

"Dear God," Balan breathed.

"Aye." Osgoode nodded solemnly. " 'Twas the most incredible thing I have ever seen."

"You *saw*?" Balan asked with horror.

"*Everyone* saw," Osgoode replied. "Without your clothes, the men were not sure who was approaching and sent for Anselm, and then Anselm called me."

"Surely you recognized us?" Balan asked with disbelief, but Osgoode shook his head.

"Nay. Understand, you were crumpled and rolled up in a ball on a multicolored litter . . . and Murie's hair was damp from both sweat and river water, and plastered to her face, obscuring her features. We all just thought her a mad woman dragging something around at first." He pursed his lips and added, "Everyone was on the wall staring, and she had nearly reached the drawbridge before Cecily gasped that it was her ladyship."

"Aye," Cecily agreed solemnly. "And then I ran into the castle and grabbed a fur from the bed and rushed out to cover her with it as the men hurried to take the litter."

Osgoode nodded and added enviously, "She must love you very much to go to such ends to see you safe."

Balan paused and stared at his cousin. Love? Had it been love that made her drag him naked from the river to the castle? Could she really love him? The idea almost made him smile, but then he recalled that, had she loved him, surely she would be here when he woke. Which she wasn't.

"Where is my wife?" he asked with a growl.

"She went below to see if she could come up with something to help with your pain when you woke. She said your head would be splitting when you finally did." Seeing Balan's irritation, Osgoode added, "But she was most worried for your well-being and would not leave until both Cecily and I agreed to stay with you."

"Hmmmph." Balan shifted in the collapsed bed. He supposed her leaving to see to his comfort was acceptable. And insisting upon two people to watch him was good. It showed more care and concern than asking only one to stay. Still, he wished she'd been here when he'd first opened his eyes. Actually, he wished she'd been there with something for his pain. The dratted woman was right—his head was splitting.

"Do you remember what happened?" Osgoode asked suddenly. "How did you end up falling in the river and hitting your head?"

"I did not fall in the river and hit my head," he announced grimly. "Someone crept up behind me and hit me over the head. I fell in the river . . . or perhaps they pushed me in after. Whichever the case, this was no accident."

Osgoode sat back on the mattress, eyes narrowed thoughtfully. They were all three on the straw-stuffed mattress on the floor. Balan lay on his back in the middle, and the maid and Osgoode were seated on either side. There were no chairs in the room.

"You do not think Murie—," Osgoode began.

"Osgoode!" Balan snapped and regretted it at once. Clutching his head, he said through gritted teeth, "You have just finished telling me that my wife stripped naked and dragged me back up the path to the castle to save my life. Do not dare suggest the woman tried to kill me first and then tried to save me. Should you be foolish enough to do so—aching head or no aching head—I shall rise up out of this bed and strike you down."

"Nay, of course not," Osgoode said quickly. "It was just a thought."

Balan started to shake his head with disgust, but paused with a grimace at the pain that engendered. Shifting impatiently in bed, he muttered, "Where *is* my wife?"

"Very well, I have arranged it so that Cecily and Osgoode stay by my husband's side. Now, what is it that was so important you had to drag me away when he most needs me?" Murie asked, her gaze sliding over the group gathered at the castle wall. Everyone was there: Gatty, her son and two daughters, Juliana, Clement, Thibault and every last one of the soldiers as far as she could tell. Murie supposed they'd chosen the wall to avoid leaving it unmanned, while also avoiding leaving anyone out. That fact made her curious, but—much to her exasperation—no one was answering her question; instead they were all avoiding looking at her and shifting uncomfortably.

Murie knew what the problem was, of course. They had seen her naked as the day she was born and were now embarrassed in her presence. She understood, though she did wonder that they should be reacting thus when *she* was the one who should be squirming. However, odd as it might seem, their very discomfort eased her own, and she was the only one not blushing.

"Anselm?" she asked finally. As the man Balan left in charge of Gaynor when he was away, the soldier seemed the most likely leader of this procession.

The man hesitated, his eyes skating to her and then away as if she were still naked rather than in a clean new gown of pale cream. She was about to prompt him again when he spoke.

"We have been thinking, my lady," he started. "And it occurred to us that the only people on the journey between court and Reynard were Lord and Lady Reynard, their men-at-arms, the Reynards' servants, your maid, Cecily, and Osgoode."

"Aye," Murie murmured, knowing where this was going. The fact had occurred to her as well.

"So . . . it has to be one of them," Godart announced, as if it were obvious. Which, she supposed, it was. But Murie frowned. Cecily had been a good and loyal servant, following her to court and mopping up her tears when the other girls had been at their worst. As for Osgoode: she wasn't as sure about him, but she liked her husband's cousin and did not wish to think he was involved. She had another culprit she would prefer it to be.

"We must consider motive here," she said at last. "Who would have a motive to kill Balan? Surely, neither Osgoode nor Cecily would have reason?"

"I do not know about your maid, but Osgoode would," Anselm said slowly.

Murie blinked in surprise. "What motive would he have?"

The soldier shrugged. "He inherits if Balan dies."

Murie scowled. "I would think Juliana would inherit should Balan die. She is his sister."

"Gaynor has always passed down through the men. A son or nephew always inherits. Juliana would inherit her mother's demesne, but Osgoode would get Gaynor."

Murie's gaze slid to Juliana, but the child seemed neither surprised nor hurt by this announcement.

"There are other possibilities," she said at last.

"Such as?" Anselm asked.

Murie hesitated. "If there were a party traveling nearby that we had not realized was there, for instance," she suggested. "Someone from that party may have put the thistle under Balan's saddle and poisoned that meat."

"Like Lord Malculinus and his sister, Lauda?" Habbie asked. "You did mention that their party must have left court on your heels to arrive at Gaynor when they did. Are you thinking they could be behind these attacks?"

"Well, there were no more attacks once we reached Reynard," Murie pointed out. "And they have only now started up again. Gatty told me they are neighbors to us."

"Aye," Erol said, but sounded doubtful. Murie understood why when he added, "While no one might have necessarily noticed anyone specifically near the horses or by the cooking meat, a stranger would definitely have been noticed lurking about." He shook his head. "It really is more likely someone in the party."

Murie frowned with displeasure. She preferred the Aldouses as suspects, and so suggested, "Mayhap they bribed one of Lord Reynard's men to perform the deeds and traveled close by to hear the results."

"That is possible," Godart murmured. Then he pointed out, "This latest attack did take place outside the gates and could be from an outsider."

Anselm nodded slowly. "Aye, and Aldous could have bribed one of Reynard's men."

They were all silent for a moment. Murie at last said, "Well, we still do not know who it is. It could be Osgoode or Cecily," she agreed reluctantly. "But it could also be Lord Aldous behind it all. So, I suggest—"

"But what would his motive be?" Gatty interrupted. "He and Balan have been at odds for years, but Malculinus has never resorted to trying to kill him before this. Why now?"

Murie wrinkled her nose. "Malculinus and Lauda apparently intended to try to trick me into marriage, but Balan stopped them, and I ended up marrying him instead. Malculinus may want revenge."

"Or to make you a widow so you will marry him after all," Anselm suggested.

Murie snorted. "I would not marry him if he were the last man in England."

"You were going to suggest something, my lady," Thibault reminded her. "Before Gatty interrupted. You said, 'So I suggest . . .' What were you going to say?"

"Oh, aye." Murie dragged her mind back on track and said, "As we are not sure who the culprit is and are short the manpower to watch all three suspects, mayhap the best bet is to set two men on Balan to watch him."

"Two?" Anselm asked with a grimace. "My lady, we *are* short-staffed. Can we not make it one?"

Murie bit her lip. She would feel better if it were two, but they were at a terrible disadvantage when it came to number Sighing, she nodded. "Very well, make it one. One man should be with Balan at all times to watch for any future attempts until this is resolved."

"Lord Balan is not going to like having a minder," Erol grumbled. "He'll order against it, and we will have to listen."

Murie's mouth set with displeasure. It was true: Balan probably wouldn't like it and would find a way to be rid of anyone guarding him . . . if he knew they were. "Very well, one man must watch him from a distance, doing his best to avoid being noticed by Balan in the process."

"That may work," Anselm admitted.

The men all mumbled their agreement, and Anselm turned to Erol and Godart. "You two can watch him in shifts, one during the day and one at night. You can decide which shift you want between the two of you.

But," he added, his gaze moving over everyone present, "I want everyone to try to keep an eye out for him. If you see Lord Balan about, take note that all is well and that no one is watching or following him or acting strangely." When everyone murmured or nodded, Anselm clapped his hands. "That is it then. We can all go back to our duties."

Feeling a little better now that she knew Balan would have someone watching over him at all times, Murie joined the others in leaving the castle wall. She was back in the keep and halfway across the great hall before she became aware that she was being followed. Glancing back, she raised an eyebrow at the sight of Juliana trailing after her. The girl was biting her lip and looking anxious.

With all the excitement and worry since coming upon her husband in the river, Murie hadn't given a thought to how this must have upset the child. Pausing, she held her hand out, smiling when the girl slipped fingers into hers.

"You saved him," Juliana whispered in a trembling voice, and before Murie could speak, added, "but what if he is killed the next time? He is all I have."

Murie's smile faltered at the child's words, knowing the incident had raised fears of what would happen if her brother died. It was a worry Murie had never had as a child . . . until she'd found herself orphaned. Kneeling, she took the girl by the shoulders and stared her straight in the face. "Nay. You have me now, too . . . and I promise you, should anything happen to your brother, I shall take care of you."

Juliana bit her lip and managed a trembling smile. "And I would look after you, too."

Murie smiled at the child and gave her a quick hug. "That is what sisters are for," she whispered by her ear, and thought to herself that she was beginning to love the sister as much as the brother. The thought so startled her that Murie simply knelt there when Juliana stepped back. She barely heard the girl say she was going to go find Frederick and run down to the stables to see if Habbie's dog had had her litter yet; she was simply too stunned by her own thoughts.

Standing slowly, she continued on toward the stairs, but her mind was racing. Did she *love* her husband? Certainly she liked him, respected him, and she definitely enjoyed their marital bed . . . but love? How could she love him already?

Murie's parents had had a wonderful marriage. They had been a loving and affectionate couple. But they had seemed to her to be the exception rather than the rule. The behavior she'd seen at court had been somewhat less than stellar: married noblemen dallying with maids in whatever dark corner they could find, while their wives took lovers of their own in more discreet but no less adulterous affairs. She'd seen men beat their wives in public after too much drink, insult them publicly after nothing to drink and just generally treat them poorly. But Balan had never treated her so, and she was quite positive he never would, though she could not have said why. There was just something too honorable about the man for her to believe he would ever sink to such behavior.

But love . . . ?

"Aye," she admitted on a sigh. She loved him. And, if for no other reason than that, she could not lose him. She would do all in her power to ensure whoever was trying to kill him did not succeed.

Balan woke slowly and opened his eyes, relieved to note that this time his head was not aching. He supposed he could thank Murie's medicinals for that. They had worked wonders when she'd finally returned. The noxious brew had tasted bitter and nasty, but his headache had soon eased. The only problem was that the brew had made him sleepy as well, and he'd soon found himself falling off to sleep again.

Wondering what time it was, he peered around the room. The chamber was dark, lit only by the fire, which cast dancing shadows across the wall. At first he thought his wife had left him alone, but then he saw her kneeling on a fur before the fire, mending something by the light cast by the flames. He watched her for a moment as she concentrated on her stitches and had just realized that the pale yellow cloth she held must be Juliana's new dress when he became aware of the pungent smell in the air.

"What is that smell?" he asked after a moment. It smelled like onions to him, but there was no good reason that he could think for the room to reek of the scent.

Murie glanced up from sewing, wide eyes swiveling his way. "You are awake." Setting Juliana's dress aside, she climbed to her feet and crossed to the bed.

"Aye," Balan acknowledged, as she settled on the straw mattress next to him and placed a hand at his cheek. Her gaze slid over his face and eyes.

"Your coloring is much better, and your eyes are clear," she noted. "The rest has done you good. How is your head?"

"Fine," he muttered, then repeated, "What is that smell?"

"What smell?" she asked with confusion.

"It smells like onions," he said, glancing around again.

"Oh. Well that would be onions," Murie answered,

bending to pick up a tankard of some liquid left beside the mattress. Straightening, she held it out. "Here. Drink this."

"Nay, it made me sleepy the last time," he protested, waving it away. "Why would our room reek of onions?"

"Because there are onions in our room," she answered simply, and held the tankard out again. " 'Tis not the same brew as last time. 'Tis a special concoction to strengthen you. It will not make you sleep. Drink it."

Balan scowled, but took the tankard and drank half of it in one gulp, only to pause and make a face. "This is worse than the last one. What is in it?"

"Rosemary, sage and St. John's wort—among other things," she answered evasively.

"Hmmph." Balan scowled but drank more of the liquid before asking, "Why are there onions in our room?"

"They will help prevent your getting an infection or fever," was Murie's answer.

"Humph," Balan muttered. He gulped the rest of the vile drink down, then handed back the tankard.

"Are you hungry?" Murie asked, taking it.

"Aye," he admitted. "I do not suppose there is any boar left?"

"Of course there is," Murie assured him, standing and moving to place the tankard on one of her chests that had been moved beside the bed to be used as a table. There was a trencher on it, which she picked up to carry back. "They saved you the choicest bits. Clement brought it up before the others sat down to eat. It has been waiting here for you to wake."

"Mmm." Balan sat up as she handed him the trencher. Murie settled on the bed as he began to eat, but shook her head when he offered her some.

He ate in silence for several minutes before she asked, "Balan? Do you remember what happened?"

"Aye. We went down to the river, washed our clothes and laid them out to dry on the rocks, then bathed. Osgoode was done quicker than I and left to head back to the castle. I had just got out and re-donned my clothes when someone cracked me over the head. I must have fallen into the river."

She was silent as he ate some more. Then: "You did not hear or see anything ere they hit you over the head?"

"Nay. There are small rapids just up from where we swam. The sound of the water rushing over the rocks would have covered for any sound of an approach," he pointed out.

"Aye," Murie murmured. "I passed Osgoode on my way down to the river. His clothes were wet."

"Aye. They did not get a chance to dry ere our getting out. Mine were still wet too when I donned them," Balan said absently, his concentration on his food. Clement had outdone himself. The boar was juicy and well-seasoned, and the man had indeed saved him the choicest bits.

"So, he was not wet from dragging you into the water?" Murie asked.

Balan stiffened, the food forgotten. Raising startled eyes, he said, "What?"

"You do not think he . . ." She paused and bit her lip, looking uncomfortable, and blinked in surprise when Balan burst out laughing.

"Nay, wife," he said when his laughter had slowed. "Osgoode did not cosh me over the head and throw me in the river to drown."

She gave a half-relieved smile, but asked, "You are

sure? I have had it pointed out to me that he would inherit everything if you were to die."

Balan frowned as he realized that truth, but shook his head. "Nay. Osgoode has watched my back since we were children. He saved my life countless times while in France. And I his, for that matter. I trust him with my life. Nay, 'twas not Osgoode," he assured her, but found it amusing that each seemed to think the other was trying to kill him. Turning his gaze back to his trencher, he reached for more meat, then paused in surprise when he realized he'd eaten it all.

"Would you like more?" Murie asked, noting his expression.

"Nay," Balan answered, and instead broke off a piece of bread from the trencher and popped it in his mouth. The hollowed out and stale bread had been softened and flavored by the meat juices, and was almost as good as the meat itself.

Catching his wife glancing toward the dress she'd been working on, he said, "Finish what you were doing. Do not let me stop you."

Murie smiled and shook her head. "I would rather visit with you."

Balan shifted restlessly in the bed. "We could play that game of chess you promised me."

His wife's eyes brightened at the suggestion, and she stood at once and started toward the door, saying, "I shall fetch it right away. Do you wish me to fetch you something to drink while I am below stairs?"

"Aye, a tankard of ale, if you would," he said, and then changed his mind. "Nay, fetch wine for us both."

Murie grinned at the suggestion and teased, "Hoping that I will imbibe too much and give you a better chance of winning, my lord?"

Balan just chuckled and shook his head.

As she slipped out of the room, he lay back to await her return, then scowled as the scent of onions immediately became stronger. Shifting onto one elbow, he peered over the side of the mattress, his eyes widening at the sight of the onions lined up on the floor beside him. There must've been two or three dozen, cleaned, peeled and halved, just lying there lined up like a small fence. His gaze drifted past them to see there were more in each corner of the room and along the walls, but these were interspersed with various other items. He recognized clover and ash leaves as well as ash-keys, but had no idea about the branches and twigs strewn throughout.

No doubt they were something considered lucky. His wife did seem to have a penchant for superstitious nonsense. Balan had never seen the like. While he was watching over Murie's sick bed at Reynard as she recovered from the poisoning, Reginald had told him that Emilie had told him that Murie had been superstitious ever since her arrival at court. Emilie seemed to think it was Murie's way of dealing with the uncertainty of life and had to do with the death of her parents. One moment she'd been the happy, laughing child of Lord and Lady Somerdale, and the next she was their orphaned daughter, living at court and being made as miserable as a child could be. Emilie suspected that Murie's penchant for superstition was her way of trying to be prepared for whatever life threw her way . . . and to combat it.

That being the case, Balan supposed he should be happy she was placing lucky charms about the room and not decorating their chamber with the white maney flower of the hawthorne, which he knew was unlucky. It was said that, when brought into a home, death followed. Except on May Day, of course.

Smiling faintly, he lay back in the bed and then glanced toward the door as it opened. Murie bustled back in, bearing the chessboard. She was followed by Cecily, who was bearing wine.

"Thank you, Cecily," Murie murmured as she set the board on the bed and began to open the leather bag that held the chess pieces. "You may go to bed if you wish. I will not need you again tonight."

"Aye, my lady," Cecily replied, and slipped out of the room after setting the wine and chalices down by the straw mattress.

"Who taught you to play chess?" Balan asked as he helped Murie set up the pieces. "The king?"

Murie hesitated, then admitted, "Nay. My father taught me. But the king also offered to teach me, and rather than hurt his feelings, I let him think I did not know how to play." Balan grinned. Catching his expression, Murie raised an eyebrow. "What are you smiling about?"

"I was just thinking that you are so wonderfully tenderhearted," he said, his smile widening as she blushed. He then added, "And that I am going to slaughter you at this game." When she stiffened in surprise, he shrugged and added, "You simply cannot possibly have the killing instinct needed to beat me."

Balan swallowed those words two hours later as his wife proceeded to take his king and win her third game. He hadn't seen it coming. Shaking his head with bewilderment, he lay back in bed and peered at her. "I am impressed, my lady wife. I can see why the king will no longer play with you."

"Oh?" She looked alarmed. "Does this mean you will

not play with me, either? I could lose once in a while if it would please you," she offered. Then she added, "I am sure you only lost because of your head injury. No doubt it is paining you."

Balan made a face. "My head is not paining me. You won fair and square. And of course I shall play with you again. I am not so proud I must win at everything. Mayhap you can teach me a thing or two."

Murie stared at him, wide-eyed. "Really?"

"Aye, really." He smiled, but it turned into a yawn at the end, and Murie quickly began to gather the chess pieces.

"You should sleep, my lord," she murmured.

"I slept all afternoon," Balan said irritably.

"Aye, but you sustained a terrible head wound," she pointed out. She paused to ask, "Are you sure it is not paining you? I could fetch you more—"

"Nay!" he interrupted quickly. The very idea of having to drink more of her special tea was enough to scare away any pain he might have felt. "I am fine. But I think I shall sleep now."

He settled back on the mattress as she removed the chess game and pieces, then scowled when she moved back toward the fire. "Are you not coming to bed?" he asked.

"I thought to work on the dress for a little bit before I retire," she replied.

"Come to bed," he ordered. Balan was too weary to make love, but for some reason he wanted the comfort of her near.

Murie hesitated, then turned back and quickly stripped down to her undertunic. She climbed onto the mattress next to him. The moment she was within reach, Balan turned on his side and snaked his arm around her waist, drawing her against him.

"Good night, husband," she whispered as he closed his eyes.

Balan's answer was a grunt as he drifted off to sleep.

He didn't wake when Murie slipped away and only knew she had because when he woke up several hours later, she was sleeping on the fur before the fire, the crumpled pale yellow dress a pillow beneath her cheek. Grumbling under his breath, Balan pushed the linens and furs aside and crawled off the mattress. Unfortunately, he'd forgotten about the onions around the bed and planted his foot on one as he rose, lost his balance and fell back to the straw mattress hard enough to draw a groan from his lips.

Cursing now, he crawled to his hands and knees and then got up again, moving more carefully this time to avoid the onions. Muttering about his wife, her foolish superstitions and basically just women in general, Balan crossed the room to scoop Murie up off the floor and carry her back to bed.

The woman sighed in her sleep, but other than that she did not stir as he slipped off her clothes and settled her beneath the linens and furs. It wasn't until he crawled into bed beside her and pulled her against his chest that she showed any sign of waking. Murmuring his name, she started to lift her head, but he pressed it back down onto his chest and whispered, "Sleep."

Balan was sure he would not fall back to sleep himself. He'd slept all afternoon and a good portion of the evening, after all; but he'd barely pressed her head back to his chest and closed his eyes when sleep claimed him once again.

When next he opened his eyes, Balan could see sunlight creeping around the furs covering the windows, and Murie was missing from the bed again. This time, however, she was not on the fur before the fire. In fact, she was nowhere in the room.

Sighing in exasperation, Balan pushed the linens and furs aside to climb to his feet. Of course, he again forgot about the onions. This time, rather than fall backward, he stumbled forward, crashing to the hard wooden floor just as the bedchamber door opened and his wife entered.

"Husband! What are you doing out of bed?" Murie cried, rushing across the room to his side. "You should not be out of bed. You are obviously still too weak from your injury."

"It is not weakness that saw me on the floor, wife," he said through gritted teeth. "It is your blasted onions. I stepped on the damn things, and my foot went out from under me."

"Oh." Biting her lip, she glanced toward the crushed wild onions he'd stepped on and sighed. "Well you still should not be out of bed."

" 'Tis not a bed, Murie. 'Tis a bloody straw mattress on the bloody floor," he pointed out with irritation. "Speaking of which, we really have to either get the men to fix this bed frame or make a new one. A new mattress would not go amiss, either. And a chair. Two of them to set by the fire," Balan said, scowling, as he regained his feet.

"Husband." Murie caught his arms and tried to turn him back toward the bed. "You should not be up. You took a terrible head injury."

"I am fine," he assured her, and really he did feel fine, although all this movement was beginning to make his head ache again. Ignoring it, he added, "Besides, I wish to take some of the dower I received on our marriage and go out in search of livestock and more servants. Osgoode and I are riding to Carlisle in the hopes of finding what we need there."

"Carlisle?" she asked with amazement, following as he moved around the bed to collect his clothes from where they were folded and set on one of the chests. "But that is a day's ride away."

"Osgoode and I can cover the distance quickly on the way there, but will be slower coming back. I expect we shall be back the morning after next—or early afternoon at the latest," he assured her, tugging on his doublet. Pausing as he saw the grass stains and small holes in it from its use in rescuing him, he scowled, but then reached for his leggings.

"But, you cannot travel now. You sustained a terrible injury to your head," she repeated, trying to take the leggings from him. "You should rest another day at least. Pray, husband, get back into bed. I—"

"I am fine, Murie," he insisted firmly. "And this needs to be done."

She fell silent, no longer protesting, but not looking pleased, either. Finally, she said, "Please, at least promise me you shall be careful."

"Aye," he muttered, shifting his leggings in his hands. They had fared worse than his doublet and now had several large holes. Shaking his head, he donned the items, thinking he would have to go fetch clothes from the garrison and change into his other pair of leggings and the blue doublet that had been his father's; these were now ruined.

Finished dressing, Balan began to look around for his boots. He noticed his wife hurrying for the door and frowned. "Where are you going?"

"If you insist on making this journey, there are a few things I need to gather together for you," she announced as she reached the door. Pausing, she turned to peer at him worriedly. "You will not leave before I come back, will you? I will be as quick as I can."

"Come back from where?" Balan asked sharply, but she was already slipping through the door and pulling it closed.

Chapter Fifteen

"Where is my wife?" Balan shifted impatiently on his mount, his gaze moving around the bailey. When he did not spot her anywhere, he cursed under his breath and turned back to the keep as the doors opened. Rather than his wife, Anselm hurried out. Balan shouted, "Anselm! Have Godart and Erol not found my wife yet?"

"Nay, my lord. But I'm sure they will find her soon." The soldier came to stand by Balan's mount. The man's gaze shifted from Balan to Osgoode and back, and he said slowly, "Are you sure you will not take another man or two?"

"We have not another man to spare," he replied impatiently. Anselm had asked the question at least six times since learning of this trip, and Balan could not help noticing that while the man was not arguing the trek was needed, his concern seemed to be with Balan going alone with Osgoode. It would appear the soldier, like his wife, had suspicions where his cousin was concerned.

"Here she comes," Osgoode said, drawing Balan's gaze toward the gates. His wife hurried across the bailey toward him.

Balan frowned. "Where the devil is she coming from?"

Not expecting an answer, he turned his horse and quickly rode to his wife's side, scooping her up off the ground and settling her before him on his mount with one smooth action. She was apologizing before he could demand to know where she'd been.

"I am ever so sorry, husband," she said, digging around in the small bag she carried. "I did not intend to be so long, but I could not find a clover leaf. I mean, I could find a clover, but I wanted a four-leafed one. They are really the best, but ever so hard to find. And then, I had difficulty finding an even ash leaf, and once I did, I could not recall what you were to say as you picked it. I think it is, 'Even ash I do thee pluck, hoping thus to meet good luck. If no good luck I get from thee, I shall wish thee on the tree.' But I was not certain."

"Wife," Balan said the moment she paused to draw breath.

"Aye?" She stopped what she was doing to peer at him.

"Why are you sticking leaves and bits of twig in my clothing?" he asked with what he thought was a display of utmost patience.

"There is no need to yell, husband," Murie said, looking hurt. "These are all charms to bring you luck. This twig is from a birch tree. It is supposed to avert the evil eye and has protective powers. And this is elder to—"

Balan silenced her explanations with a kiss. She was

blessedly silent when it was over, except for a little sigh that slipped from her lips. It was enough to make him consider delaying the trip long enough to carry her up to their room and give her something to remember him by, but he resisted the temptation. Did he do that, he would never leave, and this trip was necessary.

In fact, it was more than necessary. The things he intended to get were needed desperately. But should he not get her out of his lap soon, Balan knew he was in danger of forsaking this trip. While her superstitions and insistence on sticking twigs and leaves and other charms in every hole and spot she could find was annoying, it warmed his heart that she cared so much about him and was doing the only thing she could think of to keep him safe while he was away.

Pressing a kiss to the top of her head, he bent to the side and set her on the ground at the foot of the stairs beside Anselm. Turning solemn eyes to the man, he ordered, "Look after her." His soldier nodded solemnly in return, and Balan started to turn his horse away.

"Oh! Wait, husband!" Murie cried, making him draw his horse to a halt and turn back. She rushed to his side.

"I forgot," she explained, grabbing his foot in the stirrup. She paused and began to work her mouth as if she had a bad taste in it. Balan was about to ask what she'd forgotten, when she nodded with apparent satisfaction and . . . spat on him.

Balan simply stared with disbelief. It was Osgoode who asked what he could not.

"Er . . . Murie? Did you just spit on Balan?" his cousin asked. Anselm rushed forward, eyes wide with horror.

"Aye." Murie beamed at them as if it were the most

natural thing in the world. " 'Tis good luck to spit on someone before they take a journey. 'Twill protect them and bring them good fortune," she explained. She asked Osgoode, "Would you like me to spit on you, too?"

"Nay!" the man said quickly through laughter. Then he asked, "Did you ever spit on the king before a journey?"

"Nay," she confessed. "But I am sure the queen did. I did once tell her about the custom, and she seemed most interested."

"Murie," Balan said as Osgoode burst into more laughter.

"Aye, husband?"

"Come here."

Her eyes suddenly wary, she hesitated, but then moved closer. Bending to the side, Balan lifted her up again, pressed a quick hard kiss to her lips and whispered, "I love you." He then quickly set her back down, turned his mount toward the gates and set out. He cast one quick glance back before riding out of the bailey, saw that his wife still stood where he'd set her, a stunned look on her face.

"I got the feeling that Anselm was none too pleased that I would be going with you on this trip," Osgoode commented as they crossed the drawbridge. When Balan did not comment, his cousin added, "You do not think he suspects me of knocking you into the river?"

"I do not know. He has not said anything," Balan answered with a shrug. But he added, "Murie does."

"What?" Osgood glanced over with a start. "Never say she does. How could she suspect me?"

Balan shrugged again and pointed out, "You suspected her."

"Aye, but that was different."

"Of course it was," Balan said with amusement. Then he spurred his horse into a run. He did not wish to speak; he wanted to think on his wife and all the things he would do to her in their bed when he got home.

It was Cecily entering the room that woke Murie. Blinking open sleepy eyes, she saw the maid move quietly to her chest and sort through her clothes until she settled on Murie's favorite, a burgundy gown and black surcoat. Murie's eyes drifted shut as the maid closed the chest again. She'd been working terribly hard these last two days and had exhausted herself. She wished for just a couple more minutes sleep.

The moment her husband left the bailey, Murie had rounded up every available person at Gaynor and set to work. That first day they'd taken down all the tapestries and other decorations in the great hall and beaten or soaked them clean; then they'd whitewashed the walls, removed all the nasty old rushes and replaced them with fresh new rushes before hanging the tapestries and decorations back in their places. Everyone had been exhausted when they'd finally sought their beds for the night. But they'd also been back at it bright and early the next morning. Murie wasn't sure if it was pride fueling their efforts to make the castle look at least almost as impressive as it used to for the arrival of the new servants her husband was bringing back, or the prospect of the more varied diet that was ensured by the livestock he was also fetching.

That second morning, Murie had set them to work on several different projects. Some she'd sent to the kitchens to help prepare for Balan's return, but Clement had kept the kitchens in such good repair that few were needed there. The rest she set to work on the upper floor. She'd asked Anselm who among the men knew something about carpentry, then had sent the four he named to cut down trees and build a new bed frame. She'd set several others to making a new straw mattress for both their bed and Juliana's, and the remainder of people to work in the hall and the guest rooms, cleaning and scrubbing and righting what they could.

Despite working well into the night, the men had not yet finished making the bed when she'd retired, though they'd promised to have it done today. The mattresses were done, however, as well as most of the cleaning. Today Murie planned to have new shutters made for the windows and to have Cecily go with Gatty's daughters to collect more fresh rushes for the upper rooms. She would also set several men to repairing or rebuilding pens for the animals her husband was bringing back, while she herself worked on the gardens. Clement had done his best to keep up with that as well as the kitchens, but he was only one man.

Sudden sunlight pouring over her face brought Murie's eyes open with a start. Cecily had removed the fur from the window directly across from the bed, making it clear that her few more minutes of sleep were now done. It was time to rise and start the day. Her husband returned today.

The thought brought a grin to her face, and Murie scrambled up off the straw mattress, full of pep and vigor.

"Good morning, Cecily. Today is a fine day, is it not?" she said happily, her gaze sliding to the bright sunny sky outside the window.

"Aye, my lady. A fine day," Cecily agreed with a smile, handing her a small bit of linen to wash herself.

Accepting it, Murie moved to the basin of water, stripped off her undertunic and began.

"So, what tasks have you decided to set us to today?"

Cecily asked, moving to collect the gown and surcoat laid out on the chest. "Scrubbing the outside of the castle walls, mayhap?"

Murie wrinkled her nose and assured her, "You shall have a much easier task today. We need new rushes for the other rooms above stairs. I thought you and Gatty's daughters could go collect them. 'Twill give you a chance to lounge about and giggle without my snapping at you all to get back to work." She finished with the linen and rose water, and turned to accept the green gown Cecily held out.

"And what shall you be doing?" Cecily asked as Murie donned the gown.

"Working in the garden, I think," Murie answered. She tugged the gown into place and reached for the surcoat. "It has grown over quite badly with no one to tend it. I thought to weed and see what is usable and what is not. Some of the herbs will still be usable and can be dried for use in winter, but not for much longer. The sooner I start that the better; else we will be either eating tasteless, unseasoned dishes or purchasing herbs at an exorbitant price."

"Aye." Cecily nodded, moving behind her and setting to work on her hair. "But even unseasoned beef and chicken would be welcome rather than fish three times a day."

Murie wrinkled her nose in agreement. The boar had gone quickly, and they'd returned to their diet of fish. After just two days, Murie felt sure she could happily skip ever eating fish again.

"There you are," Cecily said as she got the last of the tangles out of Murie's hair. "Do you wish me to collect Gatty's daughters and head out straight away to search for more rushes, or is there something else you want done first?"

"Nay, go on. You shall most like have to make several trips with just the three of you working, and I would have it done ere Balan returns. Best to start right away."

"He should not be back ere sup, should he?" Cecily asked. She collected the scented water and damp linen.

"He thought closer to noon—or even earlier," Murie replied, looking for her leather pattens. She'd kicked the shoes off before crawling into bed last night, she thought, but they were not by the bedside. "He hoped to finish his business in Carlisle by early yesterday afternoon and travel halfway back, then camp and finish the journey home this morning."

"We had best get moving then," Cecily said, heading for the door.

"Aye," Murie agreed, relieved to spot her pattens. She pulled them on, hurried out of the room and rushed below stairs.

It was the same pattern for much of the day: Murie and everyone else rushed around trying to get everything done. She herself spent most of the time in the garden, but was constantly interrupted by questions. The men Anselm had set to the task of building pens came to ask how big they should make them and where exactly she wished them to go. Murie had to look at where the old pens sat rotting and to make suggestions that they pretty much ignored: They decided for themselves what to do in an open debate.

Rolling her eyes at the men, she'd returned to the garden, only to be interrupted when the men working on the bed came to tell her it was done and in the bedchamber. Of course, she'd had to stop what she was doing to rush up and inspect and praise their efforts. Then Cecily and the girls came to inform her that Juliana's room now had a new carpet of rushes. Murie had praised them for working so quickly and sent them off to find more for the other rooms above stairs. And then one of the men working on the new shutters had approached to show her what they had come up with and to ask if it would do, so that they could make the rest of them. Murie had praised the design and sent him on his way with a little sigh, hoping that she could at least get a quarter of the garden done before her husband returned.

By the time Anselm approached, Murie was growing quite short-tempered, and her voice was a tad sharp as she glanced up from where she knelt. "Aye? What now?"

The man-at-arms raised his eyebrows, but he merely said, "Company has arrived. 'Tis Lord Aldous."

Murie sat back on her heels. "Alone?"

"Nay. He has Baxley with him."

"Baxley?" Murie echoed.

"He is supposed to be Lord Aldous's servant, but is really kept around to protect him in case there is trouble. Malculinus takes him everywhere. Although, perhaps it was not necessary the man stick close at court."

Murie shrugged with disinterest. "Tell him I am too busy to see him."

"Do you think that is wise, my lady?"

She'd started to bend back to her weeds, but paused at the question. Eyebrows rising, she asked, "What do you mean?"

"Well, it occurred to me you might be able to learn something that would give us a better idea if Malculinus is behind these attacks on his lordship," Anselm said slowly. "He may let something slip, or at the very least his behavior toward you may tell us whether he has hopes of marrying you should his lordship die."

Murie hesitated. She really had no desire to even look at the man, let alone speak to him, and she had so much work to do. But if Malculinus were behind the attacks on her husband . . .

"Aye," she agreed, getting stiffly to her feet. "I shall see what I can find out."

Anselm nodded encouragingly. "I shall stay close by, in case there is trouble."

"Thank you," she said, though she doubted Lord Aldous would openly cause trouble at Gaynor. He seemed to prefer sneaky, behind-the-back methods of getting what he wanted.

"Lady Murie!" Malculinus stood and greeted her with a smile when she entered the great hall. "You have done wonders with the castle. It almost appears livable again. It had really gone to ruin since the plague."

"Thank you, my lord," Murie said stiffly as she approached the table, for truly, that was about the most backhanded compliment she'd ever received. It "almost appeared livable"? It looked bloody lovely to her eyes. Irritated, she turned her gaze to the man with Malculinus and felt her eyes narrow. Anselm had said Malculinus took Baxley with him everywhere, but she hadn't recalled him hanging about Malculinus at court. She had assumed he hadn't needed his services there. Still, the man did look familiar. He was tall and more slender than she would have expected in a body-guard, and his hair was a strawberry blond. She was trying to sort out where she'd seen him when Malculinus took her hand and pressed a kiss to it.

"You are more than welcome," Malculinus assured her, peering up from where he bent over her hand, his lips still touching it and moving against her skin. "And more than welcome at Castle Aldous anytime. In fact, I was just telling Baxley that I should be so lucky as to have a wife as industrious as yourself to grace my castle. Although, of course, you yourself would be preferred."

Murie blinked and snatched her hand away, trying to sort out whether he'd just said something terribly bold, or if she'd misunderstood completely. A glance in Anselm's direction suggested she'd not misunderstood. Malculinus had just openly claimed he would gladly take her to wife. The only problem was, she was already married.

As if reading her mind, Malculinus said, "Where is your husband? Not still sick in bed after his head wound, I hope? We did hear at Aldous of his misadventure, and I wished to come by and extend my condolences."

"Condolences are unnecessary. Balan is fine," she assured him grimly.

"Is he here then?"

Murie hesitated, unsure if telling the man where her husband was would be smart. If Malculinus were behind these attacks, he might arrange an ambush upon her husband's return. Although, she supposed that would be difficult on such short notice, and she need not say when he was returning.

"My husband is out at the moment," she answered, deciding upon caution.

Malculinus made a moue of disappointment. "I suppose we shall just have to enjoy your company alone then."

Murie very much suspected he would be the only one to enjoy the time. Still, she had to try to find out what she could and supposed she would have to be nice to do so.

"Would you care for a drink, my lord?" she asked. "Or something to eat?"

While the offer sounded polite and even friendly, Murie was aware of its punitive nature even as she spoke. Fish cakes and the rather vile ale they had at Gaynor would hardly be a treat for this man, who probably had a proper alewife with the proper ingredients to make the drink, as well as plenty of foodstuffs to make delectable treats.

"Fishcakes and bad ale?" Malculinus asked with a laugh. "Thank you, no."

Murie's eyes narrowed, but she simply said, "You seem to know quite a bit of what goes on at Gaynor, my lord."

"Aye." He smiled beatifically. "Your cook's sister is still at Aldous. Did you know?"

"Clement?" Murie asked with surprise. She hadn't realized he had family, but then, the cook wasn't the most talkative of men.

"Aye. His sister visits him quite frequently here at Gaynor, and I like to check with her and see how things are going from time to time. She was most relieved that Balan was going to find more help and livestock for his people. She was quite worried about her brother for a while."

Murie glanced quickly to the side, noting movement out of the corner of her eye. Anselm was heading for the kitchen, an expression like thunder on his face.

"Anselm," she called sharply, drawing him to a halt. He glanced back, and she shook her head. His mouth worked briefly, but then he returned to where he'd been, obviously not pleased that he could not go give Clement a telling off for speaking to his sister. But Murie would not allow it. She would speak to the cook later and tell him that Malculinus was pumping his sister for information, and then she would suggest that Balan offer the woman a job at Gaynor. She was not going to restrict the man from talking to his sibling, however.

To be honest, she very much doubted Clement had told his sister anything. The man was as grouchy as a scalded cat and silent as a stone at the best of times; she couldn't imagine that changing even with his sister. Murie suspected most of the information the woman had gained was simply by walking through the bailey on her way around to the kitchens and seeing the state of things. Or perhaps from Gatty's daughters. Estrelda and Livith were proving quite chatty.

As if her thinking of them brought them forward, the keep doors suddenly opened and Gatty's daughters and Cecily hurried in, their arms full of rushes. All three glanced curiously toward the table, and the guests and all three women did a double-take at Baxley. It made Murie glance toward the man again, and she realized what she'd completely missed the first time she'd looked. The man was extraordinarily handsome. The girls obviously thought so, too. They were craning their necks and likely to break them in a tumble down the stairs in their effort not to look away.

One of Gatty's daughters—the younger one, Estrelda—stumbled on a step. Dropping her burden, she grabbed for the rail in an effort to save herself. Cecily, following the girl up, immediately dropped her own pile of rushes to save Estrelda from tumbling back down the stairs. Fortunately, she managed. Releasing a little sigh of relief as the women bent to begin picking up the rushes, Murie started to shake her head and then turned sharply back to Malculinus. He'd grasped her hand.

"I hate to see you in such dire straits," he said, rubbing his thumb lightly over her fingers. "If there is anything I can do to help . . ."

Murie stiffened as his other hand suddenly ran lightly up her inner arm, brushing against her breast.

"Like you helped Lady Jane?" she asked coldly. There was just so much she would take in an effort to learn if Malculinus was behind these attacks. Besides, he wasn't likely to blurt a confession, and she already knew that he knew everything that went on here. She'd had quite enough of the man and had better things to do than waste time having him grope her.

"What do you know about Lady Jane?" he asked sharply.

Murie smiled. While they were playing chess the night before he left, Balan had told her what he and Osgoode had seen on St. Agnes Eve. She knew all about Malculinus's liaison with Lady Jane, and she thought the man was despicable. She had no doubt he'd convinced Lady Jane that he would marry her in order to get her into bed. Now the woman was caught in a terrible situation that would become a horrible scandal when everything came out, which it surely must do if she was pregnant.

A titter of sound drew her gaze back to the women on the stairs, and Murie frowned as she saw that Baxley was now there. The man was smiling and flirting and using every opportunity he could to touch both Estrelda and Cecily as he piled rushes back into their arms.

Like lord, like servant, she thought derisively, and watched in tense silence until the women continued on their way above stairs. Only then did she turn back to Malculinus. He'd been talking throughout her inattention, apparently oblivious of her disinterest. The moment he fell silent, she said, "I would appreciate it if you and your man would leave now, my lord. I have much to get done ere my husband returns and little enough time in which to do it. I cannot spend hours on company at the moment."

She saw fury in Lord Aldous's eyes, but then it was gone, hidden behind a wide, fake smile.

"Of course. How thoughtless of me. No doubt you shall work yourself to the bone trying to keep this place running," he said sweetly. Then he added archly, "We must hope you do not end up working yourself to the grave as well."

When Murie's only response was for her mouth to tighten and she resisted the urge to insult him back, Malculinus decided to get in a couple more blows. "I think the king made a mistake in allowing you to choose your own husband. You really have chosen poorly, Murie. While the plague greatly reduced the number of single lords out there, surely you could have found someone a little better set than this? Look at you. You were among the most beautiful at court, yet here you look no better than a filthy, common peasant. Oh, how the mighty do fall."

Murie clenched her fists, but she raised a hand to stop Anselm when she sensed him closing the distance between them. She could feel the anger vibrating off him at Malculinus's insult. Once he stopped, she merely asked Malculinus politely, "Are you quite finished?"

"Why? Are you going to cry for me, my little royal brat?"

Murie stiffened—more at the excited look in his eyes than the use of the old nickname. The man wanted her to cry. He would enjoy it if she did, and she suspected—unless she did something—Malculinus would probably stand there all day hurling insults at her to make it happen. Murie simply did not have time for that.

Without planning it out or even realizing she intended to do so, her right fist suddenly shot out, slamming into the man's nose. It hurt like the devil and her knuckles vibrated with pain, but the satisfaction of Malculinus holding a suddenly gushing nose and squealing like a little girl more than made up for it. Murie watched with a small smile as Baxley hurried the rest of the way to the trestle table and his lord's side. The man examined Lord Aldous's nose, pronounced it broken and then ripped a strip off his doublet to stop the blood. He then cast an uncertain frown Murie's way and shook his head, leading Malculinus to the keep doors. Apparently, he wasn't willing to attempt retribution.

Murie followed in their wake, aware that Anselm had moved to her side. She had no desire to have to speak to Malculinus again, but she did wish to be sure he left. She followed them outside and stood at the top of the stairs, watched as Baxley helped Malculinus onto his mount. He then took the reins and mounted his own horse, leading his master home like a child rather than a grown man suffering a bloodied nose.

"Well," Anselm murmured as they watched the pair ride out. "If Lord Aldous *was* the one behind the attacks because he hoped to marry you, I suspect they will end quite suddenly." Murie turned to peer at him, and he explained, "No man wants to marry a woman who can best him in a fight."

She smiled faintly, then shook her head and turned away. "I shall be in the garden should you need me."

"Aye, my lady," Anselm said. He added with a laugh, "And I shall be running around the castle checking on everyone's progress—and telling every last man what you just did. They will find it quite entertaining, I am sure. As will his lordship when he returns."

Murie did not bother to comment. She headed up
the stairs to pass through the keep and back to the garden. This time she got to work for quite a period before anyone interrupted. The sun was high in the sky,
suggesting it was time to break for the nooning meal
when she heard shouting.

"My lady!"

Murie straightened and peered up the path to see
Godart rushing toward her, excitement on his face.

"His lordship has been sighted," he gasped as he
paused beside her. "They are riding up to the drawbridge now, and the men on the wall say there are six
cows, as many pigs and three wagons—one holding
what looks to be half a dozen servants, and the others
holding rolls of cloth and they think caged birds."

Smiling, Murie scrambled to her feet. Balan was home.

Yes, the servants and livestock were grand news, but
more important to her was the fact that Balan was
home. The man had said he loved her before leaving
and had left her gaping after him like a fish out of
water. Now it would be her turn. She would run out
to greet him by throwing her arms around his neck,
kissing him soundly and telling him that she loved
him, too.

Laughing with joy, she hurried up the path with Godart on her heels and rushed through the kitchen, the
great hall and finally out onto the keep steps. In her
excitement, Murie didn't notice that the kitchen and
great hall were empty, but they must have been, for
every single inhabitant of Gaynor was already at the
bottom of the steps waiting when she stepped outside.

Smiling at their excitement, she tripped lightly
down the stairs to wait with them just as the traveling
party rolled through the gate. They all watched impatiently as the small convoy made its way across the bai-

ley before finally coming to a halt. Everyone began to converge on the wagons at once.

Thibault rushed to greet the new servants and welcome them to Gaynor almost as effusively as he'd greeted Murie.

Clement and Habbie went straight to the animals, examining the cows and exclaiming over two of them being milking cows, then moving to peer at the chickens, licking their lips the whole while.

Gatty rushed to the wagon with the rolls of cloth, Juliana and Frederick trailing her. She cried out with excitement that they could make new clothes. Her daughters would be ecstatic when they returned with Cecily from collecting rushes, she said, teary-eyed as she examined the cloth and noted aloud that there wasn't one roll even close to the color brown.

The soldiers and other men were also gathered around the wagon with the cloth, but their interest was caught by the barrels of ale and mead on board. Truly, every last one looked as if he might cry for joy.

While the others gathered around, chattering excitedly, Murie and Anselm remained where they were, both frowning. They looked over the party. There were two mounted men with the wagons, but they were not her husband and Osgoode.

"Where is my husband?" Murie asked with confusion, uncaring about the servants and livestock her husband had managed to find. Her gaze slid back to the armed soldiers and she frowned. "And who are these men?"

"Did you say your husband?" one of the men asked with surprise. "Did you mean Osgoode?"

"Nay. *Balan*," Murie said. "I am Lady Gaynor. Who are you?"

"We were hired by your husband to help guard the

wagons on the way back from Carlisle," the soldier answered slowly. Then he said, "How did you get back to the keep so quickly?"

Murie peered at him with confusion. "What are you talking about? I have been here at the keep all day . . . working in the gardens."

When the two soldiers exchanged a glance, Murie felt alarm clutch at her. Something was wrong.

"Where is my husband?" she asked again, demanding this time.

"He is in the village below, outside the gates. Osgoode said he saw Lord Balan's wife in one of the cottages. There was smoke coming from the chimney. Lord Gaynor ordered us to continue on to the castle with the wagons, and the two rode for the village to find you."

Murie's gaze shot to Anselm's in alarm, which she saw mirrored on his weathered face. "I shall fetch some men and look into it," he assured her, and he rushed off toward the stables.

Murie watched the man-at-arms go, her mind in an uproar. She was positive this was somehow another attempt on her husband's life and had no time to wait for horses or Anselm to round up men to check. Her gaze swung back to the armed guards who were now dismounting. Moving quickly forward, Murie snatched the reins from the nearest man's unsuspecting hands and clambered atop his mount's back.

"Hey! That's my horse!" the man cried, moving to stop her, but Murie was not willing to be stopped. Pulling hard on the reins, she turned the animal toward the gates and dug in her heels. The horse was very responsive and charged forward at once.

Murie heard the shouts and commotion behind her but did not slow. Her husband needed her.

Chapter Sixteen

"Are you sure it was Murie?" Balan asked as they rode toward the row of empty buildings that made up the village. They'd waited at the bend where the road to the castle split off toward the village to be sure the wagon train made it to the drawbridge unmolested before continuing on to meet his wife. It had been a relatively short but hard journey, and he'd spent too much money for very little return to risk bandits, or even the armed guards he'd paid to accompany them, running off with either the servants he'd managed to hire or the items he'd purchased—even for the sake of meeting his wife.

"Aye. She had on that black and burgundy gown she favors," Osgoode answered, but he was frowning as he added, "I wonder why she is in the village? You do not think she believed we would be putting the servants up there, do you?"

Balan frowned at the suggestion. It had never occurred to him that she might make such an assumption. In fact, it had never occurred to him to put up the new servants in the village, but that was a perfectly fine idea. It was close enough that they could walk up in the mornings to attend their duties, as well as walk home at night when they were finished. But at the same time, they'd have their own homes, with their own bit of gardens to work come spring. That might prevent their being lured away by another lord.

It also would have the added benefit of preventing the village from falling into complete ruin.

Balan smiled to himself and shook his head. Wasn't his wife a clever puss to think of such a thing?

"Or mayhap she arranged a special welcome home for you after your journey," Osgoode suggested with a grin. "Mayhap she has a picnic set out by a cozy little fire for the two of you."

"Oh, aye." Balan chuckled. "Fish cakes and rotten ale, in a cottage filthy with neglect and us sweltering from a fire that is not needed on such a fine day."

"You are right, cousin," Osgoode agreed with a frown. "It is far too warm today to be bothered with a fire. Whatever can she be doing in there?"

Balan shook his head, beginning to frown as he pondered. Why would she have a fire going in the cottage?

"Perhaps she is burning something sweet smelling to remove a bad stench," Osgoode suggested. He was silent for a moment before offering with amusement, "Or perhaps it is another one of her superstitions."

Balan grimaced. His wife did seem to have far too many superstitions: It was something he would have to work on. He would not have Murie going around throwing herself to the ground every time a cuckoo called or worrying that something ill was going to happen every time a curlew sang.

"I hope she has got past the ridiculous idea that I

am trying to kill you," Osgoode said suddenly, drawing Balan's attention.

He peered at his cousin curiously. "Have you ever considered it?"

"What? Killing you?" Osgoode asked, looking shocked.

Balan shrugged. "You *would* inherit everything."

Osgoode burst out laughing. "Oh, aye. I would inherit a castle with fields full of rotting vegetation, no coins to repair it and too few servants to work it—and all the headaches involved in returning it to some semblance of its former glory. Delightful! Let me just find my dagger, Balan, and I shall gut you where you sit."

Balan smiled faintly. "'Tis not so bad. 'Twill be a year or two of hard work and expense, but then we should be fine."

"Aye, but you have Murie and her dower to help. Both equally valuable I think."

"Nay," Balan assured him. "The dower is useful and will help Gaynor recover more quickly, but Murie is definitely more valuable."

He was aware of the way Osgoode stared at him, but was still unprepared when the man said, "You love her!"

Balan nodded solemnly, not willing to deny it.

Osgoode smiled and then began to laugh.

"What is so funny?" Balan asked.

"I was just recalling how you squawked at the very idea of marrying her when I first suggested it. What was it you said . . . ?" He tipped his head back and peered at the sky thoughtfully. "Oh, yes, I believe your response was, 'You are quite mad if you think I would even momentarily consider marrying the king's spoiled goddaughter.'" He grinned at Balan and taunted, "I must be quite mad indeed."

"Oh, all right, have your fun," Balan muttered. Then he grinned and added, "But I have Murie."

"Aye, you do," Osgoode said, sobering. "And you are most fortunate to have her. I hope I am so fortunate one day."

Now it was Balan's turn to grin. Eyes sparking with deviltry he said, "Mayhap I can help you with that. Murie may know one or two ladies at court with a home and demesne of their own for you to rule."

Osgoode gave a quick laugh. "Oh, dear Lord, do not even say it!"

"Why not?" Balan asked with amusement.

"Hmph. I would not marry one of those highbrow witches. Murie is the absolute only female at court who did not sneer at our garb. Well, aside from Lady Emilie, but she is already married to Reynard." Osgoode shook his head. "Nay, I am too young to settle down. Besides, you would miss me here."

"Aye, I would," Balan acknowledged. He and his cousin had been knocking about together since they were very young children. In truth, he could not recall a time when Osgoode hadn't been there, watching his back or getting him into trouble. He would miss him, but he knew the day was coming when his cousin would wish for a wife and home of his own. Balan would be sad to see him go, but happy for him as well when that day came. A smile on his lips, he said, "You could always marry Lauda. That way, you would have a wife and home of your own and still remain close by. We would be neighbors."

"And have Malculinus for a brother-in-law?" he asked with horror.

"If that is your only protest, we could always find an excuse to challenge the man and kill him," Balan said with a laugh.

Osgoode started to shake his head and then paused,

his gaze dead ahead. "That does not look like a hearth fire to me, Balan."

Balan glanced at the buildings ahead, eyes widening with alarm when he saw smoke coming through the door of the largest cottage. It had been the blacksmith's home before the plague hit, but that man and his family were among the first claimed by the plague, and it had been empty ever since.

"That is not where you saw Murie?" he asked with dread.

"Aye," Osgoode muttered, concern marring his own brow.

Balan cursed and put his spurs to his mount, crossing the remaining distance at full speed. "Murie!" he shouted as he drew the animal to a halt a safe distance from the cottage. "Murie?"

As Osgoode drew up, Balan dismounted and headed for the door. Smoke was billowing out in a constant, dark, noxious stream, and he could not imagine what was burning.

"It smells like she is burning some of those twigs and herbs she likes to collect," Osgoode gasped, running to catch up.

"Aye. Cover your nose and mouth with your doublet," Balan suggested, and did so himself as he hurried inside.

The smoke billowing out the door was nothing compared to that caught inside the cottage: a dark, heavy cloud obscured his ability to see.

"Murie!" he shouted, stumbling into furniture.

"Murie!" Osgoode shouted right behind him, then cursed. "I cannot see a damned thing."

"Neither can I," Balan admitted. He bent at the waist, wracked by a violent cough. Despite the cloth over his face, smoke was getting through and choking him.

"She could not possibly be conscious in all this smoke, Balan," Osgoode said anxiously. He was coughing violently himself.

"I shall look for her; you go back outside," Balan ordered, dropping to his knees to feel around the floor. If she were not conscious, she would be on the ground.

"Where have you gone?" Osgoode's voice sounded alarmed, directly above him. The man was nearly standing on him. "I cannot even see you anymore."

"I am down here. 'Tis less smoky by the ground." Balan began to crawl toward the back of the cottage in an awkward three-limbed maneuver, trying to hold the cloth of his shirt to his face while moving.

The building was smaller when it was first built, but the blacksmith had grown prosperous from his work for Balan's father and added on, making the cottage two rooms. The second was where the smoke seemed to be originating. It was darkest in that area, and Balan feared where he found the fire would be where he found his wife.

Hearing Osgoode coughing violently again, Balan snapped, "Get outside!"

"Nay!" his cousin snapped right back. "I am helping you."

"Then get on the floor at least," he said shortly. "You will be little help if I have to carry you out as well as my wife. Murie!"

He paused to cough up some of the choking fumes he'd inhaled as he spoke, then felt something bump against his hip. His cousin had listened and joined him on the floor he realized with a grunt of satisfaction.

"I think she must be in the back room," Osgoode gasped, crawling up beside him.

"Aye," Balan agreed, not bothering to mention that

he'd already thought of that, which was why he was headed that way. They worked their way the last couple of feet in silence, moving as quickly as they could until they reached the wall. It had been years since Balan was in the cottage, and the smoke made it difficult to judge the arrangement of everything, but he thought the door was to their left. He began to move that way on his knees, one hand holding the cloth over his face, the other feeling along the wall in hopes of finding the door. Balan knew he'd found it when he felt the heat under his hand. It was almost as hot as a poker.

Cursing deep in his throat, he moved around to the side and grabbed Osgoode's arm to drag him that way as well; then he reached up and pulled open the door.

Fire roared out like an animal, lashing above their heads in a stream of hot fury. Had they been in front of the door when it opened, it surely would have roasted them alive. As it was, Balan found himself gasping for breath and falling back, dragging Osgoode with him.

"She cannot be alive if she is in there," Osgoode said grimly as the flames died back. They could now see that the room beyond was fully aflame. It had been burning slowly before they opened the door, but the influx of oxygen had set it to a roar.

Balan was silent, his body completely still for several heartbeats. His wife was certainly dead if she had been in there, but he was suddenly quite sure she was not. None of this made sense. There was no reason for her to be at the village when there was so much to be done at the castle. And why would she have waved from the door and then come inside a burning cottage. Nay, his wife was not here, and he was a fool.

"Get out!" he shouted, turning and pushing Osgoode before him. " 'Tis a trap! Get out!"

Even as he began to herd Osgoode back across the floor, he saw the white square of smoke that was the front door begin to narrow.

Roaring in fury, Balan lunged to his feet to make a run for the opening, but it slammed shut seconds before he crashed against it. Cursing and choking, he shoved at the door, threw his weight forward, but sagged weakly against it as his lungs seized up and he began another coughing fit. He felt Osgoode tugging at his arm and allowed his cousin to pull him back to the floor, where the air was a little less polluted.

"There was no smoke coming out of the windows," Osgoode gasped, realizing what they should have noted on their approach.

"They were boarded up," Balan said once he had breath back. He'd noted that on the periphery of his consciousness as they rode up, but had paid it little attention, his concern with his wife and why she was in the cottage.

" 'Twas a trap," Osgoode repeated on the heels of another coughing fit. "And we walked right into it."

Ran, Balan corrected. They'd run right into it like fools. But he did not say so aloud; the more they talked, the more smoke they inhaled.

Leaning his back against the door, he peered around the room. He couldn't see anything in all this smoke, but he was trying to recall the cottage in his mind's eye, trying to place where the windows were, or what might be available to use to break down the door.

"I bumped into a table while still standing. It seemed heavy—solid oak, I think. If we rammed the door with it, we might be able to break it down," Osgoode panted.

"Aye," Balan agreed, thinking it worth a try.

The two men crawled silently away from the door,

finding the table easily. It was indeed solid and heavy. They turned it on its side and each knelt by its legs; Osgoode at the back and Balan at the front, staying as close to the floor as possible until they had to rise and charge forward.

"I will count to three," Balan said. "At three, take a deep breath and then stand and charge the door."

Osgoode's answer was another coughing fit. Balan started to count, had to pause at two to cough, then gritted his teeth and shouted, "Three!"

He did not suck in a deep breath. Afraid he would fall into another coughing fit, he took as shallow a breath as he could, held it and rose up to charge. They had taken three steps and nearly reached the door when it was flung open and he heard Murie shout, "Husband!"

He tried to stop their forward momentum, but Osgoode had no idea what was before them and wasn't slowing. Balan shouted a warning to his wife, but it was too late. There was a cry of pain as they rammed into her, then the faint form he'd barely been able to see through the light gray smoke by the door disappeared under the table as they ran her over.

"You are not getting up."

Murie made a face at her scowling maid.

"I am fine, Cecily," she muttered, pushing the linens and furs away and slipping her feet off the bed.

"You are *not* fine," Cecily argued. "You got yourself run over by two men and a table."

"Two men with a table bumped into me and knocked me to the ground," she corrected with exasperation. "All I have is a little lump on the head."

"Catty had to stitch you up," her maid reminded her, as if she might have forgotten that painful experience. It had been more painful than gaining the injury itself.

In truth, Murie only had a vague recollection of the actual event. She'd raced that horse down to the village, left him by Balan and Osgoode's mounts, and rushed to the door of the cottage. It had been jammed shut, a heavy piece of wood stuck firmly into the dirt and wedged against it so well that it had taken some effort for her to remove it. She'd heard shouting inside as she'd worked at the wood, and also coughing. The shouting had reassured her at first, but the coughing that followed was so violent and deep and wretched that it had erased her relief and left her frantic to free her husband and his cousin from what could have been their fiery tomb.

Finally freeing the wood, she'd thrown the door open and called out as she started inside . . . and the next thing she knew, a great misshapen mass hurtled out of the smoke at her. Murie hadn't had time to even raise her hands in front of her, let alone step out of the way. One moment she was running forward; the next, the entire front of her body was vibrating with pain, and she was hurtling toward the ground.

Murie had been told that Balan and Osgoode had tossed the table aside and rushed to her at once. Her husband had lifted her in his arms, mounted his horse and ridden for the castle as if the devil were on his heels—though it was actually only Osgoode. The two men had passed Anselm and his soldiers on their way down to the village without even slowing to explain, but there'd apparently been little to explain. The head wound she'd received had bled copiously, and her face was covered in gore. Anselm and the men had turned at once to follow their lord to the keep.

According to Juliana, who'd told her that tale with

wide anxious eyes, once in the bailey everyone thought
Balan would ride his mount right up the keep stairs
and into the great hall to get her inside. Gatty had apparently been so sure of this that she'd rushed up
from the wagons to throw the keep doors open for
him. But he'd brought his mount to a rearing halt at
the foot of the steps and leapt off, shouting for Gatty
to follow as he raced up the stairs and past her into
the keep.

Gatty had been the one to sew Murie up. Juliana
had informed her that she'd had to be cleaned up just
to find the wound. According to the child, she had
been awash in blood, her face almost unrecognizable.

That was where the narrative of events had ended,
however. There was no need for her to tell more. The
stinging pain of the needle in the thin skin of her forehead had roused Murie from unconsciousness and
brought her back to screaming life. Balan had been
holding her at the time, and had simply kept her still
and murmured soothing words as Gatty finished the
job. He hadn't really needed to hold her after the first
few seconds, as she'd regained her wits and realized
what was happening, but he'd done so anyway. While
Murie had been feeling weak and trembly by the end
of the ordeal, Balan had actually been gray-faced and
sick-looking, and had muttered an excuse, then fled
the room the moment it was done.

Murie had hardly noticed. Gatty had been busy
helping her to remove her gown and settling her into
the bed, and she'd been distracted as both her body
and head protested any movement.

While her head was the only bleeding wound,
bruises were beginning to form down the front of
her chest to her thighs where the table had struck
her. She was going to be extremely sore soon if did

she not keep moving. That was the only way she knew to ease pain—movement, so muscles didn't get the chance to stiffen and set. This was part of the reason she was now getting up despite Cecily's scowls and growls. The other part was that she'd had plans for her husband's return. She'd intended to greet him with the joyful news that she loved him. The incident at the village had rather ruined that, and she silently cursed her husband's attacker to hell for it.

"My lady, please," Cecily begged. "His lordship shall no doubt blame me for your being up, and then—"

"Guilt will not work either, Cecily," Murie said mildly, managing not to wince as she gained her feet and her body protested. The maid had been with her for ten years. It was Cecily who'd had the unenviable task of tending Murie when she was ill since her parents' death, and she'd tried many different ways to keep her abed through flus and colds and various other childhood ailments. None of them had ever worked, but the woman kept trying.

"Why do you not get back in bed and let me fetch you some of the ale his lordship brought back from Carlisle?" Cecily said. "It may ease your aching head."

"Bribery will not work either," Murie assured her. "Only time will cure the aching in my head."

She moved to the chest to find some clothes, determined not to show how weak she really felt by asking the maid to fetch them. While she'd not felt bad other than aches and pains in bed, now that she was up, her head was showing a distressing tendency to spin on her neck . . . either that, or the room was doing the spinning. But she felt sure Cecily would have mentioned the fact if it were, so she knew it must be her head.

"You are the most obstinate woman I know," Cecily

announced with irritation. She rushed over to grab her mistress by the arm to steady her.

"Aye," Murie agreed easily. She supposed she must have been swaying, for the woman to think she needed support. Shrugging inwardly, she allowed Cecily to help her kneel by the chest, then sat back as the maid began to sift through the clothing inside.

"What do you wish to wear?" the woman asked, still sounding annoyed.

"It matters little," Murie said. "Whatever is clean and available."

"Hmph. The maid pulled out a pale cream gown and brown surcoat to go over it. "You cannot work in this gown without ruining it, so at least I know you will not be able to be *that* foolish."

Murie bit her lip, but did not ask her to choose something else. She really wasn't feeling up to working. She just did not wish to be trapped in the chamber all day like an invalid. Whether she was one or not.

Cecily alternated between muttering under her breath about Murie's obstinacy and lecturing that she wasn't to do anything more strenuous than sitting at the trestle tables below as she helped Murie dress. She then insisted on helping her out of the room and down the stairs, so that she wouldn't "go faint and tumble down the stairs and break her neck."

Murie felt so weak and unsteady that she didn't argue. Truly, she was beginning to think getting out of bed had been a poor idea by the time Cecily saw her settled at the trestle table. Of course, she was too proud to say so to the maid and simply promised to remain where she was so the woman could return above stairs and retrieve the gown she'd been wearing to see if she could wash out the blood.

Murie watched Cecily go with affection, knowing

from experience that the maid would be muttering the entire time she walked upstairs, collected the gown, and no doubt would still be muttering even as she washed it.

Once the maid was out of sight, Murie peered around the empty great hall in search of something to distract herself. Unfortunately, there was no one and nothing there to keep her attention, and she soon found herself drumming her fingertips on the table and trying to think of something to do. There was plenty of mending she could turn her attention to. Balan's doublet and her gown and surcoat had taken a terrible beating the day she'd used them to make a litter and then dragged him back to the castle. His leggings were, unfortunately, beyond repair, but she might be able to mend the gown and doublet.

However, she hadn't thought to bring them down and had no intention of going up after them.

She peered around the hall again, then got carefully to her feet. When the room did not begin spinning as it had above stairs, she released a little sigh of relief and started toward the kitchens. Now that she had nothing to distract her, she was aware of a dry, bitter taste in her mouth, no doubt a result of both her head wound and the vile liquid Gatty had made her drink. A nice mug of some of that ale Cecily had mentioned sounded nice about now.

Moving at a sedate pace to keep the dizziness from returning, Murie had only crossed half the hall to the door when it opened. A woman she thought she'd seen on the wagon earlier in the day started to walk out, but paused abruptly at the sight of her and hurried back into the kitchens. A moment later, the door swung open once more and Clement was striding toward her, his expression the grimmest she'd yet seen. Thibault was hard on his heels, wringing his hands agitatedly as they hurried to her side.

Clement did not even speak. His mouth merely tightened, and he caught her arm, turned Murie and walked her firmly back to the trestle tables.

"You should not be out of bed," he said once he had her seated.

"Perhaps not," Murie allowed. "But—"

"There are no buts," Clement informed her. "You took a terrible blow to the head. You scared us all silly, and if you had any sense at all, you would be tucked up in your bed allowing your body to recover."

Murie noticed Cecily hurrying down the stairs and into the kitchen, but most of her attention was on the man before her. No one had spoken to her in such a manner since her father's death. Not even the king, her godfather. There was both concern and fear on the man's face, and it made her feel cared for.

"He is right, my lady," Thibault agreed. "You lost a great deal of blood from the knock on your head and still look quite pale. I really think you should be back up in bed."

"Aye, but . . ." Murie hesitated as Clement arched an eyebrow. His expression seemed to suggest she had best have a good excuse, so she let her breath out on a sigh and admitted, "I was hoping to have some of the ale my husband brought back from Carlisle and perhaps something to eat."

Apparently it was the right thing to say; the cook relaxed at once, but chided, "You should have sent someone to fetch it for you. I sacrificed one of the chickens to make soup, and it has been simmering these last two hours since you were injured. It could use more simmering, but should do well enough for now. 'Twill help you rebuild your strength." He turned back to head into the kitchens announcing, "I shall bring some out at once and some ale as well. See she stays seated, Thibault."

The steward watched him go, then settled on the bench beside Murie with a sigh.

"It will be delicious, my lady," he assured her sadly. "His lordship brought back some vegetables as well from Carlisle, and Clement makes the best soup in the county. The smell has been permeating the keep and driving me wild for the last hour at least, but he will not let any of us near. Not even to sample it for him. He insists it is for you and you alone." He smiled at her and added, "I think Clement likes you."

Murie raised her eyebrows in doubt. The man was rarely anything but short and surly with everyone, including herself. She found it hard to imagine he liked anyone. She asked, "What makes you say that? Because of the soup?"

"Nay. Because he said so," Thibault explained. "When his lordship learned that you had given suggestions on how better to set up the kitchens and had removed the parsley from his gardens without the man throwing a fit, he asked Clement why he would allow such with you when he'd had fits at the tiniest suggestions from his own father, and Clement said, 'Because I like your wife, my lord.'

"He did not care much for Lord Balan's father," the man went on. "He didn't like the way he neglected our Juliana. He is really very soft at heart, is our Clement. He seems tough and gruff, but I have seen him feeding birds and squirrels out in the garden. He is softer than he likes us to think."

"He is *not* softer than he likes you to think," Clement snapped behind them, making them both jump and turn to face him guiltily. The cook glared at

Thibault for a moment, then added, "I simply prefer squirrels and birds to people."

Murie bit her lip as Thibault's expression fell, then sat a little straighter when the cook turned to her.

"Your soup." He set the steaming bread bowl he carried on the table. " 'Tis not as flavorful as 'twill be later in the day, but I will have you eat every last drop. 'Tis good for you. Estrelda is bringing your ale and shall be here momentarily."

"Thank you." Murie inhaled the steam pouring off the thick soup. "It smells divine."

Nodding abruptly, Clement turned and made his way back to the kitchens.

Murie glanced at Thibault once the cook was gone and patted his hand reassuringly. "I am sure it is as you say and he is softer than he wants us to think."

"Aye." Thibault was cheered. "Did you see? I think he almost smiled when you said it smelled divine."

Murie chuckled.

"I should be about my business." Thibault got to his feet as Estrelda hurried out of the kitchens with her mug of ale. "Even with more servants, there is always something needing doing. Enjoy your soup."

Murie thanked him, and then thanked Estrelda, who set down her ale. She then turned her attention to her soup. Despite Clement's claim that it really needed to simmer longer to be fully flavored, it was the best soup she'd had in ages. It was rich and thick and full of chunks of meat and vegetables. It was more a stew than a soup, really, and Murie gobbled it up quickly and then even ate the juice-soaked, hollowed-out bread it had been served in. By the time she'd finished the last bit, she felt almost her old self again. And she was immediately ready to find something to do.

Her gaze slid around the great hall. Despite their

feverish work over the past two and a half days, there
was still much to be done, but much of it was likely to
ruin her gown and was probably too strenuous for her
at this point; but there was something she thought she
could manage. Something that would make the great
hall smell nice, as well as work as a protective charm.

Murie stood and waited a moment to be sure the
dizziness and weakness did not return. When they
didn't, she began to make her way toward the keep
doors. She would just take a nice leisurely walk around
the woods outside the castle and collect some birch
and clover to be strewn among the rushes in the hall.
Both were said to help avert bad luck. Elder too, she
thought. That was supposed to protect against fire.

Her steps slowed as she reached the doors. Should
anyone catch her leaving, they'd surely try to stop her
and most likely rush off to tattle to Balan. She needed
to be stealthy.

Easing the door open, she peered about, surprised
to see that the bailey was completely empty. It seemed
everyone was busy elsewhere, and if she were quick,
she might slip out of the keep and cross the bailey
without drawing attention. The men on the wall were
the only worry, but the surcoat she wore over her gown
was almost the same brown as the gowns Gatty and her
daughters wore. From the wall, they might mistake her
for one of Gatty's daughters . . . she hoped.

Smiling to herself, she slipped outside.

"There you are," Balan said as Clement, Cecily, Estrelda and Thibault hurried to join everyone else waiting on the wall.

"We are sorry, my lord," Thibault gasped as the
group came to a halt before him. "Lady Murie came
below in search of something to eat, and—"

"She is out of bed?" he asked with dismay.

"Aye, but she is just sitting at the trestle table eating the soup Clement made for her," the man rushed to assure him. "But that is why we are late. Clement got the soup and Estrelda fetched her some ale, and then we came out through the kitchen door and had to walk around to the wall the long way." He hesitated, then asked, "We did wonder if you wished her here as well, but—"

"Nay," Balan said, cutting him off. "She is the reason I called you all here."

"She is?" Anselm asked with amazement.

It was Gatty who asked, "Surely you are not thinking that she had anything to do with this latest attempt on your life, my lord?"

"Of course not," Balan snapped. "Why would you think so?"

"Because the last time we had a meeting up here on the wall like this, the two people we left out were the two we thought possible suspects," the woman explained.

"We had a meeting up here before?" Osgoode asked with surprise. Then his eyebrows flew up as he realized he was one of the two who had been left out. "You *all* thought I was trying to kill Balan?"

"And I," Cecily murmured quietly.

When everyone looked uncomfortable and avoided making eye contact with either the maid or his cousin, Balan said, "It does not matter. And I did not call this meeting to talk about whoever is trying to kill me. This meeting is about my wife. I wanted to talk to you all at once so that I was sure absolutely everyone understood, including the men on the wall."

When they all nodded and peered at him attentively, he said, "I want my wife watched at all times. She is not to be alone for a moment. I want at least two men following her every moment of every day until my attacker is caught. But I also want the rest of you to keep an eye on her. Is that understood?"

There was a moment of silence, and then Anselm cleared his throat. "We understand, my lord, but the killer is after you, not your lady wife. She is perfectly safe."

"She is not perfectly safe," Balan countered. "She was—"

"My lord," Erol tried to interrupt.

"Not now, Erol." Balan scowled and then continued, "She was nearly killed today trying to rescue me. And she was forced to drag me back to the castle on her own and naked after the attempt before that. 'Tis obvious—"

"But my lord," Erol tried again.

"Not now!" Balan snapped. "Where was I? Oh yes, 'tis obvious that so long as I am in danger, my wife is in danger, and I will not have it! I want her watched at all times. I will have her safe. Are there any questions?"

"Aye," Erol said, sounding a bit snappish himself. "Is that not your wife slipping off into the woods *alone*, while we stand here talking about guarding her?"

Balan stiffened, then whirled to peer over the wall. He saw his wife disappear into the woods. Cursing, he spun away and ran for the stairs.

Chapter Seventeen

Ash-keys and ash leaves were both considered lucky, but the best ash leaf was an even one—which is how Murie found herself up an ash tree when she first heard the sound of hoofbeats. Pausing in her hunt, she glanced down curiously, her eyes widening as her husband charged past on Lightning.

He was riding quickly, and looking rather upset, she noted, and decided not to trouble him by calling out. Obviously the chore he was on was an important one. Besides, she had no doubt he'd have fits if he knew she was climbing trees so soon after an injury.

The moment the sound of hoofbeats faded, Murie turned her attention back to the leaves around her. She'd just found an even leaf when she heard hoofbeats again. Letting go of the branch she was holding, she glanced down to see Balan charging by once more, this time headed in the opposite direction. She took a moment to wonder if he'd accomplished whatever chore he was on, then turned back to the branch where she'd spotted the even leaf moments ago. Of course, it had bounced back in amongst the other branches, and she could no longer tell which one it was.

Muttering under her breath, she began to examine each leaf of each branch again in search of the even leaf and had just found it when the sound of a charging horse drew her attention once more.

This time, unwilling to lose the leaf, Murie tugged it free before glancing down. Her husband charged past once more. Wondering what on earth he was doing, she shook her head as he disappeared into the woods, then quickly climbed down from the tree, collecting some ash-keys as she went.

She was on the ground before it occurred to her to wonder where his guard was. One man was supposed to be watching him at all times—either Erol or Godart. She would have to have a stern talking-to with the men when she got back to the castle. Her husband should not be out on his own. His would-be killer had only narrowly failed several times now, and they would not continue to be so lucky.

She pondered the last attempt as she made her way to the large clearing with clover she'd spotted, wondering why Osgoode had thought it was her in the village earlier that day. Had it been a woman who lured the two cousins? She found it hard to believe it was a coincidence that Malculinus and his henchman had been at Gaynor not long before this latest attack. On the other hand, Malculinus couldn't know when Balan was expected back . . . unless Cecily or Estrelda had mentioned it while Baxley was flirting with them.

She supposed that was possible. But Osgoode would hardly mistake either man for her. She'd have to ask him why he'd thought it was her.

Reaching the patch of clover, Murie tucked her precious ash leaf and keys carefully under the belt of her surcoat, wishing she'd thought to bring a basket, then dropped to her knees to begin her hunt for one of the four-leafed variety.

She was there moments later when the hoofbeats returned. Wishing she were still up the tree, Murie remained on her hands and knees in the clover patch, hoping her husband would not notice her and simply ride past. A foolish hope, she knew.

"Wife!"

Murie sat back on her haunches with resignation and peered around as Balan drew his mount to a halt in the clearing. He quickly dismounted. She smiled at her first sight of him, but then saw the scowl on his face and scowled in return, knowing he was annoyed with her.

Still, she watched him walk toward her and enjoyed it. He was a fine figure of a man—tall, well-built, muscles as sleek as a cat's moving under his clothing.

Despite how busy she'd kept herself, she'd missed him while he was gone, and the nights had been the worst. She'd lain awake long into the evenings recalling his touches and kisses and the pleasure he gave her. And she'd wondered if she gave him the same pleasure in return.

It was hard to imagine she might, not when he did all the touching and kissing, but Murie was unsure what to do herself. She'd run across men and women coupling at court, in dark hallways and corners: From that, she knew there were all sorts of ways to do it. But she'd also come across women on their knees, as she was now, doing unknown things to lords standing before them with looks of ecstasy on their faces. It had appeared to her as if the women were kissing or suckling on the man's shaft, but they'd been only a few quick glances she'd got before turning away with embarrassment and heading in another direction.

Murie had thought that on Balan's return she might ask him what the women were doing, and if he might like her to do it to him, but now, faced with the prospect, she was not sure she had the courage. Though, it would certainly be a distraction to make him forget he wished her back in bed recuperating.

"Wife." Balan came to a halt directly in front of where she knelt. He was still scowling, and she almost scowled herself, but managed a smile instead.

"Good afternoon, husband," she greeted. " 'Tis a lovely day for a ride. Are you on a chore?"

"Aye. Looking for you," he announced with irritation, propping his hands on his hips. "You should be in your bed."

"Bed is boring, husband," she said quietly. Then she added in a husky voice, "At least it is when you are not there."

That seemed to make him pause. He closed his mouth on whatever else he'd intended to say, his gaze flickering over where she knelt. Some of the anger slid from his expression. "Aye, well, that's as may be, but . . ."

"Husband?" Murie murmured when his voice trailed away. His eyes had caught on the neckline of her gown. Their positions gave him a lovely view down her top, she noted, glancing down, but the realization did not make her stand up. Instead, she reached out a hand to his upper leg as if to steady herself. The muscle under her fingers tensed.

"Aye?" he asked. His gaze slid over her once more.

For some reason her position seemed to fascinate Balan, and Murie wondered if it was suggesting certain activities to him. Like those activities she'd glimpsed at court.

She slid her hand tentatively up his legging until it disappeared under his doublet, and said, "I was wondering . . ."

"Aye?" he growled, but did not push her hand away. Murie moved it to the left until she felt his sex pressing against the gathered leather of his leggings. He was already semi-hard, but at her touch seemed to harden further, and she saw as well as heard him suck in a sharp breath.

"I was wondering if you would enjoy me doing the things to you that you do to me with your mouth," she whispered.

His eyes went wide, and his mouth opened and worked briefly with nothing coming out as she ran her hand slowly along the length of him through the bunched cloth. Taking that as a yes, Murie pushed up his doublet with her other hand. She found where the cloth of his leggings was gathered together, which she parted to allow him to spring free. The moment he did, Murie caught him in her hand. She stilled as her husband groaned. Glancing up, afraid she'd done something to hurt him—indeed, his eyes were closed, his face tight with what might have been pain, but it was also the expression he got when making love to her—she then ran her fingers gently over him, relaxing a bit when his hips bucked in response. She leaned forward to press a kiss to the tip, but curiosity got the better of her, and she ran her tongue up his length tasting him.

Balan's reaction was most encouraging, she decided, when he clasped his hands in her hair and groaned again. Recalling that the maids had seemed to suckle at the shaft, Murie held the base to keep him still and took him into her mouth, running her lips up as far as she could and then drawing away again. She hadn't a clue what she was doing and was judging her success or failure by his reactions, but as far as she could tell from the groans and moans issuing above her head, he seemed to be enjoying it; so she was quite startled when he suddenly pulled himself free, stopping her.

"Did I do something wrong, husband?" she asked with concern as he dropped to his knees.

His answer was to kiss her, his tongue thrusting into her mouth with purpose, and he urged her back onto the bed of clover and lay himself on top of her. Tearing his mouth from hers, he began to press kisses along her jaw and growled, "Where did you learn to do that?"

"Oh." She blushed. "I saw one of the maids at court doing it, and seeing as how I like it when you . . ." She paused and blushed as his head lifted and he peered at her. She rushed on with embarrassment: "I thought mayhap you would like it if I did the same for you, but I only caught a quick glimpse and was not at all sure how. Was I doing it right?" she asked anxiously.

"Aye," he growled, and kissed her again, his tongue thrusting in and forcing hers to duel. Murie slid her arms around his shoulders and kissed him back, moaning as he tweaked her nipple through the cloth and rubbed his upper thigh more firmly against the apex of hers. Then he shifted away, and she felt his hand slip beneath the hem of her skirt and ride up her inner leg.

Murie shifted her legs restlessly under the caress, her own response becoming more frantic as his hand ran along her upper thigh. She cried out into his mouth as his fingers reached her core, and suddenly his mouth was gone. She blinked her eyes open with confusion. He moved down her body, but she never got the chance to ask why; she had her answer when his head ducked beneath her skirt.

"Oh!" she cried out, clawing at the clover on each side of her as his lips moved over first one thigh and then the other. She felt his hands slide beneath her bottom to lift her as if he were about to bite into a quarter slice of melon, and his mouth settled on her, drawing another cry of pleasure from her throat.

Moaning, Murie twisted her head to the side and then blinked as she found herself staring at an elusive four-leaf clover not an inch before her eyes. Reaching out she grabbed it, then squeezed her hand tight closed around it, crushing the leaf as her husband set to work in earnest. Within moments she'd forgot all about the clover and had her eyes crushed shut as she twisted her head back and forth on the ground.

When her husband's teeth lightly grazed the core of her pleasure, her eyes popped open on a gasp, and she bucked against him; then she blinked as a droplet of water fell into her eye. When a second fell, she blinked again, her mind slowly registering that it was raining and apparently had been for some moments. Turning her eyes skyward, she noted dark, heavy storm clouds gathering overhead and caught her breath.

Murie instinctively reached down to find her husband and warn him, since he was under her skirt and would not realize it, but in the next moment she was clawing at the ground again as he slid a finger inside her, adding to the sensations already assaulting her. Murie wasn't aware she was making a long ululating sound until her body convulsed with pleasure and the noise became something of a shriek, echoing in the clearing.

Balan rose as she was still shuddering with pleasure and started to shift to his knees, but then paused and glanced skyward, his hands reaching out to the sides as he realized that, yes, indeed it was raining, and his wife hadn't said a thing and now lay half soaked and trembling.

Murie heard him chuckle; then he was scooping her up in his arms and running for the cover of the trees. She kissed his neck, his ear and anything else she could reach as they went, then happily opened her mouth for him when he turned his head to cover hers with his own.

Once under cover, he broke their kiss as he set her down on her own two feet. He then reached for her surcoat, lifted it off over her head and tossed it to the ground before bending to kiss her again and work at the lacings of her gown. Unwilling to be the only one undressed, Murie immediately set to work at the buttons of his doublet. She was working blindly, her eyes closed as he kissed her, but they shot open with a start as a crack of thunder sounded overhead.

Balan finished undoing her gown and immediately began to tug it off her shoulders and down her arms, forcing her hands to stop work on his clothing. Murie shivered as the gown pooled around her feet, leaving her naked in the storm-chilled breeze. Balan broke away to finish working the buttons of his doublet. He then shrugged it off. His boots and leggings soon followed the gown and doublet to the ground, and he drew her into his arms once more.

Murie sighed against his chest as his warm body encompassed hers, and then Balan bent to trail kisses down her throat. Moaning, she turned her head to the side to give him better access, but stilled as she caught the flash of lightning in the sky. Thunder rolled right behind it, and alarm claimed her. The storm was close.

Tugging free of Balan's hold, she grabbed his hand and turned to run through the trees, pulling him behind her. She thought she heard him ask where she was going, but another roll of thunder drowned out the question, and then they were at the tree she wanted. She'd spotted it earlier as she'd looked for an ash. Tugging him under the safety of its branches, she turned and threw her arms around him, seeking the warmth of his body again.

"What—?" Balan asked, glancing around with bewilderment, obviously not understanding why this tree would be better than the last.

" 'Tis an elder," she explained. " 'Tis safer. Lightning never strikes elders. 'Tis the wood they made the cross—"

Balan cut off her explanation with a kiss, his body herding hers against the tree. She could feel him still hard and hot against her thigh, and she sighed into his mouth, her breasts pressing eagerly against him. They kissed. His hands caught the soft orbs of her breasts and kneaded gently, and then he broke away to suckle at one as his hand slid between her legs. Finding her warm and wet for him, he left off her breast and kissed her again as he carried her down to the ground.

Murie felt the cool, dry earth beneath her back, and then his warm body pressed down on her, and he used a knee to urge her legs apart. She opened for him at once, clutching at his arms in anticipation and then arching and crying out as he entered her. All the excitement and passion he'd stirred earlier in the field of clover was immediately back, her body humming with eagerness and desire as she drew up her knees to cradle him, and she pressed her feet flat to the earth to be able to push upward and meet his thrusts.

The storm raged as they made love, their passion meeting nature's fury and surpassing it. Murie felt the familiar tension drawing tight within her, and then Balan caught her ankles and drew them up to hook them over his shoulders. He then leaned forward so that he rested against the backs of her legs and his hands were free to touch her. He squeezed and caressed her breasts, then continued to fondle with one hand while the other dropped lower to touch her again.

Murie cried out and covered his hand at her breast, clutching at it as her hips danced against him. Then the tension broke, a dam allowing the floodwaters to flow, and she screamed as her body convulsed. Balan thrust into her one more time, and then he cried out as well, his body stiffening against hers as he spilled his seed into her.

"The storm has passed."

"Mmmm," Murie murmured, and opened her eyes to see that the sky was now clearing and late afternoon sunshine was pouring down, though it wasn't reaching them where they lay under the elder tree. She turned to peer at her husband and offered a smile as she rested her chin on her hand on his chest. He'd rolled them so that he was on the bottom immediately after they'd finished making love, leaving her to rest in comfort above.

Balan smiled back, his hand lifting to catch and caress her bottom. Then his eyebrows drew together with concern. "You are cold."

"Only my back," she assured him with a grin. "My front is very warm indeed. You are better than a fire, husband."

He chuckled and sat up, forcing her to let her legs

slide to the side so that she sat up as well, straddling him, her body sliding over his. The surprise on his face told her there had been no intent behind the action, but now that they were in this position, his hands slid to her waist and he kissed her. Murie moaned into his mouth as she felt him grow hard against her.

"We need to dress," he muttered.

"Aye," she agreed, her fingers sliding over his shoulders, then scraping into his hair. Balan moaned as her nails dragged across his skull, and then both of them stiffened at the sound of a distant shout. They broke apart and peered at each other in dread.

"Was that Osgoode?" Murie asked.

Balan nodded slowly as a second shout sounded. He said, "And that sounds like Anselm. They must have worried when we did not return and started a search party once the storm ended."

Osgoode shouted again, this time sounding closer. Murie and Balan scrambled to their feet.

"Our clothes—they are still under the tree by the clover," Murie realized with alarm.

"Which way to that?" Balan asked, his mouth pulling into a frown as she glanced around uncertainly. The word was almost a warning growl: "Murie?"

"Do not 'Murie' me, my lord. It causes me distress, and I cannot think when distressed." Huffing out a breath, she tried to recall where the clover patch was from there, then pointed and said, "That direction, I think, husband."

"You think?" he squawked. There were at least six different voices shouting for them now, drawing closer all the time.

Ignoring his scowl, Murie headed in the direction she thought the clover patch lay, aware from the muttering that trailed her that her husband was following.

They had gone quite a ways, and she was beginning to think she'd chosen wrong when her husband suddenly grabbed her arm and pulled her behind a tree.

"Really, husband!" Murie said as his body covered hers. "I thought you wished to dress. We do not have time to—"

Balan silenced her by placing a hand over her mouth. Her eyes widened incredulously at the rude action, and then she became aware of the sound of hoofbeats drawing nearer until they seemed to be right on top of them.

"Balan! Murie!" she heard Osgoode shout somewhere behind her, and then the sound of hoofbeats began to fade again. The next shout sounded more distant.

Balan did not answer either call. He did, however, remove his hand from Murie's mouth, and he stepped away and gestured for her to continue.

Murie took his hand in hers and continued on. It seemed they had covered more ground in their run than she'd realized, for she was just about to stop and confess to Balan that she must have chosen the wrong direction when they broke out into the clearing where the patch of clover grew. Sighing in relief, Murie rushed toward the pile of clothes under the tree, but then glanced anxiously back toward Balan. The sound of hoofbeats began to grow again, this time sounding like more than one horse.

Balan cursed, tugged at her hand and dragged her to the side and behind a large bush on the edge of the clearing just moments before two horses broke through the trees. She and Balan watched through the leaves as Erol and Godart appeared and—quite unfortunately—decided to stop. It appeared everyone had been called out for the search.

"Where the hell have they got to?" Erol asked with bewilderment, sitting up straighter on his horse to peer around.

"Perhaps the killer has got them," Godart said unhappily. "Surely his lordship would have returned by now if not."

The two men began to debate the subject, and what would become of them if their lord and ladyship were gone, but Murie wasn't paying attention; she was peering about the clearing, wondering where Balan's horse was.

"Lightning is gone, husband," she whispered by his ear.

"Osgoode was pulling it behind him," Balan murmured back, his attention shifting from the two men in the clearing to the clothes on the ground under the tree behind and a little to the side of them.

"How did he not see our clothes?" Murie asked with surprise, but then supposed it was a foolish question. Erol and Godart hadn't yet noticed them. Somehow, thankfully, Osgoode has missed the garments as well.

Balan quickly disabused her of the notion. "He *did* see them, Murie. Do you not notice they are all in a nice little pile rather than strewn around the clearing as we left them?"

"But why did he take the horse and not the clothes?" she asked with confusion.

"No doubt, because he expected us to return for the clothes," he pointed out. "Osgoode piled them under the tree with my green doublet on top to make them less visible, then led my horse away so that none of the others would see him and stop to investigate the area. He did it so that we could return and dress," he explained. "My cousin was no doubt hoping to preserve your modesty."

"Oh." Murie sighed. She seemed to have little enough of it lately. It was just days ago that she'd been forced to walk back to the castle naked, dragging her unconscious husband on the makeshift litter. Now she was standing bare-arsed in the bushes.

"Wait here."

She glanced around sharply at that whisper to see Balan already moving away. Holding her breath, she watched him slink along the edge of the clearing, sometimes crouching behind trees, sometimes crawling behind bushes and once running from one tree trunk to another; but finally he made it to the tree where their clothes were. He paused behind the trunk, peered around at his men, and then, assured that they weren't looking, ducked quickly out to snatch up the pile of clothes and hurry back behind the tree.

Balan did not return at once but dressed very quickly, tugging on his doublet and then his leggings and tying them up before donning his boots. Then he paused and glanced toward Murie, and glanced toward the clearing and frowned. His expression made her examine the two men in the clearing as well, and she bit her lip when she saw that they were now facing the direction of the tree. There was no way Balan could sneak back without being seen.

Biting her lip, she glanced at her husband. The moment she did, he laid the clothes on the ground behind the tree, then straightened, pointed at his chest, then toward the two men in the clearing, then to her and finally at the clothes.

Murie didn't have a clue as to what he was trying to pantomime, but she didn't get a chance to clarify; Balan was already moving into the clearing.

"My lord!" Erol cried happily. "You are well!"

"Aye." Balan smiled as if he didn't have a care in the

world. It was only then that Murie became aware that his doublet was tucked into the back of his leggings. Groaning inwardly, she closed her eyes.

"My *wife* . . . will be along soon."

Murie's eyes popped open as Balan almost shouted that comment, and she peered out into the clearing to see that he'd moved past Erol and Godart, forcing them to maneuver their horses around to face him. Their backs were now to the part of the clearing where she was. Her gaze slid to Balan again, and he gestured for her to get moving and dress. She suspected he'd done it once already, and only said "wife" so emphatically when he'd realized she wasn't paying attention.

Murie began to move along the edge of the clearing, crouching here and crawling there as he'd done. This seemed to annoy her husband, however, and she noticed his hand gesturing impatiently for her to get a move on. He was doing his best to distract the men, and so it was probably safe to run straight over, naked as she was—but what if one of the men glanced over his shoulder?

"Is there something wrong with your hand, my lord?" Godart asked. "You keep flicking it about."

"Nay," Balan growled, and flicked it impatiently again.

Sighing, Murie gave up her crawling and made a straight run for the clothes. She'd nearly reached them when the sound of more hoofbeats sounded. Biting back a squeal of alarm, she dove for the clothes and rolled behind a tree just as Anselm rode into the clearing.

Murie listened absently to the men talk as she dressed, but she wasn't really paying attention. The moment she had her gown and surcoat on, she paused to run her fingers quickly through her hair. Then she tried for a serene expression and walked out of the woods just as Osgoode rode into the clearing with Balan's horse behind him.

"Thank you, cousin," Balan said, moving to take the reins and tie the animal to the exact same tree he'd tied him to earlier. He turned back and spotted Murie standing uncertainly on the edge of the clearing and immediately walked to her side. Osgoode dismounted.

"Oh, my lady!" Anselm smiled at her. "We were just telling his lordship that we became quite worried when the two of you did not return before the storm and set out to find you once it ended. He explained that you took cover under a tree and waited it out."

"Aye." Murie managed a smile, leaning weakly against her husband's side.

A distant shout made them all glance toward the woods, and Anselm frowned. "I should go round up the others and tell them you are both found and well."

"Aye," Balan said agreeably.

The man-at-arms glanced to Erol and Godart, and gave them meaningful looks. "You can ride back with Lord Balan and his wife." The two men nodded, and Anselm turned his horse and rode to find the others.

"Well," Osgoode said, laughter dancing in his eyes. "We should head back to the keep, should we not?"

"Aye. Come." Balan started to lead Murie toward his horse, but she dug in her heels, forcing him to stop and turn to face her.

"I still wish to gather some clover and elder, and perhaps some birch branches," she told him.

"Nay. You are going back to the castle to rest. You have sustained a terrible injury and are too weak to be doing anything strenuous yet."

Murie's mouth tightened. "Surely it is no less strenuous than what we were doing a moment ago," she said archly. "I should think it would be less so."

The laughter that had been dancing in Osgoode's eyes suddenly burst from his lips. "Whatever could that be, I wonder."

"You may wonder silently," Murie told him tartly.

Osgoode nodded. "Aye. By the way, cousin, your doublet is caught in your leggings. And Murie, your lacings are all tangled."

Murie flushed bright pink as she saw that was true. It seemed that none of them had been left wondering. Grimacing, she and Balan straightened their clothes. He turned and said firmly, "I do not want you out here alone, wife."

She scowled. It seemed that loving each other did not automatically resolve all conflicts and ensure everything ran smoothly. Some compromise was needed.

"If you would just send Cecily back with a basket, then I shall not be alone and need not leave," she suggested reasonably.

Balan did not look pleased. Still, he seemed to realize that he could not prove her too weak to pick up branches after the rather energetic activity they'd just enjoyed. And, as having Cecily with her would mean she wasn't alone, he gave in.

"Very well. I shall ride back and fetch her to you," he promised. Turning to the two soldiers who were still mounted, he said, "Erol. Godart. You are to stay here with my wife until her maid returns."

"Aye, my lord," they said, but neither man looked pleased by the order.

Murie understood why, and she wasn't all that pleased either. These were the two men who were supposed to be keeping an eye on her husband. "Surely you need leave only one man with me, husband. Why not take Erol with you? Or leave Erol and take Godart. Two are not needed."

"Nay," Balan said firmly. "They shall both stay."

"But—"

Her husband silenced her with a quick hard kiss, then turned and strode to his horse. Murie released a little sigh, her gaze dropping over his back as she watched him walk away, then blinking off the contentment he'd induced and scowling after him. The stubborn man was going to get himself killed.

Which reminded her of the question she'd wanted to ask Osgoode. Murie glanced to him just as he settled back in the saddle. He picked up his reins, preparing to ride over to where Balan was untying lightning, but she stepped to his side and raised a hand, placing it on his boot to stop him.

"A moment, my lord?" she murmured.

Balan's cousin paused at once and glanced down at her in question. "Aye?"

"One of the guards with the wagons said that you were the one to see me in the village as you came over the rise. Is that true?" she asked.

Osgoode blew out an exasperated breath. "Oh, pray, Murie please do not say you still think I am trying to kill your husband. That I lied to lure him to the burning cottage and—"

"Nay, of course not, my lord!" she interrupted.

"Oh." He smiled faintly. "Good."

"I was just wondering if you would tell me exactly what you saw?"

"What I saw?" he repeated with confusion.

"Aye. What made you think it was me? Malculinus and his man Baxley had just left ere your return. Could it have been a man dressed up as a woman?"

"A man dressed as a woman?" Osgoode considered the question with interest, but then shook his head. "Nay. She had a woman's figure, full and—" He started to hold his hands up to indicate large breasts, and then caught himself and offered an apologetic grimace. "Nay, it was a woman."

"Could it have been Lauda, do you think?"

He thought even less time about that before shaking his head. "Nay. Not Lauda. She is too tall and . . . flat.

"So the woman was shorter?"

"Aye, and rounded like you," he said, glancing toward Balan who mounted Lightning. He turned back, suspicion glinting behind his eyes. "In fact, I was sure it was you."

"Why?" Muric's eyebrows drew together. "Why were you so sure it was me? There must have been a reason. You were very far away, my lord."

"Aye, but I have good eyesight," he said stiffly. And she could tell by his expression that, while she no longer thought him the attempted killer, he once again thought she was.

Exasperated, she said, "You could only have seen the shape and perhaps hair color. Was she blond like me?"

"Aye." He nodded with a sudden realization. "But that is not why I was so sure."

"Are you coming, cousin?" Balan called out. Mounted and apparently impatient to be away, he scowled at the pair of them.

"Aye," Osgoode said, and shifted in his saddle. As he urged his mount into a walk, Balan turned and rode out of the clearing.

Osgoode would have put spurs to his mount, too, Murie was sure, but she still had her hand on his boot and was walking beside him.

"*Why* were you so sure?" she repeated as he glanced down at her.

"It was the color of the dress she wore that made me think it was you," he answered. "Now let me go. I wish to stay close to Balan until this is all cleared up."

"The color of her dress?" Murie asked sharply. "What color was it?"

"It was that burgundy and black surcoat you favor. I recognized it at once." He frowned. "But you were not wearing it when we charged out of the cottage and ran you over . . . and could not have possibly changed so quickly." He shook his head with a sigh, deciding, "It was not you."

"Nay," she whispered.

"Well, I am glad to hear it," Osgoode assured her. "Balan loves you, and I would not have him hurt knowing you were trying to kill him. Now, if you will excuse me, I truly do not want him without someone to watch his back."

Murie released the man's leg and stepped back from his horse. Osgoode was away at once, hurrying into the woods after Balan, but she hardly noticed. Her mind was taken up with wondering why Cecily was trying to kill her husband.

Chapter Eighteen

"Are you going to tell me what I have done?"

Balan slowed his mount and glanced at his cousin with narrowed eyes. After taking Cecily to his wife, he'd forsaken turning his attention to any of the many chores awaiting him at the castle and instead suggested another hunt. He'd bought six cows in Carlisle, but the beasts had cost him twice what they would have before the plague, and he was loath to sacrifice any. They must breed to give him more cows.

"Well?" Osgoode prompted.

"I do not know what you are talking about," he said finally.

"I am talking about the silence you are treating me to and the glares you keep throwing my way. Would you care to share with me what I have done?"

Balan glowered and suggested, "Why do you not, instead, share with me what my wife said?"

Osgoode's eyebrows flew up on his forehead. "You are jealous!"

"Nay," Balan argued. "I am curious."

Chuckling with open disbelief, Osgoode shook his head. "She was only asking me why I thought she was the woman in the village."

Balan's expression eased, but he tilted his head curiously. "Why *did* you think it was Murie? I never thought to ask you myself."

"It was the color of her dress," Osgoode explained. "I was sure it was that burgundy gown and black surcoat that Murie favors."

"The burgundy gown and black surcoat?" Balan repeated.

"Aye. In fact, I know it was, but Murie was not wearing it when we ran her over, and I really doubt she could have changed that quickly. Someone else must have been wearing it or a gown very similar."

"Someone else," Balan echoed.

"Did I tell you?" Osgoode said with a smile. "Anselm has apparently decided—from the fact that I too was nearly killed in the fire—that I am not the killer. He was telling me the theories he and the other men have been tossing around. They have decided the would-be killer is someone who must have been in our traveling party from court, else he would have been noticed while skulking around the horses and poisoning that meat."

"A woman in our traveling party who would have access to Murie's gown," Balan muttered.

"Aye, that seems to be—Where are you going?" Osgoode cut himself off to ask. Balan had suddenly turned his mount and headed back the way they'd come.

"The only person who fills that criteria is Cecily!" he pointed out harshly.

"Cecily?" Osgoode repeated with amazement. "Why would Cecily wish to kill you?"

* * *

"Why are you trying to kill my husband?" Murie blurted. She'd spent every moment since Osgoode rode off pondering the matter, then trying to sort out how to question Cecily, and this was the best she could do. She blamed it on her husband. He'd been short-tempered upon returning with Cecily, and had barely paused long enough to set the maid on the ground before announcing he and Osgoode were going hunting and riding off.

Murie had watched him go with a frown, then had peered meaningfully at Erol and Godart, encouraging them to follow. If she were right about Cecily, her husband would be perfectly safe while the maid was with her, but Murie wanted to confront the woman alone. She'd been with her for ten years, and Murie felt this was the least that was owed her. She was hoping by approaching the matter on her own, she might get some honest answers. Cecily, however, wasn't rushing to confess.

The silence that descended in the clearing was almost preternatural. Even the birds in the trees and the insects that moments ago had been buzzing around them were suddenly silent. The two women faced each other for so long that one could be forgiven for thinking time had stopped . . . and then the song of a cuckoo pierced the air.

As if on cue, Cecily swallowed and said, "I do not understand, my lady."

"Aye, you do," Murie said. "I saw you take my gown."

"Your gown?" the maid asked, suddenly wary.

Murie nodded. "I was half asleep and paid little attention, thinking you were merely taking it out for me to wear that day, and then I dozed off again. When you woke me later by removing the furs from the windows to let the light in, however, it was a different dress you had set out for me."

"I—"

"I thought little of it at the time," Murie went on, not giving her maid the chance to lie. "In fact, I did not even really recall it . . . until Osgoode described to me the gown the woman he saw in the village was wearing. It was mine. The one I had seen you taking out of my chest."

"Osgoode lied. He must have. He is the one trying to kill your husband."

Cecily sounded desperate, Murie noted sadly. She'd really hoped she was wrong and the maid would somehow prove herself innocent. Instead, Murie's certainty of her guilt grew with every word.

"What would I gain from killing your husband? Osgoode is the one who will inherit should he die," Cecily added when Murie remained silent.

Murie's gaze sharpened. "How do you know that Osgoode will inherit? I did not know it until Anselm told me, when we all met on the wall. Were you there? You must have been."

"Nay. I was with your husband," Cecily said quickly. "You insisted Osgood and I sit with him, remember?"

"Aye, I did," Murie murmured, pondering the matter. Raising her head she repeated, "How did you know that Osgoode would inherit?"

Cecily shrugged helplessly. "Someone must have told me."

"Nay." Murie shook her head firmly. "You were there. What happened? Did my husband send you to look for me? He was awake when I returned to the room, and asking you something, but stopped when I walked in." She tilted her head. "Was he asking where I was because he had sent you to find me?"

Cecily shook her head silently, but Murie did not believe her.

"And so you came looking for me, heard that Osgoode would inherit if Balan died, and heard that someone was to be watching my husband at all times," she guessed. "It must have vexed you. It would make it so much harder to kill him. But then he pulled himself out of his sick bed to travel outside and find more servants and livestock, and you thought of a way to use that. He would be alone with Osgoode. Osgoode would be the one suspected should anything happen. It was perfect, so you donned my gown and awaited their return and . . ." Murie pursed her lips. "You must have had the fire ready to go. You would have had to light it and get it burning merrily in a hurry once you saw them approaching. Then you waved from the door to get their attention and seemed to slip back inside, never expecting Osgoode would enter with Balan."

"You have lost your mind, my lady!" Cecily said harshly. "I was in the woods with Gatty's daughters, Estrelda and Livith, collecting rushes as you ordered."

"I suspect if I ask them, Estrelda and Livith will say that you wandered off on your own to collect rushes. That you rejoined them only to return to the keep," Murie said. Her mouth tightened when panic crossed Cecily's face. "Aye, that is the way of it, is it not?"

"Nay!" the maid cried, and then repeated desperately, "What would I gain by his death?"

"Aye, that is a question. 'Tis why I kept denying you could be the culprit when the others suggested it had to be you or Osgoode. There was nothing for you to gain—or so I thought," Murie admitted. "But I have been pondering the matter ever since Osgoode described the dress you took . . . and the only thing that strikes my mind is Baxley."

"Baxley?" Cecily echoed with alarm. "I hardly know

the man. I only met him the one time here at the castle, when he flirted with Estrelda and myself."

"You lie," Murie said harshly. "You met him at court. Emilie pointed the two of you out to me on the morning of the Feast of St. Agnes."

When Cecily stilled, Murie nodded. "She said, 'Oh, look, your maid has a beau.' At the time I just smiled and thought it sweet. I did not know that the man would turn you into a murderous bitch."

"Baxley had nothing to do with this," Cecily snarled, her denials at last become rage. "I am the one who wanted Balan dead. Me. Not Baxley. He would never suggest such a thing."

"Why?" Murie asked. "He has never done a thing to you."

"He married you!" Cecily snapped.

When Murie just stared at her, Cecily threw her hands up in the air. "He married you and brought you to this godforsaken place!"

"What has that to do with it?" Murie asked with confusion. "Gaynor is a fine castle. It may be having difficulties at the moment, but many castles are since the plague. It will regain its former glory soon. In a year or two or three—"

"I do not have a year or two or three," Cecily said harshly, then shook her head with disgust. "You do not understand. You do not see at all."

"Nay, I do not," Murie agreed.

"Look at me," Cecily demanded. "See me. I am growing old and am still unwed and childless. And 'tis all your fault."

"Mine?" Murie stared at her with dismay.

"Aye. Yours. I had a beau at Somerdale. William."

"The steward?" Murie asked with surprise.

"Aye. We were to marry, but then your parents died

and the king showed up and deemed your nursemaid Elsie too old and unfit to travel."

Murie's head lifted slightly. Elsie had been a dear woman, but she had been growing old, and the journey to court would have been hard on her. Murie had forgotten all about it until now.

"I had the unfortunate luck of being in the room when the king decided this, and so he pointed to me and announced that I was to be her replacement. I was to accompany you to court, all without a by your leave. There was no asking whether I wanted to go. He ordered it, and I had to obey.

"I was furious. I had no desire to play nursemaid to some spoiled brat. I was a maid in the great hall, being trained to supervise the other maids. I had little if any interaction with you at all and had no desire to. I went to William in tears, hoping he would find some way to fix things. But there was no way. All he could do was soothe me and assure me all it meant was a delay in our plans. I would go to court with you, he said, and in four or five years when you married as most girls did, you and your husband would return to Somerdale and we could be married then and start our lives together.

"So," she finished with disgust. "I accompanied you to court and suffered the gropings and propositions of drunken lords who saw me in the hall and assumed I was as cheap and easy as the other maids. And a year passed, and another and another, until five years were gone and still you were not wed. And then six, and then seven, and then eight, and still no marriage—but William and I continued to send messages to each other through servants and tradesmen coming and going from court. He kept his promise. He did not marry anyone else. He was waiting for me." Her voice cracked on the last word.

"And then the plague struck," Murie whispered with horror. She recalled the day she'd wondered aloud how those at Somerdale fared. Cecily had told her then that they'd fared no better than anywhere else, losing nearly half their people, including the steward, William.

Cecily nodded. "He was dead six months before I got word. His last words were to tell me he loved me."

Murie bit her lip. Cecily had fallen into a deep depression in the midst of the plague, but she'd just assumed it was the ordeal itself, the horror of it all, the fear, the death and the bodies piling up. She'd never known about this William or his importance to Cecily.

"I resigned myself to never marrying, to never having children of my own, to being a barren old woman stuck at that horrid court forever, for it seemed you were *never* going to wed," Cecily said bitterly. "And then the king ordered that you should.

"It mattered little to me when I first heard the news. It actually made me angry. If he'd only ordered this when you were fifteen, things would've been different. His own daughter was sent off to be married at fourteen in the midst of the plague, and she died from it, but he never bothered to order you." She shook her head with disgust.

"And then I met Baxley." Cecily's face softened. "And he was so handsome and charming . . . and he hinted that his lord was interested in you and that mayhap I would land at Aldous and we could be together. And it was like all of England opened up again for me. There was hope once more—a husband, children, a future." Her face darkened. "But you had to marry Malculinus for me to have it."

"You knew about the trick Malculinus and his sister planned to play," Murie said quietly.

Cecily nodded. "Baxley told me and warned me that if I normally slept on a pallet in your room not to scream or otherwise give away the game."

"And so you played up the St. Agnes Eve superstition, telling me about your sister who dreamed of a man she later married."

Cecily nodded again. "I was so happy that night. I felt sure the trick would work, you would marry the handsome and rich lord Malculinus and we would go to Castle Aldous and live happily ever after."

Murie's mouth twisted with anger. "You mean *you* would. You would be at Aldous happy with Baxley, and I would be there as well, but I would be miserably married to Malculinus who had tricked me."

"You would have been *happy*," Cecily insisted. "You never would have known about the trick."

"But I soon would have come to realize the man had no character," Murie pointed out. "And by then it would have been too late."

"Character," Cecily snarled. "He does not need character. What matter if he is weak and cowardly? He is rich, with lots of servants. You wouldn't have had to slave away like a peasant to right Aldous Castle."

"Nay, I simply would have had to vie for my husband's attention with his mistress Lady Jane," she snapped. She blinked in surprise when Cecily's expression turned guilty. "You knew about Jane?"

The maid shrugged. "What matter if he was faithful? Men are never faithful."

Murie's eyes narrowed. "Your William was not faithful to you?"

"He was a man," Cecily said with a weary shrug. "What does it matter?"

"I suppose it does not," Murie acknowledged, and then shook her head. "None of this explains why you tried to kill Balan. I understand why you did not warn me of the trick and why you hoped it would succeed and I would marry Malculinus, but once Balan and I married . . ." She shook her head and said, just to be sure, "*You* put the thistle under his saddle? And poisoned the meat?"

"Aye, I did it all—the horse, the meat, hitting him over the head by the river, the fire. It was all me, but every attempt went awry thanks to *your* interference." The maid's eyes turned angry again as she glared at Murie. "The thistle worked and sent the horse charging, but you charged after him and saved his life."

"Actually, it was Reginald who saved him that time," Murie corrected her.

Cecily waved that away. "But it was you who ate half the meat so that he did not get enough poison and die. And you who dragged him out of the water." She paused and scowled at Murie. "I was there watching when you did it. I was hoping that you might leave him behind while you went to get help and I could finish him off, but no, you made a litter of your clothing and walked back naked to save him. What other lady would do that, I ask you?" She threw her hands in the air again, this time with exasperation. "You even interfered with the fire, unblocking the door and setting them both free. Every time I have thought I was about to attain my deepest desire and kill the bastard, you interfered and saved his life . . . *twice* almost getting yourself killed in the process," she added harshly. "How would I have gotten to Aldous then?"

Murie peered at the woman as if she were mad—which she obviously was—and said, "You would not have gotten to Aldous in any case. Even had my husband died, I would never have married Malculinus."

"Aye, you will," Cecily assured her.

"Nay, I will not," Murie retorted. "Even had you succeeded in killing my husband, the king would not force me to marry again so soon. If at all. And if he did, Malculinus would be the very last man in England I would ever consider."

"Your husband will die," Cecily assured her menacingly. "And when he does, you will marry Malculinus. I suffered ten long years at court for you—you owe me this."

Murie gave a *tsk* of mingled disgust and disbelief. "I owe you nothing. You were paid quite handsomely for those ten long years. And had you explained things and asked, I am sure the king would have released you to return to Somerdale. All you had to do was ask."

Now it was Cecily's turn to look dubious. "You do not ask the king for anything. You obey and keep your head on your shoulders."

"Oh, bollocks!" Murie snapped. "You are a servant not a slave. Just look at how all the villeins and servants left here when more coin was offered elsewhere."

"Now," Cecily said with emphasis. "Now that half the servants and workers are gone, we have some power and may go in search of kinder surroundings. But not ten years ago. Not when the king ordered me to court."

"Why did you not simply pack up and go to Aldous yourself if you so desired, rather than spend all this energy trying to kill my husband?" Murie asked.

Cecily frowned and avoided her gaze, and Murie's eyes widened with understanding. "Because you feared Baxley would not be interested in you without your, first, obtaining me for his lord."

"Shut up," Cecily snapped. "He is mine, and I am having him. I deserve this after losing my William. You will marry Malculinus."

"Nay, I will not," Murie said. "I will not marry him, and I will not let you kill my husband."

"Aye, you will—because if you do not, then you are of no use to me at all, and I may as well kill you, too."

Murie stared at her maid and realized she'd made a huge mistake in confronting the woman alone. This was the maid who had tended her needs for ten years, and yet Murie did not recognize her—had never even really known her, she realized. The face Cecily had been showing all these years had not been the real woman. She'd hated and resented Murie for being forced to court all this time, and Murie had to wonder if that wasn't part of the reason behind her determination to kill Balan: She'd lost her William and would now see Murie suffer an equal loss.

She was trying to sort out how best to handle the situation, when Cecily suddenly produced a knife. "I think I shall kill you anyway. You have been a canker on my arse long enough."

Murie's eyes widened incredulously. This was unexpected. She'd never imagined the maid would have such a weapon on her. On the other hand, she'd never really believed the woman had been the one behind the attacks on Balan. So far, she'd handled the situation all wrong.

Cecily suddenly lunged, stabbing out with the knife, and Murie instinctively sidestepped and then swung the heavy basket the maid had brought for collecting branches. She hit her maid in the side of the head, sending Cecily slamming to the ground. Murie did not stick around to see how the maid fared, but took off at once, crashing into the woods rather than risk the path. She was younger and stronger, but her body had taken a beating today, and she'd had nothing but the bowl of soup Clement had brought. She feared in a race to the death, she would lose. She needed to use intellect—if she had any left after the blow she'd taken.

Murie ran as quickly as she could, heading in the direction she thought the castle must be. When she broke out of the trees and suddenly found herself on the edge of the village, she didn't hesitate, but made for the small group of buildings. It was a long, unprotected run to the castle from where she'd come out of the woods, and at this point she would not put it past Cecily to chase after her and stab her at the foot of the drawbridge, even in front of the men on the wall. The maid was not in her right mind, and the village was much closer; there would be places to hide while she sorted out how to get back to the castle and help.

If Murie were extremely lucky, one of the men on the wall might even see her and send someone down to be sure all was well, she thought optimistically.

The smell of smoke was heavy in the air as she drew close to the buildings. Balan had not judged it necessary to put out the fire in the blacksmith's cottage. The building itself had already been beyond repair, and so long as the fire did not spread he'd claimed he was content to let it burn.

The fire had not spread, Murie saw as she hurried into the village. But it was not yet completely out, either. The building had collapsed in on itself and was now a heap of blackened, smoldering wood and debris. Skirting it, Murie made her way to a cottage two doors down and glanced quickly around to be sure she was not seen before slipping inside.

The cottage she'd chosen was small and dark and dank with disuse. Moving to the window beside the door, Murie peered toward the woods and worried her lip, waiting to see if Cecily followed. If she were extremely lucky, the woman was presently lying unconscious in the woods, easy for Balan's men to find and capture. Murie might be standing here hiding for naught!

That thought had barely run through her mind when Cecily appeared at the edge of the woods. The maid's head turned toward the castle, then to the village. She . . . headed for the village. Murie turned immediately to peer around, relieved when she spotted a door at the back of the cottage, leading—she hoped—outside. At least she would not be trapped if Cecily found her. She might even be able to slip out and run to the castle.

Murie's eyebrows drew together as she noted that Cecily was walking straight for the cottage she was in, as if Cecily had seen where she'd gone. And probably she had, Murie realized. Just because she had not come out of the woods right away did not preclude her from lurking just out of sight.

Cursing under her breath as the woman drew closer, Murie hurried to the back of the cottage and tried the door. Relieved, she found it opened. She slipped outside and pulled the door closed, then eased to the corner of the building, ears straining for some tell-tale sound that might inform her as to whether Cecily had yet entered. She was about to risk running behind the next cottage when Cecily stepped around the corner in front of her, knife at the ready.

A startled cry slipped from her lips, and Murie whirled and ran the other way, uncaring where she went as long as it was away from Cecily's slashing knife. She managed to get past the cottage she'd been hiding in and out behind the blacksmith's burnt ruins before Cecily caught her by the hair. The maid tried to jerk her to a stop and back around.

Knowing death awaited her, Murie threw herself to the side, breaking the hold the woman had on her but landing on her stomach on the ground, terribly vulnerable. Rolling quickly onto her back, she found Cecily looming over her, a cruel smile on her face.

"Do you know how many mornings I have fantasized about shoving your head into the basin of water I brought and drowning you?"

"It was not my fault you ended up at court," Murie yelped with frustration, scrambling backward on her behind.

"Mayhap not, but if you had died, I could have left," Cecily pointed out.

"Well then, why did you not kill me?" Murie snapped. " 'Tis funny you could not approach the king for William, but are now willing to kill for Baxley. Mayhap you never really wanted William at all, and it was easier just to allow the king to order you to court. Were you hoping for other options? Other men to woo you? Did that never happen and so you blame me for all your failures?"

"Bitch!" Cecily lunged at her, and Murie prepared to roll away at the last moment—but the last moment never came. A body came hurtling seemingly out of the air and crashed into the maid, taking her to the ground.

Confused, Murie sat up and peered around. Osgoode came running around the corner of a cottage. It was only then that Murie realized who the first body belonged to: her husband. Gasping with worry, she scrambled to her feet and turned to the couple on the ground. She saw Balan getting to his feet and dragging Cecily up with him. It wasn't until they were both standing and he dragged her around that they all saw the knife she'd been holding was protruding from her chest. She'd fallen on the weapon when Balan tackled her. He released her arm and took a step back, apparently as shocked by her injury as anyone.

Cecily scowled at the three of them and staggered back a step. She then peered down at her chest with curiosity, noticed the knife there. A small laugh slipped from her lips. Shaking her head, she backed up another step and then collapsed with a little sigh.

A moment passed, and Balan moved to her side. He turned her face his way, lifted her eyelids, then lowered his head so that his ear was over her mouth and nose. After a moment, he straightened and got to his feet.

"Is she . . . ?" Osgoode asked.

Before Balan could answer, Murie said, "Aye."

"How did you know, wife?" Balan asked with a frown.

"I heard the cuckoo call in the woods. It means someone will die," she said simply. Then she turned to walk away. She was feeling a bit shaky and uncertain about her feelings regarding her maid's death. Part of her was sorry. The woman had been with her for ten years, after all. The other part was relieved. At least now she could stop worrying for her husband's well-being.

Murie had only taken a few steps when Balan swept her into his arms.

"I love you, Murie," he whispered, holding her as if he would never let her go.

"I love you too, Balan," she whispered, and laid her head on his shoulder. That was really all there was to say.

Chapter Nineteen

"How is Murie?" Osgoode asked quietly.

"She will be fine." Balan joined his cousin at the trestle table and accepted the ale pushed his way. He'd brought his wife straight back to the keep, where she'd told them all that Cecily had said. It sounded to him as if the poor creature wasn't right in the head. He'd voiced that opinion and then spent time soothing his wife in their chamber before putting her to bed and holding her until she fell asleep.

"She is weary and shocked by the events of this day, but she will recover," he added. "She is very resilient."

"Aye, she certainly is that," Osgoode agreed with amusement. His eyes found something over Balan's shoulder that made Balan turn to glance toward the stairs: his wife, rushing down from the upper floor.

Pushing his drink away with exasperation, Balan waited for her to approach him so that he could give her hell for being up and about, but she didn't. Murie hardly seemed to notice his presence and hurried across the great hall to the keep doors.

"Where is she going?" Osgoode asked.

Shaking his head with bewilderment, Balan stood to follow her. He stepped out of the keep, opened his mouth to call out to his wife, who was tripping lightly down the stairs, then paused as he noted the traveling party riding through the gates.

"What the hell?" he muttered.

"Oh, aye, I forgot to tell you," Osgoode said, suddenly at his side. "The men spotted a party approaching carrying the king's colors while you were upstairs."

Balan nodded and relaxed, then scowled at his wife, who'd joined the growing crowd of servants and men-at-arms at the bottom of the step. "Wife! What—"

He'd been about to ask what she thought she was doing out of bed, but she whirled to grin up at him, crying, "My things!" and so Balan shut his mouth, unwilling to berate her when she appeared so happy.

It was Osgoode who asked, "Your things?" as the two men made their way down the stairs to join her.

"I thought the two chests on the wagon were your things," Balan said with a frown. "There is more?"

"Oh, aye." She laughed and explained, "Those two chests were just a few gowns and such to tide me over until my other possessions arrived. The queen promised to pack it all and send it on to me, along with items I ordered just before the wedding."

"Oh." Balan stared at her, nonplussed.

Unable to contain herself, Murie clapped her hands happily as the company of men and wagons entered the bailey. She was as giddy as a child.

Balan was less so, as wagon after wagon rolled by. "Dear God. How many dresses does one woman need?"

Murie laughed and slapped his arm. "Fie, husband. There is much more than dresses on those wagons."

"There is?" Thibault asked curiously. He'd joined the other servants at the foot of the steps.

"Aye." Murie beamed at them all. "These are the things I ordered before I left. Cheese, flour and exotic herbs we cannot grow here, and—"

"Cheese, flour and exotic herbs?" Clement interrupted, with the closest thing to a smile anyone had ever seen on his face. While Balan had brought back a few vegetables, he'd not gotten cheese or flour.

"Aye." Murie grinned. "And wine, mead, more ale, wheat, and chairs and other furniture and linens, and more chickens, cloth, and there should be more servants, too; I did ask the king to have Becker hire me some and . . ." Murie broke off her recitation as everyone rushed past her toward the first wagon that was drawing to a halt before the steps.

"You have won their everlasting love," Balan announced quietly.

"And all it took was a bit of food," Murie agreed sadly.

"Nay. 'Tis not the food or wine or cloth, Murie," he said. " 'Tis you. 'Tis that you thought of them before you had even met them, just as you had a dress made for Juliana before you met her. You arranged to have all of this brought because you knew they were without."

"They are my people now, Balan. 'Tis my place to look after them."

Balan nodded and slid his arm around her, drawing her against him and out of the way. The servants and soldiers were charging up the steps to the keep with item after item.

"They shall have the wagons emptied ere night falls," he predicted dryly. "I have not seen them move so quickly or smile so widely in a long time."

"I am happy they are happy," Murie murmured. "These are the people who remained faithful and stayed behind while others left. They deserve some comfort and joy."

"Is that the king?" Osgoode asked suddenly, alarmed.

"Nay, it could not—Damn, it is," Balan realized with dismay as he saw the monarch turn and help Queen Phillippa down from her mount. "Dear God, what are they doing here?"

"You married me," Murie said with an unhappy sigh and turned to peer at him with concern. "Husband, I know my superstitions annoy you—" Balan started to protest, but she held up her hand to silence him. "My superstitions annoy you," she repeated firmly. "My maid tried to kill you, and now the king and queen appear to have decided to visit—and may do so again."

"Aye," he agreed on a sigh. There appeared to be no end of trouble in store for him.

"Are you now sorry you married me?" she asked.

Balan turned shocked eyes her way. "What?"

"Are you now—" she started to repeat, but Balan stopped her with a hand to her mouth.

"Murie," he said solemnly, "I am more and more glad I married you every day. Aye, your superstitions baffle me. Aye, your maid tried to kill me. And, aye, the king and queen are now on my doorstep. But I would suffer that—and more—for you. Truly," he continued, "I never realized how placid and peaceful my life was until you entered it. It feels like we have been married forever."

When Osgoode burst out laughing, Balan knew

he'd bungled what he was trying to say. Murie's distressed expression verified it. He tried again.

"What I mean to say is: You have brought chaos and excitement to my life, and it already seems like years since we married."

Which just made Osgoode snicker harder.

"In a good way," Balan added desperately. "I mean—"

"He means life here was boring ere you arrived," Osgoode said, deciding at last to help him out.

"Aye, my lady. We were a dull, miserable group ere your arrival," Thibault said, marching past with a barrel of ale.

"No hope, no light, no laughter," Gatty agreed with a shake of the head. She followed the steward, a roll of cloth in her arms. "You brought hope back to Gaynor, seeing the positive where we had seen only negatives."

"Aye, and you fixed my hair!" Juliana said earnestly.

Balan sighed and turned to his wife. "I told you I am no good at speaking to women. But Murie, I cannot imagine not being married to you. It seems like you have always been here. Because you belong here." He paused with frustration and then said, "Dammit, woman, I love you. Is that not enough?"

Murie's lips parted in a soft smile, and she leaned up to gently kiss him. "More than enough, my lord husband. More than enough."

Relieved, he caught her lips with his and kissed her deeply, then swept her into his arms and turned toward the stairs.

"Where are you going?" Osgoode asked with alarm. "Balan, you cannot leave me here alone to greet the king and queen. What do I tell them?"

Balan broke the kiss to say, "Tell them I love their goddaughter and shall not return below until I am sure she knows that." He took in Murie's sweet smile and then added, "Tell them that will probably be several days at least, but they are welcome to stay for the duration if they wish."

"Several days?" Osgoode squawked.

"More likely a week, my lord," Murie murmured, and when Balan glanced down at her with surprise, she shrugged and said solemnly, "Well, the king knows I can be most difficult. He shall expect it to take longer to convince me than most."

"Brat," Balan teased affectionately, his eyes fixing on her lips as they spread in a smile that promised many splendors over the next week. Clearing his throat, he glanced at his cousin and growled, "Tell him not to expect us below for a week."

"A week?" Osgoode was starting to look faint. "But—"

Ignoring his cousin's panicked bleating, Balan turned and carried his wife inside, thinking to himself that marrying the infamous Brat had been the smartest move he'd ever made.

The Immaculate Complexion

Edie Bloom

In a world of Park Avenue princesses and Botox babes, Marnie Mann stands out like last year's lip color. If one more person at her new job for LaVigne Cosmetics suggests a laser treatment for her age spots or an injection for her furrowed brow, she's going to scream. But even her organic-loving self can't resist the seductive pull of the big-name beauty biz. That pull drags her into a high-concept product launch gone spectacularly awry and a murder by makeup in which every manicured finger points straight to her. It's going to take a lot more than wrinkle cream to smooth out this mess.

ISBN 10: 0-8439-5856-1
ISBN 13: 978-0-8439-5856-0 $6.99 US/$8.99 CAN